Praise for

SO LET THEM BURN

★ "Morally ambiguous and absolutely magical Black girls take the fate of their world into their own hands in this action-packed, cleverly crafted fantasy that will leave readers clamoring to know what happens next."

—*Booklist*, starred review

★ "Via the sisters' expertly balanced dual POVs, each imbued with a lushly wrought, moving, and action-packed narrative, Cole delivers a raucously enjoyable debut that provides an insightful look into the ways in which violence and colonization can affect a populace long after a war has ended."

—*Publishers Weekly*, starred review

"*So Let Them Burn* is the best young-adult novel I've read in ages, and one of the best fantasy novels, full stop."

—*The Washington Post*

"With rich storytelling and lushly wrought narratives, Cole's debut is not only a raucously enjoyable fantasy but also an insightful exploration of the lingering effects of violence and colonization on a populace....Highly recommended."

—*SLJ*

"By turns hopeful and devastating, *So Let Them Burn* is a masterful debut with a blazing heart. I was captivated from beginning to end."

—**Chelsea Abdullah**, author of *The Stardust Thief*

"Set my soul on fire in the best way possible! Cole weaves an enthralling tale by way of an authentic and complex sibling relationship that swallowed me whole from the first page."

—**Terry J. Benton-Walker**, bestselling author of *Blood Debts*

"Gods, dragons, and mechanoids all war against one another in a deeply imaginative and fantastical twist on colonization and island history."

—**Namina Forna**, *New York Times* bestselling author of the Gilded Ones trilogy

"Clever and utterly fresh, *So Let Them Burn* takes the fantasy genre and soars into brilliant new heights, subverting expectations and hitting every mark."

—**Chloe Gong**, #1 *New York Times* bestselling author of *These Violent Delights*

"Cole weaves a powerful narrative full of captivating lore, meddling gods, and young women willing to do whatever it takes. A heart-pounding delight."

—**M. K. Lobb**, author of *Seven Faceless Saints*

"*So Let Them Burn* elevates the game, asking hard questions about the power and agency of a chosen one whose destiny has been seemingly fulfilled. By the time you see the claws, they're already around your throat."

—**Margaret Owen**, *New York Times* bestselling author of *Little Thieves* and *The Merciful Crow*

"A riveting adventure, a deft exploration of colonialism, and a deeply moving tale of a fierce and complex sisterly bond."

—**Ava Reid**, award-winning and internationally bestselling author of *A Study in Drowning*

"Kamilah Cole has crafted a captivating story.... With deft prose and stellar world-building, this is an excellent new addition to YA fantasy."

—**Tara Sim**, author of *The City of Dusk*

"A thrilling epic about family, strength, and the real costs of war.... Truly DAZZLING. I am OBSESSED."

—**Aiden Thomas**, *New York Times* bestselling author of *Cemetery Boys*

"With characters who will grip you by the throat, a skillful commentary on colonialism, and an immersive world filled with dragons, danger, and deception, *So Let Them Burn* is a remarkable addition to the fantasy canon, establishing Cole as a powerful new voice in the genre."

—**Adrienne Tooley**, author of *Sweet & Bitter Magic* and *The Third Daughter*

"Tender, witty, and with a plot that will keep you glued to the page, *So Let Them Burn* is a beautiful exploration of what happens after becoming the chosen one—and how even when the legend ends, the story doesn't."

—**Hannah F. Whitten**, author of the Wilderwood duology

BY KAMILAH COLE

THE DIVINE TRAITORS DUOLOGY
SO LET THEM BURN
THIS ENDS IN EMBERS

THIS ENDS IN EMBERS

KAMILAH COLE

LITTLE, BROWN AND COMPANY
NEW YORK BOSTON

This book is a work of fiction. Names, characters, places, and incidents are the product of the author's imagination or are used fictitiously. Any resemblance to actual events, locales, or persons, living or dead, is coincidental.

Copyright © 2025 by Kamilah Cole
Map illustration copyright © 2024 by Virginia Allyn

Cover art copyright © 2025 by Carlos Quevedo. Cover design by Jenny Kimura.
Cover copyright © 2025 by Hachette Book Group, Inc.
Interior design by Jenny Kimura.

Hachette Book Group supports the right to free expression and the value of copyright. The purpose of copyright is to encourage writers and artists to produce the creative works that enrich our culture.

The scanning, uploading, and distribution of this book without permission is a theft of the author's intellectual property. If you would like permission to use material from the book (other than for review purposes), please contact permissions@hbgusa.com. Thank you for your support of the author's rights.

Little, Brown and Company
Hachette Book Group
1290 Avenue of the Americas, New York, NY 10104
Visit us at LBYR.com

First Edition: February 2025

Little, Brown and Company is a division of Hachette Book Group, Inc. The Little, Brown name and logo are registered trademarks of Hachette Book Group, Inc.

The publisher is not responsible for websites (or their content) that are not owned by the publisher.

Interior art credits: Flame pattern © Dana Bogatyreva/Shutterstock.com

Little, Brown and Company books may be purchased in bulk for business, educational, or promotional use. For information, please contact your local bookseller or the Hachette Book Group Special Markets Department at special.markets@hbgusa.com.

Library of Congress Cataloging-in-Publication Data
Names: Cole, Kamilah, author.
Title: This ends in embers / Kamilah Cole.
Description: First edition. | New York : Little, Brown and Company, 2025. |
  Series: The divine traitors | Summary: "After her sister, Faron, is kidnapped by a brutal
  conqueror, Elara must use powers both modern and ancient to bring her home, and save
  their country from war" —Provided by publisher.
Identifiers: LCCN 2024019435 | ISBN 9780316534956 (hardcover) | ISBN 9780316535250 (ebook)
Subjects: CYAC: Fantasy. | Sisters—Fiction. | Kidnapping—Fiction. | LCGFT: Fantasy fiction. |
  Novels.
Classification: LCC PZ7.1.C64285 Th 2025 | DDC [Fic]—dc23
LC record available at https://lccn.loc.gov/2024019435

ISBNs: 978-0-316-53495-6 (hardcover), 978-0-316-53525-0 (ebook)

Printed in Indiana, U.S.A.

LSC-C

Printing 1, 2024

To Lauren.
Every book, every line,
every word, is because of you,
you dork.

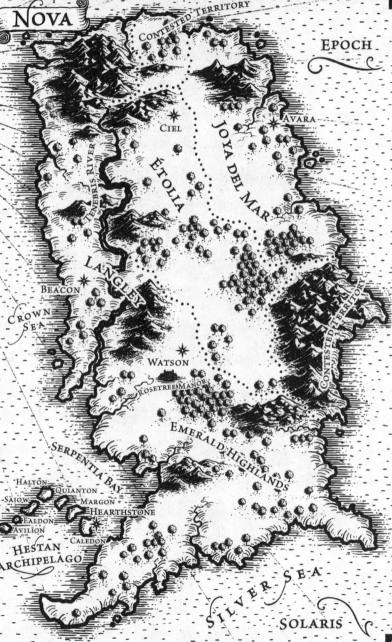

PART I

SLANDER

CHAPTER ONE

ELARA

E LARA VINCENT HAD BEEN A SAINT FOR LONGER THAN SHE'D BEEN a liar.

Even when she'd snuck out of her parents' house a lifetime ago, it had been a selfless act. She had forged herself into a weapon for her country and a shield for her sister—and, together, she and Faron had destroyed everything. Now, as the Maiden Empyrean, she was a walking fabrication. A living promise to the people of San Irie that *this* time *this* Empyrean would be everything they hoped for.

Elara did not know how to lie. Thankfully, her new title lied for her.

Deadegg, a town in the loosest sense of the word, gasped its necrotic breaths beneath the high noon sun. Broken buildings and shattered streets drew her toward the square, where the dirt roads and concrete plaza had been replaced by obsidian dust and cracked rock. That was all that remained of the dragon egg that had given the town its name, and of the squat stone wall that had separated the egg from the wary townsfolk. The sun beat down on charred soil that would never again bear life, on palm trees flattened and cleaved in half, on bodies still trapped beneath rubble that only a talented summoner could remove.

Because of her and her sister, Deadegg was a corpse reduced to bones and viscera and a river of still-flowing blood. Her sister, Faron, had dealt the killing blow to the town. Now, Elara was left to stitch the remains back together, at least long enough to autopsy the mistakes that had led them to where they were.

And she was so very tired.

"Don't overexert yourself," said the man to her right, so cautiously that Elara worried her grim thoughts showed on her face. "*Can* you overexert yourself? I was never quite sure how all that worked."

Papa's mouth twitched into a smile that vanished all too quickly. He'd always looked as if a thousand years of sleep wouldn't be nearly enough, but now he was *faded*. Like a vague idea of what a human should be, sketched by someone who had only heard sad stories about them: his skin wan, his locs limp, his shoulders slumped. Carver and Nida Vincent had been among the few to remain in Deadegg after the attack, and her father's lined eyes were hollower than the town.

"I'm fine," she assured him. "I'll be fine."

Elara didn't give him the chance to point out the waver in her voice or the trembling hands that she clenched at her side. She took a deep breath and called on the gods.

It wasn't the first time Elara had summoned a god, but it still felt novel to an eighteen-year-old girl who had grown up on nothing but faith. Fighting past her lingering awe, she sank deeper into the divine plane, which appeared to her as a thick forest that was ablaze except where she was standing. But she didn't feel the heat of the flames or smell the impenetrable smoke that shrouded the greenery; despite the roaring fire, she felt safely cloistered. Her soul swelled into a beacon of light that prayed, *Come to me, come to me, come to me....*

And the gods answered her call.

Mala, the goddess of the stars, the keeper of the astrals, the ruler of dawn and dusk, appeared before her in a swirl of rose-petal-pink fabric and twinkling silver light. Like the other two gods, Irie and Obie, Mala was twelve feet tall and had pupilless eyes. Her mahogany skin was smooth and clear, her cheekbones high, her lips full, her hair a river of thick curls that tumbled down her back. She wore a pink beaded bodice with a plunging neckline that exploded at the waist into a waterfall of tulle, making her look as if she were floating above the ground. Silver stars crowned her head, and her eyes glowed with that same color.

If Elara were impious enough to pick a favorite from the pantheon, she would have chosen Mala. The deity was usually all smiles, a playful dance of wind through leaves, as compared with Obie's enigmatic fog and Irie's unstoppable hurricane. But there was no smile on her face today, and the coldness in her eyes gave Elara pause.

Maiden Empyrean, Mala said, her voice as cold as her eyes. *What can I do for you?*

Elara blinked through the phantom smoke. Since choosing her as their new champion, the gods hadn't asked her what she needed their power for. She knew for a fact they'd never asked Faron, either. Then again, considering what Faron had done with it...

I—was hoping to repair some of the damage to the town. Anxiety prickled her skin, making her words come out sounding uncertain. *If that's all right with you?*

Mala didn't respond.

Elara shifted her weight from foot to foot. Her neck hurt from her staring upward. Time had no meaning in the divine plane, so she could have been waiting for hours or seconds. If Mala refused to share her power, it would be only a minor obstacle. Elara would do with hammers and shovels what she could have done faster with magic. She owed the town that much.

Still, her throat tightened as the time ticked by. It had been a week since she had asked the gods to lend her their power, to allow her to prove herself. It had been a week since she had channeled their magic and changed the tide of what was now called the Battle for Port Sol. It had been a week, and she had done nothing to break their trust since then.

But she didn't dare say so. After all, who was she to question the gods?

Finally, Mala smiled, and it made her pupilless eyes sparkle like shards of titanium. *Of course, Empyrean. Happy to help.*

She reached out for Elara, who promptly reached back. The tightness in her stomach loosened as their souls finally merged. Her vision whited out. Her ears rang. Her heart pounded so fast that she thought it would stop.

And then it was over. Mala's soul was beneath her skin—swelling with immense power that heated her body, her bones, her blood— but Elara was the one in control.

She blinked her way back to the present, where she stood facing the barren land where the town landmark had once been, sandwiched between her father and the Queenshield who had been assigned to her. Neither looked at her strangely, which confirmed that her tense standoff with Mala hadn't rendered her physical body stationary long enough for the interaction to be noticed. The

THIS ENDS IN EMBERS

last of her stress dissipated, leaving her free to focus on the work ahead.

Before she'd summoned Mala, the square had been empty, but now suspicious villagers had begun to emerge from their homes. Many clung to machetes, but they didn't raise them. The attack had made them wary, but Elara had the power of the gods on her side... for now. The villagers wouldn't start a fight they knew they couldn't win—and that moment of hesitation was the chance she needed to show them that they didn't need to fight at all.

Elara stretched an arm out toward the first destroyed building, holding in her mind a firm idea of what it used to look like. While Elara couldn't summon the spirits of ancestors who didn't share her bloodline, Mala's status as the keeper of the astrals allowed Elara to draw on all their energy to power large spells. Elara showed Mala the image of the corner shop, its blue-and-gold-painted concrete facade and the wooden awnings from which bunches of green bananas had once dangled, and their twined souls threw magic toward the building to knit it back together. It was a little like healing herself after a fight, except she couldn't restore the shop to what it had been. She could only restore it to what she *thought* it had been and hope that this was good enough for the owner.

After she'd fixed that one, she moved on to the next building and the next and the next. Slowly, the businesses that surrounded the town square sprouted like flower buds—perhaps a little outdated but whole. A handful had scorched storefronts and caved-in rooftops that Mala's magic slipped by like water around a boulder; Lightbringer's flame had destroyed those places, and the damage wrought by dragonfire was one of the few things the gods' magic could not touch.

Elara released Mala's soul, stumbling a little as exhaustion careened into her with the force of a tree trunk, and prepared to negotiate with Irie, the patron goddess of the island, to help clear the debris. But before she could sink back into the divine plane, a hand gripped her shoulder.

"That is more than enough for now, Maiden," said Queen Aveline Renard Castell, the twenty-two-year-old ruler of San Irie. A pearl diadem winked from atop her ink-black spiral curls. It matched the pearl-encrusted bodice of her seafoam gown. There was a pinch between her eyebrows as she studied Elara. "You do not look well."

"I can—" Elara's words were cut off by a yawn so wide that her jaw cracked.

Her skin was coated with sweat, and the silken fabric of the dress Aveline had provided clung to her damp body. It was a high-necked button-down in the colors of the Iryan flag—forest green with gold embroidered flowers, and a black ribbon belt to cinch her waist. Summoning raised the body's temperature, and it was also another unforgivably hot day, so a dress that covered this much of her skin had been a poor choice. She'd wanted to don the clothing of a respected religious figure, comfort be damned, and a respected religious figure did not give up when a job was only half done.

Aveline didn't release her arm. "Just because your sister did this in a day does not mean you have to undo it in that time."

Elara swallowed hard, hating to acknowledge that Aveline's grip was the only thing keeping her upright. Not just because of her fatigue, but also because of the ever-present reminder that she and her sister had done this. In cracking open the egg at the

THIS ENDS IN EMBERS

center of the town square, Faron had also opened a doorway to a prison between realms called the Empty. Faron had freed the First Dragon, Lightbringer, and his Rider, who was called the Gray Saint but had been born as Gael Soto. Faron had been claimed as Gael's co-Rider, her soul fused with his and Lightbringer's in a celestial bond, and she had accompanied them as they razed a path to the capital in a bid to claim the island as their own.

And she had done it all to save Elara from her own dragon bond.

Around her, the bleak faces of the people watching were rooted in the kind of pain that could come only from betrayal. Once, Faron had been the gods' avatar in the mortal world, the Childe Empyrean, capable of doing all that Elara had just done. Now Faron was a cautionary tale, a missing war criminal who had chosen to fly away with Lightbringer after their defeat.

Elara still had faith in her sister, though the world and the gods had forsaken her. But she was alone to live with the aftermath. To fix Faron's mistakes. No matter the cost to herself.

"I can keep going," she finished, even though her eyelids felt heavy and her back was as slick as a dolphin's and she was certain that if she tried to take a step, she would collapse. "We need to be able to bury our dead."

"I hardly think pushing yourself until you are among the aforementioned dead is the correct move," said Aveline, her voice soft. "This is but one stop on the reconstruction tour, Maiden. I command you to rest."

Aveline had never before commanded Elara to do anything. She had asked. She had guilted. She had even snapped. But she rarely issued a command without discussion, respecting, as Elara did, that they had once, when Elara was thirteen and Aveline was seventeen, fought a war together—something that made them more than queen and subject.

Elara couldn't imagine how worn down she looked for Aveline to be doing it now.

"All right," she said, chancing another look at the crowds. They still held their machetes close, but their grips had loosened. Papa was weaving through the pack, Queenshield trailing in his wake to hand out the relief packages Aveline had created.

Even after the war, even after the recent horrors, Deadegg was still a landlocked small town that wasn't on most maps drawn of the island. It would have been easy for the queen to forget them, focusing only on the capital and on larger towns like Highfort and Papillon. But Aveline was not a ruler who left the most marginalized of her people behind. She had insisted not only that Deadegg be the first stop on this tour but had also insisted on coming herself.

Elara eyed the mountains of rubble and debris that marked the surrounding area and cast ugly shadows across the otherwise bright day. Then she yawned again and forced herself to turn away.

"I'll meet you at my house," she told Aveline, wiping the sweat from her brow with the back of her hand. "Thank you, Your Majesty."

Aveline released her at last, a relieved smile on her face. "No, thank *you*. Take two guards with you, please. For my peace of mind."

Elara nodded, gesturing for two of the Queenshield to follow her down the unevenly paved roads that would take her to her parents' house. It was easier than saying what she truly felt: that there would be no peace of mind for any of them until Faron returned.

THIS ENDS IN EMBERS

This was not the longest Elara had gone without seeing her sister. Her unwanted trip to Langley had claimed that honor. But at least then she had left Faron in San Irie, with the queen, with their parents, with *Reeve Warwick*. Now it had been seven days—seven long but quick days—since Faron had disappeared, and no one even knew where she was. It felt like being out of step with the natural rhythm of the world, forever searching crowds for a face she would never see, forever listening for a voice she would never hear. Where Faron went, Elara had always followed, but not this time. This time, in the aftermath of battle, she filled her days with a flurry of activity that was like a single stitch on a gaping wound.

In the Battle for Port Sol, Lightbringer had fought against three drakes—the giant, dragon-shaped flying machines made from the scalestone metal mined only in San Irie—six dragons who had turned their back on their own kind to help San Irie instead, and the queen herself. Still, Lightbringer had almost won. After the battle ended, Aveline and Elara had each slept for an entire day. Then there had been meetings with the governors and High Santi—the leaders of the temples—who had flown in from across the island to assess all the damage, plan the reconstruction tour with the Queenshield, and run logistics on the remaining drakes to make sure they were still battle ready.

Valor, the newest drake to be built, had been the only one to be destroyed. The wreckage lay beyond the town lines, and Elara couldn't even *look* at it, let alone approach it. Two of the pilots had been her neighbors, her friends: Wayne Pryor and Aisha Harlow. They, along with a third pilot from Deadegg, Jordan Simmons, had been killed when Lightbringer blasted Valor out of the air.

Elara knew that Lightbringer hadn't acted alone. She knew that he and his Firstrider had renamed themselves Iya to emphasize that they acted as a single deity who expected the world to come to heel. But acknowledging the existence of Iya meant acknowledging that Reeve was gone, that Reeve had been *taken*, that—thanks to the machinations of his power-hungry parents—Reeve was being worn by Iya like a bad costume, and she could not think of Reeve without experiencing an eviscerating pain capable of bringing her to her knees.

Her best friend. Her sister. Loss after loss. Failure after failure.

Elara felt every single one of her eighteen years when she tried to parse the last week and realized it was just a small taste of more danger to come. That was why she didn't notice the scene at first, at least not until one of the two Queenshield surged ahead to block Elara's way with one buff arm. She was momentarily distracted by the swell of the woman's muscles—so much like her girlfriend's—before she saw her mother standing with said girlfriend in front of her house.

Someone had smeared TRAITORS across the front wall in bloodred paint, half the letters smudged and faded. Buckets with pink water stood sentry beneath them. Signey Soto and Nida Vincent turned, swollen sponges weeping red in their hands. Their palms were so wrinkled, it was clear they had been at work for hours. Maybe even since she'd left. The fence—the one Papa had built to keep worshippers from bothering Faron in her own yard—was in pieces across the lawn.

Elara's bottom lip trembled. She was so *fucking* tired.

"It's okay. Go ahead. I've got her," Elara heard, seconds before a pair of familiar hands grabbed her shoulders. Signey, her Langlish girlfriend and former co-Rider, watched her through shrewd

THIS ENDS IN EMBERS

brown eyes, taking in every tic of what Elara was so desperate to hide. Signey had been at the top of her class at the Hearthstone Academy, Langley's military school for dragon Riders, before and after her dragon, Zephyra, had chosen Elara as their co-Rider. Elara would have had better luck hiding a dragon beneath her bed than hiding her emotions from Langley's most promising young soldier. "Elara, you need to get some sleep. Maybe for a century or two."

"Ha ha," said Elara, swallowing another yawn before it could prove Signey's point. Even now, she wanted to blossom under Signey's undivided attention, something that had been difficult to get since the battle. Elara chalked it up to their both being busy, mainly because she was afraid to dig any deeper when she was already so stressed. "Did you see who did this?"

"No, but..."

"But what?"

Signey lowered her hands. It had been an emotional day, so Elara allowed herself a moment to marvel at her girlfriend's soft beauty. Her round face was framed by loose curls that tumbled from her widow's peak and past her shoulders, the black of a moonless sky. Her once bronze skin was now the rich brown of clay, tanned darker by the relentless Iryan sun. Her oval eyes were umber beneath naturally arched eyebrows. Her fleshy nose and crooked teeth gave her character. She was two inches taller than Elara and built differently, which was emphasized by the lace-lined house dress she wore. It belonged to Elara, and so, on Signey, it was tight in the bust and loose at the back.

Despite the storm clouds that gathered in her expression, Signey Soto was so stupidly beautiful—inside and out—that just looking

13

at her made Elara want to smile. She regretted every mistake she had made, but not the ones that had led her to Signey.

But when Signey's shoulders straightened into a soldier's stance, Elara braced herself for bad news. "They were gone by the time we made it to the porch, which likely means it's one of your neighbors."

Elara swallowed. All the sleepy houses that lined the block suddenly looked like ancient beasts, sunlight making their windows glow like wrathful eyes. Four of them belonged to families she knew: the Hanlons, the McKays, the Pryors, and the Harlows. The rest belonged to families she knew *of.* Any one of them would have just cause to do something like this. Any one of them could have witnessed what Faron had unleashed.

"Well, I'm here now," Elara managed. "Let me take care of this. Your hands look six times older than you do."

"You need to *sleep.*"

But Elara was already calling on the gods, hoping that Mala wouldn't mind such a frivolous use of her powers. The deity appeared in a shower of twinkling silver stars, her wide nose wrinkling at the sight of Signey—of a Langlish Rider—on Iryan land. Even though Signey had fought against her own country in the Battle for Port Sol, Elara had needed to plead for her girlfriend's right to stay by her side. Iryan officials thought Signey was a spy, just as they'd assumed of Reeve, and Elara was not looking forward to having the same argument with her gods.

Thankfully, Mala soon dismissed Signey to return her attention to Elara.

"You have summoned me at a fortuitous time, Maiden Empyrean." Mala's frown was as deep as a gorge. Elara's pulse was already jumping from this new form of summoning, and Mala's expression sent her heart rate to new heights. Terrifying possibilities ran through her mind, from the withdrawal of her Empyrean powers to the condemnation of her family for all the devastation they had wrought. But nothing could have prepared her for the shock wave that pulsed through her mind when Mala said, *We have finally located your sister.*

CHAPTER TWO

FARON

FARON VINCENT HAD BEEN A SURVIVOR SINCE THE MOMENT SHE'D gone to war.

On the battlefield, it had been easy to justify death. People had to die so that she, and her island, could live. It wasn't until afterward that she'd been forced to reckon with what she'd done to keep breathing. All the lives she had destroyed. All the lives she was still destroying.

Faron survived, and others suffered for it.

The bodies she had left behind in San Irie hadn't died by her hands—not like the many Langlish soldiers and Riders she had cut down during the San Irie Revolution—but her hands were still slick with their blood. Awake, she saw their charred bodies every time she blinked, brown skin burned red, then black, muscle and organs and bones reduced to putrid remains. Asleep, she woke screaming from nightmares in which the scorched husks of the Queenshield, of her neighbors' children, of Iryan civilians, reached for her with furious hands, their hollow mouths accusing her with cauterized tongues: *Your fault. Your fault. Your fault.*

THIS ENDS IN EMBERS

Once, San Irie had worshipped her as a saint. Once, she had been the voice of the gods themselves.

But now she knew she was nothing but a harbinger of death—and she had brought that death on a dragon to her island for her own selfish purposes.

By the time Lightbringer began descending toward an unfamiliar strip of land, Faron had cried for so long that her eyes felt swollen and crusted. During the journey across the Ember Sea, that infinite blue ocean that stretched between San Irie and the northern continent of Nova, Faron had remembered the look on her sister's face as Faron had taken Iya's hand and flown away from the smoking capital of Port Sol. There had been no time to apologize or explain. There had been only the sound of two hearts breaking, a sound oddly similar to that of powerful dragon wings beating on the wind.

Faron had lost Reeve. Her gods. Her people. She couldn't stand to lose Elara, too.

But maybe she already had.

The greenery below resolved itself into an archipelago of seven islands of varying sizes. It was the Hestan Archipelago, where Elara had spent two months enrolled in Langley's dragon-riding academy, Hearthstone. Faron had seen it on a map in Pearl Bay Palace, this inverted V off the coast of the hooked Langlish land that formed the bottom of Nova. She couldn't remember now if Iya had placed a clay crown atop the archipelago, marking it as a target in his upcoming conquest, but her stomach tightened all the same.

Lightbringer's forces now consisted of three dragons—Goldeye, Ignatz, and Irontooth—as well as their Riders—Marius Lynwood and Nichol Thompson, Estella Ballard and Briar Noble, and Commander Gavriel Warwick and Director Mireya Warwick—but most of the other dragons and Riders had fought for San Irie during Iya's attempt to claim it. Eventually, they would return here, and surely another battle would break out.

Faron was too tired for another battle.

"Your mental tears are being wasted unless their purpose is to irritate me," Lightbringer said through the bond he had forced upon her. *"There is only one dragon here, and he has no interest in battle."*

She hated the growl of that voice in her mind. This was the second time the dragon had spoken to her directly, and his voice was like claws slicing poisonous lines under her skin. It left behind a miasma that was hard to shake off.

They landed smoothly in a wide field on the first island, the name of which Faron had never bothered to learn. Iya jumped from the saddle onto flattened grass cupped by the golden sand of a long beach. Low tide lapped at the shoreline in peaceful waves, retreating periodically back into Serpentia Bay. Faron dropped behind Iya with a wince, her thighs unused to long flights on dragonback—or even short ones. It felt as if her skin had been scraped raw by Lightbringer's diamond-hard scales.

Then the boy before her turned, and Faron's breath caught.

Reeve Warwick gazed steadily at her, his eyes the clear blue of the Ember Sea, his red-brown curls haloed by the sun, his candle-white skin pinkened from overexposure, his dragon-eye necklace resting over his chest. But it wasn't Reeve Warwick, she reminded herself. It was Iya with his cutting smile who watched her, his appearance little more than a trap to weaken her resolve.

She couldn't forget that there were four beings staring back at her from those cold eyes: Reeve Warwick, whose body had been possessed and whose soul was caged too deep for her to reach; Gael Soto, whose soul had been corrupted and whose flashes of humanity had seduced her into dooming the world; Lightbringer, the dragon they were bonded to, whose innate malice made him a danger to two realms; and Iya, the parts of Gael that were Lightbringer and the parts of Lightbringer that were Gael, the singular godlike creature who was determined to get her to believe he was all that remained of the boys she knew.

The boys she was here to save.

Faron swallowed and forced herself to breathe. To remember why she had taken his hand, climbed on his dragon, and set fire to her reputation.

Iya may have declared himself a god, but Faron was his undoing. *You are nothing but the heart I can't seem to destroy,* he had said to her hours ago, his eyes wild and his hands tight around her throat. He could not destroy her, but she could destroy *him*—starting with his hold on Reeve and Gael.

Or so she hoped.

Iya's smile deepened, as if he could hear what she was thinking—and maybe he could—but before either of them could speak, there was a shouted welcome from above. Ahead of them was a hill with a plateau, and atop that hill was a white girl perhaps a couple years older than Faron. Her red hair was styled into a chin-length bob, and she wore a Hearthstone uniform: a marigold blouse with a standing collar, a black blazer with marigold cuffs, fitted breeches, and leather boots.

As they crested the hill, Faron realized there was a medallion dragon stretching in the grass behind her, golden with a barbed tail and belly scales the pale yellow of an old sponge. His eyes, like Lightbringer's, were green, but that was their only similarity. Lightbringer was the only imperial dragon in existence, the white of a newborn and massive enough to overshadow even a carmine, and his bulk and spikes made him a dangerous weapon. By comparison, the yellow dragon suspiciously narrowing its gaze looked like a child.

"Cruz, Margot," Iya said, greeting the dragon and then the girl. "Where's your father?"

"He's waiting in the courtyard," said Margot. "We saw you arrive while we were flying, and I thought I should walk you there."

There was a calculating edge to the way Margot looked at Iya, as though she was judging him against some silent set of expectations. Faron couldn't tell whether he fell short, however. Her expression gave little else away.

Iya nodded his agreement, and Margot paused to whisper something to her dragon—to Cruz—that sent him back into the air. Lightbringer sat unmoving in the field, now joined by Irontooth, Goldeye, and Ignatz. The Riders made their way up the hill, the Warwicks leading the throng. Had Elara felt this continual pulse of fear while surrounded by enemies and dragons? Had she lifted her chin, as Faron was doing now, and armored herself with the lie that everything would be fine if she stuck to the plan?

It was a silent walk through a verdant valley surrounding a fortress of obsidian. Walls as tall as a dragon flew Langlish flags from towers in every corner, each flag the color of one of the four breeds: red for carmine, yellow for medallion, blue for ultramarine, and green for sage. On the other side of the walls was a courtyard and

THIS ENDS IN EMBERS

a keep, and in front of the keep's raised portcullis was another white man. His complexion was ruddy, his blond and silver hair retreating from his wide forehead, and he wore a black suit with the Langlish starburst on the right breast. He and Margot had the same narrow noses, the same brown eyes, the same round cheeks.

Faron realized this must be Margot's father seconds before Gavriel Warwick muscled past her to say, warmly, "Headmaster Luxton. Always a pleasure."

"The pleasure is all mine," said the headmaster of Hearthstone Academy, his thick mustache twitching over his thin mouth. He and the commander shook hands like old friends before Luxton dropped into a deep bow before Iya. "It is an incredible honor to meet and host you, Gray Saint. I am Oscar Luxton, Wingleader for my daughter, Margot, and our dragon, Cruz. We've cleared the second floor for your forces."

Elara had explained Wingleaders and Firstriders to Faron during one of her fire calls from Langley, a connection of voices that required only an open flame to allow them to hear and respond to each other, but Faron hadn't bothered to retain the information. Her sister aside, a Rider was a Rider to Faron; it didn't matter their precise role in the colonization of her island.

"And when," Iya asked, *"will you grapple with your role in it? Five years ago, your home was in shambles because of the Langlish. Now your home is in shambles because of you."*

Guilt settled in Faron's chest, squeezing her lungs to make it impossible to breathe. Iya sounded slightly different from Lightbringer alone—it was like the buzzing of a beehive, several voices speaking at once, a war of souls within the single body of a boy. But it was his words rather than just his voice that struck her like daggers across the unwanted bond. Because he was right. Port Sol had been reduced to ashes twice in her lifetime, and the second time, it had been her fault.

"Say what you will about these people, but they are the only allies you have left," Iya continued. His tone softened with pity, and somehow that hurt worse. *"You forget that we are the same, Faron. I was once the Empyrean. I know how easy it is to fall from the very pedestal they forced you onto. And I know you hope to regain their love by stopping me. It makes me sad to see you smother your potential to protect people who want you dead."*

"You don't know anything about me and my potential," Faron shot back, sounding weak to her own ears.

"We are connected, whether you like it or not. I know you. And part of you knows this simple truth: We were meant to rule, not to be ruled." While he spoke in her mind, Iya gestured for Margot to lead his people into the gray stone keep. The Warwicks and Headmaster Luxton followed, their heads bent in conversation. Soon, Iya and Faron were the only two remaining in the courtyard, and he faced her with an intense fervor in his—in Reeve's—light blue eyes. He studied her the way Reeve once did, as if he were looking for something she wasn't sure he would find. *"Your island sees a saint. Your parents see a rebel. Your queen sees a nuisance. Your gods see an enemy. But I see you. I have always seen you. You are all of that and so much more."*

He reached for her, but Faron twisted away before his fingers could make contact with her cheek.

"Except," she said aloud, "you said I was nothing. 'You are nothing without me,' remember?" Her hands clenched into fists at her sides as she stared just over his shoulder, refusing to be taken in by the lure of his appearance. She hadn't truly realized how much time Reeve had spent watching her until now, when Iya doing the same made her skin crawl. Reeve had made her feel exposed, awkward, but Iya made her feel violated. "I told you once that you're lying to the best. I know what you really think of me."

"No," Iya murmured, his tone unreadable, "you really don't."

By the time she lowered her gaze, he was already heading into the keep, the embroidered KNIGHT OF THE EMPIRE on the back of his uniform bleeding gold in the afternoon sun.

A week passed in a blur of preparations, converting the academy from a school back to its origins as a military stronghold.

The Warwicks took Irontooth around the other six islands, conscripting civilians into Iya's army and murdering anyone who refused or rebelled. Iya established a schedule of dragons and Riders to form a perpetual perimeter guard, one group remaining around Hearthstone, the other circling the entire archipelago. The second floor—which Faron discovered had once been dormitories—was repurposed into barracks. She was given her own room, but a thorough search showed that every dragon relic, a harvested part of a dead dragon that still contained some of its magic, had been removed and every fireplace had been boarded up—just to keep her from attempting to contact San Irie in any way. Faron had expected a Rider to be assigned to her at all times, but Iya thought that unnecessary, when he could watch her every move through the bond.

Luckily, Faron could understand everything happening around her. She spoke only patois, and they spoke only Langlish, but Lightbringer's ancient knowledge included all human tongues, and his magic translated their speech accordingly. She could read written reports and understand the snide remarks the Riders—especially Marius Lynwood, Goldeye's Firstrider—made about her presence. Even if she couldn't call home, this was a weapon in her arsenal, an opportunity for espionage that she wouldn't take for granted.

At night, she would look through her window, which overlooked the bay, and see Lightbringer sitting on the beach, limned in silver moonlight. His mind was always closed to her, but there was something wistful in the lines of his body. If she hadn't witnessed his atrocities firsthand, she might have been moved.

Instead, she waited until the moon was high on the seventh night and sneaked out of her room.

It was dramatic to call it sneaking since no one stopped her, but nights were made for quiet steps and secret movements. Stars twinkled outside Hearthstone's high windows, and the only sign of life within was intermittent snoring from the off-duty Riders. It had been long enough that Faron had gotten used to the casual opulence of the so-called school, the gorgeous tapestries and carpets, the decorative suits of armor and the massive gymnasium. At this point, all it did was remind her that Langley had all this wealth and all these resources, and still they'd wanted San Irie, too.

That kind of insatiable hunger never led anywhere good.

Goldeye circled the air on night watch, but Lightbringer was right where Faron expected him to be. The closer she got to the massive war beast, the more her heart pounded. Spikes like curved teeth trailed down his back, and his tail alone was longer than she was tall. Regardless of Iya's twisted affection for her, if Lightbringer wanted to kill Faron, no one could stop him. The dragon's opinion of her had never matched that of his Rider.

Faron let that bolster her determination to at least try to resolve this peacefully.

"*Lightbringer*," she said, and only a prickle of awareness in her mind made it clear the stationary dragon was listening. "*You've done this all before. You must realize that your conquest will end only one way. I released you from the Empty. You're free for the first time in centuries. The gods are welcoming you home. Wouldn't you rather be living there than fighting here?*"

"*What do you know of my home?*" Lightbringer asked, baring his teeth in a wordless snarl. "*In the divine plane, we are little more than beasts for them to shepherd and ignore. We are not and have never been equal, even though we, too, are gods.*" His tail shifted through the sand, making the ground beneath her feet shake. Faron stumbled forward until she was near his legs, out of range of his spikes. "*You see my conquest as fruitless, but I see it as righteous. Inevitable. Where you see destruction, I see limitless potential I did not have obeying the gods. Now I am the one served. Now I am the one obeyed. And I would rather rule over the ashes of this realm than serve in the majesty of theirs.*"

Faron could barely hear him over the sudden ringing in her ears. The gods had never told her that, though she didn't know why she was so surprised. While Gael Soto had trained her to manipulate living souls, a skill he had claimed would help her break Elara's dragon bond, the gods had done nothing but prove they would always lie to her to protect their interests. Gael may have twisted or omitted some truths, but he had been more honest with her than the gods ever had—which made her more inclined to believe that Lightbringer was being honest, too.

She remembered the raw horror that had swallowed her

through the bond when Elara had opened a door between realms beneath Iya's feet. Lightbringer and Gael hadn't wanted to go back there, and, at the time, she had assumed *there* was the Empty. But maybe it had been the divine plane.

"*Still, it doesn't have to be this way,*" Faron tried, hoping she didn't sound as desperate as she felt. "*Maybe if we negotiate with the gods, they'll let you all stay—*"

"*How swiftly they damned you for making your own choices, and yet you still believe your gods can be reasoned with.*" A chuckle as low and deep as a smoker's echoed through her head. "*I have known Irie, Mala, and Obie far longer than you have, child, and they will never fold. Neither will I.*"

Faron swallowed, trying to ignore the soft heart that had gotten her into this mess in the first place. What did she care if Lightbringer feared his return to the divine realm? He had twisted Gael's mind. He had stolen Reeve's body. He had razed her island, and he planned to burn so much more before he was done.

In Faron's experience, this was how wars began: A stubborn, if not malevolent, world power claimed to see no way forward but destruction.

"*You'll lose,*" she warned him. Her mind was open for him to pick through, so she made a point of thinking of the Iryan drakes; of her sister, the Maiden Empyrean; of the Langlish dragons that had not sided with him; and of the countries worldwide that could—and would—rise up against him. "*If you don't end this now, you will lose everything. And all dragons will suffer.*"

"*Let them suffer,*" said Lightbringer, tipping his triangular head toward the full moon. "*At least then I will no longer suffer alone.*"

CHAPTER THREE

ELARA

W HEN ELARA FORCED HER EYES OPEN, IT WAS LATE AFTERNOON. Orange sunlight crept through the window of her bedroom, fragmented by the trees in Papa's garden. Shadows gathered in the corners, having watched over her as she slept. Her braids were tucked into a satin sleep cap, and someone had changed her clothes, leaving her in a pale pink nightgown. She sat up with a groan as the memory of the day before trickled back to her.

After Mala's disappearance, Elara had blurted, "Faron is at Hearthstone," before passing out in the middle of the street. Yes, she'd been exhausted, but she hadn't realized *how* exhausted until now. Sleeping for almost twenty-four hours when her sister was in danger? Guilt twisted her insides as she swung her legs over the side of the bed.

Her room was a relic of the girl she'd once been. After the war, she hadn't cared to do anything besides donate the clothes and shoes she'd outgrown. Eventually, when she'd started secondary school, she'd donated her stuffed animals and dolls, as well. But as she changed now into a simple day dress, Elara felt disconnected from the girl who had collected the drake figurines that lined her bookshelf, who had framed newspaper articles about the drake pilots on the walls, who had a small altar to Irie on the side table beneath the window. She had lived through too many things that had aged her by centuries instead of days. Everything else seemed frivolous.

"There you are," said Papa when she stepped into the hallway, wiggling her foot deeper into her button boots. "Her Majesty has been waiting for you to wake up for the meeting."

Elara blinked. "What meeting?"

Twenty minutes later, Elara was seated at the empty dinner table between Signey and Papa. Mosquitos buzzed around the window mesh, looking for a way inside. Queenshield guarded the exits, their faces impassive. Her jittery thoughts were drowned out by the sonorous *tick-tock tick-tock* of the grandfather clock in the hall. Elara was beginning to understand why Faron always did the bad thing without waiting for permission. She itched to be on dragonback, soaring to her sister's alleged location. Instead, Aveline was making it clear that no action could be taken until they had discussed the situation at length.

As if a lengthy discussion would bring Faron home any faster.

Curry goat scented the air as Mama prepared enough food for everyone. She stirred the goat meat stewing in the cast-iron dutchie, sprinkling diced Scotch bonnets into the curry. The scrape of her metal spoon against the pot's sides broke the pensive silence.

Elara's foot shook restlessly. "Your Majesty, the longer we wait—"

"How can we be sure that Faron is at Hearthstone?" Aveline asked, her eyebrows drawn together. "This could be a trap that Iya

THIS ENDS IN EMBERS

has set for us, knowing that the dragon bond shields his actions from the gods."

"Mala said their sight is obstructed in the Hestan Archipelago, and Signey confirmed that the rest of the dragons returned to the Langlish capital after—"

"Yes, so you have said," said the queen, holding up a hand. "But that merely confirms that Iya's forces are at Hearthstone. How can we be sure that *Faron* is?"

Elara's mouth snapped shut. Frustration rolled through her, but she forced it down. Aveline was asking the right questions, the questions that Elara would be asking if this weren't about her sister. Aveline hadn't seen the heartbroken and hopeless expression on Faron's face as she'd disappeared into the clouds on Lightbringer's back. The queen probably thought that Faron was in no danger at all. But these past few months since Elara had been claimed as a Rider by Zephyra had been the most amount of time that they'd ever spent apart since Faron's birth. Even though her parents had said nothing of the sort, Elara still heard their voices in her mind: *Protect your sister. Protect your sister. Protect your sister.*

"We cannot risk dispatching the Sky Battalion without more information," Aveline continued. "The pilots are still recovering from Port Sol. Families are still burying their dead. Iya is a god; he must have known they would find him and planned accordingly."

"Then don't deploy the Sky Battalion," said Signey. "I can go alone."

"No, you can't." Elara glared at her. "I'll go with you."

Signey didn't look at her. "Your people need you."

I need you, Elara wanted to say. But it was too much, too soon, even though Signey's presence by her side had made the last few months bearable. There was still an awkwardness that lived between them, curling through that space like citronella smoke. Papa sat close enough for their elbows to brush whenever he moved. Signey sat so far away that not even her wayward curls would kiss Elara's skin if she tilted her head.

Another thing that Elara didn't have time to discuss.

"What, exactly, is your plan?" she asked Signey instead. "Fly close enough for Iya to induce the Fury and then wake up in a dungeon?"

The Fury was a problem with no clear solution. When Elara had first formed her bond with Zephyra, Commander Gavriel Warwick had warned that if Faron didn't find a way to break it, the Fury would drive Elara—and her dragon and co-Rider—mad. The sudden tendency of dragons to turn feral, violent, uncontrollable— which the commander had called the Fury—had been wielded as a weapon by Lightbringer during the battle. The only thing that had kept their minds sane and whole was Faron, using a kind of magic that Elara had never seen before. A kind of magic that Gael Soto—Signey and her brother, Jesper's, ancestor, who now called himself Iya—had taught her.

Signey tucked her curls behind her ear. The scent of cocoa butter lotion wafted from her now-unwrinkled hands. "My *plan* is to pretend to defect to his side, send information about his plans through the den, and extract Faron at the earliest and safest time."

It was a good plan. Good enough for Aveline to visibly consider. But Elara's panicked heart refused to see its merits. Iya inhabited Reeve's body. Faron had chosen to run with him. If Signey and Zephyra left, too, Elara would be completely alone. Even if she was no longer bonded to them, and could thus no longer share their

THIS ENDS IN EMBERS

thoughts and emotions, they were the only ones left who knew her down to her soul. Elara wasn't sure she knew *herself* anymore.

An argument struck her like a lightning bolt, and she tried not to sound upbeat as she pointed out, "Lightbringer is connected to all the dragons, since he created the original dragon bond. He'll read your intentions before you even get close to Hearthstone, let alone if you stay there. You can't keep your walls up *all* the time."

"Just because *you're* bad at guarding your mind—"

"The Maiden has a point. A single slip would jeopardize the entire ruse," said Aveline before a full disagreement could break out. "For such a long-term mission, we'd need someone whose intentions he cannot read."

"Which," Elara said, "would be me. If we go together, Zephyra can carry me as close to the shore as she can get, and, while the two of you are stalling Iya, I can sneak into Hearthstone and find Faron."

"Absolutely not," said Mama, setting the first plate of curry goat and rice on the table. "What if you get stranded?"

"I'm a trained soldier, Mama. I was the second-highest-scoring combat student at Hearthstone!"

"I don't care if you're the highest-scoring soldier in the entire world. *I will not lose you both.*"

And so it went. Aveline, Mama, and Papa poked holes in her plan, while Signey continued to insist that she did not need Elara's help at all. Plates were cleared and tensions were high, and all the while the hours washed away like sand at high tide. It was nearing sundown by the time Elara's frustration bubbled over and she set down her empty cup of carrot juice hard enough to rattle the table.

"I am the Maiden Empyrean, not a child to be coddled." She

looked at the queen and the queen alone. "This is the compromise: Signey and I will fly Zephyra out for a scouting mission. We won't engage with Iya; we'll get only as close as we can for reconnaissance and come right back. Is that acceptable to everyone?" And then, allowing the whole room to fall away so that Aveline could see the worry and the fear and the guilt that swirled inside her, Elara pleaded, "Talking in circles like this is just wasting time, Your Majesty. My sister needs me. *Please.*"

Aveline studied her for so long that Elara expected to be turned down, followed by another few hours of pointless conversation.

Then she sighed. "All right. But you are absolutely not to engage. Do you both understand?"

"Yes," Elara and Signey said together.

"Do not make me regret this," Aveline said. She lifted her glass. "Mrs. Vincent, may I have more rum?"

Elara rose with the sun and dressed in her newly cleaned riding leathers. She hadn't slept, too anxious about the plan and everything that could go wrong with it, but she was counting on a mug of coffee to keep her awake for the two-hour flight to the Hestan Archipelago.

A half hour later, she and Signey stood at the base of the Argent Mountains, on the shoulder of the paved road that wound up the vibrant green and misty blue of its peaks. At the top was Highfort, a town named after the military base that took up most of one peak—a town that Elara hadn't been to since her failed attempt to become a drake pilot and join the Sky Battalion of the Iryan Military Forces. They had gone the long way around Deadegg to reach

THIS ENDS IN EMBERS

this road to avoid any sight of the wreckage of Valor, but, if Elara squinted far enough behind them, she could see the scorched tip of a chunk of silver scalestone.

She wanted to talk to Signey about it, but she didn't know what she would say. Besides, once she started talking, she had a hard time stopping, and no doubt she would start with Valor and end up somewhere near *Why are you acting weird and distant?*

"It's nice that I don't need the bond to tell what you're thinking," Signey said in her accented patois. Once again, there was enough space for a third person between them, but Elara tried not to focus on that. "Stop worrying. It won't change what will or won't happen."

"Easier said than done," said Elara as the wind around them picked up, a sign that Zephyra would soon arrive. "But I'll try."

Zephyra landed in front of them in a small cyclone of dirt, her wings momentarily blocking the sun. She was fifteen feet in length, her body the deep green of a palm frond, with dark spikes trailing down her back. Signey's saddle was affixed to her, strapped just above her now-folded wings. Light green scales protected her sleek stomach, and a pointed snout curved upward from her head, which lacked the horns that Elara had noticed on some other dragons.

But then, Zephyra was a sage dragon, the smallest of the four dragon breeds, built for speed rather than for war. And though Signey was fluent in patois, sage dragons like Zephyra were gifted with languages, and their bond allowed Signey to understand any human tongue, whether spoken, written, or signed. It was a handy ability, one that Elara missed having.

There were a lot of things that Elara hadn't expected to miss when Faron had severed Elara's bond with Signey and Zephyra.

The dragon carefully flattened herself on the road, laying her head close enough for Signey and Elara to step forward and rest their hands on her snout in greeting. Signey closed her eyes and pressed her forehead against Zephyra's scaly neck, no doubt in silent conversation with her mount, and Elara tried to ignore her envy as she rubbed the soft skin of Zephyra's forehead. She wasn't even sure which one she was envious of. This was the most affection she had seen Signey show anyone all week, and she wished she were on the receiving end of it. Before the Battle for Port Sol, Signey had kissed her for the first time, a passionate clash of lips that had distracted Elara long enough for Signey to drop her from Zephyra's back before the dragon succumbed to the Fury. Elara had expressed her own feelings, returning the gesture with a kiss on Signey's cheek before going to beg the gods for the power of the Empyrean. Ever since, they'd been too busy to talk, let alone kiss—but Elara wasn't sure when things had changed from *couldn't* to *wouldn't*.

So many things would be easier if she could just see inside Signey's head, could just feel that Signey still wanted this. Or if she could feel Zephyra's comforting affection, a kind of love that could never expire. But Elara had lost her dragon bond and become a tool of the Iryan gods.

That was *better*, she told herself. That was what her island needed. Her destiny was to remove dragons from this realm, not to ride or befriend them. She had to focus on issues more significant than her stalled love life.

Zephyra blinked her golden eyes, her catlike pupils finding Elara. Elara swallowed around the ache of regret, whispering, "It's nice to see you, old friend."

THIS ENDS IN EMBERS

Signey helped her struggle up into Zephyra's saddle, and that utilitarian touch felt like another kind of loss. When they had been bonded, Elara had enjoyed the Rider magic that gave her perfect balance when on the back of her dragon. Now she had to strap herself in and hope that she didn't slip off the sides as they flew, while Signey leaped higher than a normal person could, landing gracefully in the saddle in front of her. She strapped herself in as well, but it was a formality. Even if Zephyra flew upside down, Signey wouldn't fall.

Elara's front pressed against Signey's back, her arms wrapping around Signey's waist, and she inhaled Signey's honeysuckle-and-clove scent. If Signey noticed or minded, she didn't show it as they took off. So at least Elara could confirm her girlfriend wasn't *repulsed* by her.

The last time she had made the flight from San Irie to Langley, she'd been terrified. Of the future, of the cold soldier in the saddle before her, of the dragon that was the only thing keeping her from falling to her death. Even now that she only feared one of the three, anxiety twisted her stomach until she felt sick with nerves. Nine days ago, her sister had felt—for just an instant—like a stranger. Would she go home with them now? Or was whatever she had left to do more important than the worry of her loved ones?

Despite her agitation, Elara dozed on and off, drifting from stress dream to stress dream. She saw faceless people vandalizing her house again—this time going a step further and shattering windows—as Signey stood by and watched with an inscrutable expression. She saw Faron with her eyes glowing the same mold green as Lightbringer's, her sister lost to the Fury and attacking her own allies. She saw Reeve caged and begging for help, pleading with Elara to save him the way he had saved her, even as the iron bars grew smaller and smaller around him. . . .

Worse than the metaphors were the memories that her tired mind latched on to. Once, she had asked Reeve if it had ever bothered him, being the only member of his family who wasn't a Rider. His mother and father were co-Riders to their carmine, Irontooth, and Reeve had spent most of his childhood bedridden with illness after illness, his immune system so weak, it was almost as if he didn't have one. For that reason, his parents had never taken him to the Beacon Dragon Preserve, where eggs were laid in an area called the Nest and hatched into colorless dragons waiting for Riders to bond with. Considering the Warwicks were one of the four dragon-riding dynasties of Langley—alongside the Sotos, the Hylands, and the Lynwoods—Elara had wondered how that made Reeve feel, long before she'd ever learned half that information.

Reeve had considered the question as thoughtfully as Reeve considered everything, his finger acting as a bookmark in what he was reading at the time: a biography of the first Renard queen. Then he'd said, "Not as much as other things. My parents loved me—or seemed to—but I always got the impression that Irontooth thought I was weak. He protected me, but he scared me, too. And I didn't even know what he was doing to San Irie. I just thought a creature that powerful shouldn't be trusted in the hands of people so . . . small."

From his tone of voice, it had been clear that he hadn't just meant in size. Her book of choice, which she could no longer remember the subject of, had been face down on the table. They'd been at the Hanlon house, with Reeve's foster parents in the kitchen making stew chicken. The window had been open to provide some relief

THIS ENDS IN EMBERS

from the late-spring heat, and the wind had been steadily growing cooler as the sun finally began to go down.

That hot-spice smell of stew filling the house. That rhythmic *chop-chop-chop* of vegetables being diced. That comforting warmth of Reeve's foot pressing against hers beneath the table. It was those little things that made her heart seize now that he was gone.

"Isn't that blasphemous of you?" Elara had asked, amused. "You said Riders are worshipped as saints."

Reeve had glanced off to the side, out the window, his eyes slightly narrowed. "I never said that was a good thing. Being worshipped."

Elara jolted awake, just in time to find them plunging through the air.

"We're still a mile out from shore, and we've already been spotted by a perimeter guard," Signey said, snapping Elara into the present. "Ignatz, to be specific."

"We're not supposed to engage," said Elara, her mind still struggling into wakefulness.

"Oh, we're engaged. Hold on tight."

Elara barely had time to make sure her straps were secure before Zephyra shot upward. She closed her eyes against the sunlight that Zephyra was using for cover, and, behind them, she could hear the echoing roar of Ignatz. If she remembered correctly, Ignatz was an ultramarine dragon, deep blue in color, larger than Zephyra in size, and the strongest swimmer of all the breeds. Hopefully, they wouldn't need to put that to the test.

Wind sliced Elara's skin. Cloud water slicked her face. Her heart beat so fast, it sounded like static. She didn't want to think of how high up they were, how quickly she would slip if Zephyra had to roll away from an attack. Instead, she forced herself to remember that she was in the best hands. Signey was one of the top soldiers in Langley. She and Zephyra had bonded half a decade ago, and Signey had been strong enough to bear the dragon bond alone until they'd found a Wingleader in Elara. Together, Signey and Zephyra moved like droplets in a river, harmoniously indistinguishable from each other. Defensive maneuvering was as easy as breathing for them.

Especially when they had Elara to help with the offensive.

She took a deep breath of knife-edged air and called upon the gods. The sky fell away, replaced by the vastness of the divine plane, and then Irie, ruler of the daytime and patron goddess of San Irie, appeared to answer her summons. Instead of floating before her in a forest fire, the world returned in golden color as the sun goddess glided alongside them, easily keeping pace with Zephyra. Her snow-white robes flapped around her dark brown skin, and her pupilless eyes glowered amber beneath her crown. The embroidery on her robe was a gold that matched her lipstick, both shimmering in the light.

Please, Elara gasped. *Please, help us.*

Irie's expression was shrewd. *Do you see, now, why this world needs to be rid of dragons?*

Please!

Ah, of course. There is some urgency, isn't there?

PLEASE!

Elara reached out and Irie merged with her, the majestic force of Irie's soul briefly making her feel like a balloon close to popping. Despite the chill this high in the sky, she began sweating,

THIS ENDS IN EMBERS

her clothes clinging to her overheated body. Fire raced up her spine, and for a moment she thought that Ignatz had caught up with them, before she realized that it was just Irie's power settling within her. Irie, she had learned, had magic that eclipsed that of both Mala and Obie, the kind of raw power that leveled cities and created worlds. What she loaned to Elara was just a trickle of something that was vast enough to corrode Elara's weak human flesh from the inside—and that energy was exactly what she needed right now.

Though she'd have to talk with the gods about the effort it had taken to get it.

"Going down," Signey said as Elara focused on the world around her.

Zephyra dived again, narrowly avoiding a burst of fire. She dropped so precipitously that Elara partially lifted from the saddle, the straps straining to keep her from falling. But Elara's heart was no longer racing. Irie's calm confidence had become her own.

She twisted around just far enough to stick her hand out toward Ignatz. Light erupted from her palm, illuminating the morning with a destructive beam that seared one of Ignatz's horns. The dragon roared in pain and swerved away from them to regroup. His next attack came from the front, but Elara saw it coming and leaned around Signey to shoot two blasts of light at the gigantic blue target. Ignatz puffed a cloud of fire in their direction, which collided with the light beams and exploded in a blinding flash.

Zephyra was low enough that she had to pull up to avoid skimming the top of a mountain range; Elara's mental map identified it as the one that cut through the Emerald Highlands in the south of Langley. They had passed the Hestan Archipelago entirely, and, even if they turned back, they had thoroughly lost any chance at stealth. Iya would either send his other dragons after them or take Zephyra out of the equation with the Fury. That left them with only two options: fight or flight.

Die or run.

"We're made," she said to Signey, settling properly into the saddle. "We have to turn back."

"I can still drop you off—"

"They'll expect something like that now. And there's a dragon on top of us!"

Signey didn't argue further. Seconds later, Zephyra was ascending into the clouds and racing back the way they had come. The gap between them and Ignatz widened until they were blissfully alone in the sky, too far from the Hestan Archipelago for Ignatz to still consider them a threat. Then and only then did Elara expel Irie from her body, allowing the exhaustion of summoning to settle into a full-body ache. Her eyes fluttered closed, from both fatigue and shame.

Another failure to add to the pile.

"It's another four hours from here to Beacon," Signey whispered. "Jesper and Torrey would love to see you, and we could use the time to regroup."

"Okay."

Signey let the silence envelop them, and it was broken only by the rhythmic flap of Zephyra's wings. With no one but the stars to see her, Elara let the tears fall, wondering if she would ever feel like the Maiden Empyrean or if she was just going to keep failing massively and publicly until the gods realized they'd made another mistake. She wished she could talk to Faron about how she dealt with this unceasing pressure, this weight on her chest, this unrelenting dread that she was failing the world. Granted, it was an emotion that Elara was familiar with from being an older sibling, but it was heavier now that she had more than her parents' expectations to meet.

Reeve had been right. Being worshipped was hardly a good thing, and a pedestal was nothing but a clifftop to fall from.

Elara reached down until her fingers were touching Zephyra's hard scales, wishing she could hear the dragon's kind voice in her head, could lean upon the strength of Zephyra's soul to keep herself from shattering. Then Signey gasped, and Elara thought for a wild moment that she had somehow succeeded in renewing their bond just by wanting it badly enough.

Her hopes were dashed seconds later when Signey said, "It's Iya. He's—he's speaking to us. To all the dragons. We can hear him, *feel* him, in our heads."

"What? What's he saying?"

Signey listened, her curls rippling in the wind. Elara didn't need to see the expression on her girlfriend's face, because she could picture it perfectly: the clenched jaw and glazed eyes and thunderous furrow of her forehead. Things were weird between them, and Elara couldn't read Signey as well as Signey could read her, but she had seen that expression often enough in the last few months to draw it from memory.

When Signey spoke again, it was with barely concealed wrath. "He's calling for all dragons and Riders to join his faction. If we do, we'll be safe from his conquest. If we don't"—and here her voice shook, though Elara couldn't tell if it was from anger or fear— "he'll sever our bonds and just take our dragons for himself."

CHAPTER FOUR

FARON

YA'S ULTIMATUM ECHOED IN FARON'S EARS AS SHE RACED OUT INTO the courtyard, hoping that she would catch a glimpse of her sister's dragon before it was gone. But the skies were clear of everything but gold-tinted clouds and Ignatz's sapphire body circling the island Faron now knew was called Caledon. Nearing noon, the sun was high in the sky, and yellow light glittered across the whitecaps of the Ember Sea. On any other day, it might have been beautiful.

Right now, it just made her unspeakably lonely.

Her sister had been here, or near here, and Faron had been too late to see her. She would never even have known if not for Iya's announcement, which broadcast his shrewd message across their bond with a brief image of the source: a familiar green dragon twisting this way and that to avoid Ignatz's powerful flames.

She had no idea if Elara had been coming to rescue her or to stop Iya, if she had been doing reconnaissance or just been on her way to the Langlish capital, Beacon, unaware that Faron was down here at all. Her eyes burned with unshed tears as she realized she didn't know which option was better or worse. All San Irie thought she was a traitor. Elara probably did, too.

Now your home is in shambles because of you.

She shuddered at the memory. She knew the truth, and so did Reeve. Once she saved him—once she saved him *and* Gael—it would all be worth it. She had to believe this would all be worth it. Otherwise, she would shatter into a million pieces, her legacy little more than a pile of useless trash.

Faron turned back into Hearthstone, only to stop at the sight of four Riders emerging from the gatehouse entrance. Gavriel and Mireya Warwick wore crisp new riding leathers, his red-brown hair and beard trimmed and her lithe body free of decoration except for her silver wedding ring. Behind them, Marius Lynwood and Nichol Thompson wore their uniforms, which were riding leathers masquerading as fitted suits with red accents. It was clear that Luxton had treated them all well in the last nine days, because they looked less as if they were in the middle of war and more as if they were on their way to sit for a portrait.

Her hands clenched into fists. Meanwhile, her people were rebuilding the capital and burying their dead for the second time in ten years.

Because of you.

She blinked and found herself across the courtyard without having made a conscious decision to move. Iya's group had filed through the rounded mouth of the outer wall, talking among themselves unintelligibly, while Faron trailed several feet behind wondering when her surroundings had changed. Her heart pounded, both from the bone-deep knowledge that they were up to something and from the terror that she might be losing time again.

It had gotten bad, after the war, so bad that she had once woken up in the middle of a barren field, barefoot and wearing nothing but a cotton nightgown, Irie floating before her. Faron had been sweating so profusely that the fabric clung to her skin, and her pulse had still been racing with warning from the dregs of her nightmare. Instead of dragons, the sky had been filled with stars. Instead of an inferno, a light breeze had caressed her overheated skin.

What happened? Faron had asked, hating how small and scared her voice sounded. She had survived war, for gods' sake. Why should she be afraid of sleeping? *How did I get out here?*

You summoned me fifteen minutes ago, Irie had said in a gentle tone. Her hand had lifted and then fallen back to her side as she likely remembered she was only corporeal inside a temple, not on former farmland that would never grow anything again. *You said, 'We're being attacked,' but you... There's no one here, Empyrean. Everything is all right.*

None of it had sounded familiar to Faron, whose last memory had been of hugging Elara before going to sleep. No matter how hard she had tried, she couldn't fill those blanks with anything but nightmares of dragonfire. Fifteen minutes? She'd been outside for longer than *fifteen minutes?*

Faron hadn't realized she was crying until Irie's fingers passed through her cheek, drawing her attention to the fat tears leaving wet trails across her skin. *I'm sorry. I shouldn't have—I didn't mean to—I'm wasting your time.*

Time spent with you is never a waste, Empyrean, said Irie. *I withdrew because your body was weakening, but I am otherwise happy to stay. For as long as you need.*

Most days, Faron had wanted nothing more than to get rid of the gods. Her job was over. The war had been won. Their lingering presence, their infinite powers, had been more of a nuisance

THIS ENDS IN EMBERS

than anything else. But in that moment, all Faron had been able to manage was a sharp nod. And, true to her word, Irie had remained in that field with her, watching the sky for threats, until Faron had stopped shaking enough to return home. Even then, she'd had to check that her sister, her mother, and her father were safe before she'd felt close to sleeping.

There would be none of that now. No safety. No comfort. The gods had been a pain, but they had also been like parents to Faron when she couldn't confide in her own. Then they had lied to her, ordered her to kill her sister, compared her to Iya before Faron even fully understood who that was. Despite all they'd been through together, she was sure they had told Elara that Faron was the one who now needed to die to end this war.

She wished that was enough to stop her from missing them.

The sound of waves sucked her back into the present. They were at the beach, and Lightbringer sat where the grass met the sand, while the other two dragons—Goldeye and Irontooth—lay across the golden coastline with their eyes closed. It took her a moment to notice that Iya stood in the shadow of Lightbringer's folded wings. Since she'd last seen him, he had cut Reeve's hair military short, except for the red-brown curls still adorning his brow. Instead of his charcoal military uniform, he wore a new pair of riding leathers, like the Warwicks. It was so unlike Reeve that, for once, the dissonance of his face with Iya's personality didn't catch up with her.

Yet.

Iya leaned with one hand against the dragon's body, as if he were a wall instead of a war beast. Faron shuddered at the thought of being that comfortable with the creature who had killed her neighbors and set fire to her town. But if she needed to stay on his good side to achieve her goals—

"*You have never been on my good side,*" said Lightbringer. "*And your lies are transparent.*"

"*Only because you're in my head,*" Faron fired back. "*What, is the inside of yours too boring?*"

Not that she could have said that for sure. She might not have known how to build a barrier around her own thoughts, but she had spent the last week testing the one around his. She imagined the bond as a corridor between their souls, but where hers had an open door that she couldn't seem to close, his had a fence, a moat, barbed wire, and several security guards. Dusk or dawn, midday or midnight, she would inch as close as she could, her efforts going unnoticed because they were just that pointless.

Lightbringer snorted. "*I do not need to be in your head to see your weakness, Faron Vincent. I feel it.*"

She swallowed hard.

"So, why are we here?" Lynwood asked, reminding her that there were other people in the world. He was sitting in the sand between his dragon and Nichol Thompson, who Faron had since learned was his cousin. One leg was drawn up to Marius's chest. His square jaw rested atop his knee, and his dark hair hid his eyes from view. "If you're sending us out to gather recruits, we should get to it before we lose the sun."

Gavriel and Mireya hadn't bothered to join Irontooth; instead, they remained in the grass with Faron. Faron could only see their profiles from where she was standing, but Gavriel stood at ease, his arms behind his body and his eyes intent on Iya. Meanwhile, Mireya had her arms folded over her chest, her legs tensed

THIS ENDS IN EMBERS

as if she wanted to start tapping her foot impatiently. Faron wondered if they looked at Iya and tried to see their son in him, clinging to the strength that they had traded his body away for. Or perhaps they were glad that Reeve was gone, because now all that was left was the key to the power they felt they had been denied.

Their expressions gave away nothing.

Iya gestured for Faron to come closer, and she reluctantly obeyed despite the prickle of nerves that washed across her skin. And when Iya stepped out from the shadows and took her hand, Faron tensed even further. The last time they'd held hands, she had chosen to leave her home behind with nothing but the hope that she would make the most difference at his side. That had felt like diving from a cliff, but somehow this felt worse—an unknown she couldn't even begin to guess at. All she knew for sure was that whatever was about to happen here wouldn't be good.

"Once, I believed in loyalty. Friendship. Family. Courage." Iya laced their fingers together. His hand was dry, whereas hers was sweaty, his grip steady whereas hers was trembling, but if he noticed, then he'd discarded it as being irrelevant in the grand scheme of things. His gaze focused on each of the Riders in turn. "But then I was betrayed, and something about centuries of imprisonment makes one far less trusting."

The relaxed air of the meeting splintered like glass. Nichol Thompson's shoulders stiffened, his pale face even paler than usual beneath his short brown hair. Gavriel Warwick's hands dropped to his sides, an artificial lack of tension in them. Iya not only seemed to expect this change but to be amused by it.

"The reason I called you here today is that I have promised

47

power and riches beyond the pale, but those boons do not exist in a vacuum. To bring the world to heel, I will need my Four Generals. I will need you." There was a dangerous edge to Iya's smile, like a sheathed sword. That smile promised blood, to be drawn at his leisure. "Like the Hylands and the Sotos, the Warwicks and the Lynwoods are illustrious dragon-riding dynasties. When we take Langley, the people will remain loyal to you. For that reason, I am appointing you as the leader of my forces, answering only to me and, one day, Faron."

"I don't take orders from Iryans," Lynwood sneered.

"I heard you take ass kickings from them, though," said Faron automatically, because she had never met trouble she didn't want to get into. "My sister told me all about your incendio."

Color bloomed high on his peach cheeks. An incendio was a means of settling private disputes between Riders, and, though it had been her first one, Elara had thoroughly humiliated Lynwood in it. She had told Faron all about it during one of their fire calls, and Faron hadn't been able to stop laughing. Marius Lynwood reminded her of Jordan Simmons, a bully she herself had taken great joy in humiliating.

And then she remembered that Jordan was dead because she'd let Lightbringer loose, and her body went cold.

"She got lucky," Lynwood grumbled.

"*You* got lucky that it was her and not me." Faron bared her teeth in a vicious smile. "Elara's the nice one."

His unblinking green gaze was challenging, and Faron knew that she was misdirecting her anger, that Lightbringer felt like too big of a threat to tackle right now and Lynwood was an easy target. But she didn't care. Not right now. Right now, she felt in control

THIS ENDS IN EMBERS

for the first time in weeks, and she wanted to cling to that for as long as possible.

"Faron will need training to become the leader you deserve," Iya said as though the two of them hadn't spoken. "We can discuss the chain of command in detail then. For now, it's time to cement your allegiance and share in my power. Let the Four Generals rise again, firmly under my rule."

As he raised his hand, Faron began to feel strange. *More* somehow, not unlike the swell of magic within her whenever she summoned a god. It took her a moment to realize that Iya was using their bond to cast magic, their souls intertwining to power the spell, and another moment to realize he hadn't needed to ask her permission to wield their bond in this way.

The pressure beneath her skin increased, until Faron felt as if her body might explode. Her temples pounded. Black spots danced in her vision. Iya's grip was the only thing that kept her on her feet.

And then he let her go.

"The first time is always the hardest," Iya murmured. "I should have warned you."

"What"—Faron sounded as if she were speaking from the bottom of a well, her voice echoing in her ears—"have you done?"

"The four of them, and their dragons, are now tethered to us. They cannot do us harm, and their magic will amplify our own. Or, to put it more plainly"—Iya smiled in a way that made a shiver claw up her spine—"I summoned their living souls and chained them to our will."

"This was not part of the agreement," said Mireya Warwick. Her eyes were pitch-black voids, narrowed between long lashes. "We promised to serve you. You don't need to *puppet* us—"

49

"I've heard that before." Iya's smile was gone, and his voice was cold. "Believing it landed me in the Empty. You wanted power. I have given it to you. But your true ambition—for power to eclipse mine—betrays you, Director."

Mireya visibly bit back anything else she wanted to say. Lynwood and Thompson said nothing at all, their heads bowed toward the sand. The commander's hands were in his pockets, but Faron could tell from the flex of his muscles that he had clenched them into fists. Clearly, none of them had been consulted before Iya had enacted this plan.

"Now," Iya finished, "leave."

They all left, straight-backed and walking in unison. Iya watched them with the same mild interest with which he might watch a rainstorm, indifferent to the fact that he had overwritten their minds and controlled their bodies. Faron wanted to be horrified—but, after all, wasn't she the one who had shown him how easily this could be done? She had wielded this power against her own people to save Reeve's life, once. One night, they had stumbled across two drunken Iryans who had taken out their anguish over the war on Reeve, beating him so badly, Faron had thought he was dead. She'd surged into their bodies, into their souls, and ordered them to leave, to forget what they'd seen and done. Her will had become theirs, shattering their autonomy for what she'd thought was a good cause. Now, watching Iya do the same, she wasn't so sure there *was* a good cause for this power. Now it felt like a shared crime.

Because of you.

Faron stared at the two carmines who still slumbered on the beach. Goldeye had turned onto his side, baring his blush-pink

THIS ENDS IN EMBERS

stomach, his snout buried beneath one of his arms as if to protect it from windblown sand. Unless they were patrolling, the carmines were usually sleeping, the ultramarine was usually floating on her back in the lake, and the medallion was usually exploring the neighboring shorelines as if he expected to find treasure. Lightbringer had no such quirks, at least not that he'd shared with her. He'd shifted so that he was lying half on the warm sand, his wings blanketing his body, but he wasn't tired or hot or curious. *Grim* was the best way she could describe the emotion wafting from him across the bond.

Then Faron realized she *could feel him* across the bond, a shockingly open channel to his mind. She didn't know whether he was letting her in or if Iya's power surge had bound them closer together, but she wasn't going to waste this chance. Her soul rushed toward his. Maybe if she took him by surprise, she could finally command him. Maybe she could even puppet him the way he had the Riders. At the very least, she would glean some idea of his plans, and even that would be more than she had so far.

Faron's soul dropped back into her body when something yanked her forward. Iya stood before her, his grip tight around her wrist, his eyes boring into hers. Her breath escaped in a gasp when she realized his eyes were hazel, rather than Reeve's pale blue. This was not Iya who stared her down.

It was Gael Soto.

For the first time since she had released Lightbringer from the Empty, Gael Soto was looking out at her. Faron was too stunned to move, afraid to blink in case he disappeared.

"He'll *kill* you," Gael hissed. His voice was still Reeve's, but, studying him now, Faron could see the stark difference between

Iya and Gael. Even in Reeve's body, there was always a flatness in Iya's eyes, a cruel point to his smiles, a certain presence that screamed at her instincts to be on their guard. Gael was more curious about the world around him, but there was a shadow to everything he did and said, shrouded, as he was, in Lightbringer's influence, rarely allowed to be his own person. There was a fear in his face right now that she couldn't imagine on Iya's—shared body or no shared body. "You heard what he told you last time you tried to command his soul. If you try it again, *he will kill you, Faron.*"

It wasn't a guess. "Gael, how are you doing this—?"

But he blinked, and his eyes were blue again. Confusion flashed across his face, gone too quickly for her to interpret, before Iya's neutral expression returned. It was a different kind of barrier, hiding everything he didn't want her to see. His hand tightened around her wrist until her bones screamed for mercy, but Faron bit the inside of her cheek to keep from making a sound. She would not let him see her break down. Not again.

"I was serious about your training," he said, and there was so much venom in his voice that it felt almost performative. "The well of uncorrupted magic in your Iryan blood has proved useful, but you are weak in every way that matters. Once I decide the best way to strengthen you without making you a threat to me, we'll begin. In the meantime"—Iya finally released her throbbing arm—"get out of my sight."

Faron flinched automatically, expecting the words to be a magical command, but a minute passed and she was still standing there. The iciness of Iya's gaze was a warning, and for now she gave in. She would rather be in her room, figuring out whether she had a bruise, than out here with him. He was using gentle Reeve's body

THIS ENDS IN EMBERS

to hurt her, and bile rose in her throat at the thought of how horrified Reeve would be to see it. Their words had occasionally cut each other deeply, but Reeve would *never* physically hurt her. She hadn't needed to like him to know that.

But as she walked away, her mind turned the mystery of Gael's reappearance over and over, trying to make sense of it.

Or, more importantly, trying to make use of it.

CHAPTER FIVE

ELARA

Beacon—the capital of Langley—was a gorgeous city when Elara wasn't there against her will.

Elara could never get over how *massive* Nova was, how Langley was just one small part of an enormous area of land that just kept going and going. Without a drake, it was still only a two-day trip around the entire island of San Irie by cart. Nova was a continent, a landmass that Elara had never seen in person before she'd left home to attend Hearthstone; from above she felt even smaller in the face of the jagged peaks at the border of Langley and Étolia, the turquoise ribbon of the Tenebris River to the far east of Beacon, and the rolling green fields that eventually formed the Emerald Highlands.

Unlike San Irie, Langley did not wear the scars of war. Their landmarks were not newly rebuilt. Their farmland still bore fruit; their trees were in vibrant shades of red and gold as Harvest turned to Solstice. Even as they flew toward the National Hall of Honor, passing over the clogged Beacon streets and through air tinted gray and mud brown from factory smoke, no one seemed afraid. No one paused to look upward unless it was to wave. These people

THIS ENDS IN EMBERS

had nothing to fear from dragons, didn't awaken from nightmares of fire and death. Did they even know there was a war going on?

She couldn't imagine the blissful ignorance these people were living in. She'd never had that luxury.

Each of her previous trips to the National Hall had been to study under and spy on Commander Gavriel Warwick. The last time she'd been there, she had torn a hole in the building to race back to San Irie with Aveline and her drake, Nobility, in tow. Langley's Dragon Legion had splintered that day, between the Riders who declared their intention to protect San Irie from their own empire and the Riders who had decided to stand aside. Things had changed so much since then, and not just because the wall had been repaired.

Zephyra landed in the back garden of the National Hall, where a brown-eyed carmine already waited in the verdant space more than large enough to accommodate them. As soon as Signey had helped Elara safely out of the saddle, Zephyra threw herself at Azeal with a roar like laughter. The two dragons went rolling farther into the garden, wrestling playfully as if they hadn't seen each other in years. Azeal was Jesper Soto and Torrey Kelley's deep red dragon, and, as with Jesper and Signey, he was older than Zephyra—if only by a few days. But Zephyra held her own in the scrap, managing to pin him several times. Elara watched them with a tightness in her chest, wondering if she would ever see her own sister again.

"Elara? Are you coming?"

Signey was already ascending the stairs of the castle-like building. Elara rushed to join her, taking note of the differences since the last time she had walked these halls. The bodies of the

55

unconscious soldiers she'd left behind had been cleared from the hallways, replaced by black-and-gold carpeting that matched the Langlish flag and, perhaps most crucially, wouldn't show bloodstains. She still heard voices behind every door—the legislative branch known as the Conclave, the Judiciary, and the dracologist general's research department—but they were quieter than usual, as though the crowds packed into the rooms had thinned.

When they met Barret Zayas Soto in the commander's former office, Elara wasn't surprised to see the fresh exhaustion etched onto his face. He was, after all, taking command of a splintered nation. Even so, Barret looked better physically, his eyes clear and his cheeks slowly filling out. When she had first met him, he looked like some forgotten thing: overgrown facial hair, wan skin, gaunt build, and buried so deep within his own mind that even Signey had trouble pulling him out. One week away from the Mausoleum, one week of sunshine and regular meals and basic respect, had brought him back to life. She was struck by how much Signey and Jesper resembled him, their big brown eyes, their deep brown skin, their round jaws and crooked smiles.

As Signey swept into his arms, giving him the same warm affection that she'd given Zephyra, their resemblance became even more obvious. They hugged as if it would be the last time. Of course, considering Signey's father had spent the last five years in Langley's most secure prison on falsified treason charges, Elara supposed they would hug like that for a while.

"It's good to see you again, Miss Vincent," said Barret, one hand on Signey's shoulder even after they parted from their hug. He spoke patois for Elara's benefit, with a stronger Langlish accent

THIS ENDS IN EMBERS

than Signey's. There were shadows in his expression, a haunting that would never be lifted, but he smiled. He could still smile, and, as long as that was true, the Warwicks had not beaten him down. "Iya has wasted very little time."

Her stomach twisted at the understatement. Iya had been free for fewer than ten days, and in that time, he had killed her friends, burned down the capital, settled in Hearthstone with her sister as a hostage, and threatened every dragon that still drew breath. "So you've already heard."

"My son filled me in." Barret had been born a Zayas, taking the Soto name after marriage due to its political weight as a Langlish dragon-riding dynasty. Before his arrest, he had been a military dracologist, not a Rider, so he wouldn't have heard Iya's declaration directly. "The Conclave will be meeting about it in the afternoon, but initial reports are...not good."

"Are people actually considering joining Iya?" Elara asked.

"Not in as many words. But let's just say that, of all the proposed solutions to Iya's ultimatum, sending away the dragons is not among them."

Elara glanced at Signey, but Signey wasn't looking at her. The den knew what the gods had asked Elara to do, because she didn't dare keep that from them after what they'd done for San Irie. But they had yet to sit and talk about what that would mean. Despite the fact only a handful of Riders existed, dragons were the foundation of Langlish culture, a key part of their military, and a symbol of their national pride. It was far easier to do the right thing when they didn't have to lose everything in the process.

That even Elara doubted this *was* the right thing made it harder.

"Anyway," said Barret into the silence that followed, "nothing substantial is going to get done ahead of that meeting, so we may as well take a break."

"Father," Signey said with a roll of her eyes, "you're the interim commander of the empire. You can't just *take a break*."

The hand on Signey's shoulder reached up to ruffle her curls. She cursed and twisted away, which made Barret's smile widen. "I would argue that that is exactly why I need a break. Besides, Olivea can handle anything crucial that arises in my absence."

"Hyland?" There was a sudden distaste in Signey's tone. "That's even worse."

"Who's Olivea Hyland?" Elara asked, pulling the Sotos' attention back to her.

"The current leader of the Conclave," Barret said at the same time that Signey snapped, "A snake in the sand."

Barret clapped his hands together. "Let's discuss this over brunch. You two go ahead. I'll fly with your brother and Torrey."

Signey didn't pause to see if Elara was following before storming out of the room. Elara's lips parted to call out to her, but nothing came except a puff of air too much like a sigh. She hadn't felt this out of sync with Signey since before they were bonded, when she'd just been a Langlish girl across a banquet hall, as inscrutable as she was gorgeous.

"Miss Vincent?"

She realized that she was still standing there, staring after Signey like a lost puppy, and shook her head. "Sorry. Sorry, I—yes. We'll meet you at brunch."

Barret Soto said something else, but Elara fled before she could hear it, her cheeks burning.

Within the city proper, there was a tearoom that the Sotos had always favored. That was all Signey said to Elara on the short flight there, which did little to prepare her for how beautiful it was.

The tearoom sat on a historic square filled with multicolored eateries, cobblestone roads too narrow for a horse to comfortably trot through, and black iron streetlamps with electric bulbs rather than gas. Elara could smell the flowers in the beds beneath the tearoom windows, adding fragrant brightness to an already-gorgeous street. It was the nicest Langlish area that Elara had ever been in.

Torrey threw her arms around Elara as soon as their eyes met. She had cut her wheat-blond hair into a shoulder-length bob but still wore all black: a loose black button-down tucked into her riding leathers, black boots, black lipstick, and black kohl ringing her blue eyes. Her ear cuff was shaped like a silver dragon scale, and she wore an imitation dragon tooth on a black string around her neck—too small to be from a real dragon, but it had been combined with *some* piece of a dragon. Elara could feel the magic of it from here.

"Welcome back!" Torrey chirped in patois. "Missed you, Vincent."

"Even though I'm not in the den anymore?" Elara asked with a rush of affection.

"You'll always be in the den, bonded or not," said Jesper, Signey's older brother and Torrey's Firstrider. He and Torrey were nineteen to Elara and Signey's eighteen, but neither acted superior for it. His patois, she noticed, was just as good as theirs. "I'm glad you're here."

Jesper had gained an inch in height since Elara had last seen him, but he had the same puppylike smile on his round, tan face, the same beauty mark on his jawline, and the same curly tuft of dark brown hair as his sister. He wore a white collared shirt and crimson vest, completing the outfit with a black trilby that matched his slacks. Elara lifted an eyebrow at the vest. At Hearthstone, their uniforms included shirts the color of their dragon breeds. That Jesper was *choosing* to wear the red of his carmine dragon, Azeal, was adorable.

Torrey looped her arm through Jesper's. "Shall we? I'm famished."

They sat at a window table, Elara next to Signey and Torrey and across from Jesper and Barret. Barret ordered black tea, to which he added two sugar cubes and a splash of milk.

"Now that we're not in the National Hall, I'd like to say...this country is a fucking mess." He sighed into his cup. "I almost miss my cell."

"Don't even joke about that." Jesper rolled his eyes. "You've been incredibly capable as a leader, considering you were a dracologist before this."

"I've had the Hylands to help me. Their political aspirations may have been stymied by the Warwicks, but they still have all the knowledge."

"Just none of the popular support," said Torrey. "The Hylands and the Lynwoods are snakes, but at least the Lynwoods are just brutes. The Hylands are the brains. If Olivea Hyland honored the results of the election and didn't try to steal power from you after the Warwicks fled, there's a reason for it. Be careful around her."

"Torrey wanted to work in intelligence, like her parents," Signey whispered. "Her family, the Kelleys, are always the first to know about domestic or international unrest."

THIS ENDS IN EMBERS

"Nosy busybodies, the lot of us," Torrey added without bothering to whisper. But there was a twinkle in her eye. "It's up to you whether that makes me very good or very bad at keeping secrets."

Even with this explanation, Elara could only vaguely follow the conversation. During her time at Hearthstone, Elara had met members of two of the four dragon-riding dynasties: Signey and Jesper Soto, and Marius Lynwood. And before she'd left Deadegg, she'd been best friends with Reeve Warwick, the first of his lineage without a dragon. But though she had heard of Arran Hyland, a Hearthstone student who had fought for San Irie, they had never formally met, and she knew nothing about the Hylands as a whole.

"This is too heavy a conversation for such a joyful reunion," Jesper said as a server began to lay out their food. "How have you been, Elara? I see my sister's neck has some new marks."

Signey slapped a hand over her skin, her cheeks darkening. *"Stop talking."*

"There's nothing there," Torrey reassured her. "He's just taking you for a ride."

Barret sipped his tea. "I thought I sensed something between you two at the Mausoleum...."

The look that Signey gave her brother was murderous. Elara didn't know whether she wanted to laugh or drown herself in her teacup. The latter seemed preferable, given that she and Signey hadn't so much as held hands since the Battle for Port Sol. Instead, she tucked into her eggs on toast, the only food that seemed safe on a menu full of pickled haddock and odd puddings and jams she'd never heard of. But even the eggs were bland and flavorless on her tongue, as if Langley had yet to discover spices. Or salt.

After the meal, they took a walk around the neighborhood,

Barret in front to speak Langlish with Torrey, and Jesper strolling alone with his hands in his pockets. Behind him, Elara and Signey were side by side in a silence too thick to be comfortable. Several conversation starters clamored for attention, but none of them made it out of Elara's head.

Then Signey grabbed her hand, and Elara's heart leaped into her throat. Her touch was so gentle, her calluses brushing over Elara's skin lightly enough to make her shiver. Signey tugged Elara down a narrow side street, apparently unaware of the riot she had caused in Elara's chest. "We'll catch up with them later," she whispered, "but I want to show you something first."

Elara threw a concerned look over her shoulder, wondering if she should say something so the den didn't worry, but she wouldn't have interrupted this moment for anything. They emerged onto another block lined with colorful storefronts. More flower beds and more cobblestones ribboned between the gray sidewalks and around a fountain with a massive dragon statue in the center that shot water into the air to pool in the basin. Two men walked hand in hand into a bookstore, and a person bent down to feed a stray dog that had warily come closer.

"We used to live in Beacon," Signey explained as they came to a stop in front of the fountain. She'd dropped Elara's hand, but at least she hadn't done it as if Elara's skin were made of poison. "Whenever I was on summer holiday from Hearthstone, I'd always find my way to this square."

"To swim in the fountain?" Elara asked.

"Ha ha." Signey gestured toward the statue. "I just liked this monument. It's called the Regis Draconis. All four of the dragon breeds—carmine, medallion, ultramarine, and sage—are working

THIS ENDS IN EMBERS

together to create that waterspout. Which dragon you see depends on which direction you approach the fountain from. And if you look around the basin of the fountain, it lists every Rider who has ever lived."

Elara squinted enough to see that Signey was right. The basin, which had just seemed textured to her at a glance, was actually covered in names carved into the otherwise-smooth stone. She searched, but she couldn't see Signey's, Jesper's, or Torrey's names on this side of the fountain.

"It's supposed to be a reminder of the legacy we're a part of. The might and majesty of Langley and the dragons we've been blessed with. As you can imagine, it's largely used to drum up patriotic fervor." Signey rolled her eyes. "But for me, it was more of a reminder that we serve the people, not the country. This bond and the gifts that the dragons gave us aren't blessings that we need to conquer other countries to share—no, they *really* did teach that at Hearthstone at one point," Signey added at Elara's shocked expression. "This bond, these gifts, the dragons...We should be using them to protect and uplift our people. To give them something to believe in again."

Her tone turned shy. "Anyway. That's why I always loved coming here. It reminded me to believe. Even after we lost Mum and Celyn. Even after Jesper found his co-Rider before I did. Even after Dad went to the Mausoleum. I found peace here. And I know that dragons haven't exactly brought San Irie peace, but...I hoped that maybe you would find something here, too."

Elara stepped closer to the fountain. She didn't feel the same kind of peace that Signey described—not from this monument, anyway. Because the truth was that she had already found something here,

63

in Langley, and that was the girl behind her. When she had first been forced to travel to Langley, Elara had thought only of returning home. Instead, Signey and Zephyra had become a home. Her reminder that, even in this enemy country, there were still people who were good, who did the right thing even when it was hard.

She had found her peace in Signey's support during her incendio, in their conversations to and from Beacon, in their teamwork to escape their captivity at the Warwicks' ancestral estate, Rosetree Manor. She had found something to believe in through the bond, through Zephyra's steadfast advice and Signey's wry humor. She had found hope for a better world in Signey, who loved her country without wanting to destroy others—even if that sometimes meant standing against it.

Elara turned to face her now. Signey's gaze shifted from the fountain to Elara, and the sun shone through the clouds, illuminating her warm brown eyes from umber to dark honey.

"Why are you sharing this with me?" Elara whispered.

"Well," Signey whispered back, "you were forced to live in my head for months. Now I want to invite you in."

"Then why have you been acting so weird and distant?"

The words fell between them like a broken bottle, an accident with the potential to cut them both. Signey's eyes were wide, and Elara was overcome with a desperation to snatch the words back. This was the first time in a long time that Signey had let her in, and of course she had to ruin it with her inability to keep her mouth shut.

But then Signey swallowed, and Elara knew in that moment that it hadn't all been in her head. Signey really *had* been putting distance between them. Her chest hurt.

THIS ENDS IN EMBERS

"Did I do something wrong?" Elara asked hoarsely. "I know there's a lot going on, but I thought— Was I wrong? About us?"

"I've...I've never..." Signey straightened her shoulders and met Elara's eyes head-on, a soldier ready for battle. "I've never done this before. When I kissed you, it was my first time kissing *anyone*. And I thought—well, I thought one or both of us might die."

Silence tumbled down on them.

"I like you," Signey finally said. "I do. I wouldn't lie about something like that. I just have no idea what I'm doing, so I guess I've been too focused on what I *do* know how to do."

"Okay." Elara didn't know which part of that to tackle first. She didn't want this distance between them, but she also didn't want to push. "I don't want to be a distraction."

Signey's hands clenched into fists at her side. "I don't think there's anything about you that I don't find distracting. Even with the war, with our bond severed, and my ancestor threatening all the rest, you're all I can think about."

She said it as if it were painful. As if it destroyed her. Signey had never handled vulnerability well. Her walls came down in fits and starts, every honest word costing her more than Elara could imagine. The stronger she felt about something, the harder it was for her to speak. Elara knew that this should make her happy, but instead the distance between them now felt insurmountable.

"We don't have to do anything or be anything right now. Like you said, there's the war to think about." Her heart was so loud that it was almost all she could hear. "I like you. You like me. That's enough for now. All I'm asking is for you to stop shutting me out. We don't have to be together to win this, but we do need to work together."

"Elara—"

"*There* you are." Jesper emerged from the side street, a knowing smile on his face. "I should've known you'd bring her here. We have to take Father back to the Hall, but he's inviting us all to sit in on the Conclave meeting. Are you done having it on?"

A red-faced Signey turned on her brother to point out that there were children present. Any raw emotion was now shuttered behind that wall. Elara used the temporary reprieve to pull herself together, pushing down her disappointment. She'd once asked Faron to keep Signey alive long enough for them to go on a date. That date seemed uncertain now, and understanding the reasoning didn't make it hurt any less.

At least she knew what was going on and could act accordingly. She clung to that as she painted a smile on her face and followed the bickering Soto siblings back to their dragons. There was a war going on, a long stretch of uncertainty more important than her love life. This was nothing in the grand scheme of things.

Absolutely nothing.

CHAPTER SIX

FARON

FARON HAD SAT THROUGH HER FAIR SHARE OF WAR MEETINGS. During the San Irie Revolution, they'd had them wherever they could find shelter and privacy: loaned barns and patrolled clearings, cramped inns and roadside food shacks. Three children—Faron, Elara, and Aveline—sitting in places of honor, surrounded by uniformed officers, discussing things like supply lines, access points, artillery stock, and army sizes. Of course, Aveline had seemed, to her, like another adult, but now that Faron was the same age as the queen had been back then, she knew better.

They'd all been too young to be there. They were still too young.

Iya's war meeting was worlds away from the ones that Faron remembered. Instead of gathering between battles, alert to smoking skies and well-armed Langlish soldiers, they met in the Hearthstone dining hall. The world map that Iya had stolen from Pearl Bay Palace was unfurled before him at a long table that easily seated Iya's officers. Faron sat beside him, eyeing all the officers she didn't recognize, the ones who had defected from Langley to follow the commander into this madness. Their names didn't matter to her, but she would never forget their faces or the way they gazed at Iya with that terrifying fervor in their eyes. As if it would be an honor to die for him.

Faron had never felt that way about anyone, except perhaps her sister. And, even then, she knew that Elara would never ask her to. Iya would sacrifice these people in an instant and forget they had ever existed.

"Why," Marius Lynwood asked, "is *she* here? She's a spy."

Iya shrugged. "A spy with no way to escape and no means of reporting to her handlers. What does it matter if she's here or not?"

"She'll sabotage our plans, my saint," said Nichol Thompson in a more measured tone than his cousin's. He was the shyer of the two, Faron noted, content to let Marius lead and generally unwilling to challenge him. "It might be safer to lock her up during war meetings. The less she knows, the better."

"She may look free," said Iya, "but I assure you that she is in a prison of her own making."

"She's also sitting right here," Faron pointed out, glaring across the table at the two Riders. "If you have something to say about me, say it *to me*."

Lynwood sneered. "Our saint may trust you, but I never will, you gru—"

Faron slammed her hands on the table so hard that the clay figurines on the map shook from the force. Magic swirled around her hands, pulled from the bond, a yellow-orange light that made the map edges flutter. Power that answered only to her rage. "Finish that sentence, and it will be your last."

"Now, now," Iya said mildly. "There will be plenty of time for infighting later. For now, may we begin?"

THIS ENDS IN EMBERS

Lynwood said nothing. Faron stared him down as the magic retreated, silently begging him to give her a reason to attack. When he didn't, she clenched and unclenched her fists under the table, trying to work out her now-restless muscles.

"Thank you all for your prompt attendance," Iya said as though nothing had happened. His glacial eyes swept from one end of the table to the other. Though he appeared only eighteen, this group blossomed like flowers under the light of his attention. Faron shuddered. "I expected to have this meeting in the National Hall, the whole empire at my command, but for now this will do."

Commander Warwick's jaw tightened almost imperceptibly. His original plan—to burn San Irie to the ground five years ago, revealing the entrance to the Empty so he could free Iya, and to return home as the war hero responsible for resurrecting their most famous saint—would have done exactly as Iya had expected. Instead, his son, Reeve, had alerted the Iryans to his schemes, Langley had lost the war and control of the island, and he had been forced to wait and improvise. Now here they were, with Langley torn between those who supported Iya and those who didn't.

Faron hid a smile.

"Our first move should be to unite Langley," said one of the officers, a man in his sixties or seventies with silver hair and ruddy skin. "If the rest of the Riders join our cause, the people will, too. Have you had any response to your message, my saint?"

"I don't anticipate we'll hear back for at least a week," Iya said. "They'll need to meet about it, assess the seriousness of my threat. A show of power may be necessary. But I am confident that they will fall easily enough that we can turn our focus to Étolia and Joya del Mar for now."

He stood to bend over the map, using those little clay crown figures he'd also stolen from Pearl Bay Palace, to outline his plan for an initial volley that would test the strength of the other empires' defenses. Faron kept half her attention on the plan, but the other half was on observing Iya and how he seemed in his element here, leading humans into battle even in unfamiliar territory. The officers, the Riders, and his Generals chimed in with their knowledge of the terrain, of the people, of the magic they wielded, and he easily tailored his plans to incorporate their suggestions. There was a magnetism to him, even in this young body, that made the people around them eager to impress him.

Which meant they would not be easy for her to manipulate with her own charm. She'd have to resort to extreme measures.

That night, she snuck out of her room again, noting that Lightbringer was both awake and aware of her movements. He did nothing to stop her, as usual, because her small rebellions remained beneath his notice. Hopefully, he would keep thinking that until she'd done what she needed to do.

The sky was a cloudless spill of ink overhead, stars splashed across it like glitter. It was different here after dark than it was in San Irie. Even in Deadegg, there was noise, whether it was the snuffling of sleeping stray dogs or the chirping of hidden tree frogs. Here, the silence was broken only by the occasional sigh of a dragon, the occasional slosh of the water over the shore, the occasional whisper of footsteps across the lawn.

Tonight's perimeter patrol was being done by Estella Ballard, Briar Noble, and their ultramarine, Ignatz. The Luxtons rode their

THIS ENDS IN EMBERS

medallion, Cruz, in a circuit around the archipelago, handling the air patrol. And then there was Lightbringer, his green eyes forever on the sky, while Reeve's body slept in a dormitory in Hearthstone.

Ballard noticed Faron first. She stopped midstride, her eyes narrowing. Her short sandy hair and freckles lent her a youthful appearance that wasn't matched by the hatred in her brown eyes. "Don't try anything. I'm bored, and I'd love to make that your problem."

"Your posturing is unnecessary," said Faron, folding her arms over her chest. "You aren't allowed to hurt me."

"We're not allowed to *kill* you," Ballard corrected. "There are all kinds of ways to hurt people."

Noble approached from the opposite side of the island, coming to a stop before them just in time to hear the end of his co-Rider's threat. He bared his teeth in an unfriendly smile. "I, for one, would love to try, *Empyrean*. You murdered my mentor."

Faron glared at him. "I don't know your mentor. For Irie's sake, I don't even know *you*."

"Sebastian Edwards," Noble continued, his voice wavering. His black hair was pulled back into a ponytail at the base of his neck, and, when he shook his head as if to clear the bad memories, it snapped like a whip. "He and his sister, Kenya, were the Riders of Raisel—a dragon *your army* drowned in the Ember Sea, and their Riders along with him. Sound familiar?"

It didn't, but Faron knew better than to say that much when it was two against one. She didn't think they would care, either, that it was hardly *her* army, that she had only participated in the final year of the revolution. But though she hadn't come out here to argue with them, she couldn't stop herself: "That was war. They were attacking our island!"

"They were *following orders*, you savage bitch," said Ballard. Noble put a quelling hand on her shoulder, but Ballard shook it off. "Sebastian and Kenya were just following orders, and so are we. Whatever you've come out here to do, Vincent, it's not going to happen on our watch."

Faron looked from one hard face to the next and sighed, her indignant anger sliding away. They would never agree with her, and she would never agree with them. The tally of lives lost and crimes committed would only rise as they entered a second conflict. At least this circular argument had bored Lightbringer enough that he'd retreated from her mind—and that was the opening she needed.

This is war, she told herself, stomach churning. Then she reached out for their living souls.

For most of her life, Faron had been taught that Iryan summoners could command only the souls of the dead, and even then, only the souls of their ancestors, the dead with whom they had shared a bloodline. Gael Soto had shown her that she could impress her will upon living souls, as long as she was stronger than those whom she was trying to control.

The first time she had used this power, she had done it to save Reeve's life—but she had been saving him from her own people. She still felt conflicted about that and what it said about her that she had done it so unrepentantly. Now, however, she was skimming the edges of Langlish souls—souls brighter than usual thanks to their connection with Ignatz—and she refused to feel guilty about it.

Give me your relics, she commanded. *Let me call my sister.*

Unlike her first two victims, Noble and Ballard weren't drunk

THIS ENDS IN EMBERS

and pliable. They fought against her influence, as angry as a disturbed flock of ducks. Faron fought back, pushing harder against the force of their defiance, the force of their dragon. A dark tear ran down Noble's cheek, and it took Faron a moment to realize that it was blood. A vessel in his eye had popped from the strain of shielding his mind. Beside him, Ballard's nostrils bled, and red smeared above the thin line of her lips.

Stop fighting, she commanded. *You're only hurting yourselves. And Ignatz.*

Faron couldn't see the dragon, but she knew that what she did to the Riders would happen to the dragon and vice versa. If they were bleeding, then somewhere in the bay, so was he. Noble and Ballard seemed to realize this, too, because it was this that broke them. Faron's own soul withdrew from theirs as blankness curtained their faces.

She was breathing hard, but that did nothing to stop her triumphant smile. Even with the added magic from Iya, she had worried that she had grown weak since the battle. Or that she could command dragons but not the solid combination of dragons and their Riders. Worse, she had worried that Noble and Ballard would prove stronger than her will, that they would control *her*—and, through her, control Iya.

But she was strong. She had won.

Pain exploded across the center of her face. Faron saw red and then black, staggering backward and blinking spots away from her eyes. She shouted, but the sound was weak compared with the sudden ringing in her ears. She touched her nose. Her fingers came away bloody.

"What the—?" she asked sluggishly.

Standing before her was Margot Luxton, holding her own fist. Crimson stained her knuckles—blood. Faron's blood.

She blinked. "Did you just punch me?"

"What did you do to them?" said Oscar Luxton, joining his daughter, his face slack with shock. Behind them, Cruz was still folding his golden wings from a sudden landing. "I've never seen magic like that."

"*Faron? Are you injured?*" Iya sent through the bond. His voice was a fuse waiting to be lit. "*WHO DID THIS TO YOU?*"

Her senses expanded. Just as Iya was attempting to see and feel through her, so, too, could she see and feel through him. The throbbing in her head doubled as Iya suffered from her broken nose, from the fatigue of her attempt to control Ballard and Noble. She felt a cool breeze on her face, as if she were standing at a window, and his anger pulsed through her until it became her own.

Whatever they saw on her face made Oscar and Margot Luxton take a step back.

"He's coming," she managed, breathing hard. Black spots danced at the edge of her vision. "Leave."

Faron didn't wait to see if they obeyed. She turned and took a step toward Hearthstone. One single step.

And then she collapsed.

CHAPTER SEVEN

ELARA

E LARA COULD FEEL THE BEGINNINGS OF A HEADACHE DRILLING AT her skull. Outside the divine plane, her body sat on a bed in Nobility's upper cabins as the drake flew them to Joya del Mar—a roughly two-hour flight from Beacon. The queen had picked up Elara in the Langlish capital and, before retiring to a neighboring cabin, had suggested that Elara call on the gods for advice. Elara had been willing to wait until after the trip, until she could go to an Iryan temple and speak to all three of the gods at once, but Aveline was right about the urgency of their situation. No more Riders from their side had joined Iya yet, but that *yet* loomed larger with each passing day.

And each passing day, they got closer and closer to his deadline.

Within the divine plane, the goddess Irie looked as exhausted as Elara felt. Cold fire raged around them, consuming a forest that would never truly burn. Irie's pearl-white robes rippled wide enough to brush Elara's face, as gentle as a mother's caress.

Iya has given the Langlish an ultimatum, Elara said. Pleaded, really, because she already knew how this conversation would end.

Unless they join him, they'll lose control of their dragons. We can't let that happen.

And how—those golden eyes were heavy with judgment—*do you propose we stop it, Maiden?*

Iya can break dragon bonds. If you could show me how to do that—

Irie made a sound that was just shy of exasperated. *You could use our power to tear a seam between worlds, returning the dragons to our realm and avoiding this entirely. Yet you ask for more power?*

We're at war against the most ancient dragon of them all. We can't win without the rest of them!

That was why they were going to Joya del Mar to begin with. Iya had raised the stakes beyond San Irie's and Langley's abilities to deal with him alone—dragons or no dragons. Joya del Mar rested on the opposite side of Étolia, as far away from Langley as it was possible to get while still being on the continent, which made it their last hope of keeping Iya from conquering his way to the Silver Sea that wrapped around the southern and eastern coast of Nova. Aveline had proposed a conference with representatives from all the major powers to discuss the threat that Iya posed, but, after Elara's failed mission and Iya's announcement, she was no longer willing to wait for them to write back to her.

She'd also insisted that the Maiden Empyrean needed to be present in both Joya del Mar and Étolia for these discussions, unknowingly saving Elara from the unholy awkwardness that followed her and Signey around like a bodyguard.

I thought, Elara said, daunted though she was by the prospect of having another of these conversations, *that you trusted me to be your new Empyrean. I thought you agreed to lend me your power and let me decide what to do with it. I thought*—

THIS ENDS IN EMBERS

We thought you and every Empyrean before you would do as you were told, Irie interrupted. The anger in her voice was enough to shake the ground beneath Elara's feet. *The longer you take, the more chance there is for you to be corrupted. Why should we continue to pour our magic into a weapon too dull to cut?*

Elara's throat closed at the idea of disappointing the very gods she had revered her whole life, just as she had disappointed the people of Deadegg, just as she had disappointed Reeve. Had Faron ever felt like this? Had she felt constantly weighed down by a pressure that threatened to cleave her in pieces? Or was it the very feeling of eyes on her that led her to disappoint them before they could expect too much from her?

Please, Elara whispered. *I plan to do as you have asked. I do. But the situation is delicate right now. If we tear the Langlish away from their dragons like Iya has threatened to do, they'll think we're no better. They'll attack San Irie again. You'll be sated, but my home will be imperiled, and I can't do that to them. We've been through so much.* She slid to her knees, her head bowed. *I know you have little reason to trust me, but I have always been faithful. If you heard Faron's prayers, then surely you heard mine. To end this war of dragons, I need to make sure they aren't the catalyst for further unrest. And for that I need time. Please . . . help me.*

Irie was silent. Elara didn't dare stand or lift her head. If the goddess could hear her rapid heartbeat, hopefully she would take it for passion rather than simply fear. Then: *We cannot help you break the dragon bonds, Maiden. Iya created the bond through a bastardization of summoning and draconic magic, such that each is indistinguishable from the other. Our powers do not extend so far into your realm.*

There has to be a way, Elara said, scrambling desperately to her feet. *If Iya can do it, even now, there has to be a way.*

77

We have told you the way, Irie said without sympathy. *If you insist upon stumbling down another path, you will be walking alone. And that is your mistake to make.*

Please—

Irie's answer shook the world again, suffused with an ancient anger that Elara tried not to take personally. *Iya is a creature of the past. Perhaps that's where the answer lies.*

In the past? What should— The burning forest of the divine realm began to swirl out of view, replaced by gray metal and seafoam sheets. "Wait! Irie, wait!"

But the goddess was gone, and Elara's soul was back inside her body, miles above the ground. Her discomfort escalated into anxiety that made her heart race and her skin buzz with prickling energy. The gods wouldn't help her. They *could* help her, she knew that they could, but they wouldn't. Not after two failed Empyreans. Not after Iya's emancipation. Elara didn't believe she could do this alone, but there was no winning against Lightbringer without the dragons. She closed her eyes, pressing her fists against her eyelids to keep from crying.

All right, then. If the answer to breaking dragon bonds was in Iya's past, there was only one person besides Iya who might be able to find it.

Although he was a dracologist, one of his proudest research projects was only tangentially related to dragons: the Soto-Zayas family tree.

Signey had told her that once. Lindans, the people from the Ember Sea island of Isalina, had been conquered by Joya del Mar for longer than Elara had been alive, but Barret's family tree was one of many ways he had kept Signey and Jesper in touch with their culture. Now it might be the key to their victory. Just as soon as Elara could find a fireplace.

It was nighttime when the carriage trundled into the courtyard of the Palacio Real in Joya del Mar, which was surrounded on four sides by high brick walls with a tower in each corner.

A small group of soldiers already waited on the stones as Elara and Aveline exited; the squad featured at least twice the number of guards as they had brought with them. The carriage was led away to the stables, and Elara tried to study her surroundings without looking distracted. To the left and right of them were gardens, both walled away by large boxwood hedges with arched doors clipped into them. Winter jasmine, bright yellow blossoms on slender branches; hellebore, with its plum-colored roselike folds; and deep orange pansies thrived indifferently against the frost. It must have been magnificent in the daytime, but the starlit blooms were breathtaking in their own way.

When she turned her attention back to the soldiers, they stepped to the side to reveal a familiar face. Or as familiar as someone could be after being seen in profile from across a room.

"Maiden Empyrean, Your Majesty," said Doña Pilar Montserrat, dipping into a bow. She spoke patois like a native. "Welcome to the capital city of Avara."

Doña Montserrat was around Aveline's age, with skin the color of wet sand, freckles dusting the bottom half of her oval face, full lips, thick eyebrows, and medium-sized brown eyes. Instead of wearing the colorful dresses the Joyans seemed to favor, with their three-quarter sleeves and flowing skirts, the doña wore a fitted suit: a short-fronted black jacket over a loose white shirt, high-waisted pale blue trousers with a fall front, a sapphire waistcoat peeking out from the jacket's lapels. Her wavy hair couldn't seem to decide what shade of brown it wanted to be beneath the moonlight.

The last time Elara had seen Doña Montserrat had been at the San Irie International Peace Summit, where she had attended as a representative of her cousin Rey Christóbal. It seemed that she represented him in more matters than Elara had thought.

Aveline smiled a counterfeit smile. "Good evening, Doña. Thank you for your warm welcome."

Doña Montserrat straightened from her bow. Elara would have made her own greeting, but the lady hadn't taken her eyes off Aveline. "It's been quite some time."

"Two months, in fact."

"Nearly three," Doña Montserrat corrected. "I thought we'd hear from you sooner."

"I had nothing to say to you."

The two women stared each other down. There was a tension in the air that Elara couldn't put a name to, like seeing swollen gray clouds for hours before a thunderstorm.

Elara blinked. "Are we going inside . . . ? It's cold."

Doña Montserrat and Aveline turned to face her as one. From their expressions, Elara could tell they had forgotten she was there.

The doña cleared her throat. "Yes, of course. My cousin is waiting. If you'll follow me."

The inside of the palace was lavish. In the main hall, stone walls were covered with mosaics, the ceiling bare and the floors light brown marble. Doña Montserrat took them through an arcade

THIS ENDS IN EMBERS

that lined one of the gardens that Elara had seen before. Through the shadowy trees she could glimpse cerulean reflecting pools coated in thin layers of ice and elaborate sculptures on marble pedestals. Then they were in another corridor, with cream walls and portraits of former reys and reinas that watched from gold frames, before the doña finally threw open the doors to a reception hall.

Rey Christóbal Montserrat sat atop a dais on a simple high-backed chair of gold and crimson. He appeared to be in his late forties or early fifties, his brown hair oiled into neat waves beneath his crown and his full beard speckled with silver. His eyes were brown like Doña Montserrat's, but they sloped downward at the corners beneath his thick eyebrows, making him look tired. His peach skin had a red flush, and he was wearing all black—black jacket, black waistcoat, black shirt, black trousers. Around his neck was a heavy gold brooch shaped like a tree with an eye in the bark, each leaf intricately carved—the symbol of the House of Montserrat.

The mosaic behind him, Elara noticed, was a large tiled portrait of that same symbol.

Doña Montserrat joined her cousin on the dais as Elara and the Queenshield dipped into bows. But Rey Christóbal stood up and walked down the two steps to greet Aveline with his arms out as if expecting a hug. "You honor me with your presence, young queen." His patois was colored by a Joyan accent. "I hope your trip was comfortable."

Aveline clasped her hands in front of her. "Very much so, thank you. Have you received any threats from Iya?"

"And here I thought you would be tired from your travels." The rey looked bemused by Aveline, watching her as if she were a jester who had asked to be crowned. "Not as yet, but I don't doubt that we

81

will soon." He lowered his arms, coming to a stop a polite distance away. "At least we were prepared for the eventuality of a dragon war. I'm sure Pilar took you through the gardens we've newly replanted for Solstice. Keeping our plants and flowers in bloom all year round strengthens our various nature spirits—a necessary precaution these days. Rather land hungry, the Langlish."

Elara thought this was a wild assessment coming from the king of another empire, the very empire that had colonized Signey's ancestral island of Isalina, that had been one of the empires that brought slavery to San Irie, but she kept her mouth shut about that. Filing his words away as a reminder to read up later on Joyan magic, she straightened from her bow and said, "Thank you for having us, Your Majesty."

"Have you had time," Aveline broke in, "to consider our request?"

"It was kind of you both to come all this way to invite us to your conference in person," said the rey. "But I hate to discuss such matters on an empty stomach. My cousin will show you to the chambers we have set aside for you, and we'll talk over dinner."

Aveline looked as though she wanted to argue, but ultimately all she did was nod. "Thank you for your generosity."

CHAPTER EIGHT

FARON

FARON AWOKE TO REEVE STARING DOWN AT HER, HIS PALE FACE even paler.

There were dark circles beneath his blue eyes, and his short hair was a mess of brown curls illuminated by the electric lamps that brightened the room. When he saw that she was awake, he smiled radiantly, and Faron smiled back, relief cutting through her disorientation. Once, she would never have felt comforted by the presence of Reeve Warwick, but everything was so different now. She *felt* so different now. She touched his cheek, desperate for even that small point of contact. As her brain struggled toward wakefulness, she allowed this—him—to ground her. Her guiding star.

"It's you," she said faintly, tracing the line of his jaw. Hair bristled under her fingers, stubble that was not yet shaven. Something about that tickled the back of her mind, but she was still too lethargic to think. "You're here."

Since they had left Port Sol, she had seen no sign of Reeve in his own body. Iya maneuvered Reeve's body from place to place, but Gael, not Reeve, was the only one who had previously emerged to help her. She had worried that he was too weak to control the body, that maybe he no longer existed at all. She'd felt him there, the one time she had skimmed Lightbringer's soul, but that didn't mean he was still there. It was a thought she hadn't wanted to face, a failure she hadn't been able to accept the possibility of. She hadn't known just how scared she'd been until she saw him there, now, and tears stung her eyes.

"Are you all right?" Reeve asked, and for a moment it seemed as if his eye color was shifting from blue to hazel and back again. Light spilled into the room from behind him, making it hard to figure out if she was just hallucinating. "How do you feel?"

"How do *I* feel?" It took everything she had not to let those tears fall. His skin was so warm. His tone was so caring. It was more than she deserved. "I'm fine. I just—I missed you."

"Aw, how sweet." He reached up to catch her hand, yanking it away from his face. "Worry not. I've punished the two responsible for your injury."

The words slapped Faron in the face like cold water. Her hand shook in his bruising grip. "Iya."

"The very same." That cruel slash of a smile appeared. His eyes were a blue as cold as death. How could she have ever mistaken that frost for the petal-soft lignum vitae blue of Reeve's eyes? "Did you think I was Reeve Warwick? How humiliating for you."

"Let go of me."

He released her at once, letting her push herself up. Her arms trembled from trying to hold her weight, but she managed without his help. She was in a bed in the Hearthstone infirmary, swaddled in white walls and white sheets and the familiar smell of antiseptic. Her memories came flooding back, but, when she reached up to

THIS ENDS IN EMBERS

touch her nose, she found no broken bones or bleeding trails. Iya was sitting in a chair beside her bed, a notebook open in his lap. He closed it when she tried to sneak a peek.

"I healed you with a dragon relic," he explained, leaning back in the chair. Behind him, a window was open to let in the moonlit nighttime air. "One of the very same you tried to acquire tonight." Faron flinched, which only made his smile widen. "I'm not angry with you. I assumed you would try this sooner or later. The reason you found their souls so difficult to command is that I had already implanted them with an order to resist you. Had you kept going, all you would have done is kill them as our powers raged within their pliant minds."

"Piss off," said Faron.

"You grow more and more powerful every day. Tell me"—his voice lowered to a whisper, his face incandescent with glee—"how did it feel to control them? To taste their weakness and turn it to your advantage? How did it feel to play god?"

That hurt Faron worse than the punch. "I don't know what you're talking about."

And yet she thought of how victorious she had felt after that rush of power, how Noble and Ballard had been *dying* and she hadn't cared at all. *They're the enemy,* she told herself, but that defense sounded weak to her ears. Elara had gone to Langley for two months and had not only made friends but defeated Marius Lynwood without actually harming him. Faron had been with Iya for two weeks and she had already drawn first blood.

"I'll let you get some rest," Iya said in a smug tone. There was nothing else to say. His point had been made so sharply that Faron was still bleeding. "But I'll have some free time in the afternoon if you'd like to continue gazing longingly at my vessel, hoping for what will never again be."

"Ass," Faron muttered.

"They really should," Iya shot back—his face then mellowed into something mischievous, his eyes the clear blue of morning mist, affection dancing there, so familiar it made Faron's heart clench—"write more books about your charm."

They both froze. Iya looked lost for a moment before his expression closed off and he swept out of the room. But Faron was shaken down to her core.

Those words. Reeve had said them to her months ago, in response to the same insult. They had been at her house, and Elara had brought Reeve home with her. Faron had been unable to resist the chance to insult him, and his drawling sarcasm had infuriated her even more than the sight of his stupid face. The few times he decided to rise to her bait, he was casually witty and lightning fast in his retorts, as if he didn't even need to think about them.

They really should write more books about your charm.

That was not Iya. That was Reeve. *That was Reeve.*

Just as Gael had come to her before, stopping her from incurring Lightbringer's fatal wrath, Reeve had instinctively risen to her bait. He was alive. His soul was alive.

Iya was trying to hide it by lashing out and retreating, but he was losing control over the other souls in his body. She didn't know how and she didn't know why, but twice was a pattern that she could exploit. The fact that he hadn't killed her for this yet meant that he still needed her—which gave her the opportunity *she* needed. If she could find the weakness in the prison he'd trapped Reeve and Gael in, she would have allies. She would figure out how to stop him, or at least incapacitate him. She would be a step closer to returning home a hero.

Faron lay back on her pillows, turning her face toward the winking stars and imagining that Mala was gazing down at her in approval.

CHAPTER NINE

ELARA

T HE FIRST THING ELARA DID WHEN SHE RETIRED TO HER BOR-
rowed chambers was take a long soak in the bath, a claw-foot
tub with carnation-scented water. The second thing she did was
wrap a woven blanket around her shoulders and wander out to
the balcony to gaze over the gorgeous lawns and elegant pools
that made up the dark courtyards. Her hands shook on the railing
from something other than the cold, and she forced herself to take
a breath. And another. And another.

She felt so out of place there, in someone else's palace, with the
future of her island in her hands. But she just had to remind herself
that her scores in etiquette, history, and politics at Hearthstone
had been worth bragging about, as well. Aveline needed a partner,
a support system, a piece she could move across the board to keep
the other nations in line. Elara could do that. She could be that.

Still, Elara couldn't help being glad she didn't have to do it right
now. For the moment, she needed to just *be*.

Two Queenshield guarded her door. A third patrolled the area
beneath the balcony, to prevent any threats from climbing into
her room. Elara sat in a wooden lounge chair and drew her legs

up to her chest beneath the blanket. Late Harvest season in Joya del Mar was cooler than San Irie. Even without a wind, there was a bite of chill in the air. Moonlight beat down on the plants, edging each flower with a line of silver. The flowers that, apparently, lent strength to the nature spirits that Joya del Mar channeled for magic.

She was sure that Reeve had told her that once. A throwaway fact from one of his books.

In the years after the war, Reeve had become fluent in patois from reading, asking Elara to pronounce or translate words. In exchange for her favorite novels, he would teach her Langlish phrases, tell her what he knew about dragons, share his complicated feelings about his family and his former home. Elara hadn't even noticed their slow slide into friendship. One day, she had just woken up feeling as though she had known Reeve Warwick her whole life.

Now he was gone, and she missed him. She missed him so much, it hurt. Elara's eyes began to burn, so she closed them in an attempt to ward off tears. If she could just talk to Reeve...if he could reassure her that she was what the queen needed...gods, if she could even just find out if he was all right...

Faron is with him. With his body, she told herself. *She'll bring him back. She does the impossible all the time.*

But she still *missed* him.

"Elara."

She jumped. Aveline stood in the doorway between the bedroom and the balcony, dressed in a simple cotton dress with long sleeves and a high collar. Its vermilion color brought out the red undertones in her deep brown skin, and it covered enough to keep her warm as she approached the outdoors. Amusement flashed in her eyes at the sight of Elara holding a hand to her chest.

"It's a good thing I brought as many guards as I did," Aveline said, "though I suppose it won't matter if you die of fear before a real threat sneaks up on you."

"I consider you a real threat, Your Majesty."

Aveline raised a hand to stop Elara from getting up, instead settling in the chair beside her. "Well, thank you. But I'm here for advice, not threats, if you don't mind talking friend to friend."

"Friend to friend," Elara echoed, trying to tamp down a smile. From the twinkle in Aveline's eyes, she didn't succeed. "Okay. What's going on?"

"We have a real opportunity with the Joyans, Elara." Aveline leaned back in the chair, speaking only just above a whisper, as if she didn't want to risk even the slumbering birds overhearing. "Not just for the conference, but for a potential alliance. They have a larger military than San Irie does, and their spirit magic has grown all the more powerful with the new gardens and parks they've built into their city planning from border to border."

"Why would they help us, though? Before we fought Langley, we were at war with them."

"Lightbringer—Iya—is not just an Iryan problem. If the Joyans leave us to fall first, they'll have no chance of standing against him alone. If I can't get Rey Christóbal to see reason, I'm almost positive I can get through to the doña."

"I didn't know you knew the doña that well."

Aveline stiffened. "We have a certain history. She's . . . susceptible to reason."

It sounded as if the queen wanted to add something else. Elara

THIS ENDS IN EMBERS

got the sense that she was missing a key part of all this, but asking questions that Aveline wasn't prepared to answer was the fastest way to get her to shut down.

"I think it's a good idea," Elara said carefully. "I mean, if we can get all the Novan empires to ally—"

"I see you're finally starting to develop a mind for politics." The tension slowly seeped out of Aveline's shoulders, until she was crossing her legs at the ankles and sliding her eyes shut. "You're already ahead of me."

"Wait. What do you mean?"

"I'll remain here to sway the Joyans to attend the conference and plant the seed for a treaty. I'm sending you ahead to Étolia to do the same."

Elara twisted in her seat, her eyebrows leaping toward her hair. "*Me?* Aveline, I don't even speak Étolian."

"That won't be an issue," said Aveline dismissively. "You're the Maiden Empyrean, the voice of the gods in the mortal realm, and second only to me in power. You will make a fine representative. Think of this less as politics and more . . . as a mission."

"With all due respect, Your Majesty, I failed miserably at the last mission you sent me on. I'm a soldier, not a diplomat."

"And yet, thanks to you, we can fly in and out of the Langlish Empire at our leisure, with the same dragons that once attempted to wipe us out now on our side."

Elara's lips parted, but she had no defense against that. It wasn't the way she would have put it, but she couldn't deny that it was true. Still, discomfort hummed through her blood, her mind already grasping at a myriad of ways she could mess this up. The headache she had fought off earlier returned with a vengeance, hammering at her brain stem until she felt it all over her body. Her resolution to be a useful pawn had relied on the queen being there to guide her. Could she do it alone without causing an international incident?

"I know I seem very good at this, but it's only because of practice. This life was never something I wanted for myself." Aveline's smile faded into something more thoughtful. Her eyes opened, and she stared blankly at the stars. "I wanted to be a dancer."

"You—what?"

To her surprise, the queen blushed. "When I lived on the farm, I wanted to move to Port Sol and be a dancer. To perform onstage, if the war ever ended. I was planning to leave once I turned eighteen, but, as you know, your sister found me first."

"I didn't know you could dance!"

"You don't need to sound so shocked. Am I not graceful?"

Of course you are, Elara almost blurted. After all, she had noticed Aveline's grace and elegance under the context of pining for her at the tender age of thirteen. Aveline Renard Castell didn't walk, she glided. Her every movement was refined. But Elara had thought Aveline had trained herself in sophistication while alone in Pearl Bay Palace, ruling a country before she was in her twenties. She had never imagined this.

"Anyway." Aveline sighed, that heavy, fatigued sigh Elara had become familiar with. "I just wanted you to know that you weren't alone in being surprised at the twists that life has taken. For what it's worth, I think you would have made a fine soldier. But you are also a magnificent Empyrean."

Aveline had expressed a similar sentiment ahead of the Summit, even after Elara had snuck away to enlist in the Iryan Military

THIS ENDS IN EMBERS

Forces behind her back, but it meant just as much now as it had back then. Elara had grown disillusioned with the life of a soldier after failing to become a drake pilot, but she still wanted to help people and protect her home. She hadn't imagined becoming the Maiden Empyrean, but the title would help her do what she'd set out to do. It would help her rescue her sister and defeat Lightbringer. It would empower her to bring Faron and Reeve home, to San Irie, where they all belonged.

It was hard to think of what she would do after. But for now, she could do this.

"All right," she said, proud that her voice did not shake. "I'll go to Étolia and win them over. I won't let you down, Your Majesty."

"I know," said Aveline. "I've always known that."

CHAPTER TEN

FARON

FROM THE MOMENT THIS WAR MEETING BEGAN, FARON COULD TELL it was different. There was an anticipation in the air, a restlessness among Iya's followers, that hadn't been there before. No one looked at her except Ballard and Noble, whose swift recovery from their head wounds seemed to have made them even more volatile. They sat beside Lynwood and Thompson, and the former smirked as though he knew something Faron didn't.

Once again, a map of the world covered the tabletop. This time, the clay crowns had been cleared from the space, except for a single one over the Emerald Highlands of Nova. The south of Langley was roughly an hour to two hours away from the archipelago by dragon, depending on where, exactly, they landed. Instead of squat tenements and precarious high-rises, the Highlands boasted verdant countryside claimed by those rich enough to measure their property in thousands of acres.

"We'll begin the conquest here," Iya said, his fingers resting atop the crown. "Even if news of our arrival reaches the capital, it would take them over an hour to mobilize the Dragon Legion and

THIS ENDS IN EMBERS

reach the Highlands. We'll also have the benefit of cutting them off from the Silver Sea as we move farther south."

"Rosetree Manor is fortified against dragons, my saint," said Mireya Warwick. "If we take Watson, we'll be in a perfect position to hold our lands from there."

It took Faron a moment to place the name Watson, and then she scowled. It was the name of the town where the Warwicks had briefly trapped Elara. With Signey and Zephyra, she'd managed to escape, to warn the queen of the impending attack and return to San Irie. But across the Crown Sea, Faron had freed Lightbringer from the Empty, severing Elara's dragon bond at the worst-possible moment. It was a wonder that Elara had made it out, when she had no longer been able to communicate with her dragon.

"What information do we have on the town?" asked Iya. "It's far closer to Beacon than I would like." He moved the crown deeper into the Highlands, resting over a city that hid in the shadow of a short mountain range. "What if we take Arledge instead and spread north?"

"Arledge is more densely populated," Gavriel Warwick pointed out. "And their people are vicious fighters. They live too close to the Contested Lands not to be."

"*Their* people'?" Faron lifted her eyebrows. "Don't you mean *your* people?"

"Watson may take away our advantage on time," he continued as if she hadn't spoken, "but I believe it would be easier to bring the population to heel."

Their people. The population. Hearing the commander of Langley speak about his empire as though they were targets to be taken out instead of humans who had once looked to him as a ruler was horrifying. Even before she had won the throne, Aveline had thought of Iryans as her people, her family, her reason to fight. Everyone in this room—Faron excluded—looked between the Warwicks and Iya with mild interest, indifferent to the destruction this would cause.

They were Langlish. It was none of her business. But Faron's stomach twisted as the conversation carried on without her, turning to scouting parties and predicted fatalities. She had forgotten this aspect of war, this . . . casual disregard for the reality of human suffering. This dehumanization of the opposition, to justify what would be done. This rationalization of even-accidental deaths as casualties of a necessary conflict. Hadn't she used that same reasoning just the other day to skirt San Irie's culpability for Sebastian Edwards's death? *That was war*, she had said. This was war.

But Iya spoke of killing innocents. There could be no war against innocents. Only an unjust massacre.

And she was just letting it happen.

Faron stood up. Words hovered on the tip of her tongue, but, in the end, she fled.

The hallway was cool in comparison with the heat of that oppressive room—or maybe it was her, just her, burning from the combination of wild emotions she felt. The Langlish weren't her people, but they didn't have to be her people to deserve to live. But what could she do? She could ask Iya to order the citizens of Watson to evacuate, but that was only a temporary solution. Even if they had somewhere else to go, he had no intention of giving back their homes, and she could hardly ask them to trust her long enough to defeat him.

Her back met the wall. She slid down until she was on the floor,

THIS ENDS IN EMBERS

her knees drawn up to her chest, her forehead pressed against them. The air was thin. Their voices tornadoed through her mind: *cutting them off...what if we take...bring the population to heel...* It wasn't as though she had thought that being on the offensive side of a conquest would be easier in any way, but she was in this room and she wasn't in this room, the inevitable result of Iya's scheming playing out behind her eyelids every time she blinked. She had seen it in San Irie during the war, and her throat burned with the phantom taste of acrid smoke and putrid corpses. She remembered it too well. The fire and fear. The hunger and helplessness. The death, always death, so much death.

Get up, she told her leaden limbs. *Stop him.* But the memories were paralyzing. Her body was not her own. Her chest was tight. It was only when she registered footsteps that her heart stopped pounding in her ears. She tensed, ready for a fight, but the footsteps of the rest of the members of the war meeting trailed past her as though she weren't even there. Except the final set, walking alone, pausing less than a yard away from her. Close enough for her to strike—*ankle sweep, groin punch, victory in two moves*—if she needed to defend herself.

"Faron," said Iya. "The meeting is over. You should return to your room."

Not that she knew how to defend herself from him.

"What did you decide?" she asked in her most acidic tone. Her voice remained blissfully steady. "Who will be first to die?"

"We'll start with Watson." Iya sat down beside her. She could feel the line of his arm against her shoulder, but she refused to look at him. She felt too raw right now to see those words come from Reeve's lips. "You can come along, if you like."

"I don't want to watch you massacre your own people."

"You watched me massacre *your* people with little protest. What makes this so different?"

Faron's head snapped up. "That's unfair. That's not—"

Iya withdrew something from the inner pocket of his jacket and passed it to her. It was a folded copy of the *San Irie Times*, black-and-white front page emblazoned with her face—or, rather, her younger face. She was twelve years old, her fist raised over her head, the sky dark with a dragon twisted into an unnatural position. She remembered the photo from the same paper years ago, and the triumphant write-up of the battle that had followed.

This was not triumphant. CHILDE TRAITOR, the headline read. THE GODS' CHOSEN DESTROYS THE CAPITAL. Along the side were two smaller photos, one of Port Sol as it had looked before, surrounded by crystal-clear waters and divided by crowded streets, and a second one of Port Sol in the wake of Iya's temporary takeover, reduced to destroyed buildings and smoking craters.

Faron's hands shook as she turned to the page with the rest of the article. The version of her the Iryans described sounded worse than Iya, somehow—a sociopath elevated to divine status by her people only to wield her power against two nations. Was this how San Irie saw her?

Was this how the gods saw her?

"You may think my current methods are cruel, but I once *tried* to build a legacy based on something other than fear," Iya said. "In return, history forgot my name. 'The Gray Saint,' I believe I was called?" He leaned closer, lowering his voice to a sinister whisper. "When you're gone, do you think they will remember Faron

THIS ENDS IN EMBERS

Vincent? Or will they remember the Childe Empyrean and how far she fell?"

She couldn't take her eyes off the article, and was sliced by the devastation and rage in every word. She'd done that. She hadn't meant to, but she'd done that. And here it was in print, a permanent record of her shattered reputation.

Faron's breaths knifed out of her, painful and sharp. "Where did you get this?"

"The market, one island over. I can take you there later if you suspect I've tampered with this in any way." Iya pried her clawed fingers from the paper and took it back. He folded it carefully in half before setting it on his other side. "Breathe with me before you pass out, Faron. Inhale...."

Her body instinctively followed the familiar instructions. Her eyes slid shut as she inhaled, held the breath, exhaled, then repeated each step. She and Elara had often done this together in the dark of night, Faron's forehead pressed to Elara's collarbone, their heartbeats slowly syncing as they calmed from whatever nightmare had gripped them in its talons. *Where are you?* Elara would ask. *In my bedroom, in Deadegg*, Faron would reply. *With you. I'm safe. We're safe.*

We're safe, Elara would whisper, a prayer and a promise. *We are safe.*

"You try so hard to be good," Iya murmured from somewhere above her, fingertips tracing over her frizzy baby hairs, "and it seems to do little but exhaust you."

Faron swatted away his hand and straightened. The article had left her in pieces, but she was used to wedging them back together into a facade of strength. She glared at Iya, sweeping her vulnerabilities behind her mental armor. "Just because you tried to be good and failed so badly, it was legendary doesn't mean the rest of us will follow in your footsteps."

Instead of responding with anger, Iya chuckled. As if she were *amusing* him. "The sooner you accept that you've already followed in my footsteps, the sooner you'll stop feeling like this."

"Don't pretend to know how I feel—"

"We're *connected*, Faron. When you feel something strongly enough, I feel it, too. You're exhausted. You're miserable. You're angry with yourself, and you're angry with me, and you're angry with the world for placing these burdens on your shoulders." Suddenly, she could no longer hear the serrated edges of Lightbringer in Iya's tone. She could hear him and him only. Gael Soto—or as close to Gael Soto as she could get with Lightbringer corrupting his soul. "I know exactly how you feel. I've felt it myself, in the past." His fingers tipped up her chin, until all she could see were those eyes. Instead of the usual coldness, she saw understanding. "If you cannot be their saint, why not be their villain? Why chase fame when you could live in infamy?"

He was close, close enough that she could study his chaotic eyebrows, feel the warmth of his breath, smell the black tea he'd had with his toast-and-jam breakfast. She could count his stubby eyelashes, follow the uneven line of his curls across his forehead. His eyes were trained on hers. They were no longer Reeve's blue but hazel, and, even still, as she watched, his pupils slowly consumed that hazel until there was only a ring of it left. Desire was etched into every line of his face, thick in every breath.

Lightbringer had lost control again. It was obvious to her now.

THIS ENDS IN EMBERS

This was Gael Soto watching her as if he wanted to swallow her whole.

"You are an unstoppable, overwhelming, indescribable force, Faron Vincent," he said softly, "and they do not deserve you."

Faron's traitorous body wanted to surge closer, but her heart held her firmly in place. Her shallow breath, the thrum of her pulse—none of it was for him. It was for who he looked like. It was for Reeve. She remembered how Gael had once appeared—black hair, milk-white skin, hazel eyes, all sharp angles—and she felt nothing but wistful regret. She looked at the boy in front of her, at Reeve, and, even though his eyes were *wrong, wrong, wrong*, her lips parted with the desire to feel his again. To kiss him better, longer, deeper this time, until there was no one in his mind but her.

"Faron, I..." Gael's lips were parted. His expression was both hungry and lost, as if he didn't know where he was or what he wanted except for her. Faron swallowed, unsure of what to say to keep them suspended in this moment that Lightbringer couldn't seem to pierce.

And then it was over. Iya surged to his feet in a wave of movement, swiping a hand over his mouth. He left without looking at her, his thundering footsteps echoing down the quiet hallway. Faron deflated against the wall, her heart fissuring from a hundred disparate emotions. She was uninterested in Gael's want, but she was terrified of his understanding. Why was the only person who truly saw her the biggest danger her world had ever faced?

He was right. She had tried to be good. She had tried so hard. She was not like her sister, who seemed to be a natural hero. She always had to try. And it had blown up in her face so badly that it was front-page news.

"I miss you, Elara," she whispered into the silent air.

But above all, she missed who she used to be. A girl who knew right from wrong. A tool for independence. A saint with a purpose. Whoever she was—whoever she was becoming—was not someone she recognized. And with each new day, she feared she'd passed the point of no return.

CHAPTER ELEVEN

ELARA

THE CHÂTEAU WAS THE PRIDE OF CIEL, THE CAPITAL OF ÉTOLIA. Elara had spent the hour-and-a-half-long drake flight reading as much about the country as she could, but even the pictures had not done the beauty of it justice.

Ciel was like something out of a picture book, all cobblestone streets choked with people and framed by pine trees, colorful storefronts down alleys too narrow for carriages, and street artists in thick coats and long scarves perched on overturned buckets advertising portraits in Étolian. A carriage had conveyed a wide-eyed Elara and her Queenshield through the heart of Ciel, giving Elara ample time to admire how different the city was from anywhere she'd ever been.

Étolia had carved out a foothold in the Ember Sea by conquering the island of Marién, the way Joya del Mar had claimed Isalina and Kaere, and Langley had ruled San Irie. Since Étolia had lost that colony in the Mariéni Revolution a century ago, they hadn't made any further attempts to settle in the Ember Sea. But their empire hardly seemed to be suffering from lacking land that wasn't theirs. In fact, Ciel seemed to be flourishing by minding its own business.

Despite all the sights she had passed, Elara found the real treasure standing at the entrance to the Château gardens. "Professor Smithers!"

Damon Smithers was a tall white man in his late fifties, with shoulders as wide as a mainsail, a square jaw on a square head, and a broad smile that made his laugh lines deepen. In the midafternoon sun, he leaned against a lamppost, dressed in a fitted gray suit with an indigo waistcoat that made his narrow blue eyes pop. A blue scarf protected his neck from the cold. At Hearthstone, he had taught history, one of Elara's two favorite classes. Here, with a gray wool cap atop his silver hair, and his mustache grown out into a short salt-and-pepper beard, he looked like a force waiting to be unleashed.

"Miss Vincent," he said warmly in patois. "You're early."

"So are you." Elara wanted to throw her arms around him, but she wasn't sure it would be appropriate. When Aveline had assured her that a translator would meet her at the Château, she hadn't imagined it would be her former professor. "How have you been? How's Mr. Lewis?"

Professor Smithers dipped his head with a shy smile at the mention of his husband. "He's well. We're both as well as can be with all the upheaval." The smile faded into something brittle. "For all our studies, we underestimated how exhausting it is to live through unprecedented times."

Elara's smile froze on her face. She reminded herself that the professor meant well: He had praised and encouraged her in her studies, and he and Mr. Lewis had ridden their sage dragon, Nizsa,

THIS ENDS IN EMBERS

into battle to protect San Irie from their own country. She was sure he hadn't meant to remind her that, while San Irie had always existed in unprecedented times—war after war, with ingenuity and community as their only shields against total annihilation—Langley had known peace and stability.

Peace and stability that had grown from the blood of the conquered.

Smithers's expression changed, as if he realized he had said something wrong. Elara pushed forward before he could apologize. Or, rather, before she could feel obligated to accept an apology. "So, who will we be dealing with in there?"

Since there was nothing a professor loved to do more than lecture, Elara was treated to an overview of the Étolian royal family—including their host, twenty-six-year-old Orianne Lumiére. As the second daughter of the House of Lumière, she was a tournesola, or heir to the throne, and acted as a diplomat for her sister, Reine Anjou, protecting her local interests. Her sixteen-year-old brother, Guienne, typically represented their family abroad. If Elara remembered correctly, he had been the one they had sent to the San Irie International Peace Summit months ago.

Smithers wrapped up his lesson just as a small group of soldiers—musketeers, he reminded her—exited the Château to bring them inside for the meeting. They wore the gold-lined blue cassocks she remembered from the Summit, along with wide-brimmed plumed hats. Elara followed the bobbing feathers into the massive building, up a carpeted staircase illuminated by a gorgeous skylight, and through marble-and-bronze corridors.

The salon they ended up in had several paintings on the ceiling in gilded oval frames, scenes of battles that Elara didn't recognize, and marble columns. There was a long dining table in front of a fireplace, and several cushioned chairs were scattered around it. Sitting in one of them, reflected in the large square mirror over the mantel shelf, was Tournesola Orianne.

Her skin was white with golden undertones, her hair was shoulder-length and yellow, her eyes were long-lashed and blue, and her lips were full and pink. She wore a tan gown that brought out her hair's darker highlights, with a gold medallion at her neck.

An unknown person stood just to her left—likely her translator. Étolia, Reeve had once told Elara, was the only country where none of the Ember Sea island languages were spoken in some capacity. Before losing Marién, they had forced the Mariéni to learn Étolian, brutally stamping out any existing language, culture, or magic. To this day, the island still spoke a dialect of Étolian.

Behind them, the doors closed. Three musketeers remained inside to protect the tournesola, standing shoulder to shoulder with the Queenshield. Smithers bowed, and Elara quickly copied him. She could do this. She had to do this, and so she would.

The tournesola's voice was lower and raspier than Elara had expected. "Welcome," her translator said after she finished speaking, their patois nasal from their Étolian accent. "I hate to waste your time, but I have considered your proposal and I do not see the point."

"The point in a conference?" Elara blinked. "To discuss the threat that Iya poses to the world?"

Smithers translated that, his eyebrows knitted together.

Tournesola Orianne snorted. "As far as I can tell, Iya is a problem made by you and for you," she said via translator. "Why should we waste our time at an international conference when we could be safeguarding our people from your mistakes?"

THIS ENDS IN EMBERS

"You share a border with Langley," said Smithers, once in Étolian and then again in patois for Elara's benefit. "Do you think that Iya will stop his conquest with one empire? If he overtakes us, he'll come for you and your people next. Do you want to stand alone when he does?"

The professor and the translator continued to volley back and forth, but Elara was no longer listening. She hadn't expected the conversation to be quick, but she felt naive for expecting that the Étolian royal family wouldn't need to be convinced that Iya was a danger to them all. When he had been unleashed, she hadn't hesitated to stand against him, to protect everyone, with or without the power of the gods on her side. That had made her ignorant to the fact that there were people in this world who needed to be *persuaded* to care about others.

Once again, she found herself thinking about Reeve. He could recite every branch of the House of Lumiére off the top of his head, with facts about each member that he'd read in the newspaper or in the library. What had he told her about Tournesola Orianne?

When her sister became the reine, the queen, Orianne was called to the Château from a convent. It was almost as if he were here beside her, his lightning-blue eyes sparking with new information. Even Elara did not love learning as much as Reeve did; sometimes, absorbing knowledge seemed to breathe life back into him. *She's reportedly inflexible and proud, but, above all, she is pious.*

The book Elara had read in the drake had confirmed as much: Étolia, like San Irie, had religious institutions all over its major cities. Their god, Pére Divin, blessed their royal family with wonder working—the power to heal—which they claimed as their divine right to rule. Elara's eyes narrowed on the tournesola and the medallion around her neck as she and Smithers lobbied back and forth via the translator. It had a symbol of two glowing hands etched into its face. If she was as pious as Reeve claimed, political reasoning wouldn't work on her.

The queen had been right. This *was* a job for the Maiden Empyrean. And, finally, Elara knew exactly what to say.

She cleared her throat, stopping Smithers midsentence, and locked eyes with the tournesola. "You're right."

The conversation screeched to a stop. Tournesola Orianne's expression gave away nothing, but there was a shine to her eyes that hadn't been there before. Elara hoped it was respect.

"Iya is a problem we created, but he's not one we can solve alone," she continued, speaking slowly enough for the translator to keep pace. "You know who I am. You know I am the Maiden Empyrean, the weapon of the gods. The *Iryan* gods," she corrected when the tournesola's eyebrow lifted. "Stopping Iya is not just an international mission. It's a holy one. And I know that if we all don't join together to stop him now, then he will win. The best way to protect your people is to stand with us, starting with attending this conference. I beg you, on behalf of my queen, my island, my gods, to please consider our proposal."

In the ensuing silence, Tournesola Orianne continued to stare at Elara as though she were a horse that had learned to walk on just its front legs. Elara's heart began to beat faster, so fast that she was breathless, but she froze in place. She wanted this victory so badly, every second added new weight to her shoulders, but she feared that any sign of vulnerability would weaken her argument. The longer the tournesola remained quiet, the harder it became for Elara to keep her expression blank.

THIS ENDS IN EMBERS

And then the tournesola looked away with a clipped statement conveyed by her translator: "I will consider this matter further."

"Your Highness, there is no time—"

"My musketeers will show you out."

"But when will you—?"

"Thank you for coming." She stood, a clear end to the conversation. "It was enlightening to meet you, Maiden Empyrean."

With those final words, her translator fell back, hands folded behind them. Elara felt sick. She bit the inside of her cheek to keep from flinging more pleas in Orianne's direction. *Reeve would have been able to secure this alliance,* she thought. Even Faron, for all her stubborn rebelliousness, was well-versed in politics; she probably would have had talking points. Elara was a soldier, not a diplomat. Her words would never be enough.

She would never be enough.

Outside, Elara and Smithers watched the musketeers retreat into the Château while the Queenshield went to get Elara's carriage. She would have to fire call the queen to find out if she was free to return home or if she would have to remain in Ciel to take another meeting with the tournesola...whenever the tournesola was ready. Her insides twisted at the thought of telling Aveline how badly she'd failed.

Then Professor Smithers said, "That was rather shrewd maneuvering, Miss Vincent."

"What?" Elara paused at the smile on his face. "She didn't agree."

"She didn't disagree," he pointed out. "The meeting began with her refusal, and you argued her into a deliberation. That's better than I thought we would get, if I'm honest."

Elara's need for validation flared up at once. Every dark thought she'd been having evaporated in the face of the compliment, until she had to fight back a smile. "Well. All right."

Smithers led the way toward the street, where her carriage idled. The crowds of people had slowed to a trickle, but he still paused before they made it to the sidewalk. He rubbed at his beard, glancing down the lane at the trees casting the stones in shadow. Pine needles littered the sidewalk like a carpet of emeralds.

"I know I said earlier that we are living through unprecedented times, but that's not quite true," Smithers finally said, his hands falling to his side. "Iya is recreating the circumstances of his first rise, which Rupert and I have been studying in detail since I was... relieved of my teaching post at Hearthstone."

Elara remembered, just then, that Mr. Lewis was a historian, so he likely had access to the very books and records that the Sotos were probably using to learn more about Iya. The first time Elara had met Barret Soto, he had recited a Langlish nursery rhyme with prescient information about Lightbringer's plans to rise from the Empty. Perhaps Mr. Lewis and Barret had read the same books. "Is there another nursery rhyme about this, Professor?"

"Not as such. This is just a story we all know by heart yet seem incapable of learning from." Smithers sighed. "It begins like this: A young and charismatic leader, a hunger for power, and the annexation of lands expedited by the sheer volume of people who believe this is, simply, not their problem."

"And how does it end?"

"Historically?" The professor opened the carriage door. "Some people—good people—speak out. They rally, and they organize. They fight back, with or without the support of their hand-wringing leaders. In the light of day or the dead of night, they hold the line."

THIS ENDS IN EMBERS

A fervor appeared in his eyes that Elara wanted to ask him about, but it quickly disappeared. "And the tyrant falls, sometimes as brutally as they rose to begin with."

But it wasn't a story, Elara wanted to say as she stepped into the carriage. Stories had endings. This was an endless cycle. This was the Warwicks trading Reeve's autonomy away in exchange for power. This was Wayne and Aisha's parents burying their children decades too soon. This was Iya tearing apart countries and families to build an empire on their skulls.

This was an unlearned lesson that always ended in destruction.

"How many people have to die," Elara whispered, "before a tyrant falls?"

"Even one is far too many."

Smithers closed the carriage door, and it pulled away from the curb, leaving Elara alone with her thoughts.

CHAPTER TWELVE

FARON

FARON DID NOT FEEL WELL ENOUGH FOR BATTLE, BUT SHE DIDN'T have much of a choice. The invasion of Watson would take place whether she was there or not, and if she couldn't stop it, then she should at least bear witness to her failure. Still, she felt nausea unrelated to how high Lightbringer chose to fly so they would go unseen during the two-hour flight from the Hestan Archipelago to the northernmost town in the Emerald Highlands.

By the time Lightbringer finally broke through the clouds, Faron's nerves were as steady as they would get, and she could appreciate the beauty that sprawled out below them. Manor homes claimed endless acres of land, delineated by hedges and wrought-iron fences, but nature otherwise ruled from the Silver Sea north to the Tenebris River. They flew over a patchwork of greens—olive and pine, sage and mint, moss and fern—all the shades smearing into one another like mixed paint on a palette. Here and there, Faron saw the pewter of mountain ranges, the sepia of dark hills, and the cobalt of ponds and lagoons. Sun-dappled clouds hung above them, their color almost grimy compared with the arrant white of Lightbringer's beating wings.

THIS ENDS IN EMBERS

It was too nice a day for conquest. Lightbringer probably loved that.

Watson was a sprawling agricultural settlement pressed between one of the many mountain ranges that sprawled through the Highlands and a grove of pine and ash trees that clustered together like gossiping elders. They landed just outside the town line, marching past acres of flat farmland, crops in various states of decay, and browning grass preparing to be covered by a blanket of cold snow. Faron was reminded, inevitably, of Deadegg, her small agricultural town, with its farms that were slowly going out of business and the misty Argent Mountains watching over them from the center of the island. Her landlocked home with the people who had watched her grow up . . . and now hated her.

She tried to stop thinking of Deadegg, but she heard the bleating of goats and she smelled the pungent fertilizer and she could almost *feel* the Deadegg dirt still caked under her nails. Her town might not welcome her back, but she carried it with her even now—her love for her town as fixed and immutable as her love for her sister, her parents, her island. It might be too late to prove herself to them, but she had to try. She had saved them once with powers they didn't understand. In a way, this was no different.

If her mistake had made her a villain, she would perform a hundred thousand conciliatory acts until she could go home again. She didn't care what the history books would say about her. She only wanted to go home.

"Hm," said Iya, his first sound since they had landed.

Faron followed his line of sight to see they had reached the town line—and the town in question was empty. Cows weren't grazing near the windbreaks in the enclosed fields. Horses swaddled in rugs weren't tied to wooden posts or slumbering in the stables. There were no carriages in the streets, no sounds of life, nothing but the echoing silence periodically interrupted by the rattle of the wind.

Estella Ballard found them first, jogging up from one of the side streets with her co-Rider, Briar Noble, inches behind her. She scowled at Faron and then, with effort, dragged away her gaze. Faron was brimming with too much tentative excitement to scowl back. The town was empty. *The town was empty.* It would not be a massacre after all.

"Did they evacuate?" Iya asked without giving Ballard a chance to catch her breath. "And, if so, how did they know we were coming?"

He didn't look at Faron, knowing as well as she did that she had no means of contacting anyone, let alone the people of Watson. She hid a smile anyway. It was delightful, seeing Iya's careful planning crumble so quickly.

"There are no tracks leading out, my saint," Ballard said. "Our dragons have scented nothing, but we're making a full search of every building just to be—"

From deeper into the town, there came a scream. Faron winced. Damn it.

Ballard and Noble ran back the way they'd come. The shadow of their ultramarine dragon, Ignatz, passed overhead. Iya told Faron to stay put, before charging after them, a dangerous look on his face. Lightbringer remained on the outskirts of town, watching for any attacks from the north, and Faron briefly considered waiting with him. As much as she hated being told what to do, she didn't want to be a part of whatever was about to happen.

THIS ENDS IN EMBERS

Fire flashed against the blood-orange sky. Her hands clenched at her sides at the next round of screams.

Didn't it make Faron complicit, to be able to help and yet close her ears to the suffering? Iya couldn't hurt her, and, if he was distracted by stopping her, then the villagers could still get away. She could *help*. She *should* help, no matter the consequences.

Faron made it halfway down the street before she heard a noise.

It was too soft to have come from a dragon, but too loud to be a scavenger. To her left was a small ancient brick house with dark windows, surrounded by a half fence that separated the house from a dying cornfield. Ballard had said they'd made a sweep of the buildings, but it would be easy to hide within the wilted stalks that hadn't been cleared in time for Harvest. Maybe the bulk of the residents were close by, waiting for the dragons to go farther into town so they could get away. Faron could distract Lightbringer long enough for that.

She had no weapon save her bond magic, but hopefully she wouldn't need one. In fact, that was likely for the best, if she was to convince them that she was on their side.

She crept toward the source of the sound, only to find a child staring at her from behind a scuffed black bin. It smelled of straw and day-old milk, and it was large enough that Faron and the child could both stand behind it without being seen from the street. Standing in the dirt between the bin and the cornfield, the child watched her with wide blue eyes, her saffron hair divided into two pigtails. She couldn't have been more than six or seven, though Faron had a hard time judging the age of children.

After all, it wasn't as though she'd had much of a childhood herself.

The noise hadn't come from the cornfield. It came from a single crutch the girl had tucked under one arm. Her opposite foot had a brace on it, and the sound of the crutch moving from the dirt to the concrete surrounding a set of cellar doors had been what had drawn Faron's attention. Basements and cellars were a rare sight in Langley. Langlish towns flooded as often as San Irie's seaside cities, and, as a result, they avoided underground floors in favor of keeping all their old belongings in storage rooms and garages. This building must have been at least a century old, from when they'd used cellars to stock fuel for the winter.

"Is your family down there?" she asked. This part of Watson was quiet for now, but she was well aware of how quickly that could change. Lightbringer had flown in with Irontooth and Ignatz. Cruz was on standby in case the people proved too difficult for three dragons to overcome. And if he wasn't enough, Goldeye was at Hearthstone, eager for blood. "You should—"

The child threw the crutch with a high-pitched grunt. Faron ducked just in time to avoid getting hit in the head. It clattered against the bin, and the child darted over the fence to limp into the darkened field beyond. Either she was trying to get away or she was trying to lead Faron into a trap.

Faron didn't follow her. Instead, she inched closer to the metal doors of the cellar, which were closed but unchained.

"Is anyone in there?" she whispered. "I just want to help."

Faron tugged at one of the doors and it opened, though it was heavier than she'd expected because there was something affixed to the underside of it. The steps to the cellar were dark, but in the dying light she could see that there were rocks and drywall firmly attached to the door itself. More pieces were scattered across the steps and

THIS ENDS IN EMBERS

lining the interior walls, which were nowhere near as dusty as they should have been in an unused cellar. Something about it felt *off.*

"Of course."

Faron jumped, dropping the door. It clattered against the frame, louder than her heartbeat.

Gavriel Warwick stood behind her. A quiet anger radiated from him, lending him a predatory air. "These are pieces of my home, Rosetree Manor. It was built with dragon relics embedded in the wood and stone, to prevent . . . unwanted spying." He shoved Faron out of the way and pulled open the other cellar door. "Demolishing my house and using pieces of it to deceive us. Clever. Infuriating, but clever. Whatever they're hiding down here must be very valuable indeed."

Faron remembered the little girl—the decoy, she now realized—and her stomach twisted. "It's probably nothing. You should get back to the fight."

"Iya sent me to find you," said the commander, summoning a ball of flame to his gloved hands. "I have time enough."

He threw the fire down the stairs.

Faron screamed, stumbled forward, dropped to her knees.

The fire sputtered and went out before it even hit the bottom, smothered, she assumed, by the magic in the stones. But it illuminated a crowd of children gathered in the cellar, clinging to one another with wide eyes. They hadn't made a sound, wouldn't have been seen at all if not for the fire, and now they looked at the commander *and* Faron as if they were monsters come to consume them. Fear made them tremble. Faron trembled with them.

"Well," Commander Warwick said smugly, "this should resolve things faster."

Faron wished she had just followed that little girl into the fields, pretended to get lost for a few hours, and minded her own business for once in her life. Instead, she watched the commander draw a sword on the children she had inadvertently damned, evacuating them from the cellar to be used against their parents.

The way they looked at her. Her fingers curled against the packed ground and loose stones.

"I didn't mean—I only wanted to help," she whispered.

"Thanks for your *help*," one of the boys sneered.

"We know who you are," said a redheaded girl, clinging to another's hand. "You're the Empyrean. A monster."

"I—"

"We won't hurt you," the commander assured them with such faux kindness that Faron felt sick. "As long as your parents surrender immediately, we won't hurt any of you."

Faron glanced over her shoulder. His eyes were on the group of children, seemingly counting them. They were well trained, these kids. Not a single one of them glanced toward the field, where one of their number had disappeared. Those who weren't watching the commander in fear were glaring at her with hate in their eyes.

Hate she deserved.

She turned back to the cellar, pretending that she was closing the doors behind them.

And she slipped a loose stone, still warm with magic, up her sleeve.

As soon as they had seen their children wedged between Commander Warwick and Faron, most of the adults of Watson had

THIS ENDS IN EMBERS

surrendered. Some lives had already been lost in the battle, but the rest had dropped their weapons as quickly as Warwick had hoped.

"How could you?" an adult had asked as he'd turned over his pitchfork to one of Iya's soldiers. "They're just *kids*." His eyes had caught on Faron, and his expression had changed to something so hateful, she felt it like a punch. "I should've known. *You*—you're immoral. You've always been a savage."

This wasn't my idea, Faron had wanted to scream, but what had it mattered? Whether he'd thought her a savage because she was the Childe Empyrean or because she was Iryan, she had been standing with the people who had threatened a group of children. She'd had no moral high ground to stand on.

Iya had waited hours before allowing the anguished parents to reunite with their children, first confiscating their blades, drafting the able-bodied farmers into his army, and interrogating the mayor about any incoming reinforcements. By the time Iya's forces dragged themselves back to Lightbringer and flew the two hours to Hearthstone, it was nearing midnight. And still he called another meeting in the war room before dismissing anyone.

There were two empty chairs at the table this time. Estella Ballard and Briar Noble had remained in Watson with Ignatz to "maintain order," along with a small contingent of soldiers in case of retaliation. Faron didn't want to think about what they were doing to the people who had refused to bow to Iya, children or no children. She didn't want to think of the role she had played in their downfall.

"Once we secure the Highlands, our next phase should begin with Joya del Mar," Gavriel Warwick said. "The Dragon Legion would be split between coming to their aid and minding the south, which would make them easier to eliminate. Besides that, Joyan magic is derived from nature spirits. By razing their forests and drying out their lakes, we could render the people powerless."

"My current goal is not to eliminate the Dragon Legion," Iya said, his chin resting on his steepled fingers. Soot caked the side of his face, but he was otherwise uninjured from the battle. "I want to command them. To show them how powerful they can be when truly unleashed."

"That would require them to heed your threat, my saint," Oscar Luxton chipped in from the other end of the table. Beneath the electric lights, a bald spot was visible near the back of his silvering blond hair. "Two days from now will make a week since you issued it, and we haven't received word of any deserters."

"Hm. Well, I hardly blame them for not taking me seriously when I reside in the body of an eighteen-year-old boy."

"It's not just that," said Mireya Warwick. "The Sotos and the Hylands have been surprisingly capable leaders in our absence. According to my spies, they've assured the people of Beacon that they are taking steps to neutralize the threat you pose to their way of life." Faron's ears pricked at the word *spies*, and she filed away that information for later. She had thought those loyal to the Warwicks were only among their army here at Hearthstone, but *of course* they had left a few in key places to pass along information. "Whether that's true or not, they've kept the empire together well enough that everyone is taking them at their word. Or at least waiting to see what happens next."

"What happens next," Iya drawled, "is that we pay Beacon a visit."

"And what?" Faron asked with a glare. "Burn it down? That didn't work out so well when you tried it on San Irie."

THIS ENDS IN EMBERS

"Burning down the capital of a dragon-riding empire isn't as easy as you think. I'm aiming for something more subtle."

"Like *what?*"

"We could raid the Preserve," Nichol Thompson suggested. He faltered a little when all eyes turned to him, but his voice remained strong. Faron wanted to burn *him*. "The dragon eggs there are still incubating, but we shouldn't risk them hatching into new enemies."

Marius Lynwood smirked. "We can handle that one alone, if it pleases you, my saint."

"A sound idea." Iya leaned back with a smirk of his own, nodding at each person in turn. "Warwicks, you'll be with me in Beacon. Lynwood and Thompson, you take the Dragon Preserve. Luxtons, you'll hold Hearthstone and identify if any other cities are being shielded from us with the wreckage of Rosetree, so that I can plan accordingly. We leave in two days."

Everyone murmured their assent and began to leave the table in a cloud of yawns and stretching. Oscar Luxton and Mireya Warwick left together, speaking in quick whispers. Marius Lynwood was attempting to flirt with Margot Luxton, who thoroughly ignored him, as Nichol Thompson trailed silently behind them. Gavriel Warwick was the last to leave, and he did so reluctantly, as if expecting Iya to ask him to stay. Faron's lips thinned. *How pathetic.*

"*He is loyal only as long as it benefits him,*" Lightbringer said through the bond. "*Does that make him pathetic or me pathetic for needing such a snake?*"

"*You're an overgrown lizard,*" Faron pointed out. "*Should you be using* snake *as an insult?*"

121

"Hilarious."

"So, what preparations will we need to do before we go to Beacon?" Faron asked aloud, her voice dull with resignation. News of what had happened in Watson would surely have spread by the time they made it to the capital, and that howling emptiness threatened to swallow her emotions. The way those parents and children had looked at her. The way they'd called her a monster and a savage. The way their clever plan to face Iya's forces had been ruined in seconds by her errant curiosity. She was a danger to others just by being around them, but maybe she could sabotage the planning somehow. Maybe she had lulled Iya into a sense of security that would keep him from noticing what she was doing.

"As much as I'd love to give you the opportunity for sabotage," Iya said, getting to his feet with a snort, "you won't be coming."

"What are you planning to do to them?" she demanded. "And what's the point of letting me sit in on these meetings if you're going to keep secrets? You either trust me or you don't."

"I don't," Iya said without hesitation. "And even if I did, your amateur efforts to get in my way have proved that I can't. You'll remain here with the Luxtons until you see reason."

Faron stood, scrambling for something to change his mind. "With the Luxtons? One of them punched me in the face. How do you know they won't take the opportunity to get rid of me once and for all?"

"I told you I've already dealt with that. They know now that hurting you hurts me." Anger simmered in Iya's voice like a pot about to boil over. "They wouldn't dare touch you and expect to live."

She swallowed. "What if I hurt *myself*?"

THIS ENDS IN EMBERS

"How morbid." Iya checked to make sure there was no one at the door before those wrathful eyes turned on her. He stepped closer, until there was no more than a hand's breadth of distance between them. "I know that you've noticed that my souls are... unruly. Have you realized yet why?"

Slowly, Faron shook her head. She had her theories, of course, but none that she was willing to share.

Iya smiled, small and sharp. "These fool boys love you, Faron Vincent. It is the one thing that they agree on, the one emotion they feel so strongly that it enables them to unite against my influence. I will take this body to Beacon, and it will not matter how much their souls yearn for you. Your death may kill them, but not Lightbringer. It would be a minor setback at best." His hand lifted as though to touch her, and Faron ducked away. He chuckled. "You cannot stop me. You cannot stop the Warwicks. You cannot stop what is already in place."

"I don't believe that," Faron said, her voice stronger than she felt. "I've saved the world before, and I can do it again. I *have* to."

"You can certainly try." Iya headed for the door and then paused. "You know? I think I will take you with me to Beacon. But not so you can prove yourself." His expression was unreadable when he glanced at her over his shoulder. "I will take you to Beacon so the world can prove that I told you the truth: You can never make them love you again. You can only make them bow."

CHAPTER THIRTEEN

ELARA

I N THE END, AVELINE GAVE ELARA PERMISSION TO RETURN TO SAN Irie until the tournesola reached out again. "There's nothing more you can do," the queen had said during the fire call, "and Tournesola Orianne may react unfavorably if she thinks your presence is pressuring her." And then, almost as an afterthought, she'd added, "Why don't you go to Highfort to check in with the officers about their research and their defense strategies? It might help you, to be back in your element."

Elara had taken the idea of being back in her element a little too far by stopping in Deadegg first. But between Joya del Mar and Étolia, she'd been gone for just under a week, and she missed the security and confidence that she could get only from being home. If she landed in Deadegg to see her parents, took a carriage through Papillon to talk to the gods, and finally settled in Highfort, she would still be ready when Aveline summoned her again. Even more so, really, because her problems always seemed smaller with a belly full of her mother's rice and peas and oxtail.

But there was tension on the streets of her small town. There were no fresh insults painted on her house—unless her parents had

THIS ENDS IN EMBERS

already cleaned them off—but there were flyers affixed to every tree and lamppost, advertising a rally in the square. Half-hidden in an alley, Elara had shaken off her Queenshield escort to avoid a scene. Instead, she wore a head wrap over her unbraided hair and the most nondescript day dress she could find in her closet. But if someone spotted her, she knew she would still be recognizable. These people had watched her grow up, after all.

A fact that made the swollen crowd before her all the more terrifying.

Elara swallowed around a dry throat. Her skin felt too small for her body. The last time she had faced down a protest, it had been on horseback in the capital while her countrymen spoke out against the Novan presence on the island. Now she was on foot, in her hometown, while her neighbors spoke out against *her*.

Her fist tightened around the wrinkled flyer in her hand, which read NO MORE EMPYREANS above the protest's date and time. The market that usually spilled across the square with wooden carts and colorful awnings had been replaced by a raised wooden platform. A man walked onto that platform now, stopping in the center to face the crowd. Elara's heart seized when she recognized him.

Desmond Pryor.

Wayne's father.

Desmond had skin the color of tree bark and one amber eye. The other had been lost in the revolution; all that was left were his closed lid and the scar that sliced from his hairline, through his eye socket, down his face, to the base of his neck. His hair had grown out into an afro of tight curls, and his hands were gloved to hide the first-degree burns the dragons had left him with. Wayne had always said his father hadn't returned from war better off, and

Elara knew that went deeper than the injuries he'd been left with. Even from here, there was a hollowness in his eye that she recognized. As if even this rally were just another battle.

"Let's begin," he said without raising his voice. A hush fell over the crowd anyway, conversations easing into rapt silence. Desmond held himself like an officer, with the commanding voice to match. It was easy to imagine him leading squads to victory. "For too long, we have placed our fates in the hands of children, based on only their word that this is the will of the gods. A sword without an experienced hand to wield it can cut us just as easily as it cuts our enemies. We need only look around to see these wounds."

Elara had repaired the shops that bracketed the square, but he stood in front of the crumbled stone wall that had once surrounded the dragon egg for which Deadegg was named. The soil was black, swallowing shards of stone and concrete. Grass grew in an unnatural oval around the area, clearly delineating where nothing would ever grow again.

"I don't know about you," Desmond continued, "but I cannot believe this is Irie's will. Or, if it is, her will has been corrupted by the impulsiveness of adolescents. We deserve better than a queen who lies in bed with Novans."

"YES!" the crowd shouted in answer to a question he hadn't needed to ask.

"We deserve better than an Empyrean who attacks the very people she's meant to protect."

"YES!"

"We deserve better than a successor who brings dragons to our shores. Who worships a Langlish soldier. No," Desmond spat,

THIS ENDS IN EMBERS

"who dates *a dragon Rider*—the very kind of people who murdered our children."

"YES!"

His eye lifted, and for a wild moment Elara was sure he could see her there, tucked in that narrow space between a restaurant and a clothing store. She imagined the zealous crowd reaching for her and dragging her into the street to answer for her crimes. She didn't believe they would hurt her—she couldn't—but they would demand explanations that she didn't have. Explanations they were too hurt to listen to anyway.

"With each passing day, I fear we won't have an island to live on, or family to live with. The reign of the Renard Castell line must end here," Desmond Pryor finished. "And the time of the Empyreans is over!"

The crowd erupted with applause and cheers. "NO MORE EMPYREANS," they chanted. "NO MORE QUEENS!" Their cries rose into a cacophony, swirling and merging until they flattened into a single wall of sound: "NO MORE, NO MORE, NO MORE."

Desmond looked out at them without joy. It was as if he didn't even see the masses he had riled up. His gaze was only on the past. On the dead.

Elara pressed her back against the wall, clenching her eyes shut as the horde began to disperse. She was paralyzed by the fact that they were right. Desmond Pryor was right. For all their efforts to make San Irie better, she and Faron had done little but make it worse. They were just kids. Stupid kids. Even the gods were sick of them.

From a young age, Elara had learned to fear failure. The trickle of praise from parents and teachers made her feel as if she could fly without magic. The hammer of disappointment from those same figures could shatter her completely. She was in pieces now, bearing the resentment of an entire town, an entire nation. *Hold it together. Hold it together.* A tear slid down her cheek. She scrubbed it away.

"Hello, Elara," said Desmond Pryor.

She froze. Wayne's father stood at the mouth of Blind Alley, blocking the light from the sun. With his face in shadow, Elara couldn't read his expression. "Hello, Mr. Pryor."

"I didn't see you at the funerals."

She swallowed. "Yes, I—no."

Anything she could say—that she'd been reconstructing destroyed buildings, that she'd been chasing ways to defeat Iya, that she'd been bouncing from country to country to gain allies— just felt like an excuse. Reeve was unquestionably her best friend, but she had spent most days with Wayne and Aisha—and with Cherry—even if only from sheer proximity. She should have been at Wayne and Aisha's funerals. They shouldn't have *had* funerals.

Desmond stepped into the alley, and Elara barely stifled her sigh of relief. The last thing she wanted was for someone to notice him standing out there and come to see who he was looking at. With the two of them in the narrow space, she somehow felt safer.

At least until he said, "What did you think of the rally?"

His tone had no inflection, but she felt targeted anyway. Her shoulders hunched.

"Um, I don't think I'm allowed to have an opinion."

"Why wouldn't you be allowed to have an opinion?"

"People should be allowed to grieve, to rage, to turn their pain into action without my judgment."

Desmond Pryor tilted his head. "Even if it means treason?"

THIS ENDS IN EMBERS

Elara hadn't said that, but she pressed her lips together rather than answer the question. It felt as if she were being baited into making a statement. She could practically hear Reeve in her ear, telling her that sometimes there was no winning, there was only surviving.

"Wayne spoke fondly of you," he continued, taking a step closer. His eye was bright, and the cloud of his grief filled the spaces of the alley until Elara felt trapped. "He spoke of your discipline and your power. He looked up to you, in many ways. And you couldn't even be bothered to attend his funeral or answer for his death."

Elara's pulse raced, throbbing at her temples. "I don't—I can't possibly answer for that. It never should have happened. He never should have—"

Desmond Pryor was close enough now to back her against the wall. "It should have been you. Both of you. Not my son. *You.*"

"Mr. Pryor, please." Fresh tears ran down her face. "Wayne wouldn't want this for you."

"YOU DO NOT GET TO TELL ME WHAT HE WOULD HAVE WANTED."

"Empyrean?"

Queenshield stood at the mouth of the alley. They had found her not a moment too soon. One had a hand near the hilt of her scalestone sword.

"Everything all right?" she asked without taking her eyes off Desmond Pryor.

"It—it was nice to see you again," Elara stammered, slipping toward the safety of the Queenshield. Her heart raced faster than her feet. "I'm sorry."

He didn't reply, but as she allowed the Queenshield to surround her, she heard the clatter of a trash bin being kicked into a wall.

"That was dangerous and irresponsible," Papa said when she made it home, pacing in front of the curtained windows. It was his night to cook, and he had made stew peas—one of her favorites. But when her parents had asked about her day over dinner, the whole story had come spilling out, and now she was in deep trouble. "Desmond has been volatile since the war. What if he'd hurt you?"

"His son is dead because of me," Elara whispered now, her belly full of food and guilt. "I think it'd be understandable if he hurt me."

"You and your sister always do this, and it's precisely why we worry," said Mama, her legs crossed at the ankles. She was sitting on the couch, sewing a button back onto a dress, but it didn't seem to be going well, with how agitated she was. "You take the burden of the world on your shoulders with no regard for the people who care about you. We already had to wake up one morning to find your beds cold and you long gone to a war you had no business fighting in. Now I have to worry that you'll let your own countrymen hurt you out of—what? Some misguided penance? *Iya* killed Wayne Pryor, not you."

Papa stopped pacing. His back was to her, his locs tumbling past his shoulders and blocking his expression from view. Elara didn't know where to look or what to say. Her parents' frustration and disappointment bludgeoned every thought from her head except apologies.

Papa's sigh was a deep and broken thing. "Your mother and I have spoken many times about the pressure we've put on you from a young age. You're our firstborn, Elara. We've so rarely had to worry about you that we fear you've built your personhood around

THIS ENDS IN EMBERS

being undeserving of worry. As if concern is a sign of your failure to handle everything on your own." When he turned, the sadness on his face made Elara want to cross the room and hug him. "I just want to make sure that you know you don't have to. Trying to parent two young women whose destinies are bigger and more dangerous than we could have comprehended is . . . difficult. We've made many mistakes, and we'll make many more. But we're here for you. We love you. We're so proud of you. And we don't want anything to happen to you."

"If Desmond Pryor or anyone else tries to lay a hand on you, they'll have me to deal with," said Mama. She set the dress to the side, giving Elara the same grave look. "You and your sister may be the Empyreans, but you're still our children. Let us be there for you. Please."

Elara's eyes stung. "There's just so much going on."

"We're listening."

It was harder than she expected, opening up to her parents. But then everything spilled out of her, from the gods' reluctance to lend her their magic to her diplomatic trip to Étolia, from her failure to get anywhere near Faron at Hearthstone to Signey pulling away from her just when she needed her most. By the time she finished talking, her throat was scraped raw, and she felt like an old jar of all-purpose seasoning with nothing left to give.

"I don't think there's anything to do about Étolia but to wait. But as for the gods," Papa said slowly, "they want results, not reasoning. I think that you're right: Lightbringer cannot be defeated without the help of the dragons. But after Empyreans who said one thing and did another, you won't convince the gods with anything but your actions. You don't need their validation, Elara.

You're a smart, responsible woman. Trust your own judgment." He paused. "May Irie bless us."

Elara's mouth twitched with the sudden urge to smile. Her father had taught her to make her first altar. To speak about the gods this way, even to reassure her, was likely killing him. "But what if I'm wrong?"

"Then you try something else. Again and again until you get it right. It's the Vincent way."

"And as for Signey," said Mama with a roll of her eyes, "your father was the same way. He kissed me in the schoolyard and then tried to tell me we were just friends."

"*Nida*," Papa groaned.

"It took him four years to get his act together, and it took a lot of groveling and grand gestures for me to give him another chance," she continued as though he hadn't spoken. "Signey seems far smarter than Carver, so let her get there in her own time. But remember that you deserve someone who loves you as fiercely as your father loves me. Who makes you feel special. Who earns their place by your side. Don't settle for less."

This time, Elara *did* smile. "How much groveling, exactly?"

"For Irie's sake," muttered Papa. "There's no need to reminisce about all that."

"Does that help, baby?" Mama asked, ignoring him once more. "Even if we can't fix it, we're also just happy to listen."

Elara's smile wobbled as she felt a wave of love for her parents. They were the reason she was the person she was today, and though war had changed her relationship with them to something more fraught, she had forgotten what it was like to feel as if she could lean on them. No matter what the gods or the newspapers

THIS ENDS IN EMBERS

said, they would love her. Even if she failed. Perhaps especially if she failed.

"Can..." Elara's cheeks heated. "Can I have a hug?"

Mama's arms opened immediately. "Come here, pickney."

In seconds, Elara was bundled in her mother's warm embrace. She felt like a child again, from a time before the war when her nightmares did not have teeth and the monsters that lurked under her bed weren't yet human. Her father came up behind her, hugging her as well, and Elara could feel months of stress melting from her body. Still, she couldn't help remembering that one person was missing. That Faron should be there. That Faron should have this comfort, too.

They weren't a family without Faron.

With a shaky breath, Elara pulled back. "I have to fire call Barret Soto. And tomorrow I have to go to Papillon to talk to the gods. But maybe tonight we could just...spend time together?" Elara glanced over at the wall that lined the hallway, as though she could see through it to Faron's empty bedroom. "Even though..."

"Even though," Papa repeated wistfully. "All right, let's do that."

Mama picked up the dress and her sewing kit. Papa returned to the kitchen to wash the dishes. Elara got to her feet, feeling better than she had in days. Feeling more like herself than she had in months. Papa was right. She was a Vincent. All she could do was try and try and try.

Eventually she would succeed. Faron would be back in her room, and her family would be whole again. Anti-Empyrean protests and inscrutable allies, diplomatic trips and irritable gods, evil dragons and impossible tasks—it all may have risen to challenge her, but Elara was stronger.

With her family at her back, there was nothing she could not do.

CHAPTER FOURTEEN

FARON

BEACON WAS A GRIMY SMUDGE OF A CITY. THE AIR WAS STAINED gray-brown from the factories that handed out jobs in exchange for pumping noxious fumes into the sky. The streets were so jammed with carriages and horses that, looking from above, they resembled fat black veins. Most of the trees had shed their leaves in preparation for Solstice and looked less like lush herbage and more like wizened hands clawing for help.

Faron hated it.

She hated even more that she still had to save it.

Lightbringer flew unimpeded to a massive structure called the Saint Tower, named, Iya was sure to tell her, for the Gray Saint. It was a clock tower made of brick and limestone, topped by a tiled spire. The four glass clock faces were illuminated from within, and the silvery iron dials informed her that it was midafternoon. Above them, close to the top of the spire, was the belfry, which contained no fewer than four bells that chimed on the hour. The entire building was the first thing Faron had seen in Beacon that could reasonably be described as beautiful.

THIS ENDS IN EMBERS

Lightbringer wrapped his colossal body around the spire and belched a cloud of fire over the congested city. *"The time for deliberation is over,"* Iya said, voice echoing through her head like a roar. *"Who will join me?"*

"A bit dramatic, don't you think?" Faron sent back to get ahead of any suspicions. *"I'm sitting right behind you."*

"I realize this will be difficult for you to process, but not everything is about you."

Faron resisted the urge to pinch him and watched the sky instead. If his message had been meant for all the other Riders and dragons, they would soon appear on the horizon and everything would begin.

The stone from Rosetree Manor felt warm in the pocket of her riding leathers. Until now, she had kept it wedged in a hole in her pillow while she figured out how to use it and when. She could have put it anywhere else, but Rosetree Manor hadn't just been Gavriel Warwick's home. Reeve had been raised there, too. It felt as if she were carrying a part of him with her.

Sometimes she liked to lie in bed and imagine he were there, giving her an unwanted lecture on the architecture of the building and the theory behind the magic that protected it. She'd yawn, as if he were boring her, and he'd roll his eyes at her, and they would both smile, amused by each other's quirks now that they had found common ground. She had never been in a relationship—and she hadn't paid attention to the boys and girls Reeve had dated—so all she had now was her imagination. Iya had stolen any chance they'd had to explore what they could be. Keeping the stone in her pillow felt like stealing something back.

Besides, she'd slept dreamlessly since she'd stashed it there, as if the stone kept out Iya from her head at night. That magic alone was useful. Useful enough for her to carry the stone with her today.

She hoped the warmth of it meant that it was keeping her thoughts—her nervousness—from wafting Iya's way. If this didn't work, she'd just have to hope her overall plan went off without a hitch before he finally murdered her.

A sage dragon flew from the direction of the National Hall, lightning quick. A carmine followed at a more measured pace. From the direction of the distant Tenebris River, a medallion approached, bobbing like a dandelion on the wind. Iya's mouth stretched into a grin that Faron could see from his profile, and Lightbringer sprang from the tiled spire to greet them all.

She expected him to launch a wave of fire down on Beacon to begin his destruction. Instead, he dropped beneath the approaching dragons and flew past them, toward the National Hall. His wings pumped hard to outrun the swifter sage, making the ground blur into a rush of dark colors. The brief flashes Faron caught of the city showed none of the panic and dread her people would feel with this many dragons in the sky. Life, peaceful and unremarkable, carried on here despite the war.

Her hands fisted around Iya's waist.

Instead of attacking, Lightbringer landed in what looked like a massive field designed for that purpose. Faron saw flower beds, cobblestone paths, and a topiary clipped into the shape of dragons in flight. The Hall itself was a castle not unlike Hearthstone, with a sloped roof, and marble steps that led up to the back entrance. People were surging from the open doors, though many changed

THIS ENDS IN EMBERS

direction or stopped in their tracks when they saw the bone-white dragon staring them down.

"*You*," said a tan-skinned man in a dark suit with silver pauldrons, his voice thick with loathing. Something about him seemed familiar, but Faron couldn't figure out what. "How dare the two of you show your faces here."

The two of you? Faron's mind echoed. Iya did not respond, which was a relief. It meant he couldn't hear any thoughts she didn't specifically direct toward him. It meant the stone was doing its job.

That was the only relief from those venomous words.

Iya tilted his head. "Have we met?" When he spoke again, the curiosity had been replaced by delight. "Ah, my key to freedom. You look well."

Faron studied the man again, but Iya saved her the effort. "*This is Barret Soto, who created my dragon relic and aided the Warwicks in making contact with me,*" he explained through the bond. "*Former Mausoleum prisoner turned leader of Langley.*"

"Your descendant," Faron realized.

"*Not as such,*" said Iya. "*He married into the family. But my descendants will catch up with us soon enough.*"

"Please," Faron said aloud, locking eyes with Barret Soto. "Tell my sister—"

"Stop allying yourself with Iya," Barret interrupted, "and you can tell her whatever you like."

"You don't understand—"

"You waste your breath on your enemies, Faron," Iya drawled. "They'll only understand you when you speak in chains. If even then."

137

Iya stood up in the saddle, and four of the people with Barret Soto immediately drew dragon relics from their pockets and beneath their clothes. Barret's pauldrons were glowing, and his hands gestured until that golden light resolved itself into a translucent shield that protected the entire crowd.

"Iya and Faron Vincent, you are under arrest," he said coldly, "for a long list of crimes that amount to treason. Come quietly and—"

Lightbringer roared, and it sounded almost like laughter.

"I wish I had the time to see you try," said Iya. "But I am not here for you."

Iya climbed the column of Lightbringer's neck, turning his back to the group. Faron followed his line of sight to the sage dragon plunging toward them.

The very familiar sage dragon.

"Zephyra," she breathed. Her sister's former dragon. Faron hadn't seen Zephyra since they had left San Irie, but she felt as if she'd known the war beast her whole life. After all, she had skimmed Zephyra's soul three times before, each in a desperate bid to keep Zephyra from succumbing to the Fury. Now the dragon's soul felt like an old friend. Her chest warmed even though she knew that Elara wasn't here, not now that her dragon bond had been broken.

Then her stomach dropped. She twisted her head to look at Iya and his outstretched arm. "Wait, what are you—"

He closed his fist. Zephyra jolted, landing hard. Her wings carved holes in the lawn, and her Rider—Signey Soto, Elara's girlfriend—jumped free of the saddle to keep from being buried beneath the dragon's weight.

THIS ENDS IN EMBERS

"Stop it!" Faron said, unstrapping herself from the saddle and climbing toward Iya. "STOP IT!"

"It is done," Iya replied, settling between Lightbringer's neck spikes. His smug expression made her want to punch him in the face, so she did. His head snapped back, and when he looked at her again, blood spilling from his nose, there was a feral smile on his face. On Reeve's face. "Do it again. It changes nothing."

Her own nose ached as she felt his pain through the bond, but nothing hurt as much as the guilt that twisted in her stomach. Hurting Iya hurt Reeve. Her anger had made her forget, and now Iya seemed delighted that she'd lost control, which just made her angrier. How many times would she lose to him before this war was over?

A roar as loud as a gong rent the air. Zephyra was back on her feet, snarling like a wild animal. Her eyes rolled from one person to another, her talons digging into the grass as if she were deciding who was the biggest threat. It was so unlike the gentle, intelligent creature Faron remembered that dread filled her.

"What did you do?" she whispered.

"Her bond is broken," Iya murmured back. "She is free."

Zephyra roared again and took to the sky. Flames sparked from between her teeth. Signey Soto was on the ground beneath her. Faron saw the disaster that was about to happen with perfect clarity. The cataclysmic flame, searing and unstoppable. The nauseating smell of burning skin, putrid and sour. The charred remains of Signey dropping like a brick to the blackened ground. And then the massacre: a feral dragon, surrounded on all sides by prey, ready to consume. To destroy.

Iya had not just broken Zephyra's bond. He had transformed

her from partner to predator. A beast of war returned to her martial instincts.

And they would all suffer for it.

Faron gripped the stone in her pocket. Her soul surged toward Zephyra.

The first time she had connected with the dragon's soul, she had felt overwhelmed by the state of feral rage, the Fury that gripped Zephyra, brought about by Faron's connection to Lightbringer and his own rage at being trapped in the Empty. She had never felt anger like that, power like that. It was like the magic of the gods, but destructive where theirs was creative. It was the kind of fire that demolished, not the kind that warmed.

This time was worse. Beneath the wrath, there had been a mind—lost to the Fury, but still present to take over once Faron had eased that pain. This time she felt nothing, or worse than nothing, because there was an *absence* of what should have been there. Zephyra's thoughts were not simply buried; she was now incapable of rational thought. Her intelligence, her wittiness, her personality—gone. Her soul was a jumble of instincts and hunger.

She was an animal. Faron had never tried controlling the soul of an animal.

At least the stone kept her efforts from the grinning god behind her.

Stand down, she pressed into the cosmic force that was the dragon's soul. *These are your friends. Your people. You don't want to hurt them. Stand down.*

Zephyra released her flames in a blinding column of red and yellow.

Faron screamed, their connection severed.

THIS ENDS IN EMBERS

When her vision returned, Signey was still there in the grass, her hands gripping her own head. Casting her in shadow were the broad wings of a carmine dragon, whose body was unaffected by Zephyra's flames. Strapped to the dragon's back were Jesper Soto and Torrence Kelley, two more of the Riders who had fought for San Irie. Jesper reached down toward his sister. Faron couldn't hear them from here, but she assumed he was asking Signey if she was all right.

Barret and his group had scattered, some racing back inside to evacuate the building and others racing toward Zephyra to neutralize the situation. Another stream of fire from Zephyra arced across the grass, cutting off Barret from his daughter. Faron could hear his pained shouts of Signey's name, could hear Jesper's answering plea for him to stay back. Dragon relics glowed like stars as the Langlish soldiers drew on the magic to fight the flames.

Zephyra was no less pleased by the appearance of another dragon than she was by all the humans. She spewed fire a third time, and the carmine—Azeal, if Faron remembered correctly—blew flames right back. They collided in the air, throwing light and sparks across the garden. The dragon topiary was next to catch fire, only for fountains of frigid water to bubble up from their heads and put out the flames.

Through the blaze and the smoke, Faron looked back at Signey. Signey, who was still crumpled on the ground like a discarded ball of paper, pulling at her own curls as if she wanted to tear them out of her head. She was finally facing in Faron's direction, and her expression wasn't horrified. Not even close. It was hollow. Haunted. As if she'd forgotten how to feel, how to think.

As if the breaking of the bond had also broken her mind.

"I warned you," Iya announced as a medallion dragon was next to arrive, distracting Zephyra from the rear while Jesper released his straps and dropped to the ground to check on his sister. "Join me or lose your dragons. You have two weeks before I come for another. Then one week. Then..."

He didn't finish that sentence, but he didn't need to. Instead, he shoved past Faron to climb back into the saddle. She couldn't drag her eyes from the scene. Zephyra wove past Azeal and the gold dragon, avoiding their flames. The colliding blast pushed the dragons apart, leaving Zephyra to fly free.

"Take them," Iya said over the bond. Once again, he was not speaking to her, but she could hear him as though he were. He *wanted* her to hear him. *"And let's go."*

Zephyra zipped toward the Sotos. Jesper shoved his writhing sister out of the way seconds before Zephyra's talons gripped him as if he were a rag doll. Zephyra pumped into the sky, too high for him to struggle without risking a fatal drop, then hovered as though she planned to dive a second time. Lightbringer rose at a slower pace, belching fire toward the medallion dragon and Azeal to keep them from interfering.

"Leave her," Iya said. *"For now."*

Zephyra soared toward the Hestan Archipelago with Lightbringer close behind.

Faron tightened her grip around Iya even as her soul slipped from her body again. This time, she flew toward Signey. It was like feeling broken glass, if the shards could dissolve back into celestial matter on contact. The parts of Signey's soul that had been interwoven with Zephyra's were in pieces. If Faron let it carry on like this, Signey would have nothing left of herself. She would be

THIS ENDS IN EMBERS

nothing but an empty shell. She had to fuse Signey's soul back together before it was too late. She had to *try*.

Faron drew on the enhanced power that Iya had knitted together for them and pumped that into Signey's body, into Signey's soul. Even if he couldn't hear her intentions, he would soon feel the drain, so she worked quickly. Magic flowed from their bond, through her body, to her soul and into Signey's, welding her soul back into one whole, commanding it to be unbroken, and giving it the power she needed to follow the command.

Signey, she said, pressing her words into the girl's very being. *Tell my sister I would never betray her. Tell her that I love her. Tell her—*

Signey's soul surged like a wave, slamming Faron's consciousness against an invisible barrier. It felt like the shield she had found in the minds of Estella Ballard and Briar Noble, but even more hostile. The control that Signey exerted over herself was stricter, and returning her to full consciousness had weakened Faron too much to overcome it.

GET OUT OF MY HEAD! Signey screamed seconds before Faron was flung back into her own body. She collapsed against Iya, dizzy from the force of Signey's fighting spirit and from the depth of the hatred Signey felt for her intrusion on her soul. If she had heard Faron's commands at all, she'd shown no sign. In fact, Faron feared she had just made an enemy.

"Exhausted?" Iya asked cheerfully as they breached the clouds, Zephyra little more than a green spot before them. "We'll be home soon."

Faron let her eyes slide shut, hoping for sleep to claim her. Hearthstone was not her home, and never would be. But did that matter if she would never be welcome home again?

143

Her throat tightened. She thought of the newspaper from San Irie. Barret's condemnation. The death of Zephyra's personality. Signey's hatred. The way her own silent actions looked like complacency.

Maybe she didn't deserve to be welcomed home.

Maybe she never would.

CHAPTER FIFTEEN

ELARA

AFTER A QUIET EVENING WITH HER PARENTS AND SLEEPING IN UNTIL midday, Elara and her guards reached the mountain city of Papillon by sunset, when the sky was indigo and vermilion. Built into the mountain, Papillon boasted slanted buildings and paved roads that curved farther up the Argent Mountains to Highfort. Gas lamps lit the way to the Papillon Temple, where Elara's carriage released her to meet with the gods. Temples closed when the sun went down, but the High Santi made an exception for the Maiden Empyrean.

At least there were *some* people who still believed in her.

Once she'd been left alone in the sunroom, empty but for the garden of herbs the santi were growing at this time of year, Elara called on the gods. All three of them appeared before her, one after the other: curly-haired Mala in her petal-pink gown, stone-faced Irie in her lacy white robes, regal Obie with his head forever shaded by his hood. The sunroom of a temple was the only place holy enough for Elara to summon the three gods at once without dying and the only place in the mortal realm they could be corporeal. Deadegg was too small to have a temple, and Papillon was the closest city to both Deadegg and Highfort.

The first time she'd seen all three of them like this, they'd been so majestic, she'd fallen to her knees before them. Now, she straightened her shoulders and remembered what her father had told her: *Trust your own judgment.*

"We've done research into Gael Soto," Elara said, raising her gaze to meet theirs. "I called Barret last night, and he told me that Gael was the son of a toy maker and a knight from a small fishing village in Joya del Mar. He was nineteen when he disappeared, leaving behind a son. His lover eventually married his brother, Maceo. With Eugenia and Celyn Soto dead, Signey and Jesper are the last of the direct bloodline."

No one spoke.

"Is that significant?" Elara frowned. "Irie told me to look to the past for answers, but so far we haven't learned anything that would actually help us defeat him."

Irie gazed through the glass panes of the sunroom. Outside there was nothing but darkening trees, smooth boulders, and a sky streaked with stars. "The Soto family, as we knew them, were very close." Her smile had a bitter edge. "The power that blood holds over the Empyreans has always been stronger than our own."

Something about the way she said it made Elara's frown deepen. As much as she wanted her sister back and her family safe, she was not *just* trying to safeguard her family. The world was at stake, and she understood that. She just didn't believe that her sister needed to die to protect it.

"Did you try to get Gael to kill his brother?" she asked. "Or are Faron and I the only ones lucky enough to be at odds?"

"Maceo died of old age, but," Irie said dryly, "I don't doubt that Iya would have taken his life if given the opportunity."

THIS ENDS IN EMBERS

Elara bowed her head again. "We have bigger problems at the moment. Protests are erupting across the island again: calls for the Renard Castell line to end with Aveline, and for the Empyrean line to end with me."

"That won't be a problem much longer," said Irie, her gaze heavy. "The Empyrean line *will* end with you."

Elara's blood turned to ice in her veins. "Wait, what?"

"Once the dragons are gone, there will be no further need for the Renard Castell line or an Empyrean. You'll be free of divine missions and godsbeasts. What mortal disputes you have after that will be yours to handle however you like."

"You're—you're going to abandon us?"

"It's hardly abandonment," Irie said, her golden eyes sparking as though Elara had offended her. "We have never and will never involve ourselves in the wars of man. Like the dragons, we have remained in this realm far longer than we should have. It's made you all complacent."

Elara's mouth worked, but no sounds came out. A chill was spreading throughout her body, freezing everything but her racing mind. How could she be the last Empyrean? She had done nothing worthy of the title, and a cruel voice at the back of her mind whispered that she never would. She felt as lost as she had when Aveline had told her to go ahead to Étolia without her, as if her foundations had lost a pillar of support she needed to keep from collapsing. At eighteen, Elara was technically an adult, but she was a child. She was a *child*, expected to influence the rulers of countries and to save the world without guidance.

This is what the gods wanted.

Desmond Pryor would be pleased to know that she was the last of the Empyreans. He would celebrate every mistake she made because it would further his cause. Elara's hands shook, and she clenched them tighter, hating that this dress had no pockets. Every time she thought she was no longer alone, she was faced with another loss. Reeve. Her sister. The gods.

Alone, alone, alone.

Elara gasped as she was swept into a hug that was all pink tulle and warm brown skin. Mala knelt to hold her tight, and Elara's eyes slid shut involuntarily, pressing her face against the god's shoulder.

"Everything will be all right," Mala said, drawing back to run her thin fingers through Elara's braids. "We will still be able to hear your prayers, Maiden. San Irie will always be under our protection. But once we withdraw, you shouldn't have need for divine magic to solve your problems. You're more than capable of solving them on your own."

Elara took a deep, shaky breath. She was tired of having to be capable.

"I have to go," she said, because she couldn't lie. It wasn't okay. She didn't feel fine. She certainly didn't think herself qualified for much. But she had gotten all that she would get from the gods right now, and she wanted to lie down in the inn the Queenshield had prepared for her. "I'll keep you informed."

Elara left the temple with her chin up, managing weak smiles and dry eyes. Inside her was a tempest of insecurity. Once, Elara had asked the gods to lend her their power. She had promised to show them what she could do. She hadn't known she would be the final Empyrean. If she was going to be the last, then she had to be the best.

The world depended on it.

Elara swallowed. On her.

The inn the Queenshield had chosen was a homey scalestone-and-concrete building whose exterior was painted the bright yellow of a sunflower. The first floor was a restaurant and grill, with oval tables, cushioned chairs, and the mouthwatering scent of jerk chicken filling the space. People milled around the tables, drinking fruit juice and light beers, talking and laughing.

It was such a contrast to how low Elara felt, that her presence hovered like smog in the clear air. She kept her head down and escaped upstairs before anyone could recognize her.

A soldier waited outside the room at the end of the hall. He nodded once at Elara's approach. "You received a fire call while you were away, Maiden. We've also left dinner for you inside."

Elara nodded back. "Thank you."

"*Finally*," said Signey Soto when Elara sat down before the fireplace, her stomach full of green banana, rice and peas, and jerk pork. "We have a problem."

Elara frowned. "All we have is problems. What's one more?"

"Your sister attacked the National Hall."

Her dinner threatened to make a second appearance. She forced it down. "No, she didn't."

Signey told the story as if Elara hadn't spoken, her voice even until she got to the part about Zephyra and Jesper. Elara's ears were ringing, her shock so whole and complete that it was as if the world were frozen around her, but the crack in Signey's voice brought her back to her own body. It was easier to deal with Signey's emotions than to think of Faron. In fact, she preferred it.

"I just . . . I feel so . . . I feel lost," Signey admitted. As always, she sounded as if the words were ripped from her throat. As if it cost her to be this open but was a price she was willing to pay if she was opening up to Elara. "I don't even remember the exact moment it happened. One minute, we were united, ready for a fight. The next minute, Zephyra had been torn out and I—it's—" She made a sound like a sob. "I couldn't reach Zephyra. I've never seen her like that—so wild and destructive. And it's so quiet in my head. I hate how *quiet* it is. I can't remember the last time I was this alone."

"You're not alone," Elara murmured, wishing that Signey were here. She wanted to pull Signey into her arms, to hold her there, where she would be safe. "You have me, remember? You have Torrey. You have your father. No one can replace Zephyra; trust me, I know. But there are people who want to be there for you, if you'd let them."

"Do I? *Do* I have you? It was your sister who did this."

Elara's sympathy melted like an ice cube. "Picking a fight with me isn't going to bring back Zephyra and Jesper."

"Are you *serious*?" Instead of being close to tears, Signey sounded as though she were close to committing murder. "My best friend and my brother, Elara. She took my *best friend* and my *brother*. She would have taken me, too, if Jesper hadn't . . . if he hadn't . . ." Her voice cracked. "I can't let this stand."

Elara stared down at her lap, where her hands were clasped together so tightly that half-moon indents had appeared on her skin. She loosened her grip before her nails drew blood, trying

THIS ENDS IN EMBERS

to formulate a response that wouldn't upset Signey further. But she knew Faron. She *knew* her sister. This wasn't her. Faron would never have done something like that without a good reason, and, after the last couple days that Elara had endured, it annoyed her to have yet another person casting doubt on them.

"*Iya* took Zephyra and Jesper," Elara said firmly. "Let's lay the blame where it belongs."

"Your sister was there, Elara," Signey snapped back. "She's no captive. She wasn't even chained to the saddle. She tried to invade my mind!"

"Of course she's a captive. They're bonded! It's not as though she could hurt him—"

"She doesn't *have* to hurt him to stop him."

"With what power? You're being unfair—"

"*Elara!*"

Her mouth snapped shut. Her hands were shaking. She slid them beneath her thighs. Even when they had been enemies, Signey had never yelled at her before. Elara looked at the wall, so furious that she was close to tears. "I know her. Okay? I know her, and you don't."

"Your friends are dead. Your capital was razed. Zephyra and Jesper have been kidnapped. Iya did all of that—and your sister didn't stop him. It's been weeks, and she sits at his side and flies with him into battle, and she does *nothing to stop him.*"

"Just because you can't see what she *is* doing doesn't mean—"

"What is it going to take for you to realize your sister isn't who you think she is?" Signey was shouting again. Elara got to her feet, pacing away from the fireplace. If the Queenshield guarding her door could hear any of this, then he didn't see fit to intervene. Elara pressed her ear against the door anyway, because she was afraid of what she would say if she didn't. "The gods warned that Iya would corrupt Faron. They knew this would happen. Why won't you accept it?"

"*Because she's my sister!*" Elara whirled around, murder in her eyes even though Signey couldn't see her. "*I* grew up with her. I know her better than anyone in the world. If Jesper is in danger, he'll find an ally in her. I'm sure of it."

"You're a fool."

"*You're* an asshole."

Signey said nothing. Elara was breathing hard, and her attempts to calm down weren't working. Tears slid down her face, and she didn't bother to wipe them away. Even with the facts laid bare, she couldn't—wouldn't—believe that Faron had truly joined Iya's side. She knew her sister's flaws as well as she knew her own. Faron was reckless and impulsive. She was disrespectful and childish. She was stubborn and selfish and dishonest and difficult. But when San Irie had needed a hero, a hero she had become. She had swallowed her social anxiety to always come when the queen called. She had abused the power of the gods, but she had followed their every command during the war. She hadn't given up on Elara when everyone else had, when it had meant doing the impossible, when it had risked the safety of the rest of the world.

How could Elara give up on her?

She took a deep breath, slowly wiping at one cheek and then the other. The fireplace still flared, making it clear that Signey had not ended the call. But even after a handful of months, Elara knew how stubborn her girlfriend was. She would not be the first to

THIS ENDS IN EMBERS

break the silence. If Elara didn't take control of the situation, who knew how long it would be until they spoke next?

"If it were Jesper," she asked softly, "if all this had happened with Jesper at Iya's side, would you be so quick to think he'd been corrupted? Or would you believe, in defiance of everything to the contrary, that he was doing the best he could to stop Iya?"

Signey remained silent for a long moment. Then she sighed. "I'm getting my brother back, Elara. No matter what the cost."

"I understand." Elara gazed deep into the fireplace. Her pulse fluttered in her neck, but there was a certain peace within her— the kind of confidence that came with knowing, beyond a shadow of a doubt, where she drew the line. "As long as you understand that anything you do to my sister, you're doing to me. And I'll react accordingly."

There was another silence, during which Elara listened to the crackling of the fire and the muffled laughter from the restaurant below. Her room was on the third floor, but the crowd had gotten so noisy that she could still hear them. She crossed to the window and propped it open to let the chorus of whinnying horses and passing carriages join the din. Life moving on defiantly.

The fresh air also kept her from throwing up. From nerves or from rage. Either was enough to make her nauseous.

"Okay, Elara," Signey said, resigned. "Whatever you say."

And that was that.

Elara stared up at the stars. "Could you ask Barret to look further into Maceo Soto? I spoke to the gods today, and there might be something there...."

Soon after, the conversation ended, and the fire went out. Elara's mind drifted back to Faron and the possible reasons she

153

might have for using the power Iya had taught her against Signey. Maybe she'd been trying to send a message. Maybe she'd been trying to help Signey fight better. Maybe Elara *was* biased when it came to her sister.

But it was starting to feel as if the world was biased against Faron. What was she meant to do? She and Iya were bonded, so it wasn't as though she could attack him directly. Without her Empyrean powers, she had no magic but what Iya lent her, as Iryan magic was incompatible with the dragon bond. Any act of defiance that Faron engaged in had to be small and invisible, or who knew what danger she would find herself in? Did everyone want Faron to kill herself for a temporary victory? Were Elara and her parents the only ones who cared about getting Faron home safely?

She thought of Zephyra and her steadfast warmth, and Jesper and his mischievous smile. One feral and one missing, all because this war still raged on. And all around San Irie, a different war brewed, one sparked by the discontent of a traumatized people who just wanted peace when their leaders, their Empyreans, had brought only war.

It didn't matter how many people thought Faron had been corrupted. The gods, Signey, or even the queen, though Elara had been afraid to ask. She would always be on Faron's side. She would never lose her faith. And, together, they would defeat Iya once and for all. She had to believe that.

The alternative was just too painful to bear.

PART II
SHADOW

CHAPTER SIXTEEN

FARON

To welcome their captive, Iya had tightened the security measures around the Hestan Archipelago—and particularly around Hearthstone Academy. The raid of the Beacon Dragon Preserve had turned up four dragon eggs, which the Warwicks had hidden deep within the fortress where they could incubate in peace. Faron had thought the plan was simply to steal them so new Riders could not be bonded, swelling the enemy army and thwarting their plans, but that didn't explain the incubation.

Her mental note to investigate that, however, took a back seat to the presence of Jesper Soto.

Jesper had been imprisoned in the boathouse, where anyone could track his movements. Marius Lynwood volunteered to guard the prisoner before anyone else could, which made Faron immediately concerned. Lynwood would have gone to school with Jesper, and the sharp glint in his eyes said as much about their relationship as his eagerness to play jailer did. The only reason Faron didn't protest was that she would love to wipe the stone floor with Lynwood if she had to. Or even if she didn't have to.

The stone trail that led to the boathouse was on the other side of a thicket of trees. Docks stretched around it, jutting out into the bay, where Ignatz floated on his back in the water. His cerulean scales were stark against the gray of the filthy water. Taking up most of the dirt shore was Goldeye, whose fiery coloring screamed a warning to anyone who dared come too close. Even as he lay flat on the ground, his back spikes reached the second floor of the two-story boathouse, making it near impossible for anyone but his Riders to jump down from one of the windows. And whether or not both dragons were present, the narrow windows of Hearthstone overlooked this stretch of land, which left nowhere to hide between the boathouse and the trees.

Goldeye lifted his head as Faron approached. Today, she had opted for riding leathers instead of a dress, just in case she needed to fight her way out. She also had her Rosetree stone in her pocket, to keep her whereabouts as secret from Iya as possible. The dragon stared her down as if he could tell she was up to no good, and she stared right back. "Go on. Try something."

He snorted, a curl of smoke jumping from one nostril. But she could feel his amber eyes on her as she marched inside.

The first floor was nothing but docks and boats and water, and was massive enough for a dragon to swim right in if they wanted to. But the second floor looked almost like a home: vaulted ceilings, inlaid glass doors, and a balcony. The doors were locked, the balcony inaccessible. Nichol Thompson stood with his back to it, his arms folded over his chest.

On the floor in front of him, Lynwood and Jesper were trading blows.

"Hey!" Faron shouted, running over. "Hey, stop that!"

Lynwood managed to get Jesper pinned, with his hands around

THIS ENDS IN EMBERS

the other boy's throat. The skin around Lynwood's eye was turning an ugly shade of purple. There was blood on his teeth as he snarled, "You think you're so much better than everyone."

"I think you're a weak little shit," Jesper rasped out, hands clawing at Lynwood's shoulders, "grasping at relevance and failing."

Faron yanked Lynwood by his stupid short hair. The distraction was enough for Jesper to fling Lynwood off him. Arms grabbed Faron from behind, and Thompson cursed into her ear as she struggled.

"Don't interfere," he hissed. "They need to work this out."

"I'll work your head off your shoulders if you don't—"

Jesper smashed Lynwood's head against the wood floor hard enough to leave cracks. The other boy went limp. Panting, Jesper fell back into a sitting position. There was a bruise on his copper-brown cheek, more were forming around his neck, and blood was drying beneath his nose. Thompson released her to check on his cousin, so Faron crawled over to Jesper.

"Are you all right?" she asked. "I'd heal you, but I don't know how."

His dark brown eyes met hers. "I don't want to be healed. I want to go home. But I don't suppose you're going to do anything about that, are you?"

Faron flinched.

"No one's going to do anything about that," said Thompson, his arms around a dazed Lynwood. Such a blow would have been enough to kill a normal person, but Riders were resilient. Thompson didn't even look concerned that Lynwood might have a concussion. "Iya wants you here, so here you are."

Jesper muttered a sentence in Lindan that translated to something anatomically implausible. Two red spots appeared high on Thompson's cheeks, as though he'd understood. But all he did was help Lynwood back onto his feet.

"I've told you before and I'll tell you again," Lynwood said, dragging a hand over his mouth and smearing blood over the bottom half of his face, "your worthless family never deserved their dragons or their standing. If any of you survive the Gray Saint's wrath, I'll personally make sure you never ride again."

"Can I get a different guard?" Jesper asked. "I am so tired of listening to you."

Lynwood sprang forward, only to be stopped by Thompson. "It's done. You fought. He won. Now, it's done."

Faron shifted between Jesper and Lynwood, expecting Lynwood to ignore his cousin and start a second fight anyway. To her surprise, his shoulders dropped, and he turned away. Jesper said nothing, but there was a calculation to the way that he watched Thompson.

Thompson's blush deepened before he dragged his gaze to Faron. "What are you doing here, Vincent?"

Iya wanted eyes on the prisoner was her prepared lie. *He's listening right now, so watch how you talk to me* was her flavorful addition to cow them into behaving. But before she could say either line, the deity himself appeared at the top of the stairs with a leather satchel thrown over one shoulder and an amused smile on his face.

"I see you've learned to guard your thoughts from me," he said as he passed the satchel to Thompson. "Thankfully, you're still predictable."

"It goes on and off," Faron replied, taking another step toward Jesper. But at least that was good. If he had tried and failed to enter

THIS ENDS IN EMBERS

her mind, he was unlikely to try again for now. "If someone had trained me like they said they would, you'd know exactly what I was and wasn't capable of."

"Quite so. Let's begin with a test." Iya nodded his head toward the boy still sitting cross-legged on the floor. "I'll need you to hold him down so I can draw his blood."

"What?" asked Faron.

"*What?*" asked Jesper.

"Shouldn't you have Thompson and Lynwood do that instead? I'm almost half his size. How am I supposed to—?"

Iya's grin widened as he watched her realize what he actually wanted to test: her power to command living souls. He wanted her to command Jesper to be still, to intimidate him with the knowledge that he could lose control of his own body at any time. He wanted to make sure that Jesper hated her as much as his sister did.

And, like his sister, he would be right to.

"*Come now, Faron,*" Iya cooed as Thompson handed him what looked like a syringe with a silver dragon wrapped around the barrel. "*I'd rather not murder my descendant for this, and I won't have to as long as he doesn't fight.*"

Faron turned to Jesper. He had scrambled to his feet and was standing with his back against one of the walls, eyeing Thompson and Lynwood, who stood in front of the balcony exit, and Faron and Iya, who blocked the way to the stairs. He would definitely fight. He would fight right to his death.

"*Do this,*" Iya continued, "*and we can begin your training. My power will be your power. You will finally know the depth of all I can do, all we can do. And if, then, you still wish to stop me, we will face each other as equals.*"

161

Faron didn't move. *"Why do you need his blood?"*

"You'll find out soon enough."

"If you don't tell me, I'm not going to help you."

Iya shrugged. *"If I don't fill this syringe, I'll just have to kill him to get it all. It's up to you."*

Faron cursed, not simply because of the threat but because she could feel from his end of the bond that Jesper's life didn't matter to him. Yes, Jesper was watching her as one would an ambushing predator. But she didn't want him *dead*—and Iya would kill him, even if it ruined his plans, just to make a point to her. There was one other Soto, after all, and it would only be worse for Faron if Jesper died on her watch. Right?

"Okay," she said aloud, refusing to take her gaze off Jesper. Hoping he could read the apology in her eyes. "The more you fight, the more this will hurt."

Her soul slipped free of her body and soared toward his. Like his sister's, it was glittering, bright, a human soul enhanced by its connection to a dragon. And, like his sister, he immediately fought back. A stream of curses erupted from his throat in Langlish and Lindan, his fingers curling and uncurling at his sides. Blood gushed from his nose, and veins stuck out in his neck as he tossed his head from side to side in an attempt to stay in control.

But unlike his sister, he was not a locked safe of emotions. She could feel it. She could *see* it. Jesper Soto was as passionate in his happiness as he had been in his anger. He was open, friendly, a boy with a charming smile and a warm hug. He had no defense against her. Against this.

His eyes glazed over. He slid down the wall until his long legs were stretched out before him and he sat staring at nothing. Faron

THIS ENDS IN EMBERS

was breathing hard, but she pressed the words *stay still until your blood is drawn* against his soul and withdrew before she passed out. The temptation to leave another command was too great, and she didn't think Jesper would appreciate being made to do anything else he didn't choose to do.

"Amazing," Iya said warmly. "Simply amazing."

Before she could see if it was truly Iya who had spoken—or if that was Gael again, surfacing in awe of her—he pushed past her to kneel by Jesper's side. The boy did not react when his shirt cuff was unbuttoned, his sleeve rolled up, and a rubber tourniquet applied to his arm. He did not react when the needle of the syringe was buried into his vein or when the barrel filled with crimson blood. He did not react when Iya withdrew the syringe, leaving Thompson to bandage the small puncture wound in his arm.

Only once everything was packed back into the satchel did Jesper Soto jolt back to life with a gasp.

"What the hell," he breathed, "was *that?*"

"Heal him," said Iya, heading for the door. "We should treat our guests with the proper respect, and that means"—he paused to shoot Lynwood a dark look over one shoulder—"no brutality. If that happens again, I'll replace you as his guards. Understood?"

"Yes, my saint," Thompson and Lynwood chorused, neither meeting his eyes.

Faron still stood there, shriveling under the disgust on Jesper's face. She toyed with the buttons on her vest, but she didn't break the held gaze. She owed him that much.

Slowly, she approached. She drew a handkerchief from her pocket and bent over him. "Here. For your nose."

"From the moment I met her, I could see that Elara has nothing but faith in you," Jesper said without taking it. Faron's heart leaped, only to plummet at his next words. "So far you've done nothing to deserve it."

Her eyes stung. She had no idea whether to hope that Elara still believed in her or to hope that Elara hated her as everyone else did. Surely, she had heard about Beacon by now. Surely, she'd spoken to Signey Soto. She didn't want Elara to be hated for the crime of believing in her sister—but she didn't want Elara to hate her, either.

She shook off those thoughts and placed the handkerchief on Jesper's lap. "I'm sorry."

"It's so much easier to apologize than to do the right thing." His voice was cold, colder than the Langlish Solstice season. "Isn't it?"

Faron scurried to Iya's side. He placed a hand on her lower back and ushered her in front of him as they descended the stairs. "Your lessons," he said, "will begin tomorrow. Dress for a fight."

"I'll fight in anything," Faron replied, proud of her voice for remaining even.

Though she knew the gods weren't listening, she sent a prayer up to Irie anyway. *Please let Jesper find the stone in the handkerchief. Please let him know what to do with it.*

Please let him survive.

CHAPTER SEVENTEEN

ELARA

Elara's last visit to Highfort had been a secret, nerve-racking trip where she'd sloshed around inside a donkey-drawn cart along with the rest of the drake-pilot hopefuls. Now, riding into the military base in a horse-drawn carriage, protected from the heat and from prying eyes by a sheer curtain over the side window, she was able to ignore the pit in her stomach. The drake Valor was no longer on display in the center of the fort, newly commissioned and waiting to find her pilots. Valor had been destroyed by Lightbringer.

In another life, she might have been one of Valor's pilots, protecting San Irie from one of the three cockpits in every drake. In this one, it felt as if the ghosts of Wayne Pryor and Aisha Harlow were in this carriage with her, castigating her again for not saving them. She wondered what Desmond Pryor would say if he knew this had been her ultimate destination, if he would think she was spitting on his son's memory.

So much for ignoring that pit.

Aveline had assured her that she would be interested in the research going on at the Highfort base and had asked Elara to check on the defense strategies for the island while she was there. It was busywork, but it was the kind of busywork Elara enjoyed. That said, given how her trips to Deadegg and Papillon had gone, she was almost terrified to be here, terrified that some new problem would present itself. She needed the world to pause for a moment so that she could strategize. She needed her churning emotions to calm long enough for her to decide what to do.

Elara didn't fully relax until the carriage came to a stop in front of the guest manor. While the soldiers who were present slept in barracks, there was a three-floor residence outfitted for officers and royal guests. It was painted sea blue near the base, then transitioned to off-white, like clouds before a storm, and the top floors had balconies that overlooked the rest of Highfort. There wasn't much to see, as the city only consisted of the land cleared to make room for the base, but Elara imagined that watching a drake take off from one of those balconies must have been quite a sight.

Then her disembarking Queenshield called a greeting, and Elara looked up to see Cherry McKay standing on the guest manor's wraparound porch.

Her flat twists were dyed the same burgundy shade that Aisha's hair once was. Her brown eyes sparkled with familiar mischief. The freckle on her throat winked from above the low collar of her uniform. It was almost like seeing a ghost, considering the last time Elara had seen her ex-girlfriend had been when they were rejected drake pilots sent as cadets to keep order in Port Sol. Now Cherry wore the pristine green uniform of a military medical summoner.

"If it isn't our runaway cadet," she drawled, coming to a stop in front of Elara. "I see you found a way to leave that mark."

THIS ENDS IN EMBERS

"Cherry," she breathed. "What are you—?"

"I requested the honor of greeting you. We're long overdue for a chat, *Maiden Empyrean*."

The Queenshield curved around them, carrying Elara's bag into the manor. Cherry didn't even glance their way—she must have been accustomed to soldiers running around her. Her plump lips twisted farther downward the longer it took Elara to find something to say. She wanted to start with an apology. She wanted to burst into tears. She wanted to throw her arms around Cherry and never let go. It all felt inappropriate and trivial.

She'd been back to Deadegg twice, and not once had she thought of Cherry McKay.

"How have you—" Elara managed. Licked her lips. Tried again. "How have you been?"

"You mean since you abandoned me in the capital or since your sister killed our friends?" Cherry asked, as blunt as ever. Elara winced, but it wasn't as if she could argue. "I've been okay. It turns out that I absolutely hated being a foot soldier, so I requested a transfer to the medical department." She gestured at her new uniform. "The change of pace was better for my nerves."

Once the Queenshield had retreated to the manor, the silence between them felt thick with words unsaid. The way Cherry watched her didn't feel expectant, but it made Elara's skin prickle anyway. "Did you... ever actually want to enlist?"

"I think so." Cherry sounded thoughtful, as if she had given the question real weight even though her answer had come fast. It wasn't the first time she had considered it, clearly. "But it's easy to want to enlist in the military in peacetime. When the battle broke out in the capital, when we lost Wayne and Aisha, I realized that

I didn't want to kill people. For any reason. I want to help them. Heal them. You know?"

"I do." Elara had once thought the same thing, months ago. It was Signey who had told her there are many ways to help people and in so doing changed the way Elara had thought of choices. Thinking of Signey after their argument *hurt*, and Elara dragged her mind back to the situation at hand. "Listen, I'm really sorry—"

"I know, Elara. I know you, remember? I understand that you were in the middle of something—and kind of still are." Cherry's eyes were now like flint, cold and hard. "It's just awful that I had to find out about Wayne and Aisha from someone other than you. That I had to attend their funerals alone. That I had to mourn them without so much as a fire call from you. That's all."

"I—"

"Come on," Cherry said, turning her back on Elara and the conversation. She'd been that way all their lives; once she'd said what she needed to say, she shut up tighter than a clam. Pushing her only pushed her away. "I want to show you what I've been working on."

Elara glanced mournfully at the manor and the bed within before she followed. As they walked, she caught Cherry up on the last few days of disasters and revelations. Cherry had already read about the Beacon attack in the papers, but she was surprised about the rally ("I don't read much local news. We're at war right now, you know?"). It was an odd thing, to see her ex-girlfriend so confident and commanding in a military setting. Cherry McKay had once been too easily distracted to ever win a spar with Elara, and now she worked out of a lab in Highfort's medical building.

The lab looked near identical to the ones Elara had toured in

THIS ENDS IN EMBERS

the National Hall, during those weekends she and Signey had been forced to go to the Langley capital to study under Commander Warwick. It was smaller, but it was the same sterile white. The room was scented like antiseptic and herbs, with tables packed with tools that were largely foreign to Elara. A door off to the side, according to Cherry, led to a small bedchamber, where she could rest if she was working overnight on something. Otherwise, she slept in the dorms with the rest of the soldiers.

From there, she went immediately to a table at the other end of the room. Elara lingered over everything, trying to take it all in. It was a huge change, but it was a welcome one. Cherry, a tactless but hardworking girl from Deadegg, had managed to achieve great things without needing the gods or a drake to give her life value. Elara felt as if she were still waiting for her accomplishments to feel like enough, while Cherry moved through the lab with such easy, enviable assurance.

"Hurry up!" Cherry called. "I don't have all day."

Elara rolled her eyes and joined her at the table. It was laden with several vials filled with red fluid, vials she knew contained blood even before Cherry confirmed it. Still, she was surprised when Cherry explained that it was the blood of people from various countries: Langley, Étolia, and Joya del Mar, Kaere, Marién, and San Irie.

"Different countries have different magic systems," Cherry continued, her face bright with excitement. "And despite the natural overlap between people, the magic they can access varies. We've been trying to study why. Is the Étolian royal family the only set of people to possess magic because it's in their blood, or is it because they slaughter any magic wielder who refuses to marry in? Can Iryans one day gain the power to see one another's astrals rather than just their own? And if an Iryan can become a Rider to a Langlish dragon, is it purely a matter of the soul, or is there something in their body that gave them a predilection toward Langlish magic? We have more questions than answers right now, but our sample size is growing every day."

Elara's eyes narrowed at the vials. She had that sensation again, as if there were something her mind was trying to put together. When it didn't come to her, she turned back to Cherry. "You're about to ask me for my blood, aren't you?"

"Consider it your apology."

"I'm remembering again why we broke up."

Cherry beamed. "Get up on the table, please."

Elara let Cherry fill a vial, bandage the small puncture wound on her arm, and then smugly hand her a peppermint to eat. Cherry withdrew an orange lollipop for herself.

"I've been in contact with the Sotos and the Smithers-Lewises," she said, the lollipop stick waggling like a cigarette. "I know all about your quest into Iya's past, and it's fascinating information, but we have science. Our legacies are built on the shoulders of our ancestors, and in our blood runs their blood. Literally." She tapped one of the vials until Elara noticed that the small label on the side read SIGNEY SOTO. "If the past is our present in more ways than one, then we should explore every avenue—especially biological ones."

Elara gasped. "The power of blood."

"That"—Cherry blinked—"is not how I expected you to react."

"I spoke to the gods yesterday," she said, her words tumbling together in her excitement. "They said something along the lines

THIS ENDS IN EMBERS

of the power of blood being stronger than the power of the gods. What if that has to do with all of this?"

Cherry blinked again. "How?"

Elara picked up the vial that held Signey's blood, turning it over to trace her girlfriend's name. "This all comes down to bloodlines, in the end. Gael Soto was chosen as the first Empyrean and became the first Rider. Because of his line, Signey and Jesper became Riders. Faron was chosen as the second Empyrean, and now she's bonded with Iya. Because of our bloodline, I was able to bond with Signey and I became the third Empyrean. The power of blood."

"Hm. Well…I don't have a sample of your sister's blood, but hopefully I can run some tests with yours." Cherry murmured to herself. "I may need backups of Signey's, as well. If she's the last Soto left—"

"Jesper's not *dead*, Cherry."

"Well, he's not here, is he?" she said breezily. Then she leaned back against the table with a somber expression. "About Reeve."

Elara's heart clenched. She had been too stressed to think about Reeve lately, and she hadn't realized what a relief that was until her grief came rushing back. He would love this lab. He would love asking Cherry questions about her work. He would love being a research assistant, just to have something to do.

He would have the advice Elara needed to keep from giving in to the doubts that screamed in her mind.

"I assume you'd tell me if you'd heard anything about getting Iya out of his body…?" Cherry trailed off as Elara shook her head. The sadness in her eyes was a reflection of Elara's own. It felt like years since it had been the five of them—Cherry, Elara, Wayne, Aisha, and Reeve—sitting in an abandoned field and talking about their dreams for the future. Now only three remained, and one was impossible to reach.

"I should get to work on this," Cherry finally said, running a hand over her twists. "It was nice to see you, Elara."

"You, too," Elara said. And then, "I'm sorry."

Cherry smiled a brittle smile. "I know. I'm sorry, too."

CHAPTER EIGHTEEN

FARON

FARON WAS USED TO BEING A POOR STUDENT, BUT TODAY IT WAS NOT her fault. Today, she had Gael Soto as her teacher.

She didn't even need to see his eyes to know that the boy who came for her was Gael. For one thing, his smile was not a drawn weapon whetted with Lightbringer's self-satisfied cruelty. It was still smug, but there was a quiet intimacy to that smile. The smile of a boy who knew her, and *wanted* to know her, not an ancient creature reluctantly babysitting her as part of his plans. Instead of wearing his midnight military dress, he wore riding leathers as she did. He leaned rakishly against her doorjamb, gazing down at her with sparkling hazel eyes.

"I have far better things to do than teach rudimentary magic tricks to a weakling," Lightbringer explained before she could ask. *"But I will be taking you to the training ground. And rest assured that I will be listening."*

Faron found it hard to believe that he would trust her and Gael Soto alone together, even with his surveillance. Several times now, Gael had briefly escaped the tight leash of Lightbringer's control, as if the parts of him that had been swallowed by the dragon were forcing their way back up. Maybe Lightbringer was lending Gael the reins in an attempt to bring him back to heel, or maybe he was lobbing Gael as a distraction so that she didn't interfere in what he really planned to do with the eggs and Jesper's blood.

Either way, Faron found it impossible to concentrate on anything but how to work this to her advantage.

Lightbringer left them at the Snowmelt, a river that sliced from the Silver Sea through the bottom of the Emerald Highlands and up a mountain range in the northwest that touched Serpentia Bay. It was the kind of day that made it hard to remember they were at war: a cloudless blue sky with a sun so bright, it reflected blinding gold on the surface of the Silver Sea. When the dragon tore back toward Hearthstone, Faron briefly considered taking Gael prisoner and trying to make it through the war zone of the Emerald Highlands to Beacon. If she turned herself and him in, perhaps Barret Soto could help her save Reeve.

Then she remembered that she had given her piece of Rosetree Manor to Jesper. Lightbringer would invade their minds and find them before the day was out. Her fists clenched at her sides.

"Shall we begin?" said Gael from behind her. "He expects a status report when he returns."

"I don't care what he expects, and you shouldn't, either." Faron turned to face him, hiding another wince at seeing Reeve's face without any of Reeve's warm intelligence. "I know you've been fighting him. I know you've been trying to protect me. Why are you doing what he says now? You're free."

His smile faded. "You're always in control of your own body. Do you feel free from him right now?"

"Is that his game? To make me think I have an ally in you, that

THIS ENDS IN EMBERS

we're both victims of his plans, so you can betray me?" Faron snorted. "I already know how this story ends, Gael. You're a liar and a coward."

"I'm a coward?" He advanced on her, but Faron didn't give an inch. She lifted her jaw and tipped back her head to keep their gazes locked. There was a whisper of space between them. And she was there, with him, but she was also in a library in Renard Hall, needling her way beneath Reeve Warwick's skin the way he lived under hers. It had been a heady delight, to make Reeve lose control. Gael's anger was different. It was infuriating. "You're the one who always smells like fear, Faron. Fear you made the wrong choice. Fear you'll never find Lightbringer's weakness. Fear you'll never be forgiven. Fear you're too angry, too bitter, too selfish, too *much*—"

Faron shoved him. He didn't move, but it made her feel a little less like tearing his head from his body. Only one boy had ever known her this well. Only one boy was *allowed* to know her this well. And that boy was in a grave built of his own body because she'd made the mistake of trusting this bastard. This bastard who was now lecturing her about her own feelings.

"At least I'm doing something about it!" she pointed out, her hands still on his chest. His heartbeat raced beneath her fingers, despite his stubbornly set jaw and blazing eyes. "What are *you* doing?"

"*Trying to keep you alive.*"

"I can keep myself alive. I need you to do more. To be *better*."

"*You* need to be better," Gael snapped. His hands gripped her wrists like shackles. He leaned closer. "You forget that I was an actual soldier. I know a thing or two about strategy. Blundering around—making enemies like you have been?—is bad strategy."

"Better than letting a dragon enslave me, mind and soul." She yanked herself free, but she didn't back away. "What are his weaknesses? What is his ultimate plan? What's your so-called strategy?"

Faron could feel his frustration as if it were her own. He was breathing through gritted teeth, harsh exhales that spoke of far more effort than a simple conversation should take. He turned away from her abruptly, and a wall dropped between the two of them. Her anger receded now that it was no longer fanned by his flames. She blinked, feeling as though she'd missed a step in their dance.

"You need," Gael finally said, "to get stronger before Lightbringer returns to pick us up, or we'll both suffer for it. Let's start with putting a permanent wall around your thoughts. You think so loudly, it feels like you're still yelling at me."

Any further attempts at conversations or arguments were shut down as he shifted into teaching mode. Gael observed her, sitting on one of the smooth boulders that lined the riverbank, with one leg drawn up to his chest. As it turned out, Faron was very good at guarding her own mind—likely from lying all the time. That part of the lesson was so easy that it lulled her into a false sense of security.

For the rest of the morning, Gael made her summon fire until she stopped singeing her eyebrows. Large flames the size of a bonfire floating before her chest. Small flames the size of a candlewick bouncing around her like fireflies. Ropelike flames that wound up and down her arms. Again and again, until the sun was high in the sky and she only sometimes lost control.

"Very good," said Gael. His hand covered her own, smothering her flames. "This certainly brings back memories."

THIS ENDS IN EMBERS

His palm against her palm, his gaze steady on hers...He was right about it bringing back memories. She remembered the sun drawing sweat from her overheated skin and the smell of salt and brine. She remembered Renard Hall, its marble walls and stone paths, Seaview and the glittering ocean beyond the cliffs, lies she swallowed from Gael and feelings she developed for Reeve. She remembered the frustration and determination. Her naivete.

Back then, she'd been learning to command living souls, a forgotten extension of the magic she'd been born with. Now she was learning a magic foreign and strange, gifted to her by the dragon holding her hostage.

How quickly things changed.

"Come," Gael said, releasing her to walk toward the Snowmelt. Faron shook out her hand as if that would erase his touch, but she still felt it. The river tripped along sluggishly, indifferent to their presence. Though it was the middle of the day, she could hear frogs croaking. Bugs zipped from reed to reed, almost too fast for her to catch. The weather had grown colder, and it felt colder still closer to the water. Somehow, this didn't stop Gael from standing close to the bank and facing her with an expectant look on his face. "Now try aiming for me."

"*What?*" Faron gaped. "Why would I—?"

"You're unlikely to actually hit me," said Gael.

That made her roll her eyes. "You're in Reeve's body. I don't want to hurt him."

"But you want to hurt *me*, don't you?" Gael's tone lowered into something dangerous. "I tricked you into releasing Lightbringer. I wrecked your home. I'm wearing your boyfriend like a suit. I know it makes you angry."

177

"Not *that* angry," Faron insisted, even though that was a lie. She didn't hate Gael, but she *did* hate Lightbringer. She hated this entire situation and every choice she had made to lead her here. She hated the doubts, the endless doubts, about whether she could save Gael Soto or if he was just the sweetest lie that Iya had ever told. She hated that she had doomed Reeve to his half existence, that she hadn't been able to stop the plan his parents had laid out for him long before she'd ever grown to care for him.

But she didn't hate Gael. They were too much alike. He had been the first person to truly understand the burden she carried as the Empyrean, the pressure she was under and the temptations she faced. In turn, she understood how bleak his future felt, how exhausted he was from fighting Lightbringer for centuries in the Empty. She had felt the weight of Lightbringer's soul and maliciousness, and she knew how much it had cost Gael to keep his own soul from being shredded beneath a creature so ancient and evil.

No, she didn't hate Gael. She wanted to save him, not hurt him.

"Surely there's another way," Faron tried. "I can run through the drills again—"

"There are plenty of other ways," Gael agreed. "But this one will make you feel better. I know it will." His tone and expression were solemn. Almost reverent. It made her heart trip in her chest. "I'm not afraid of you, Faron. I'm not afraid of what you could do or who you could be. Your power, the fierce, unbridled, wild force of you . . . It's always been radiant to me."

"I don't know—"

"Reach for that anger, and wield it. Make it bow to you. Make *me* bow to you." Trouble danced in those earthy hazel eyes. A

THIS ENDS IN EMBERS

smirk tugged at his lips. He slid into a defensive position, all lithe muscle and coiled strength. "If, of course, you even can."

It was a challenge. One he knew she'd want to rise to.

Faron's hands ignited with red-orange flames.

And then she attacked.

Gael dodged every blast with a warrior's grace. She couldn't so much as scorch his hair, and her sole attempt at doing so resulted in him bending so far backward that she was shocked Reeve's spine didn't snap. He seemed to know what she was going to do before she did it, blocking her burning fist, twisting under her overhead punch, and coming up behind her with a soft laugh. She whirled around, flames-first, and he leaped out of the way, the fire illuminating the planes of his face until he looked like the god he claimed to be.

Faron snarled.

Gael's smirk widened. "There you are."

Her attacks became wilder, more vicious. Every time he evaded her, she moved faster, faster, *faster*, until she realized that her surroundings were a blur and he was the only real thing she could see. He summoned fire around his own hands, flaring it into a makeshift shield that swallowed her every blast, forcing Faron to dart in close. Block and parry. Block and parry.

He caught her wrist and twisted her flaming hand away from his face. She snuffed the fire out before her clothes could catch. He repeated the move with her other wrist, trapping her between the risk of setting herself ablaze just to take him down with her or accepting defeat.

Faron was breathing hard as she grumbled, "I yield."

"Soon, you won't have to," Gael said, voice warm with affection.

His breathing was even. "What you lack in technical skill you more than make up for in raw power. You did well, Faron."

"Don't patronize me."

"I'm not. I'm in awe of you."

Faron pulled away. Her cheeks were warm, she noted with some frustration. Even when she tried to be impervious to Gael's charm, she found herself falling for it like some inexperienced babe. His charm was a knife he had cut her with once before. She didn't want to let him do it again.

"Did I hurt Reeve?" she asked, giving his body a once-over. "Don't hide the fact that his body needs healing just to lord it over me."

"He's fine," said Gael. "Do you want to try again?"

"I think I need water and a break."

"Take your time. I think I've just figured out the best way to teach you quickly, and I'll need a few days to get it all together."

Faron squinted at him. "Am I going to like this?"

"Oh," Gael said without hesitation, mischief dancing in his eyes again, "you're going to love it."

CHAPTER NINETEEN

ELARA

A WEEK AFTER ELARA HAD ARRIVED IN HIGHFORT, THE CONFERence was held in Joya del Mar's capital city of Avara, a right that Rey Christóbal had claimed as his empire was first to see the necessity of this international alliance. Aveline and Elara would speak on behalf of San Irie. Signey and Professor Smithers would represent Langley. Étolia sent Tournesola Orianne Lumiére with a legion of musketeers to protect her. And Marién, the only other independent island in the Ember Sea, had sent no one at all.

At home, backlash to the announcement of the international conference swirled into a hurricane of vitriol. Protestors had taken to the streets, angry faces emblazoned in black and white on the front page of the newspaper that Elara read every morning before spending the day in Cherry's lab. She couldn't imagine how Aveline was dealing with it all—the queen had not been forthcoming on their fire calls—but she could guess that the answer was *not well*. After all, there was nothing that broke Aveline more than letting down her people, and it seemed as if every major decision she had made in the last few months had made her rule more and more unpopular.

Sometimes Elara wondered if the only thing keeping San Irie from dissolving into civil war was the lingering threat of Iya.

But the one time she *had* brought it up, Aveline had said, "We'll deal with San Irie's problems when we're in San Irie. Until then, nothing matters more than this conference." And so, until Aveline had sent Nobility to pick her up, Elara had buried her concern, hoping with all her heart that the other countries would feel the same.

Elara and Aveline arrived at the meeting room early, by Aveline's request. The queen sat beside Rey Christóbal while Elara waited by the window with a glass of water, dressed in the elegant bronze gown that Aveline had provided for her. Rey Christóbal and Doña Montserrat had already been present at the circular table when they had entered the room, and there were only six chairs present for the attendees—forcing Elara to stand with Tournesola Orianne's translator. The king's chair was grander than anyone else's, high-backed and gilded. His cousin had been allotted the same cushioned chair as everyone else.

Still, the doña was in high spirits, though Elara got the feeling that it took a lot for her to share what lay behind that smile. In a strange way, she reminded Elara of Faron. There was chaos in her dark brown eyes.

On the other side of Aveline was Signey. It was the first time Elara had seen her since their argument, but not the first time they had spoken. With Cherry at her side, Elara had fire called Signey to ask for more blood samples, which Signey had claimed to be too busy to send. The conference was coming up, and she and Professor Smithers had been meeting frequently with Barret and government officials to prepare for it.

Now Signey was in conversation with Professor Smithers as he

THIS ENDS IN EMBERS

glanced thoughtfully down at his ring. Elara wished she had found the time to talk with her before this, but she was also glad she hadn't. Seeing Signey now, her freckled skin and lovely eyes, made Elara's heart pound unevenly in her chest. They both needed to focus on something other than each other to get through this day.

Tournesola Orianne Lumiére sat between Professor Smithers and Doña Montserrat, rounding out the group. Elara considered it a victory that the tournesola had actually shown up, but she kept her expression blank. They were after a bigger victory than just everyone's presence. They needed promised soldiers, a signed alliance, and a declaration of war before the conference was over. Then and only then, Aveline had said, would they share San Irie's research into blood magic and Iya's past. Until then, Elara would observe and support.

Trust your own judgment.

Rey Christóbal cleared his throat before speaking in patois: "Thank you all for coming on such short notice. You've surely seen the stories of the damage Iya has caused, first to San Irie and then across Langley. If left unchecked, his power will only grow, until he poses a real threat to the continent. For that reason, I think it best if we all work together to contain the situation."

Elara stifled a scoff. *His idea. Right.*

"We've heard the rumors," Tournesola Orianne said through her translator. "This Iya you so fear is a teenager. You have called us here to deal with the petulant whims of a child?"

"I told you that this is no mere child," said Professor Smithers. "This boy is a god, bonded to the most powerful dragon in existence, and they both believe this world belongs to them."

"I heard," Rey Christóbal said, "that it is Langley's fault that we are in this position to begin with. Is that true?"

183

"I don't think assigning blame is productive right now," Signey said. "We need to form a plan and begin sharing resources—"

"There are far more young people in this room than I was expecting when you summoned us, Christóbal," said the tournesola. Her eyes found Elara again. "This one is the Empyrean, but why has Barret sent his child to speak for a nation?"

"I'm in the diplomacy track at the Hearthstone Academy," Signey said with a surprising amount of calm. "I'm here to shadow Professor Smithers, but I also have personal experience with Iya, since I successfully fought him off from his attempted conquest of San Irie. I'm here to fill in any gaps in the collective's knowledge, based on what we observed of his strengths and weaknesses. If you'd rather go in ignorantly, we're happy to leave you to squabble."

The tournesola tilted her head. "Iya is a Soto as well, is he not? How do we know you're not here to spy on his behalf?"

"Weren't you listening? Miss Soto just defended San Irie from her ancestor. She is no spy. She is a savior." When Aveline finally spoke, everyone in the room turned to listen. Her face and voice were cold, but her eyes were alight with a magnetic fury. "Iya cannot be defeated by one country alone. If we don't stand together now, one by one we will all fall. We are here to discuss his current strategies and powers so we can formulate a plan to foil his worldwide conquest before it goes any further, and nothing else. Put aside your petty disagreements, and think of your *people*."

"Your people have only been yours for five years and you think you can lecture us," Tournesola Orianne muttered. "I will not continue this meeting until the Soto girl is removed from the chamber."

Aveline opened her mouth to say something no doubt scathing,

THIS ENDS IN EMBERS

but Doña Montserrat placed a hand on her arm. The queen calmed at once, though she didn't look happy about it. The doña nodded toward the door. "It's a reasonable request. Miss Soto, please leave. Professor Smithers can handle Langlish interests in your stead."

"*No.*" It took Elara a moment of thunderous silence to realize that she was the one who had spoken. But with everyone's eyes on her, including Signey's, she refused to take back the words. "Don't dismiss Signey because she's a child or because of who her family is. The San Irie Revolution was won by children: me, my sister, the queen. It was won by a child who knew that his family was in the wrong and took steps to defeat them: Reeve Warwick. Our nation is our nation because we didn't dismiss someone as too young or too biased to make a difference. If we expect to work together to stop a threat much larger than ourselves, then we need to trust one another. If we can't do that much, then why are *any* of us here?"

Tournesola Orianne smiled, as though Elara had played right into her hands. "Aren't the two of you in some sort of relationship? Perhaps you should both leave."

"This is getting ridiculous," said Rey Christóbal. "No one is leaving. The Empyrean is right. If we begin to doubt that anyone in this room is against Iya, then where do we draw the line?"

One by one, everyone looked away from her except for Signey. Her dark eyes seemed darker with some emotion that Elara couldn't read from so far away, but it wasn't anger. It looked closer to guilt. Elara wondered if Signey had thought their disagreement about Faron was enough to break them, if by choosing Faron's side then Elara would never be on Signey's. She tried a smile, small and confident, and her smile widened when Signey returned it. They had a lot to talk about, but, at least in this moment, they felt okay.

KAMILAH COLE

The conversation finally, finally turned to Iya. But even riding the high of being heard by the adults in the room, Elara could tell after the first twenty minutes that this meeting would have no immediate resolution. Tournesola Orianne had nothing but barbed comments to make. Rey Christóbal seemed determined to cast blame on Langley, as if their admission of guilt would change the circumstances. Professor Smithers took the lead on the conversation, but he was on the defensive. And Aveline and Doña Montserrat were involved in a small argument of their own, leaning across Rey Christóbal to take verbal swipes at each other.

Elara looked around the room bleakly. Her hope seemed naive in hindsight. She should have known this was what would happen when you gathered this many people with this many large egos in the same place. She had, after all, been on the wrong side of the gods' own stubborn pridefulness when they had named her the Maiden Empyrean and tried to get her to kill Faron as a condition of saving the world. When things were hard, when they required time or sacrifice, most beings would choose the easiest path—no matter who else was burned in the process.

But there was a difference between knowing that and seeing it in action. The fate of the world was on the line, and the rulers and representatives of four different nations couldn't work together even long enough to have a *discussion*.

She spoke up again, stomach churning with disgust. "Please, can we talk about a treaty and declaration—"

"Empyrean," said Rey Christóbal, "while I appreciate your presence and your wisdom, your constant interruptions have worn out their welcome. This is politics, not theology. Your opinion is unneeded."

186

THIS ENDS IN EMBERS

"But we're short on time to—"

Aveline silently shook her head as she stared down Elara, a warning in her face. Elara's words died in her throat, her cheeks hot with embarrassment. Signey met her eyes again, and this time her expression was easy to read. She looked as disgusted and hopeless as Elara felt, as if she wished they *had* kicked her out so that she could still pretend to respect the rulers in the room.

Elara bit the inside of her cheek as the arguments carried on. Otherwise, she feared she would say something she would regret.

By the time the meeting ended for the day, dinner beckoning them all to the ornate dining room, Elara was so exhausted that she asked Aveline if she could eat in her room. She wasn't sure she could make it through a meal with all the rulers after that, especially with Tournesola Orianne's smug *Aren't the two of you in some sort of relationship?* still burning in her ears. Elara didn't regret anything she had said today, but she needed a better strategy for tomorrow. Especially if even the queen thought she had spoken out of turn.

She turned a corner and stopped. Signey Soto was leaning against the wall, her hands in the pockets of her wide-legged trousers. Elara hadn't had much time to admire her before, and she was too exhausted to do so now. But the camel-colored pants and white button-down, paired with her curly hair and plum lip paint, made it hard to take her eyes away.

"You stood up for me," said Signey, straightening. "Why?"

"It was unfair of them to try to kick you out. Especially because of your last name."

Signey's eyes narrowed.

"What?" Elara demanded.

"I thought you'd say it was because I'm your girlfriend," Signey admitted after a moment. "I thought—well, it was unfair, too. What I thought."

"We haven't exactly been on the same page lately." Elara stifled a yawn. "But this conference"—another yawn—"it's too important for personal grievances."

Signey reached out, and Elara froze like a startled cat, watching intently to see what she would do. But her hand just closed around Elara's shoulder and tugged her forward. "You're exhausted, and you're still making time to talk to me? You need to take care of *yourself.*"

"What was I meant to do?" Elara asked, her skin warm beneath Signey's fingers. "Just walk past you?"

"I would have understood, all things considered."

"I wouldn't do that to you. To anyone, but especially not to you."

"I know."

Elara wanted to say something else, but then Signey's arm slid around her shoulder, tucking Elara in close to her side, and she didn't dare breathe a word that would draw attention to it. Part of her felt as if she were dreaming. Maybe she had fallen asleep during the conference, dipped into a world where all her problems fell away because a pretty girl was touching her. But then they were in front of Elara's bedroom door and Signey let her go and the dreamlike haze of the walk faded back to her imperfect reality.

"Thank you. For sticking up for me. For being you," said Signey. "Let's get through this conference, and then maybe . . . we can talk? Properly talk."

Elara smiled. "I'd like that."

CHAPTER TWENTY

FARON

FARON SPENT MUCH OF HER TIME WANDERING HEARTHSTONE, BUT now she did it with a purpose. Lightbringer was paying her little attention. Gael was setting up some new lesson plan. This was as much freedom as she was going to get, and she wanted to use it to find the dragon eggs.

Wherever the Warwicks had placed them, they were well hidden. She searched every floor and every room. She checked tapestries and shelves for hidden corridors. The only reason she didn't start digging holes in the lawn was that Lightbringer would see her doing it. Thinking of simply following Gavriel Warwick around took her longer than she was willing to admit: With a treasure so important, the Warwicks would not trust anyone but themselves to guard it. Sooner or later, there would be a shift change. Sooner or later, she'd have her answer.

Shortly after dinner, she followed Gavriel Warwick as he left his room. He went down to the first floor and then slipped into Oscar Luxton's office, using a burst of flame from his palm to open the door. Faron hurried forward to jam a torn piece of her shirt between the door and its frame, keeping it from closing all the way. She waited until she no longer heard sounds from within and then tentatively pushed at the door.

When it was open a crack, she stared inside. Gavriel Warwick was nowhere to be seen, but there was another open door at the far end of the office. There was a chance that he was waiting there for her, well aware that she had followed him, and she debated if she was ready to take that risk. Soft voices floated out, coming closer to the main office.

Faron let the door slide shut and hurried back to her room.

The next day, Faron followed Mireya Warwick. She waited until Gavriel Warwick had emerged from the office and gone upstairs, relieved from his shift. The slip of fabric still kept the door from closing completely, and this time she quietly let herself into the office. Oscar Luxton was a tacky decorator, she noted derisively. He had portraits of white men in gilded frames, and he had dying plants in cauldron-like pots. His carpeting was black, and the walls were paneled in wood. It looked as if he were trying to impress, rather than being actually impressive.

Faron crept toward the second door, which hung open like an invitation. She couldn't hear anything from around the corner, but she had come prepared with a kitchen knife and a jagged piece of a shattered mirror. She glanced in; nothing but shadows greeted her. Rows of filing cabinets stood against the wall like soldiers, and the wood floor matched the paneled walls of the office. She bit back a curse. Wood floors were noisy if you didn't know where to step. And she didn't.

She eased off her shoes and took the risk. It was a slow, tentative

THIS ENDS IN EMBERS

trip down the hallway as she tested each wood plank before she dared to put her full weight on it. Every few seconds, she would glance at the third door at the very end, waiting for Mireya Warwick to appear and catch her. There was nowhere to hide in this stretch of her journey. She just had to hope that the director wouldn't emerge unless she had to.

Faron reached the door, which was labeled with a small plaque that read RECORDS. Student records, she assumed, though that didn't explain why there were so many cabinets in this hall. She touched the doorknob only to find it hot, as if there were a contained fire within. Was that how they incubated dragon eggs? Was that Iya's plan? To hatch the eggs quickly and find their Riders himself?

It seemed too convoluted for him. The Riders these dragons chose could very well elect to stand against him, and it would be too much work to keep breaking bonds until he found Riders who would join him. She was missing something. She knew it.

"You are far too curious for your own good," Lightbringer snarled across the bond. *"Leave, or I will make you leave."*

"I can't get in there anyway," said Faron, feigning a lack of concern. *"Are you trying to hatch them here?"*

She leaned back against the door, which was only half as warm as the knob, and tried not to smile. If it had taken Lightbringer this long to find her, then her lessons with Gael were good for at least one thing: She could hide her thoughts with or without the stone from Rosetree Manor. Their bond still allowed him to sense her presence, but he actually had to try. That gave her even more freedom than she'd thought.

Gavriel Warwick appeared at the other end of the hall. He

rolled his eyes at the sight of her. "I don't want to know how you got in here, but we'll make sure it doesn't happen again."

Faron maintained her smile, even though this was a minor setback. She had been hoping that if she lingered, Mireya Warwick would open the door to chase her off. Then she could have at least caught a glimpse of what was going on inside—and seen whether Jesper's blood was in there. Could one even store human blood at such a high temperature? Was Rider blood different?

Commander Warwick grabbed her arm and yanked her toward the office. "I told our saint that it was a mistake to keep the eggs here with you around. All you do is poke your nose where it doesn't belong, and he refuses to discipline you."

"You seem angry," Faron said as she stumbled along behind him. "Upset that you're not your god's favorite?"

"This war may be fought by children, but this is not a game, Empyrean." The commander shoved her against the wall by the office door. His gaze was sharper than a scalestone sword. "I don't know what my son sees in you, but you are nothing and no one now. The second you become more of a liability than a boon, I will kill you myself."

"You'll kill your son if you do," Faron whispered, shaking both from the commander's proximity and from the fact that he'd even noticed that she and Reeve were...what they were. "You'll kill your saint."

Gavriel Warwick smirked. His hand came up to close around her throat. She clawed at his hand, but he was strong, so strong, though bruises began to appear on his own neck, black and blue circles that bled together until he couldn't breathe, either. He dropped her, and she fell to the floor, panting.

Above her, his own breathing was heavy. And still he sounded delighted. "You're right. I don't have to kill you."

"Gael will—"

"Gael is dealing with the dragon you've just pissed off. I don't know about you, but I think the latter will win."

Faron pushed herself back onto her feet, still gasping for air. Her larynx hurt, but not as much as her pride. "Whatever power you have now, I gave you," she managed, shoving past him before he could grab her again. "One day, you'll be powerless and alone. You'll be afraid, and you'll die afraid. I just hope I'm there to see it."

CHAPTER TWENTY-ONE

ELARA

As Elara got dressed for another long day, she thought of how far she had come from that little girl who lived in a small farming town miles away from the ocean. Once, her world had been no bigger than her island. Now that it had widened, she missed that comforting smallness and that illusory sense of control. But, at the same time, she didn't regret most of the choices that had led her to the center of international politics. That little girl had been shy, ignorant, young. The woman she saw in the mirror had a voice.

And she planned to use it.

Doña Montserrat and Queen Aveline were the only two in the room when Elara arrived. Their chairs were pushed so close that their knees touched, and they spoke to each other in soft Joyan. Aveline had dressed Elara in a long-sleeved silver gown with golden appliqués; she had dressed herself in a gold gown with puffed sleeves and a matching head wrap. Doña Montserrat wore another one of her fitted suits, but by wild coincidence her vest had gold pinstripes.

They flinched apart when Elara cleared her throat.

"I wanted to talk about yesterday," she said. "You silenced me.

THIS ENDS IN EMBERS

I mean no disrespect, Your Majesty, but if you trust me enough to send me to Étolia alone, then you should trust me enough to speak during this conference. Why didn't you support me the way I support you?"

Aveline blinked, clearly thrown. Beside her, the doña hid a smile that was gone by the time Aveline glanced at her. "They were trying to manipulate you into an emotional response, Maiden. They wouldn't listen—"

"You don't know that. I wasn't feeling emotional." Elara paused. "Well, not so emotional that my points weren't sound. We are both here on behalf of San Irie. In that, we are equals. If what happened yesterday is going to happen again, then I'd rather return to Highfort. Where my opinion is respected and I can make some real progress."

"I'll...go and get us some water," said Doña Montserrat, disappearing before Aveline or Elara could point out that there were already filled glasses of water on the table.

Only once she was gone did Aveline sigh and rub her temples. Elara's hands trembled, but she clenched them into fists. *Breathe in. Breathe out.* She *refused* to apologize or console the queen, even though Aveline looked both tired and hurt. Elara wasn't wrong, and she was sure that the queen knew it. She just had to wait her out.

"Elara," Aveline finally said, her tone so thoughtful, it was clear she'd been waiting a while to say what she was going to say, "you have weathered a lot in a very short amount of time, and, in the future, your strength will be called upon even—and especially—if you do not have it. You are a light to the people of our island as the Maiden Empyrean, but you must take care to keep some of that light for yourself."

Aveline looked as though she had little light left. When they had traveled the island together during the war against the Langlish Empire, Aveline had seemed untouchable thanks to Elara's precocious crush. After the war, after she'd taken the throne, the queen had become untouchable in a different way, locking away any vulnerability to project the air of confidence that her young nation needed in a leader. It was only recently that Aveline had begun to set aside that mask when she and Elara were alone, and it never stopped feeling like a privilege to see those lines of exhaustion, those slumped shoulders, that lopsided diadem.

They were alike in many ways, Elara and Aveline. The crushing responsibility on their shoulders was one they couldn't set down, even for a second, without feeling guilty. Their lives had never been truly their own. And they were tired. So very tired.

Elara shifted her weight from one foot to the other. "Did I do something wrong, Your Majesty? If I've given you reason not to trust me—"

"That is not it at all. It's more that"—the queen paused for a long moment, her jaw working soundlessly—"I saw what this constant performance did to your sister. I know what it's done to me. And I—there were times during the revolution that I didn't know how I would bear it all until I saw your smile, so sunny and sincere, and it would seal the cracks of my damaged hope for the future."

"I—"

"I won't hide my preference for working with you for the protection of the island over your sister, but, if I treat you more cautiously, it's not because I think you're weak. It's because I want to protect that smile. I know we're not blood, but we emerged from those flames as family"—Aveline's eyes flashed—"the only family I have. Do you understand?"

THIS ENDS IN EMBERS

Elara took a deep breath, because if she gave in to the urge to sob at this show of kindness, then she would never stop. "So you silenced me because we're family? I don't understand that."

"You're right. I shouldn't have silenced you. I promise that I do trust you. It's only that"—Aveline stood up and crossed the room until she was standing in front of Elara—"the more I ask of you, the more I see your light dimming. Your confidence eroding. Your entire *self* retreating behind a mask of your own. You're too genuine for that." She took Elara's hand. Her calluses—from farm life, from battle—felt rough against Elara's skin. "Promise me you'll try to get it back."

A tear slipped free despite Elara's efforts to stop it. Relief warmed her body. She hadn't realized how tightly wound she had been, between the protests and the gods, Signey and Cherry, her sister's alleged criminal activity and the kidnapping of Jesper, until she squeezed the queen's hand and some of her nerves settled, too. She and Aveline *were* a united front, two matching shields to protect San Irie as best they could. Aveline had different priorities, but in the end, they carried the same weight.

The queen was just carrying it better.

"Does that go for Faron, too?" she whispered, because she had to know. "Is Faron still your family?"

Aveline frowned. "Where is this coming from?"

"Signey and I had a fight. She thinks that Faron's been corrupted, that she's joined Iya's side. And I—I appreciate your trust, Your Majesty, I do. I want us to be on the same side. But I can't trust you completely unless . . . I know where you stand on Faron."

The queen's frown deepened. She glanced at the door, listening for something she didn't find. Then, she lowered her voice and said,

197

"Your sister is many things, Maiden, but a traitor is not one of them. Whatever fool plan she has, she's doing it for you. For San Irie."

"I know," said Elara, smiling. "I'm just glad you know it, too."

Aveline returned her smile. Minutes later, the rest of the group filed into the room: Doña Montserrat carrying a tray of water glasses, Tournesola Orianne and her musketeers, Rey Christóbal and Professor Smithers, and, in the back, Signey Soto with a tentative smile. That smile was the final confirmation that last night's conversation hadn't been a dream, and it settled the last of Elara's nervousness.

The soldiers took their places against the wall as the seats were pulled out. But as everyone settled into their chairs, Aveline lifted a hand.

"We'll need one more," she told one of the Joyan soldiers. "The Maiden Empyrean needs a place at the table." The soldier glanced at the rey, who nodded. "Thank you."

All eyes were on Elara now, but she didn't shrink away.

Professor Smithers gave her a small smile, and Elara smiled back.

"All right," said Rey Christóbal, taking the lead once more. "Let's begin."

Even with Elara's many attempts to focus the conversation, the second day of the conference was as disastrous as the first. A discussion about supplies and capacity—what percentage of their forces each country could reasonably commit to the cause—had dissolved into another argument about personal responsibility. If Iya had been created by Langley and unleashed by San Irie, shouldn't they contribute more soldiers, whether they had them or not? Since Étolia was likely to be the next country attacked, shouldn't some of those soldiers go toward bolstering their country's defenses? And if Joya del Mar was the farthest away from Iya's current territory, should they have to spare any soldiers at all?

These details *didn't matter.* But these adults, these so-called politicians, wasted hours picking one another apart. By the time any sort of alliance was formed, there wouldn't be a world left to protect.

The very thought made Elara grouchy even after she retired to her room for the day. Orange sun rippled through the curtains, bringing out the red undertones in her skin as she loosened the buttons of her dress's high collar. Before her, the fire roared and Cherry McKay's voice twinkled a greeting. Elara's frown deepened.

"If this is a social call," she said into the fireplace, kicking off her heels and dropping onto the edge of her bed, "I'm not in the mood."

"*You're* not in the mood to be social?" Cherry sounded downright gleeful. "You really have grown."

"*Cherry.*"

"Oh, fine. I'm calling because we've finished running some preliminary tests. Signey has an anomaly in her blood that isn't shared by other Langlish samples. Or Lindan samples, for that matter. So I used various samples—magical and unmagical—as our controls, and I managed to isolate—"

"*Cherry.*" Elara groaned. "I'm glad you found your calling, but I'm so tired. Please skip the methodology and get to the point."

"The power in Signey's blood is most similar to yours. It's *divine.*"

Elara blinked. "Signey is a god?"

"Not *exactly*, but she shares the same magic as a certain someone who has the power of one. Elara, I think—I mean, more testing would be needed, of course, but I theorize that…well, it's possible that Signey—that all the Sotos—should be able to break dragon bonds."

"*What?*"

"I know! It sounds impossible, but—imagine if it's true." The glee was back in Cherry's voice, but this time it was a giddiness that accompanied a potential victory. This, Elara realized, was Cherry's version of a battle. And unlike in their backyard spars, these were fights she could win. "When Gael Soto first bonded with Lightbringer, it changed him in ways large and small, mental and biological. In his blood was the power of an Empyrean and a Rider, and he passed that blood down to his descendants. That might be the reason you and Signey were bonded to Zephyra months ago. She has the diluted power of an Empyrean inside her, except instead of summoning astrals, she might be able to manipulate dragon souls. And if she can do that, then she can definitely break bonds."

Elara got to her feet so she could pace the length of the room. It would make a strange sort of sense. Signey had been able to bear the weight of bonding with Zephyra for years before meeting Elara and in the weeks after Elara's bond had been broken. Signey and Zephyra had moved as if they were one person in two bodies, rather than dragon and Rider. Signey was the strongest warrior in Hearthstone Academy through sheer force of will, yes, but could it also have been because she was genuinely more powerful than anyone else?

"I need to talk to the queen," Elara finally said. "If this is true—if you're right—"

"This is just a theory! I have to run more tests, and I will," Cherry promised. "But even if I'm wrong, I do think I'm on to something, that the Sotos are the key to ending all this."

"I should call—"

"Barret has already been notified. Signey's there with you, right? Can you tell her I'll need those samples sooner rather than later?"

After ending the call, Elara poked her head out the door to send a Queenshield for Aveline. Then she paced her room again, mind racing. A Soto to end what a Soto had begun. But could Signey actually break the bond between Gael Soto and Lightbringer, dividing Iya back into two halves they could individually take down? Could Signey break any bonds at all, or were all Cherry's tests inaccurate? Would Signey *want* to break a bond after losing her own?

Despite everything, Elara didn't doubt that Signey would do whatever it took to save the world. It was one of the first things they had bonded over, this incessant need they both had to do the right thing. Signey had perfected the kind of heroism that Elara felt she struggled toward, and yet one starlit night, on dragonback, with wind on their faces and danger in their path, she had said that Elara was *her* inspiration.

"Why are you smiling like that?" Aveline asked as she entered the room. The door slipped shut behind her, and she folded her arms over the gold gown she still wore. "I hope it's because you have a treaty in your back pocket."

"This dress doesn't have pockets," Elara said. And then: "I just received word from Highfort that Signey Soto might be capable of breaking dragon bonds."

Aveline was quiet for a long moment, her expression blank. "Do you really think she'll pursue that option?"

"Why wouldn't she?"

"Dragons are an intrinsic part of Langlish culture and national identity. Signey did not give up her own bond willingly. Why would she force that fate upon anyone else?"

"The gods have been clear that this only ends with the dragons returned to the divine realm." Elara had the sudden urge to pace again, but she didn't want Aveline to think she was uncertain. "She knows how high the stakes are. Once Cherry confirms this theory, we can put together a plan—hopefully one that ends with breaking the bond between Lightbringer and Gael once and for all."

There was another silence. Elara had no idea what her face looked like, but whatever Aveline saw there made the queen sigh. "I think it's best if we put together a plan now. I'll summon Miss Soto."

"I need to use the bathroom anyway."

By the time Elara emerged, Signey was present in her riding leathers, speaking quietly with the queen. The conversation came to a stop when they both turned to look at her. But when Elara sat on the bed, Signey sat down beside her. As if they were united. It felt...good.

Aveline gestured for Elara to speak, so she explained everything that Cherry had told her. Signey stared at the floor between her feet, her face blank until Elara was done. She didn't speak right away, giving Elara and Aveline enough time to exchange a glance. Elara wondered if Signey was thinking about this news, or if she was thinking of Zephyra, who was, for once, not somewhere outside waiting for her. Aveline looked as if she wanted to say something, but Elara held up a hand.

They needed to let Signey process this in her own time.

"What if it hurts them?" Signey finally said in a small voice. "If

I can break bonds like Iya can, what if it hurts them? What if what happened to Zephyra happens to the rest?"

"There's definitely that risk," said Elara, placing her hand on the bed between them. Her palm was turned upward in invitation, but she didn't push. "But I think it will be different. Iya broke my bond and yours at different times. When he broke mine, I didn't even feel it. Not like you did. So there *must* be a way to do it without that trauma. You felt that pain because he wanted you to. I know you wouldn't wield this power the same way."

Signey's hand found Elara's. Their fingers intertwined. "I can't do that to my people. If—I mean, I'd want to have their permission."

"Do you think they'll give it?"

"It doesn't matter. I'll explain. I'll convince them. But they have to be willing, or I won't do it." Signey finally raised her chin, and the determination that blazed in her eyes made her all the more beautiful. "It wouldn't be right."

"This does lead perfectly into the other thing I wanted to discuss," said the queen. Elara and Signey both jumped, and Aveline smirked. "You forgot I was here, didn't you? Ah, young love." Her amusement filtered away. "I've been thinking about what you said, Maiden. About making progress elsewhere. And today made me realize that you were right. You need not be here. Either of you."

Signey looked at Elara. Elara looked at Signey.

Her eyebrows furrowed. "I don't understand, Your Majesty."

"I believe that the other rulers are purposefully talking in circles because the two of you are present. They wanted you gone, and we refused, and now they are refusing to come to a decision on the treaty terms. I know this game too well to play, especially when there are more important things you could be doing." Aveline sat on Elara's other side, her hands folded in her lap. The skirt of her dress spilled over the floor in a puddle of fabric. "Signey, I think you should return to Beacon and begin strategizing with your father about how to approach the bonds—and the Riders—once we hear back from Cherry. Elara, you should return to San Irie and aid in the research. We can't move forward without answers, and, once the treaty is signed, we'll need a plan in place."

Elara expected to feel failure, disappointment, shame, but instead all she felt was excitement. "I'll ask Rey Christóbal if I can borrow some books from his library before I go. If blood magic was ever a thing in Gael Soto's day, we'd find information about it in a Joyan history book."

"A brilliant idea, Maiden." Aveline's smile returned. "I will fire call you with any updates from here."

Signey was still holding Elara's hand. She gave it a squeeze. "I guess this is goodbye again." She brought their joined hands to her mouth and pressed a kiss to the back of Elara's. "Good luck and stay safe."

Elara's face was warm. "You, too. Um, with the luck. And the safety."

When they were both gone, Elara flopped back on her bed, smiling triumphantly at the ceiling. They had action items and a future full of possibilities. It felt so good to no longer be standing still, trying to be heard in a room of people or gods who refused to listen. She was ready to run, step by step, until the world was safe again. Until Faron and Reeve were home again.

And now she knew just where to start.

CHAPTER TWENTY-TWO

FARON

STILL REELING FROM GAVRIEL WARWICK'S THREATS, FARON practiced her magic alone, without Gael to watch her.

She ran through the drills on the beach, using her fire and the exercise as a way of keeping warm. The invisible line between Harvest and Solstice had snapped, releasing a cold front the likes of which she had never experienced in San Irie. There was talk of snow, and Faron hoped to be long gone by then.

It didn't help that Lightbringer was there, his body blocking the weak sunlight that escaped from between the pallid clouds. The dragon eggs had been moved, last time Faron had dared to check, and Lightbringer watched over her as an unwanted guardian. At the moment, however, his gaze was directed toward the bay.

Ignatz and Cruz were having some kind of aquatic fight that involved disappearing beneath the surface and then breaching in a wave taller than her head. Ignatz—who, as an ultramarine, had a particular affinity for water—cut through the whitecaps as though they were as insubstantial as air, swimming circles around Cruz. But every so often, Cruz would use his superior size to slam into Ignatz, both purring as they sank in a blur of blue and gold scales.

Lightbringer held himself apart as always. Faron was uncomfortably reminded of her schoolyard days, walking the open corridors alone while her classmates played cricket or ran races or bought snacks at the cart just beyond the gate. They had always seemed so young to her, their laughter uncomplicated, their lives untouched by bloody battlefields strewn with burning flesh.

She wondered if Lightbringer felt the same disconnect when he watched the younger dragons play. The thought made her uncomfortable.

"You're staring," said Lightbringer blandly. *"What do you want now?"*

"You know what I want," Faron replied, summoning another wall of fire and attempting to split it into different columns.

"Ah, yes." Now he sounded amused. *"My swift and total defeat. You know, you remind me so much of him."*

"Of who?" Faron asked, though she already knew.

"The boy who faced me in what is now known as the Cinder Circle was just as stubborn. Just as arrogant." Lightbringer adjusted his weight, sending a cloud of sand flying into the air. *"You will learn."*

Faron clenched her fist, smothering one column of fire and the next and the next. She still had to bite the inside of her cheek to keep from snapping out a retort.

"In the stories they tell about us, they say we went mad," Lightbringer continued. *"That I drove their precious hero mad. But I bore no grudge against humanity when I entered this realm. I was thinking only of my freedom, and Gael Soto was the first creature to show me true kindness."* The dragon tipped up his head, squinting at the sky. *"But when I carried him home, he was praised for taming me. He became the Gray Saint, and I became a monster turned mount. I had escaped one cage only to enter another, worshipped only for what I could do, not for what*

THIS ENDS IN EMBERS

I was. A footnote in an insignificant human's story. If I went mad, it is because they drove me there."

Faron's hands fell to her side as she studied Lightbringer. He wasn't looking at her, but his jaw was clenched. Maybe he wasn't squinting at the sky. Maybe he was staring down the sun—and the goddess who ruled it.

Gael had made his disdain for Lightbringer clear while manipulating her into opening the Empty. *"That dragon... is a dangerous creature,"* he had said to her once. *"No one can control that beast."* But this was the only time Faron had heard Lightbringer hate him in turn. Theirs was the first bond ever forged between dragon and human, and she had personally witnessed that it was volatile. A chaotic swirl of warring consciousness, with Lightbringer mostly in control. But this was even worse than she'd thought. This wasn't just unstable. This was a schism.

She could use that.

Lightbringer finally turned to her, green eyes glittering like acid. *"I tell you this as a cautionary tale, Faron Vincent. The very world you long to save will drain you, betray you, and forget you once your usefulness has expired. You are a martyr without a cause. A traitor without a home. A villain masquerading as a hero. And one day you will exhaust yourself. Or"*—and Faron imagined if the dragon could smile, then he would have—*"you can give up on your inane schemes now and know true power and belonging. The choice is always yours."*

With that, Lightbringer's wings fanned out behind him and carried him into the air. Faron threw an arm over her eyes to protect them from the cyclone he left in his wake, but it was sand, so it buried itself in places she would never be able to reach. Her flash of irritation took her back to another time and another beach. A bowl of guinep and a boy with loose suspenders. The rising sun and the whispering waves.

Grief pierced her heart like a blade. She missed Reeve. *Gods*, she missed him.

Would he hate her, too? Would he regret their kiss? Would he look at her and see Iya—someone just as irredeemable?

She thought of Jesper Soto and Zephyra. The Hestan Archipelago. The Emerald Highlands. Maybe his contempt was exactly what she deserved.

"Are you crying?" Gael Soto was somehow in front of her, a furrow between his brows. "Did something happen?" His eyes darkened. "Did some*one*—"

Faron swiped at the dampness on her burning cheeks. "It's fine. I'm fine. When did you get here?"

"I called your name," Gael said. "Several times."

"I'm busy."

"Well, now you're busy doing something else."

Once her face was dry, he took a step back to reveal they weren't alone. Estella Ballard and Briar Noble stood behind him in their riding leathers, with matching blue shirts and belligerent expressions. Faron scowled back, daring them to say something to provoke her. Anger was preferable to grief. Anger was her armor. Anger was her weapon.

But they did nothing but stare.

"Stella and Briar have kindly volunteered to help you with your summoning," Gael said. Both looked as if they wanted to argue against the concept of being any help to her but didn't dare disagree with their saint. "They're very sure that they can keep you out of their minds."

THIS ENDS IN EMBERS

Noble cracked his knuckles. "I'm looking forward to this."

"Ooh, scary." Faron snorted. "I could beat you with my pinky finger."

"Let's have it on, then," Ballard said. Though not as performative as her co-Rider, her ire bled tension into the cold air. "I've got better things to be doing."

"The rules are simple." Gael moved far enough away that he had to shout to be heard. He waited until Faron was looking at him to smile, wide and proud. Faron had made Reeve smile so rarely that her breath caught to see it even now.

Then the sun caught the green flecks in Gael's hazel eyes and snapped her back to the present.

"Faron," he continued, "make them bow."

Trouble called to Faron, as much a part of her as her heartbeat. It drove out the grief, the anger, the distractions. It made her feel powerful in a way few things did. Faron was a creature who thrived in chaos—and Gael had brought it to her.

Her smile was a warning. One they ignored.

Ballard and Noble attacked, all red fire and wild swings, and Faron danced out of the way. They were trained, but she was experienced. Gods, at this point, Faron was probably the top expert on Langlish fighting styles. Her vision split between the furious Riders in front of her and the battlefield that had forged her. Aveline and the soldiers—enlisted and conscripted—had done their best to insulate Faron and Elara from the worst of the war. They had failed, but they had tried. Faron was brought out as a last resort, a decisive end to an overdrawn battle. Even when she'd actually listened, even when she'd actually stayed where she'd been told, she could still hear everything. Buildings collapsing into splinters, revealing scorched stone. Dragons roaring loud enough to shake the world. Soldiers weeping through their death throes.

But death was never the ending. Not for those who witnessed it. It was the beginning of a new life for a new person, a fragmented person, whose future was a thousand disparate pieces fused back together because or in spite of what they'd seen. Faron would never know who she could have been if she'd never been touched by death. If she'd never learned how to cause it. Life, for her, was defined by tragedy and pain that ricocheted further than she could even imagine.

The heat of a punch blocked by her fireproof armguard brought her back to the present. *Make them bow.*

Ballard's and Noble's movements were coordinated, a push and pull of offense to the other's defense, and Faron caught the rhythm of it within a few minutes. Sweat slicked her skin, but she fought off the chill, and adrenaline pounded through her blood. When they adjusted their strategy, she adjusted hers, skipping backward, jumping over fiery ankle sweeps, and narrowly avoiding a blade to the ribs.

It was impossible to concentrate long enough to reach for their souls. Which, she realized, was the lesson.

Faron clenched her eyes shut and kicked up sand at her attackers. When she'd put some distance between them, she reached out for their souls. Despite them charging her from opposite sides, it was easier this time. Last time, they'd been focused, their souls buried beyond the barrier of a deep and bitter anger against her. They were still angry, but they were weakened from the fight, and their anger was more active, frenzied. It was easy for Faron's influence to dip through the cracks. To wrap around their pliant souls

THIS ENDS IN EMBERS

and squeeze until they froze, inches away from tackling her to the ground.

Bow, she commanded.

They fell to their knees. Noble's forehead hit the ground first, followed seconds later by Ballard's. His black hair was loose today, falling ruler straight across his shoulder blades, and there was something satisfying about seeing him get sand in it. She hoped granules rained from his head for the rest of the day. No, the rest of the week.

Faron reached up and wiped the corner of her mouth with the back of her hand. It came away bloody. "Still looking forward to this?" she spat.

They didn't answer, but she didn't expect them to. All their energy was going toward looking for weaknesses in her control, weaknesses they wouldn't find. She fed another surge of power into their bodies, making them press themselves flat against the sand. She could make them eat it. She could make them bark like dogs. She could make them—

"Faron," Gael said from right beside her. "You're killing them."

Faron, she's drowning!

The sand beneath their heads was dark and wet. Red stained the ground. Everything smelled of salt water and bile. Noble and Ballard coughed violently, their bodies trembling from the effort of staying still. From the force of her power. Faron blinked, and they had gone still, paralyzed as if they were in the water. Faron blinked, and Elara was lying in Reeve's arms, her face pale as he extracted the water from her lungs with his dragon relic. Faron blinked, and Ballard was wheezing, every broken breath a silent cry for help.

211

Whatever you're doing to the dragon, you have to stop. It's happening to Elara, too!

Faron blinked, and Gael was touching her shoulder. "Are you going to kill them?"

He didn't sound as if he would be upset if she did, and that more than anything dropped her back into her body. She released her hold on their souls with a gasp. Her eyes burned. Her cheeks were damp. At some point, she'd started crying. Exhaustion brought her to her knees. Exhaustion and guilt.

Behind her, she heard a dragon—Ignatz—surging above the water's surface. Everything she'd been doing to his Riders had happened to him in the bay, and when he had started drowning, so had they. Another minute and...

Ballard and Noble scrambled onto their sides, coughing up water and sucking in air. Blood was smeared across their chins and beneath their noses. Sand littered their skin along with lingering sick. Exhausted, Noble wiped a hand across his mouth, doing little to clean the mess, and then he passed out. Ballard struggled into a sitting position, swaying dangerously. Faron twitched forward to help her, but she threw up a hand.

"Stay away from me," she snarled. "You act like you're so much better than us, but you're worse. You lie about it. You lie to yourself. You—" She leaned over and vomited onto the ground again, her hair clinging to her sweaty face.

Faron tried to take a step back, but Gael was still holding on to her. Her skin felt cold. Her chest felt cold. What had she almost done?

"I'll take them both to the infirmary," Gael murmured. "Lightbringer will be back soon, and you can update him on your progress."

Faron was shaking. She wrapped her arms around herself, but

THIS ENDS IN EMBERS

she still didn't feel warm. Her brain latched on to the only thing it could, in the wake of the horror she'd almost caused. "Back from where?"

Gael's hand slid from her shoulder, brushing needlessly over her arm. She didn't, couldn't, look at him. She could only imagine what Reeve would think of what she had done. She couldn't bear to see his face right now, or she would fall apart.

"Beacon's two weeks are up," Gael said. "He's gone recruiting."

CHAPTER TWENTY-THREE

ELARA

AFTER THE POINTLESS MEETINGS ELARA HAD SAT THROUGH, THE official declaration of war from the three nations would have come as a surprise. However, Iya's latest attack had made it a necessity that they stop arguing and put their signatures to paper.

As promised, Lightbringer had returned to Beacon after two weeks—and as promised he had severed another dragon bond. This time, however, when an ultramarine named Alzina had flown off with him after destroying a bridge and setting fire to several carriages, her Riders, Petra Rowland and Hanne Gifford, had ended up in the hospital. Unlike Signey, their souls had not survived being torn from their dragon bond. Unlike Signey, combat Professor Rowland and her daughter were now comatose.

In the aftermath, two Riders named Tonya Mantle and Grady Rivas had abandoned Langley to join Iya. Which meant he now had their dragon, Blaze, at his disposal, as well. Langley was down to three dragons: Stormborn, a sage dragon bonded to Giles Crawford and Arran Hyland; Nizsa, the sage dragon bonded to Professor Smithers and his husband; and Azeal, the carmine dragon

THIS ENDS IN EMBERS

bonded to Torrey and Jesper. Iya had eight: Lightbringer, Blaze, Alzina, Zephyra, Ignatz, Cruz, Goldeye, and Irontooth.

No one in their right mind would risk having to face down eight dragons without allies. The declaration had followed swiftly.

Signed by the leaders of each country, it promised swift and unforgiving retaliation against Iya if he didn't immediately cease his hostilities against Nova and its surrounding landmasses. Elara thought it a bit strange that they would leave the door open for him to attack the other continents—Epoch, Solaris, and Luna—or the islands of Kaere, Isalina, and Marién, but that part was at least predictable. After how hard Aveline and Professor Smithers had worked to get the leaders to care about their own people, it would be near impossible to get them to care about anyone else's.

Instead of going home, Elara had headed to Beacon with Signey. Torrey and Azeal had picked them up, their expressions grim, and Elara spent her days in meetings with Barret that she recapped for Aveline in a fire call at the end of every day. Luckily, Cherry had reacted with predictable indifference to not having Elara's help. "You would have just gotten in my way," she'd said on one fire call. "Just let me know if you find anything interesting in those Joyan books."

And so, four days passed without Iya's surrender. Elara sat in an armchair with her feet tucked under her, the fireplace roaring before her as she fire called the queen to discuss the upcoming retaliation. The National Hall was even emptier now that Iya had attacked Beacon twice, but all the fireplaces were lit whether a fire call was happening or not. It was the cold season, after all.

"For the flight to Hearthstone," said Aveline, "how many drakes will you need?"

"I don't think it's a good idea to send in any drakes," Elara replied, smoothing her skirts. "They take a long time to rebuild, and we'll need them all if this goes south."

"We cannot beg the empires for military aid and then refuse to send any of our own."

"We're not refusing. *I'm* our military aid."

Aveline was silent for a long moment. Then she laughed. "How did that feel to say?"

"Weird," Elara admitted, a smile tugging at her lips. "But I really do think we'll be fine. Joya del Mar and Étolia are sending armies. Torrey, Signey, and I will fly in on Azeal. I already know how to fight from dragonback, in case they can't get me on the ground. As long as we maintain the element of surprise, this could turn things in our favor without the drakes."

"I will trust your judgment then. And Elara?"

"Yes, Your Majesty?"

"Good luck."

Elara closed her eyes as the fire call ended, wishing she were back in San Irie like Aveline. Then again, Aveline was likely more equipped to deal with the protests there than Elara was, and Hearthstone was far closer to Langley than it was to San Irie. It made the most sense for her to be here to call on the gods if Iya came back, but there was so much going on. She was homesick for a home that would never again exist. Homesick for her simple, peaceful life, with her best friend and her sister.

"There you are," said Torrey, before raising her voice to someone out in the hallway. "I found her!"

That someone turned out to be Signey, who waltzed into the room in her riding leathers, her dark curly hair in a messy side

THIS ENDS IN EMBERS

braid. She and Torrey wore matching dragon ear cuffs, but while Torrey was, as always, wearing black lipstick and dark eye shadow to contrast with her pale skin and gold hair, Signey's lips were rose pink and her lids were lightly darkened with eye shadow. Her freckles were visible across her almond skin, making her look younger than usual.

Torrey darted across the room to grab the chair next to Elara's. Signey sank down on the arm of Elara's chair, engulfing Elara in her honeysuckle scent. Every breath was exquisite torture. They were no longer at odds, but they hadn't had the time to talk, either. She didn't know whether to lean in or away.

"Elara," said Torrey, her legs thrown over the side of her chair, "tell Signey she's a delight."

"You're a delight," Elara said automatically.

"I rest my case."

Signey rolled her eyes. "Torrey thinks the other Riders will let me break their dragon bonds if I just ask nicely. No one is *that* delightful."

"You met with them?" Elara asked.

Now Signey was looking down at her lap, tracing a seam in her fireproof trousers. The light in her eyes was smothered, like a candle blown out. "Right before Tonya and Grady left. It . . . went poorly."

"You can't blame yourself for those cowards switching sides," Torrey said fiercely. "Anyone who would join a genocidal dragon to keep their bond doesn't deserve one."

Signey curled in on herself. "I'm just . . . Maybe I could have said it a better way. If I'd been better—I practically drove them into the arms of the enemy. This isn't—I'm not—I don't know."

"I offered to let you break my bond first. That show of trust might be enough to sway them."

Signey was shaking her head before Torrey had even finished her sentence. "One broken bond is just a liability. Either we break all of them or none of them. I won't experiment with you on the *hope* that others will follow your lead. I can't even get them to follow mine."

The self-loathing that wrapped around Signey was so thick, Elara feared she would choke on it. Torrey's face was full of protective anger, but Elara just felt sad. Sometimes, she forgot that beneath Signey's walls and confidence was someone vulnerable and insecure about her ability to live up to her own standards.

She placed a hand on Signey's arm. "Torrey's right. You didn't turn them into traitors. They chose that path." She paused. "And you *are* delightful."

The corner of Signey's mouth curled upward. Just a little, but it was enough.

"I know Jesper would make some sort of grand speech," said Torrey. "So, in his absence, I'll do my best. You're a born leader, Signey. You hold it together when the rest of us are collapsing." Her blue eyes flicked to Elara. "Sometimes, you hold it together a little too well. But whether or not you trust us to catch you when you're falling apart, there isn't a person alive who can doubt how much you care about people. If you talk to them again, they'll see reason. I know it."

Elara was struck by the sudden realization that Signey and Torrey might have talked about her. About *them*.

Her cheeks reddened, but she forced herself to smile and nod. "That was a very good speech, Torrey."

THIS ENDS IN EMBERS

"Thank you." Torrey beamed. The smile didn't quite reach her eyes as usual, but Elara wasn't going to be the one to point that out.

Signey rolled onto her feet, her movements as sinuous as water. When she caught Elara watching her, she paused, uncertain, before giving her another small smile. Elara's longing was like a physical ache, and she couldn't muster up a smile in return. Instead, she watched as Torrey got up as well, too quickly to be natural. Elara glanced between them, wondering if either of them had been alone since Signey had lost her bond and Torrey had lost her co-Rider. If they were both compensating for the silence in their den by spending even more time together.

Her chest ached. She'd been so busy with the state of the world, she had forgotten to worry about her friends. Even now, beneath the part of her that was concerned and guilty was a part of her that hoped the two of them would be able to fight separately when the time came. Her empathy had become another casualty of war.

The thought chilled her to the bone.

Signey paused at the door after Torrey had left. "Are you going to be okay tomorrow? With your sister and everything?"

"Are you?" Elara volleyed back.

"Probably not."

"Yeah. Probably not."

Signey nodded as though that was the answer she had expected, and then she was gone. Elara stayed there long after her footsteps had faded, just staring into the fire. But no matter how much time passed, she couldn't get warm.

CHAPTER TWENTY-FOUR

FARON

ZEPHYRA WAS CHEWING ON A COW. OR, RATHER, WHAT WAS LEFT of a cow.

Luckily, Faron couldn't see her or the poor creature she'd likely picked up from the Highlands, but she could feel flashes of sensations. The faint taste of raw meat. The coppery smell of blood. Strong bones crushed beneath stronger molars. Her own dinner threatened to come back up, but Faron forced herself to cling to the faint string that connected her soul with Zephyra's—or, rather, Lightbringer's soul to all theirs.

It had been four days since her last lesson. She saw Briar Noble's pale face every time she closed her eyes, and, every time she drew a breath, smelled the blood and bile smeared across Estella Ballard's jaw. Iya had added two more dragons to his army—Alzina and Blaze—and Alzina, like Zephyra, spent most of her time as a mindless beast. Faron was not as familiar with Alzina's soul as she was with Zephyra's, so if she wanted to help them—if she wanted to help any of them—she had to start with Zephyra.

But just like the first time, there was nothing of Zephyra's soul for her to hold on to. She had one, but there was nothing but

THIS ENDS IN EMBERS

instinct driving it. Instinct and sensation, the brief flashes of an animal who could not be directed to act against its nature. Faron had believed, her whole life, that it was a dragon's nature to destroy, but now she knew better. Without a bond, dragons wanted only one thing: to survive.

And Faron still wasn't strong enough to override that with empathy.

She withdrew from Zephyra with a sigh, exhausted by her own uselessness. She had tried commanding Lightbringer's soul and abstaining from his kills. She had tried forcing his Riders to help her and shadowing him to Beacon to ensure he didn't burn it down. She had given his prisoner a piece of debris that served as a way to guard his mind from his captors. And it all felt like a spectacular waste of time, like trying to sabotage a military base by throwing pebbles at the fence. Nothing she did would make a difference until she found out what Lightbringer was really up to. Where did he go while he had Gael Soto teaching her the magic of the bond? And why did he want her to get stronger at all?

You forget that I was an actual soldier. I know a thing or two about strategy.

Faron tried to strategize. If she got stronger, Iya got stronger. Their souls were connected, and right now Iya considered her pathetically weak. With Jesper's blood and the right equipment, he could likely assess how strong a threat his descendants were to him. But that didn't explain the stolen dragon eggs or what Lightbringer was doing while Gael gave her lessons.

The pieces just weren't coming together for Faron. She wasn't like Elara and Reeve, who, combined, had read enough books that they were able to piece together a likely plan for Iya. They hadn't stopped him in the end, because there was only so much guesswork they could do when so much of their opponent was a mystery, but they had figured him out long before Faron had. Now, without them as resources, she felt as if she were groping in the dark, trying to find something to punch.

Had she really been effective only because she'd had someone else—the gods, the queen, even Gael—telling her what to do?

Before she could wade too far into self-loathing, Gael Soto's voice echoed across the bond: *"Your next lesson will be in the gym. See you soon."*

On the first floor of Hearthstone Academy was a gymnasium large enough for even a carmine to hover off the floor. Mats covered the metal floor and the walls, and high windows let sunlight stream in. Between each window was a gas lamp, presumably for practicing long after the sun had gone down. A small door led to what Faron assumed was a bathroom.

Gael waited inside with Marius Lynwood and Nichol Thompson. Her next opponents.

"The empires have united for a declaration of war," Gael told her as she came to a stop in front of them. "So this will be a short lesson."

"We're at *war*?" Technically, they had been at war this entire time, but she hadn't thought the empires would actually unite to declare it. "Do we even have time for lessons? Shouldn't we be having a meeting or—"

"That's not for you to worry about. Goldeye and Lightbringer are patrolling, and the other Riders are ensuring that we're

THIS ENDS IN EMBERS

prepared for a siege. All you need to focus on is your lesson." Faron opened her mouth, only for Gael to press two fingers to her lips. "That's not focusing. If you're not careful, they'll actually beat you."

"Thanks for your confidence," Lynwood sneered. Unlike Noble and Ballard, he didn't seem inclined to show Gael any respect just because Gael shared a body with his saint. "Just promise me again that we won't be in trouble if we put her in the infirmary."

Thompson, as usual, said nothing to either back up or stop his cousin. He just watched Faron with a furrow between his dark eyebrows.

Faron tried to spark the anger she'd felt with Ballad and Noble, the anger that staved off the empty hopelessness that gripped her when she thought of how long she'd been among these people and how little she'd actually done to help anyone. How even the empires had managed to mobilize quickly enough that Lightbringer was concerned, while she was no closer to figuring out his ultimate plan. She had nothing but her will to live, and, when Lynwood and Thompson attacked her, every move she made felt automatic. She barely had the energy to reach for their souls, and they fought her off easily.

"*What's wrong?*" Gael asked. He stood with his hands behind his back and his head tilted curiously. "*You're not even trying.*"

Faron ignored him to duck out of the way of a fire-wrapped kick. Saying *everything* felt far too dramatic, even for her. After the first real time she had wielded her power to command living souls, on the two Iryan men who were just drunk enough to beat Reeve to death if she hadn't stopped them, Gael hadn't understood her concerns. He'd questioned why she would worry about two men she didn't know and would never see again, and she'd had to explain to him that it was normal—even encouraged—for her to care about other people.

With the world against her, Reeve trapped, and Elara far away, Faron didn't have the energy to have that conversation again. Her own faith in humanity was too weak.

Her faith in *herself* was too weak.

She yelped as the side of her face exploded with pain. Jumping back, she touched her cheek and flinched at the burn already twisting her skin. Lynwood grinned, all teeth, so proud of getting past her guard.

"Power is wasted on people like you," he said, fire winding around his arms in tendrils of red and gold. "You have no idea how the world works. You want it to be 'fair,' which just means you hate it when anyone stands out." The fire traced his shoulders and surrounded his head like a halo of flames. "But you need to realize that some people were just born better than others. Stronger. More powerful. There are things you can never grasp, no matter how hard you work for it, because it's an inherent skill. Like the right to rule."

"I hope you're not talking about yourself," Faron spat, falling back into a defensive stance on the mats. "You're not even fit to rule a nursery."

Lynwood chuckled, though there was no humor in it. "My family goes back generations. We can trace our lineage to the first dragon Riders. There has never been a Lynwood who wasn't chosen by a dragon, as long as there was an open dragon to bond with. The blood of rulers runs through my veins. And you? You are nothing and no one."

THIS ENDS IN EMBERS

"And whose fault is that?" Anger finally cut through the numbness like a hot knife through butter. It was easy for Lynwood to be proud of where he came from—*who* he came from—because he knew. Faron didn't even know what her family's name had been before they'd been taken to San Irie to be enslaved. An entire history had been erased by imperialists like him, who bred all over Nova like rabbits. Faron, her eyes narrowed, snuffed out the flames that wrapped around her fist. "Of course you don't respect hard work, if everything has always come so easily to you. My ancestors worked and bled and died for me to be standing here today, and that doesn't make them lesser than you or me. Their hard work made them strong. It made me strong."

She reached for his soul with the force of what felt like generations of rage. Existing in a world built by people who thought like Marius Lynwood would always leave a stain, an anger that could never be healed. She wielded that anger against him now, submerging his soul beneath her will. He twisted, his face growing redder the harder he tried to fight her off, but Faron's fury was as uncontainable as a dragon's.

"You're the one who's nothing," she hissed. *"Say it."*

Blood dripped from his nose and then from his eyes. He gritted his teeth, but the words still fell out of him. "I'm nothing."

From behind him, Thompson ran forward, but Faron threw up a hand. A circle of flame surrounded him, keeping him busy until she was ready for him. Lynwood was on his knees now, screaming. His soul was still fighting, but she was stronger; she was so much stronger than he had ever imagined, and she would make him regret making her sister ever feel small. Making *her* ever feel small.

"You don't deserve anything you were born with," Faron

225

continued, reaching as far down into his soul as she could. There was a tangle of light there, the part of him that was connected to Iya and the other Generals, the part of him that was connected to Thompson and Goldeye, and the part of him that was commanded not to help her contact her sister. She couldn't get close enough to even touch that part of him, not without losing herself in the process, but she pressed a command of her own into his very being: *Suffer. Every second of every day, I want you to suffer.*

She withdrew just in time for Lynwood to collapse on the mats, his head covered with blood.

Faron dropped the flames that trapped Thompson and stared him down. His eyes jumped between her and his cousin, and she wanted to take him down, too, so badly, it was as if someone were commanding *her.* But Lynwood was the bigger pain in her ass. Thompson was just as dangerous, thanks to his inaction, but that same inaction meant she had nothing specific to punish him for. She lowered her hands and nodded once; he raced to his cousin's side, calling Lynwood's name and checking his pulse.

Gael came up beside her. "Your methods are getting more brutal."

"I suppose you like that," Faron muttered, not taking her eyes off Lynwood. Even his ears were bleeding. Had she pickled his brain? "I was just angry."

"I understand. Believe me, I understand better than you might think." He looked down at his hands, clenching one into a fist. "When Lightbringer and I first bonded, my temper grew. I'd saved the world, and it felt like everyone was ungrateful because of how I'd done it. My family was wary of the bond. The people were wary of the dragon. The gods refused to speak to me. I'd won, and in so doing, I'd lost everything. And it made me furious."

THIS ENDS IN EMBERS

Faron swallowed. "Is that why you became a tyrant? Because you didn't get thanked enough?"

"Realizing that caring what people thought was holding me back from my full potential isn't tyranny, Faron," Gael said with a small smile. "Being bonded with a megalomaniacal dragon who decides that if we cannot be loved, then we can certainly rule through fear is, however." His hands dropped to his sides, and he turned away from the carnage she had wrought within Marius Lynwood. "I never wanted to rule over anyone. I just wanted to be powerful enough that no one could hurt my loved ones again." He glanced at her over his shoulder. "It's a slippery slope, isn't it?"

Faron felt as if she'd been punched. Wouldn't she have made the same choice? To give in to a power stronger than any she had ever known if it meant keeping Elara safe?

Wasn't that what she had already done?

"Now, look at yourself," Gael continued. "Look at how you suffer. You don't know how frustrating it is to watch you tear yourself apart to satisfy people who only care about what you can do for them. No one cared about Deadegg until you became the Childe Empyrean.

"No one cares about you now that you're not the Childe Empyrean. If you're not perfect every second of every day, then you're their villain. Don't you find that maddening?"

She wanted to clench her eyes shut. She wanted to run. She wanted to cry. She felt flayed open, her nerves raw and open for him to see. Emotion erupted from her like the hot lava of a volcano, devastating every other thought.

"Of course I find it maddening," she snapped. "I find it *infuriating*, actually. I go to bed and wake up screaming. I go through my day biting back a scream. I know there's no winning. I've lived it. I'm living it."

Her breathing came in harsh pants. She had made mistakes, ones she could never make up for, but Elara and Reeve were the only ones who hadn't immediately thought the worst of her. And Iya, she supposed, but every mistake she had made had helped him in some way, so she didn't think to count him.

Faron wanted penance. She wanted absolution. She wanted Lightbringer stopped. She wanted her sister back. But that didn't mean there wasn't a small, cruel part of her that raged against this new box they had wedged her into—that raged against how easily she had been discarded by people she had risked her life for at the tender age of twelve. She hated that Gael was the only one who saw that. Who felt it.

A sting of pain made her realize she was clenching her fists hard enough for her nails to break the skin. She flexed her fingers, swallowing back a wave of shame so thick, it could drag her under.

Gael had the nerve to smile. "Temper, temper."

"Piss off."

He chuckled as he walked away, pausing just long enough for Thompson to drag Lynwood's unmoving body through the entrance.

Once they were gone, Faron sat down right where she stood. She didn't recognize herself these days, and she feared that Elara wouldn't, either.

CHAPTER TWENTY-FIVE
ELARA

A SENSE OF FINALITY FOLLOWED ELARA THROUGH THE MORNING OF the battle. The empires may have dragged their feet leading up to the treaty and declaration of war, but they had wasted no time in moving on Hearthstone. Elara put on her riding leathers with a smile on her face, ready to fight in a way she never had been before. She had no love for war, but she didn't think of this as a war.

It was an ending.

Now, she was sandwiched between Torrey and Signey, strapped into the saddle as Azeal flew them down the coast toward their first stop, the Emerald Highlands. The Crown Sea was a silver-and-cerulean line against the gold and jade of the continent. It writhed like a snake, consuming the shore before spitting it back out. The glimpses she caught of the sea between the clouds took her breath away, but her anxiety was like a living thing in her chest, straining to get out.

They could get Jesper and Faron back today.

They could stop Iya today.

Everything could end *today*.

Unless she failed again, of course. But even if she did, they were not the only ones headed to the Highlands right now. The Étolian, Joyan, and Langlish armies were marching on the occupied cities, and their navies were making their way to the Hestan Archipelago. She, Torrey, and Signey were just the first wave, meant to distract as many dragons as possible while rescuing the prisoners if they could. Elara just hoped she could turn that *if* into a *when*.

She tightened her arms around Torrey's waist and sent up a prayer to the gods, even while knowing she would be channeling them soon. *Please let us weaken Iya's forces. Please let us find my sister. Please let us win.*

As if he could hear her, Azeal spread his wings wider and glided below the clouds, where the Highlands unspooled before them like a green blanket interrupted by blue-silver mountain peaks. And already waiting for them, like shadows beneath the setting sun, were four dragons.

Alzina and Zephyra hovered at the flank of the V formation, snarling at the prospect of hunting a new meal. Blaze, ridden by Tonya Mantle and Grady Rivas, was in the left center, his golden wings pumping in excitement. Beside him was a second medallion, one Elara recognized as Cruz, who was bonded to Headmaster Oscar Luxton and his daughter, Margot. She had often seen him poking around the beaches in search of something shiny to play with during her time at Hearthstone.

Azeal drew up short, hesitating in a way Elara had never known the dragon to do. "He doesn't want to hurt Zephyra," Torrey called back to them. "Or make Signey watch as he hurts Zephyra."

"Can you land us? Elara and I can handle the B mission," Signey said.

There was something off about her voice, but Elara had no time

THIS ENDS IN EMBERS

to sort through it. The dragons were approaching, and Azeal was already soaring out of their reach. He'd crested the clouds again, and his massive wingspan ate up several yards before he dived. Elara's stomach dropped as they did, but she forced her eyes to stay open behind her goggles so she could keep track of the dragons. She didn't want to call on the gods until they were closer to Hearthstone. She didn't want to risk being exhausted by the time she faced Iya.

Fire followed them down, raining from the mouths of the medallion dragons. Zephyra zipped after them, quick as lightning, until she came up alongside Azeal. Her teeth were bared, her eyes cold. She twisted toward them, slamming into Azeal's side and knocking the carmine off course. Alzina waited for them, loosing flames that scorched Azeal's hind legs. He roared and dropped again, leaving Zephyra to collide with Alzina on the next strike.

"Come on, come on," Torrey whispered under her breath. Her hands tightened on the reins, but she and Azeal were clearly communicating across the bond. He banked abruptly, making Elara and Signey bounce in the saddle as Zephyra appeared in front of them again.

Once, Zephyra's speed had been an asset. Now it was their greatest threat. They would never make it to the ground with a sage in their way.

"Go," she heard Signey shout, seconds before the wind gushed up Elara's back.

Elara twisted in the saddle to see Signey jumping off Azeal's side, her arms out wide. Elara screamed, but Signey had given herself an extra kick on the launch. She landed on Zephyra's side, skidding down a few inches before her fireproof gloves found purchase in Zephyra's scales. The sage roared indignantly, twisting to shake loose the new weight, but Signey was climbing with the kind of stubborn determination that said she would die before she let go.

"What are you doing?" Elara shouted. "This isn't the plan!"

"I'm not leaving her!" Signey shouted back. "And you can't leave while she's here! Just go!"

"Signey!"

"GO!"

Torrey went, urging Azeal into another dive against Elara's protests. Zephyra had no saddle, and Signey did not have the magic of the bond to give her perfect balance on dragonback. They were so high up that if Zephyra dropped her, Signey would die. She would die, and Elara suddenly regretted the way they had left things, regretted that Signey could die here without knowing that Elara . . . that Elara—

"She'll be okay," Torrey said as the ground rushed up to meet them. "She's the best soldier we have, remember?"

"Did you know about this?"

Instead of answering, Torrey brought them down hard. Azeal landed at a run, coming to a halt inches away from the ocean. Elara unstrapped herself as quickly as she could, her eyes on the sky. Cruz and Blaze were only yards away, and she could see their mouths were open, revealing their razor-sharp teeth, their darkened maws. As soon as she jerkily slid to the sand, Azeal took off again, leading the other dragons deeper into the Highlands.

Elara couldn't see Zephyra. She and Signey were too high up. Anxiety crawled over her skin, but she had to trust Signey to take care of herself. She had to stick to the dregs of the plan.

THIS ENDS IN EMBERS

She dragged her eyes back to the ground and broke out in a smile. The plains weren't empty. Soldiers in the colors of their respective countries had joined the fight. Joyan soldiers lifted whole chunks of the ground into the air and sent them hurtling toward the dragons. Alzina, who had been felled by one such attack, was surrounded by twenty Étolian soldiers who swung at her with swords. Langlish soldiers with fireproof shields covered their heads as Cruz rained down blasts upon them, and every break in his attack gave them the opportunity to return fire of their own. Their relics were like a thousand little suns.

Elara, Torrey, and Signey had been successful. The dragons had been so focused on Azeal, they hadn't noticed the soldiers crossing into the Highlands until it was too late. And now Torrey and Signey didn't have to fight alone.

Elara had to do her part before the tides began to turn.

Across Serpentia Bay, she could just see two dragons, the size of birds at this distance, as they soared across the sky, likely patrolling for threats like her. She didn't see Lightbringer, whose body would be at least twice as large, so she had to hope that he and Iya were there. That Faron was there. And, if not, that she could find Jesper and free him before they returned.

Elara took a deep breath and called on the gods. Irie appeared to her in an instant, nodding once before settling beneath Elara's skin. Her raw power obliterated Elara's anxiety, leaving her nothing but fierce determination. Her ears were full of roars and growls. Her body still felt the heat of the dodged fireballs. And her heart was racing from adrenaline and fear. But with Irie's magic at her fingertips, she could do anything. She would do everything she could to bring her sister home.

Fishing boats were tied to a dock. Elara loosed one and climbed in. The oars were tossed to the bottom as she leaned over to place her hands in the rippling water. Irie's magic flowed through her—down her arms, and out of her fingertips. The force of Irie's light sent the boat jetting across the bay, much faster than if she'd rowed it herself.

A shadow passed over her head. Alzina had enough time to tip back her head before Azeal slammed into her side, stopping her from setting Elara and her fishing boat aflame. Elara poured more magic into the water, her eyes on the shore of Caledon, the first island in the archipelago.

Her mind worked quickly. She was an easy target for any dragon that Torrey couldn't catch in time, and Alzina was already recovering and chasing after her. She could stop and fight back, but that might draw the attention of the two dragons at Hearthstone. If they destroyed her boat, she would have to swim, and even with Irie's power that would exhaust her. The element of surprise was still on her side, for now, and she needed to keep it if she wanted any chance of getting to Jesper.

The dragons collided again. One of them yelped in pain.

Elara's boat scraped across the sand before coming to a rattling stop near the landing field. She jumped out, checking the sky again.

Irontooth and Ignatz—a carmine and an ultramarine—were already flying toward her. She saw no sign of Goldeye or Lightbringer, but Hearthstone was a massive fortress. They could easily be hiding within the courtyard or somewhere on the other side of the building. They could even have been on one of the other islands, rallying those who had joined their forces for the ground offensive that would soon follow.

THIS ENDS IN EMBERS

It was just like the San Irie Revolution, except that she was more powerful this time. She was older, better at analyzing her enemies. Every fight had felt like her last back then, and she'd been shaking as she summoned, waiting for the blow that would take her down. She had been a child in oversize armor, sick with fear and trying to ignore it because if her sister could do this, then she *would* do this. At eighteen, Elara was still that scared little girl, but she was also a determined young woman. She was the Maiden Empyrean. She had seen that dragons could be defeated and that she could survive even the most impossible odds.

That kind of knowledge was powerful. It made her powerful.

She would not let an enemy take anything else from her.

She would fight for her country, her sister, her best friend. She would fight for herself.

Elara surrounded her hands with discs of conjured light, each as sharp as blades, and threw them back-to-back in the direction of those dragons. If they thought her easy prey because she was alone, they would quickly learn just what a nuisance she could be. She was already running for Hearthstone by the time they dodged, and their world-shaking roars chased her before she heard the flap of their wings on her trail.

I'm coming, Faron, she thought as she darted across the grass, her heart in her throat and anger in her blood. *I'm coming.*

CHAPTER TWENTY-SIX

FARON

"T HEIR FORCES HAVE ARRIVED ON THE SHORE," IYA SAID CALMLY. "Would you like to come, or would you like to sit this one out?"

They were in the gymnasium, Faron running through more drills designed to refine her control over her flames. Gael had wanted to set up a lesson with Tonya Mantle and Grady Rivas or Oscar and Margot Luxton, but Faron was getting tired of making people bleed. Faron loved to win: games and bets, races and arguments. But sending Iya's Riders to the infirmary didn't feel like a victory. It felt like a step into a spreading darkness that kept her awake at night, terrified of what she was becoming. Terrified that this kind of power was never meant to be used on human souls at all.

Gael had rejected her request to practice her soul magic on the dragons instead, and so these drills were their compromise. Once again, he had refused to tell her where Lightbringer had gone and what Lightbringer was planning, while insisting the most important thing was for Faron to focus on getting stronger. Once again, Faron had pretended to listen, if only because she wanted to be able to set Iya on fire without him being able to fight her off.

THIS ENDS IN EMBERS

Right now, it would barely delay him, would hurt her more than it hurt his plans. But one day, if she waited until the exact moment it would make a difference, Iya *would* burn to ashes. Even if it meant she burned with him.

Faron had no idea how long they had been there, but she'd spent enough time with Gael Soto to know that he was no longer the one speaking. Iya was already walking toward the door, giving her no time to check if his eyes had returned to Reeve's blue, but his voice had that edge to it. That jagged point that promised danger for anyone in his way.

"I'm coming," Faron said, jogging after him with only a second's hesitation. If nothing else, she might be able to use the distraction to send a message to her sister.

Lightbringer was waiting in the courtyard, his back to them. The entrance, Faron noticed, was on fire, and the portcullis lowered so that anyone who tried to come through anyway would find themselves trapped. Iya climbed into the saddle and helped Faron up; they took to the air before she could even strap herself in. Behind them, Goldeye took their spot in the courtyard, looking like a spill of blood before the keep.

Lightbringer flew in an arc around the island, allowing her to see the scale of what they were dealing with. Black, blue, and gold dots resolved themselves into Étolian soldiers, swarming through the streets like marbles spilling from a cloth bag. They came from the bay and they came from Margon, the next island in the archipelago. The conscripted on the other islands were fighting back, clearly afraid of what Lightbringer would do if they didn't. But the black ships anchored on all sides of the island were releasing a second wave of soldiers to march on Hearthstone. More boats with billowing sails approached from Nova, and each one flew the flag of Joya del Mar.

"*Is Langley here, too?*" she asked Iya through the bond.

"*They're on the continent, not here,*" he replied. "*I'd rather resolve this before that changes.*"

"*You let them get pretty close,*" Faron noted.

"*The cruelest defeat is when you think you're close to victory.*"

Disturbed, Faron turned her attention back to the ground below. Ignatz was in the sky over Margon to provide support to their soldiers. Lightbringer's massive jaw widened as he flew toward the city and belched fire over the platoon crossing the bridge that spanned from Margon to Caledon. Faron's stomach dropped, but when the flames cleared, they were all still there, their faces upturned to assess the dragon's position. An off-white barrier shimmered over their heads, and Faron could swear she saw eyes and a mouth in the swirls of light before it disappeared.

Was that a Joyan nature spirit?

A squad of soldiers broke off, making complex gestures with their hands. Fire erupted in columns around them, shooting upward. Lightbringer swerved to avoid the blasts, but the flames moved like a snake, trailing him through the air with a flickering gullet. Another squad broke off and pointed their hands at boulders, wiggling them loose from the beach to fling at Lightbringer. These were no inexperienced civilians protecting their homes as best they could with the resources they had. These were people acclimated to war, with the power and reflexes to match.

San Irie had never fought all the empires at once, and Faron was suddenly, profoundly grateful for that. The kind of magic being wielded was unlike anything she'd seen before, and there were so

THIS ENDS IN EMBERS

many soldiers, they actually stood a chance at winning. Instead of being happy, a hard pit formed in her stomach. There was something she didn't like about the empires doing what she had been trying to do, but it was hard to put a finger on it with everything going on.

Iya twisted in her arms, but she didn't need to see what he was seeing. She could feel the heat from the fire still chasing them, making sweat roll down her back and her clothes stick to her damp skin. He threw his own flames around her, misshapen lumps of heat meant to sweep the others off course. Lightbringer dipped beneath them as a boulder connected with his stomach, and the roar that followed shook Faron to her core.

This was the end. This really could be the end. The combined nations could defeat Iya here and now, and she would be free to return home.

Home to an island that hated her.

In the custody of people who considered her a conspirator.

Without Reeve free to go with her.

Faron clenched her eyes shut. It was better for them to stop Iya now, she told herself. It was what Reeve would want. Maybe it was even better for her to answer for her crimes. She'd thought she could do more good at Iya's side than at home, but all she had done for weeks was cause more pain. Maybe the Warwicks should finally get their wish to see her imprisoned in the Mausoleum, where she couldn't hurt anyone ever again.

Her very soul rebelled against the idea of them winning, even in this small way. Everything she had done was for nothing if she didn't save Reeve. She had fought the war for nothing if she fell right into Langlish hands.

The pit in her stomach grew even harder. Her throat closed at the realization that plunged through her. Iya could not lose here. Because, if he did, Faron would lose everything. Her life. Her love. *Everything.*

She opened her eyes and drew on the power of their bond.

Iya snuffed out the fireball growing in his hand and met her gaze. He studied her, *felt* her, in the span of seconds. Then he faced front and began aiming his flames at the oncoming rocks instead. Faron twisted in the saddle and sent a wave of fire at the red-orange snake still curving through the sky toward them. It tried to dodge, but she shot another with her free hand and then brought the two waves together with the flame snake in the center. Her dragon-fire collided with the nature spirit's fire, and it felt like punching a brick wall.

Her palms burned. Her bones shook. Her breath stuttered.

"Hang in there," Iya said, feeding her more power. *"You're doing so well."*

Her flames burned hotter. She heard a high-pitched shriek, and then the fire snake collapsed into ashes that fell like snowflakes down onto the path. They would only conjure another, she was certain, and she would run low on energy eventually. Lightbringer might have been the First Dragon, but nothing was infinite but the gods— and even, still, she was only human and far from infinite herself.

She unstrapped herself from the saddle, telling herself one more time that she was doing the right thing. Or the wrong thing, but for the right reasons.

Lightbringer dived as low as he could without taking a boulder to the face, and Faron leaped to the ground before he pulled back up. She landed flame-first, slapping her burning palms against the

THIS ENDS IN EMBERS

ground. The earth split beneath her, cracking in a honeycomb pattern outlined by bubbling red, and racing beneath the feet of the oncoming soldiers. She smelled burning leather, burning skin. She heard curses; she heard screams. She saw the ground blackening beneath the onslaught of dragonfire, never to yield life again.

Heat wafted into the air, making it ripple, as the soldiers whose feet weren't welded to the ground tried to scramble back the way they'd come. She had poisoned the ground and the air, rendering it useless for the spirits they needed to summon. She had made it too hot for them to risk conjuring another flame, and they were too far from the ocean to do anything about it.

Faron stood up, staring down the soldiers who remained, the ones assessing her as a threat they could still take down in hand-to-hand combat.

"My name is Faron Vincent," she said, "once called the Childe Empyrean. Langley learned to fear me when I was only twelve years old. Do you really want to know why?" Her fingers flexed at her sides before she summoned two fireballs around her rising fists. "Or do you want to go home to your families alive?"

Above her, Lightbringer unleashed a mighty roar, his shadow large enough to swallow them all.

The crowd rippled, but no one approached her. Faron had just begun to conjure another flame when the soldiers parted to reveal the one person she wanted to see and the last person she wanted to see her like *this*.

"Faron?" Elara breathed out. Her hair was newly braided into a side ponytail, her body wrapped in Langlish dragon leathers like Faron's. Her brown eyes were wide, so wide, and there was fear in them. She was *afraid* of Faron. "What are you *doing*?"

"I'm—" Faron smothered her growing flames. Her pulse pounded loud in her ears. "Reeve is still trapped in there. I can't leave him, Elara."

"We can save him together. We can do this *together*." Elara lifted her hands, the way one would before a startled horse. She took a step closer, and Faron stumbled back. "You don't need to work with him, Faron. Come back with me. Please come back."

"I—I can't."

"What?"

Lightbringer roared again, a thunderous threat. Faron could see what he was going to do before he did it, the spill of fire, the smoking flesh. Her sister, too focused on Faron to look up. Her sister, a casualty of her bad choices.

"I can't leave him," Faron said again. She lifted her hands. "I know how it looks. But I'm the only one who can do this, Elara. Our lives are connected. I'm the only one he'll let this close, so I *have* to stay. I need to save Reeve. For both of us."

"Faron, you *don't* have to do this alone!"

"You have to go. He'll kill you!"

"Faron!"

"He took Jesper's blood. I don't know why. Follow the blood!"

Lightbringer opened his maw, and fire erupted from his gullet. Before Elara could say another word, Faron turned her head away and slammed into her sister's soul. Elara gasped, stumbling backward into the arms of a soldier, and Faron hated it, hated how just the feel of Elara's soul was enough to comfort her, hated that she was using this power against her sister at all. There was no coming back from this. There was no forgiveness. There was just Elara, her mouth open, staring at Faron as though she were a stranger,

THIS ENDS IN EMBERS

and there was Faron, burrowing past her sister's defenses, telling her, *Go. Go now.*

The flames approached as if in slow motion. Faron's stomach twisted.

With seconds to spare, Elara—sweating and breathing hard—ran away. The soldiers retreated with her, but only some of them made it. The field disappeared beneath the smell of smoke and burning flesh.

Faron gagged. At some point, she had fallen to her knees. The lingering feeling of Elara's soul—all that warmth, all the goodness—only served to remind her of how cold and corrupted her own soul was. Of course she was Iya's co-Rider. Their souls were the same. They were the same.

When it came down to it, they would always choose to exert their power over those weaker than themselves—no matter the cost.

She'd known that rewriting her sister's free will was wrong, and she had still done it. To keep her safe. A well-intentioned betrayal was still a betrayal.

"I'm sorry," she said, her voice breaking. She didn't know when she'd started crying, but she buried her face in her hands and continued. "I'm sorry, I'm sorry, I'm sorry. . . ."

Let the soldiers take her. Let Lightbringer burn her. Her life was meant to end in embers. It was all she deserved.

CHAPTER TWENTY-SEVEN

ELARA

ELARA FELT AS IF SHE'D BEEN BLUDGEONED WITH THE WOODEN END of a machete.

The pain hit her body first and then consumed her heart until she was bent over trying not to cry. It was devastating, to live in a world where she and Faron were on opposite sides. It was shattering, to see Faron attacking her own cavalry to keep Iya safe—to keep herself and Reeve safe. It had broken her heart to leave Faron behind, so close yet so far, because her sister believed that she could do the most good by Iya's side. Even if she was right, Elara couldn't get over how worn down Faron had looked. That fire that lived inside her had been reduced to a single ember. There was no hope in her eyes, no confidence in her appearance.

Faron was destroying herself for other people. And she refused to let Elara help her.

Elara wasn't even angry that Faron had taken control of her body. Maybe she should have been, but that was the least of her concerns. The hold that Iya had on her sister was almost complete, and Elara hadn't gotten the chance to tell Faron that she loved her.

THIS ENDS IN EMBERS

If she had stayed any longer, Lightbringer would have reduced them all to ash.

Elara remained hunched over until her breath didn't come out shaky. Then she assessed where she was. It was an infirmary of some kind, and she was in bed. Someone had changed her out of her riding leathers and into a nightgown, though she still wore her underclothes. A satin sleep cap protected her braids from the cotton pillow.

She was physically safe, but her emotions felt out of control. It had taken weeks. Weeks to set up the conference. Weeks to reach a resolution. Weeks to plan the offensive against Iya. She had sat through some of the most pointless arguments in the world, just in the hope of the leaders seeing reason and coming together for a greater good. She had been berated and mistrusted by the gods, she'd been miles away from her home and her parents, and she'd listened to accusations against her sister that made her want to vomit. And for what? *For what?*

They had recovered some of the towns in the Emerald Highlands, but the rest was still occupied and Faron, Reeve, Jesper, and Zephyra were still gone. Every time she tried to make a difference, Elara was forced to acknowledge that she was a *failure*. She couldn't save the world. She couldn't save her own family.

Maiden Empyrean? No. She was a child dressed as a saint, leaving nothing but wreckage in her wake.

Elara reached behind her for a pillow and buried her face in it. It smelled of mint and herbal soap. She screamed until her throat felt raw.

"You're up," said Signey.

She was standing in the doorway for the briefest second before

Torrey pushed her farther into the room. Right behind Torrey were Professor Smithers and Barret Soto. Barret was carrying a folder that he kept checking, as if he'd been called from a meeting. Professor Smithers just looked relieved, though his suit implied that he, too, had been attending a meeting. Torrey's eyes were hollowed, the shadows beneath too deep to have been caused by her kohl makeup; nonetheless, she smiled to see Elara awake.

It wasn't Faron and Reeve, her parents and the queen, but Elara somehow felt as if she were surrounded by family anyway.

Then she remembered they'd all seen her scream into a pillow, and her face burned. She put back the pillow slowly, blushing even harder when Signey sped up to fluff it for her. Signey's own cheeks looked redder than usual, as if she didn't want an audience.

"Listen, before anything else, I want to apologize," she said, her voice low. It wasn't low enough for Torrey not to hear, but she made a show of looking at the walls to give the illusion of privacy. "What I said about your sister—"

"She manipulated my soul, too," Elara said dully. "I understand why you were upset. It feels very invasive."

"No. Well, yes. But no. The doctors caring for Professor Rowland have reported some interesting findings. Her soul is in tatters from having her bond ripped away, but mine isn't. Why?" Signey stared her down, then made an impatient sound when Elara didn't come up with an answer. "The only difference between what happened to Professor Rowland and what happened to me is your sister. Faron wasn't trying to manipulate my soul. She was the only thing that held me together when I lost Zephyra."

Elara blinked. "So, that means..."

"You were right. Iya is intentionally severing the bonds to cause

THIS ENDS IN EMBERS

as much damage as possible," said Torrey, sitting on the edge of Elara's bed. At least she didn't pretend she hadn't been listening. "If you think of our souls as pieces of fabric, Iya is tearing them, leaving them frayed and unusable. To save Signey, your sister turned it into more of a cut, all even lines and smooth recovery."

Elara wanted to cry again. While Elara had been trapped at Hearthstone, Iya had taught Faron how to command living souls; Elara didn't know if Iya was still training Faron, but it was clear that she had found another beneficial use for that power. That didn't make Faron any less trapped, but it was still a relief to have a concrete way she had been resisting Iya's influence.

"Wait." She sat up straighter. "Did Cherry call while I was out? Before she—before we parted, Faron said that Iya took some of Jesper's blood. Do you think—?"

"As a matter of fact, Lance Corporal McKay *did* fire call us," said Barret, leaning against the doorjamb. "With the additional samples we provided to her, including from our remaining dragons, she was able to confirm that Signey can, in fact, break dragon bonds. When Signey's blood was added to that of bonded dragons and their Riders, it consistently resulted in the two samples losing any similarities. Or, put another way, the dragon blood retained its magic while the human blood, well, did not."

Elara looked at Signey. Signey stared back, allowing Elara to see the flicker of fear in her eyes.

"I've been reading your books for any clues about how it works," Signey whispered, "but no one seems to have written down any instructions about blood magic. But I'm still willing. Especially since Jesper is still..."

The mood in the room dropped as Barret and Torrey looked

away. Elara felt the guilt of her failure all over again, but for once she let it motivate her instead of paralyze her. The rescue mission may have been a failure, but they had dealt the first blow against Iya and established themselves as a threat. Even better, they had enough information to start piecing together his ultimate goal—and use Signey as a weapon against him.

The time for brooding was over. She cleared her throat until everyone's attention was on her again.

"Faron also said we should follow the blood," she said. "Is it possible to track the vial of Jesper's blood somehow?"

"If we use a dragon relic for tracking, maybe...," Torrey murmured. "We might be able to figure out what he's done with it and why."

"I'll get some relics from the lab," Barret said.

"I think it's better if we use some scales from Azeal," Elara pointed out. "Jesper's connection to Azeal hasn't been severed yet, right? Which means that's the closest we can get to using his blood ourselves."

Professor Smithers nodded. "A sound idea. In the meantime, we'll have the scientists look further into the kind of magic that blood could be used for, beyond severing bonds." He gave Elara a small smile. "I'm glad to see you're all right, Miss Vincent. I know you're quite used to risking your life, but that life means far more to us than you can imagine."

The three of them went off to their assigned tasks, leaving Signey and Elara alone in the infirmary room.

"Do not cry," Signey said.

"A teacher likes me," Elara said wetly. "I'll cry whenever I want. You're not my mother."

THIS ENDS IN EMBERS

Signey rolled her eyes and moved toward one of the tables. She returned with a bandage, which she handed to Elara to use as a handkerchief.

"Your sister isn't the only thing I want to apologize for," Signey blurted. Elara, who was usually the one blurting out things, found this unspeakably endearing. "Zephyra didn't recognize me at all. I didn't realize that part of me expected her to, until she dropped me in the ocean, but I had a lot of time to think while I was falling. I'm fine—I healed more quickly than you."

Elara dragged her eyes up from Signey's body to her face. She realized she'd lifted the bandage, as if Signey could still use it with her snot in it, and dropped her hand.

"Anyway, I had a lot of time to think, and what I thought about was how much time I've wasted. I could have died. You could have died. And instead of spending any time together, I've been avoiding you. Avoiding this." She gestured between them. "At first, I thought it was better not to risk disappointing you when there was a war going on. And then I thought that with Zephyra and Jesper gone, why did I deserve to be happy? But in those two seconds I thought I was going to die, all I could think about was you."

Elara had no idea what to say to that, so she just said nothing. Hope beat like a bird's wings through her chest.

"I'm going to be more than a bit crap at this," said Signey, drawing closer step-by-bashful-step. "I'm never going to be good at the feelings and the opening up. But I don't want to risk losing you before we can see what this could be. Because I think...I think we could be something pretty amazing."

"I think so, too," Elara said weakly. "Stop talking about your feelings and kiss me."

Signey leaned over to kiss her, and Elara melted into it. She poured everything she had been feeling into that kiss, and she felt Signey give her the same right back. More, perhaps. Signey's hand held her cheek so gently, her mouth a furnace, and Elara simply allowed herself to be cherished and kissed within an inch of her life.

At some point, they fell backward, and Elara was trapped between her girlfriend's lithe body and the soft bed. She could think of nowhere else she'd rather be.

Signey pulled away, breathing as if it were optional. "Thanks for giving me a second chance."

"You kiss me like that again, and I'll give you a third one."

Signey sat up with a laugh, leaving the front of Elara's body cold. She realized her fingers were still tangled in her girlfriend's curls and slowly extracted herself, even though it was the last thing she wanted to be doing. With Signey on top of her, kissing her, holding her, everything that had led her to this infirmary bed felt a little more manageable.

She hadn't wanted to become a drake pilot because she enjoyed working alone, after all.

"No strenuous activity until you're fully recovered," Signey said, smoothing down her curls as she stood. "We need you for something important, and you'll want to be in peak health for this one."

Elara tipped her head back with a groan. "Please, no more blood."

"I can't promise that. We're at war." Signey's eyes burned like kindling. "But there are some people it's time for you to meet."

PART III
SISTER

CHAPTER TWENTY-EIGHT

FARON

FARON JOLTED AWAKE WHEN SHE FELT A SUDDEN DRAIN ON HER energy, as if it were being tugged from her body strip by strip. She had fallen asleep curled in an armchair in her room, still dressed in her riding leathers from the battle. Her mind swam for a moment, trying to remember the night before, but exhaustion dulled her senses. Shame mingled with the exhaustion until her body felt heavy, and she wanted to go back to sleep. When she was awake, all she saw was Elara's face on the battlefield, before Faron forced her to go.

At least when she was asleep, she dreamed of nothing at all.

There was another drain on her energy that made her surge to her feet. She swayed for a moment, almost tumbling back into the armchair, before she placed a hand against the back of it to steady herself. *"What are you doing?"* she sent across the bond.

Neither Gael nor Lightbringer answered.

She stumbled into the hallway, still seeing Elara's face every time she blinked. Elara had come for her, and Faron had sent her away. Faron had used her newfound power against her own sister. Faron was the monster she had always feared she could be. If it weren't for the drain on her magic, she would have stayed in that chair until the war ended and they came to arrest her. But she couldn't sit by wondering what Iya was doing. The least she could do was keep watching him.

Though she had no idea where Iya was, she could follow the pull of the magic whether she was fully conscious or not. It led her down the stairs, through the corridors, and toward an empty classroom with a locked door near the back of the school. She tried to summon heat to her palms to melt the lock, but even that much effort made her eyes flutter as she nearly passed out.

Hours or seconds later, the door opened and Faron fell into a pair of unfamiliar arms. Unfamiliar only in the sense that she had never been held by them before, because, when she drew back, she saw Jesper Soto looking down at her with shadows in his eyes. Even his smile radiated the kind of malice common in the soucouyants from Iryan storybooks. But though he wasn't a shape-shifting old hag, this boy somehow had the dark energy of a creature that sucked the blood of sleeping humans.

It was so different from the Jesper Soto she had met that she put some distance between them. "What...?"

"You don't recognize me in this body?" The smile widened. "And here I did this for you."

Faron stared. "Iya...?"

Iya spread his arms as if to say, *What do you think?* "You asked what I planned to do with his blood. Well, here it is. I am a Soto once more." He smirked. "Twice more, I suppose."

Faron's back hit the opposite wall, her eyes roving his figure in horror. He had used their combined magic to transfer his soul into Jesper Soto's body. Instead of killing his descendant, he had

THIS ENDS IN EMBERS

overwritten his soul, trapped him in the same prison that Reeve had been in. It shouldn't be that easy for him to just *take* people like this, even if they were dead. It shouldn't be something he could present to her as a gift, as if she'd asked for this. It shouldn't—

Wait.

"Where's Reeve?" she asked.

Iya gestured behind him. "Right this way."

He backed into the room, allowing her to step past him. Instead of desks, inside were two beds: one was empty, the sheets removed to leave behind a bare mattress, but in the second, Reeve slumbered, the slow rise and fall of his chest the only thing that kept her from crying out. On one wall was a long chalkboard. On another wall was a window. Beneath the window was a long table on which there was a bowl smeared with red and several dragon relics, illuminated by the sun that reached through the curtains.

"What is this?" she asked around her rapid heartbeat.

"I recreated the circumstances of my original rebirth," Iya said from behind her. "But instead of the blood of a santi and dragon relics, I combined the relics with the power of two former Empyreans. My blood and your power."

"Jesper's blood," she breathed. "You used Jesper's blood, because he's Gael's descendant."

"Blood magic was common in my time. Even now, though it's no longer practiced, magic continues to run through bloodlines. Jesper Soto was always able to bond to Lightbringer, as I once was." He raised an eyebrow at her. "My initial attempts weren't fruitful, and I couldn't figure out why at first." He reached into his pocket—Jesper's pocket—and withdrew the stone from Rosetree Manor. "Until I found this. I have no proof you had anything to do with this, but the spell went more smoothly once I relieved him of it."

As she watched, Iya clenched his fist until she heard a series of cracks. The stone, now reduced to dust, trickled from between his fingers to the floor. Useless.

Faron laid her hand over Reeve's chest to feel his steady heartbeat. She was sure her own must have been wild, racing, as she was, between fear and revulsion, between relief and horror. But if Reeve even knew she was in the room, his lashes didn't so much as twitch to show it. "You said you did this for me, but I never asked for this. I would *never* have asked for this."

"We're connected, Faron. Gael Soto knows how much you hate us because I looked like *him*." Iya was standing at her shoulder now, his shadow bisecting Reeve's body. "You can see past my conquest, past the atrocities, but you could never see past *that*. He doesn't just want you to know him." His voice was soft, but there was an edge of steel that made her finally look up. "He wants you to see him."

"And you're suddenly in the business of giving him what he wants?"

Iya shrugged his broader shoulders. "I know you've noticed a certain... disharmony between my souls. This resolves the problem. As Lightbringer's Rider, I am strongest in a body that shares my blood. If we remain on the same page, there will be no further issues."

All the work she had done to berate Gael for his lack of courage, to plant the seeds of his rebellion—it all had been undone. If Gael wished for Faron not to hate him because of Reeve, and

THIS ENDS IN EMBERS

Lightbringer had granted it, they would be of one mind again. She would never draw him out from Lightbringer's control again.

Faron blinked back tears. "Is Reeve going to be okay?"

He was, after all, only alive thanks to the deal his parents had made to trade his body to Iya for power. Once, he'd told her that he had been sickly as a child, but he had never gone into detail about what that meant. Without the sliver of connection between the two of them, the link that had allowed Iya to control Reeve's body once Iya had been freed from the Empty, would he be that sick again? Would she get him back only to watch him fade away?

Her eyes burned at the thought, but she refused to cry in front of Iya. If she started, she wouldn't stop.

"His body has been through much," said Iya. "He just needs to rest. I'm not sure for how long."

Faron looked back at Reeve. His paper-white skin looked translucent, and his breathing was so soft, she could hardly hear it. She ran a hand over her face, overwhelmed. Something about all this just wasn't connecting in her head. Kidnapping Jesper Soto only to use his blood to invade his body, just because Gael... what? *Cared* for her? That was not a side of Iya she was used to. It was a lot of effort for very little gain, as Gael's moments of mild lucidity had done nothing to threaten Iya's conquest.

Faron was being lied to.

"Why did you really need Jesper's body?" she asked, positioning herself between Iya and Reeve's slumbering form. "You didn't have to take over his body to sever his bond with his dragon. You were already stronger than anyone when you were still in Reeve. And I refuse to believe you did this for me or Gael. I'm not that stupid."

257

"And why wouldn't I have?" Iya shot back. "That body means nothing to us and everything to you. I've been clear with you about my goals, Faron. What you choose to believe is none of my concern."

Hearing Reeve referred to as nothing more than a body rankled. Faron's cheeks burned, but she refused to be diverted.

"Jesper's body must offer you something more important. There has to be a reason you wanted *him* badly enough to kidnap him." Her eyes scanned him again. "What could it be?"

The realization hit her so hard, it knocked the breath from her lungs.

"Blood magic. You can do blood magic again. And the only other person who could possibly match you with that power is Signey."

Iya tilted his head, a slow smile spreading across his new face. "And she wouldn't dare attack her own brother."

"You have my summoning magic, you have Rider magic, and now you have blood magic. A kind of sorcery that hasn't been seen in centuries." Faron covered her mouth with her hand. "With this much power...you're not planning a conquest. This was all just a distraction. You're planning a *massacre*."

"And what if I am?" Iya's every word dripped with Lightbringer's endless capacity for cruelty. His brown eyes flashed green, his pupils narrowing to catlike slits, as the dragon swelled within this body, consuming every other soul left within. "Sometimes, we must destroy the old to make room for the new. This world needs a resurrection. A rebirth."

"People will *die*."

"Dying is what mortals do. It's what defines their ephemeral

THIS ENDS IN EMBERS

existence, the knowledge that it will one day end. If they'll die regardless, why not have their deaths serve a greater purpose?" Iya gestured toward the large windows letting sunlight into the room. "You cannot tell me this world is worth saving. Your island was thrice colonized. Your childhood was defined by a war you were too young to fight in. Even before dragons entered this realm, your species were inventing new methods of harming one another every second. Would it really be so bad, Faron? To burn it all down?"

"No," Faron admitted in a hoarse whisper.

She should have felt ashamed. Iya was a megalomaniac, who cared only about the flaws of the world because he wanted to remake it in his malignant image, and it should have made her feel filthy to agree with him. But it didn't. He was right. The endless wars. The disrespect to her sister, her hero, even by her own gods. The politics and the selfishness, the imperialism and the idea that there was a divine right to rule—all mortals did was hurt one another. Hurt *her*.

And, yes, she had made mistakes, and she had done some of the hurting. She had likely hurt her sister worse than anyone had before, and she would always have to live with that. But she was so tired of living in a world that forced her to whittle down her edges until she was smooth and palatable, until she was what everyone needed her to be instead of who she was.

She was not good or evil. She was not young or old. She was not powerful or weak. She was simply Faron Vincent, a girl who defied definition.

A girl who sometimes wanted to burn it all down.

"You must be so exhausted, playing at morality. *Their* morality."

Iya stepped closer, his eyes returned to their dark brown shade although his voice still sounded like two intertwined. "Imagine a world where you get to decide what's good. A world where something is right because you've decided it's so. Instead of playing god, imagine a world where you have *become* god. You have suffered so much, Faron. You deserve that which you have always been denied: control."

Their gazes locked. Faron swallowed. "Not like this."

"Think about it," Iya said, moving away, so she could finally breathe. "I have a prior engagement, but you know where to find me when you see the truth."

Faron stood there, frozen, for far longer than she should have, her mind restless. Reeve. *Reeve*, she finally decided. She would watch over Reeve. It was the one good thing she could do right now.

But in the back of her mind, a snakelike voice whispered: *Don't you just want to burn it all down?*

CHAPTER TWENTY-NINE

ELARA

ONCE ELARA WAS CLEARED TO LEAVE THE INFIRMARY, SHE TOOK a shower and changed into a new set of riding leathers. The reprieve from being around a crowd gave her the chance to cry again, just once more, for all she'd lost and all she'd failed to do. For her sister's dimming light and the absence of Reeve's calming presence. For a world that was a casualty of the power plays between people with too much authority and not enough sense. And for the child she had been, who had believed in right and wrong, in good and evil, in heroes and villains, and been launched into a war where the only real difference between the good guys and the bad guys was what side of the battlefield they were standing on.

Then, as always, she pulled herself together for the people who needed her.

Signey led her to the chamber where the Conclave typically met, though today they were not in session. When Signey opened the door, Elara was blinded by the lavishness of the spacious room: mahogany walls and gilded decorations, stained-glass windows and long benches. The ceiling was gold with frescoes of dragons, electric lights illuminated the cavernous space, and a small crowd of people waited inside, staring at her with the same surprise that she felt.

"Elara, meet the Night Saints," said Signey once the door had closed behind them. Then she leaned closer to whisper, "I didn't name them."

Torrey sat on one of the black-cushioned benches. Across from her, on the right side of the room, two boys who Elara faintly remembered from Hearthstone Academy sat in quiet conversation. On another bench was Rupert Lewis, Professor Smithers's husband. Elara tried not to show how puzzled she felt, but she must have failed, because Signey smiled with obvious amusement. She nodded at Torrey, who skipped over with her usual flurry of energy.

"We didn't want to tell you before, because you—like Barret and Professor Smithers—needed plausible deniability," Torrey said, laying a hand on Elara's back to steer her to the center of the room. "But the Night Saints are sort of a covert-operations team. It was all Signey's idea."

Signey shrugged modestly. "After the attack on Beacon, I wanted to take a more active role in stopping Iya. All I did was find a disparate bunch of people who felt the same."

"Even before we formed the Night Saints, Giles and Arran took Rosetree Manor down to studs and distributed parts of it to the free cities so they could cloak themselves from Lightbringer," Torrey explained. Elara assumed Giles and Arran were the two boys, who had finished their conversation and were now watching her with the same curiosity she felt. "Now, with Signey's help, we're leaving packages of dragon relics with instructions for use across all the empires."

"Especially Étolia," Signey added. "If they can only rely on someone like Tournesola Orianne to protect them, they're in deep trouble."

"We're hoping to send more aid to Joya del Mar, too," Torrey finished. "Apparently, Iya's forces set the countryside aflame this morning. No one was hurt, but much of their farmland is blighted."

Elara knew they were waiting for a response from her, positive or negative, but she couldn't wrap her mind around the fact that Signey had done all this. While they had been awkwardly hovering around each other, unsure how to let each other back in, Elara had taken command of the research and strategy, while Signey had formed a guerilla group to bring direct aid to those who needed it most. Even apart, their minds had been one—working, in their own ways, to make a tangible difference.

Let the most powerful people in the world argue their way to the end of the world. The true power to save everyone was right in that room.

Elara had never felt so inspired.

"Damon told us about your conversation in Ciel," Mr. Lewis said of his husband. His dark brown hair had grown out since she'd last seen him, and he was sporting a beard that looked as if it had a mind of its own. Silver was threaded through it now, but his moss-green eyes were as warm as she remembered. "'In the light of day or the dead of night, they hold the line.' Sound familiar?"

Elara's eyebrows lifted. "He was talking about the Night Saints."

"He was talking *around* the Night Saints," Mr. Lewis corrected, a twinkle in his eyes. "Technically, as acting ambassador of the Langlish Empire, he doesn't know that we exist."

Elara loved the fondness with which Mr. Lewis and Professor Smithers discussed each other. After living through one war, she'd stopped thinking too far into the future, but, in that moment, she thought she might want something similar: someone to grow old with. Maybe that could be her and Signey one day. If, of course, they survived *this* war.

She cleared her throat before she could stumble too far down that path. "This is incredible. How do I get involved?"

"Just by knowing our identities, you're involved," said Signey, smiling so widely that the rare dimple appeared in her cheek. "As far as my father knows, I'm delivering security instructions to the remaining Riders. But we're here to discuss options for our next mission and—"

Her voice faltered. Her eyes skidded over to Torrey. There was a solemn expression on her face that Elara still wasn't accustomed to. Despite Torrey's love for black clothing and sharp jewelry, she was one of the most upbeat people Elara had ever met. But ever since Jesper had been kidnapped, it had become more and more common for her to look as if she were at a funeral.

"It's all right," Torrey finally said. "We've all agreed to allow Signey to break our bonds. Starting with myself and Azeal."

"Oh," Elara said.

"I still think it's too soon," said one of the two unfamiliar boys. He was red-haired and brown-eyed, with freckles that seemed to line his stout body. His riding leathers had green accents, marking him as a sage Rider. He wiggled his fingers in greeting when Elara looked at him. "Giles Crawford. It's a pleasure to meet you, even though you obliterated my combat scores at Hearthstone." His gaze turned back to Torrey. "You're handling your Rider's kidnapping suspiciously well, and now you want to give up your dragon?"

"I've been ready for this every time we spoke about it," Torrey

THIS ENDS IN EMBERS

said without looking at anyone. "Iya could be forcing Jesper to spy on us through the dragon bond. He could kill Jesper, killing me in the process. Even now, I..." Her hand came up to press against her chest, right over her heart. "I can't feel him at all. If he's hurt or happy, if he's alive or dead, if we're even still bonded at all. There's n-nothing." Torrey cleared her throat. "I can't live like this. *We* can't live like this."

Signey's eyes were damp. Elara swayed closer, and Signey immediately turned to wrap her arms around Elara's waist. Her body trembled as Elara held her, tears dripping against Elara's neck. "We've talked about it. A lot," Signey whispered so that only Elara could hear. "I worried...I don't want Jesper to feel like we've abandoned him. But if he were here, I know he would make the same choice. That's what...That's what makes this so hard." She sniffled. "What if I'm wrong? What if we're wrong? What if I hurt them, hurt *him*, and leave him defenseless out there? What if—"

"Hey. *Hey.*" Elara turned them around so that her back was to the still-arguing Night Saints. It was the closest she could get to hiding Signey from the world at that moment. "Remember our fight?"

Signey laughed wetly. "How could I forget?"

"I told you I trusted that whatever Faron was doing or not doing, it was for good reason. The same is true of her. And of Jesper." Elara ran her fingers through Signey's curls, pushing them behind her ear so that she could press a kiss to her hairline. "We have every reason to try this. And if it turns out to be the wrong move, Jesper will understand why we had to do it. He knows you. He loves you. He trusts you. You have to trust yourself."

Signey lifted her head, silver tears still glistening on her brown cheeks. "When did you get so wise? You were always smart, but now you're... You're so different."

"I just finally found myself, I think. And, honestly, it's about time," Elara said, pressing another kiss to Signey's forehead. "Now, let's do this."

Signey's smile was weak, but it reached her glittering eyes. "Okay. Let's do this."

Before they reached a consensus on when they would all meet again, they went to the garden. Torrey stood in the crescent of Azeal's body, saying her goodbyes, while Elara waited with a nervous Signey. It was one thing to attempt a new skill in front of a small crowd, but it was another thing when there was this much on the line. If Signey did this wrong, Torrey could end up in the hospital alongside Professor Rowland and Hanne Gifford. Even if she did this right, it would go against everything she had ever believed in.

"I think it will be okay, though," Signey said more to herself than to Elara. "We all received the same training at Hearthstone. Jesper and Torrey don't *need* a soul bond with a dragon to defend themselves." She paused. "Right?"

"Is this the part where I remind you that when we were kept at Rosetree Manor, when we couldn't communicate with Zephyra even though she was right outside, you killed a bunch of full-grown men with your bare hands?"

Signey's lips twitched into a smile. "It wasn't with my bare hands. But I see your point."

Late afternoon was turning to early evening. The sun was just

THIS ENDS IN EMBERS

above the tree line, bleeding red-orange over the foliage. Fluffy clouds limped across the indigo sky, and there was a sharp chill that made Elara wish she'd thrown a coat on over her riding leathers as everyone else had. Even near Solstice, San Irie never got cold enough for her to need even a sweater. Langley, by contrast, seemed to hurtle toward the season by turning itself into the inside of a freezer, except without the frost.

Snow was coming, though, a nearing threat of ice and rime. Elara had never seen snow before, not in real life. She hoped not to be on the continent long enough to see it.

Elara shivered again, and a blanket fell over her. She looked up to see Signey settling her coat over Elara's shoulders. It was fur-lined and black, with the texture of dragon scales. "Dragonhide," Signey confirmed. "It'll keep you warm. I forgot you can't handle a little breeze."

"This is 'a little breeze'?" Elara complained. "I can't feel my nose."

Around her, the Langlish began to chuckle at her misfortune. They all looked fine, but they were all wearing coats similar to Signey's. Without hers, Signey looked as relaxed as if she were lying on a beach, even though the latest surge of wind pierced the tips of Elara's ears like a frigid knife.

"Are you ready?" Signey called to Torrey. "My girlfriend is about to freeze to death."

"For Irie's sake—" But Elara was grinning. *Girlfriend.* She couldn't remember the last time she'd been so happy to hear the word *girlfriend.*

"Her little nose is *cold.*"

Elara pinched Signey in the side, an action that was completely ineffectual considering she was wearing padded leathers. "I hate you."

Signey winked at her before standing at attention. Her dimple was slow to disappear. Elara supposed she couldn't complain if her *girlfriend* was ejecting some levity into a serious situation for herself, even if it was at Elara's expense. Still, she burrowed deeper into the warmth of the coat as another gust of cold wind cut through the garden.

Torrey was facing them, a hand in the pocket of her riding leathers. It was time.

"Before he loses the ability to communicate with us, Azeal has something to say to everyone," Torrey said, her voice just loud enough to carry across the open space. Behind her, the dragon was a tense line of red. Even though, as a carmine, Azeal was the largest and most dangerous of all the dragon breeds, in that moment he carried himself as though he were...small. His sadness and resignation thickened the air. "He says that...that losing Zephyra, his sister, was the worst pain he's ever felt in his life. Not because her connection to the den was severed, but because her soul was shattered. The Zephyra he faced in the Emerald Highlands was not the dragon he knows and loves; she was a creature of destruction, a version of herself that would horrify her if she still knew reason. It's devastating. It's also terrifying."

Torrey closed her eyes, as though she were feeling the wave of grief that Azeal had described. She might well have been; after all, Zephyra had been den for her, too.

"He says that, 'Up until now, we have feared little more than to lose our humans,'" Torrey continued. "'Even with our strength and magic, our humans are fragile. Their lives are short. And yet they fill those short lives with so much love, passion, and indescribable strength. They lend us their rationality, their empathy, and

THIS ENDS IN EMBERS

their great capacity for emotion, and in exchange, we learn what it is to truly live. But now Lightbringer has given us something worse to fear: losing ourselves. Without that reason, that empathy, that emotion, we are little more than predators, and humans little more than prey. Life becomes not about living, but only about surviving. We deserve more than that. And if there is even a small chance that severing our bond will allow us that, I would make this choice again and again. I love you.'"

Torrey's free hand was on Azeal's hide. She pressed her forehead where her fingers had just been, whispering something too low for Elara to hear. The carmine curled more tightly around her, as if he wanted to protect her from the world. Elara's eyes stung. She remembered well the love and loyalty she felt from Zephyra long before she had wanted to accept the bond, but she had lived her whole life without being connected to a dragon. Her severed bond had allowed her to reconnect with her Iryan summoning magic. It had been bittersweet.

Now her friends were experiencing the pain of losing their version of Iryan summoning magic, and her heart broke for them. The emptiness where her magic had been . . . she had felt that every day at Hearthstone.

"Saints, I hope this works," she heard Signey whisper. Then she raised her voice. "Torrey, can you come over here? I don't want you near Azeal just in case . . . anything goes wrong."

Elara felt eyes on them and turned. Not only were the rest of the Night Saints present, but so were Barret Soto, Professor Smithers, and several Langlish politicians, who watched through the windows and from doorways. If she could feel it, Signey could feel it. The pressure she had to be under . . .

But not a drop of discomfort showed on Signey's face. She bowed her head, took a deep breath, and then looked up as she straightened her shoulders. One hand reached out to Azeal, her fingers slightly bent.

Nothing happened.

Signey closed her fist, so tightly that her knuckles blanched.

A bird chirped overhead.

Signey's jaw was clenched as she opened and closed her fist a few more times.

Someone cleared their throat, but nothing else happened.

Elara could hear her own heartbeat. The situation reminded her of her first time summoning—and how different that had been from her first time summoning the gods. Reaching across realms to signal them, containing all that volatile power, channeling it into magic large and small without exhausting herself... it had felt both intuitive and complicated. The same skill, but done a different way.

She moved closer to Signey. "Close your eyes. Envision the bond as a tangible thing: a rope you can cut or a faucet you can turn off. The magic is in your blood, but it's your soul that has to do the work."

Signey nodded slightly before doing as she was told. Her hand fell to her side. She took another deep breath, relaxing her jaw, her shoulders, her arm. A glow, the deep red of an ember, appeared in the center of her chest before spreading throughout her body, as if she had fire in her veins. Glowing lines crisscrossed her hands, forming a matrix of subcutaneous fire. Signey flexed her fingers and then made another fist.

Light erupted, a single blinding flash that forced Elara's eyes

THIS ENDS IN EMBERS

shut. Something hit the ground. Azeal howled—but not in pain. Torrey called Signey's name, and that was Elara's cue to look.

Signey was lying in the grass, unconscious. She was no longer glowing. Instead, she was pale and breathing shallowly. Barret was already at her side, with Torrey standing over them. Even Azeal had approached, and he was nudging Signey's body with his snout. He seemed no closer to eating her than he had been minutes ago.

"Is it—?" Elara asked, glancing at him for signs of feral behavior.

"Yeah," said Torrey, as Barret hoisted his daughter into his arms and stood up. "The bond is broken. We can't hear each other anymore."

People seemed to be frozen in place, as though the sight of an unbonded dragon was an impossibility. Or maybe Torrey was the impossible one, a Rider without a bond who was still close with her dragon.

Then again, it could have been both of those things. After all, the last two bonds broken had resulted in those involved losing a crucial part of themselves.

"I guess you were right." Torrey's concern for her friend creased the skin on her forehead, but still she found a smile for Elara. "The magic really is in our blood."

Elara brushed a stray lock of Signey's curls away from her clammy forehead.

"What's that face for?" Torrey asked.

Elara stepped back, gaze shifting to Azeal once more. "Nothing. I just think I have an idea."

CHAPTER THIRTY

FARON

FARON DIDN'T NOTICE TIME PASSING UNTIL A WEEK HAD GONE BY. Every day, she had woken up to sit by Reeve's bedside, leaving only for meetings and meals, for baths and books. Every day, she sat beside Iya in Jesper Soto's body and silently checked him over for signs of injury or struggle. It felt as if she held two lives in her hands, and she was juggling them disproportionately. She wanted Jesper safe, but she *needed* Reeve. She spent more time in the infirmary than she did watching over Iya.

She might not have been a reader, but Reeve was, and she read him story after story in the hopes that he would hear them and wake up faster. Langlish folklore differed from Iryan folklore in one major way: Their stories were about human saints, giant serpents, and great magic. People wielded magic swords or turned into plants or slumbered in hidden locations waiting for the right moment to awaken. In Iryan folklore, everything was a fable, an allegory, or a metaphor: Anthropomorphic animals starred in creation myths, ancestral advisors appeared when they were most needed, and duppies and soucouyants acted as warnings to misbehaving children.

THIS ENDS IN EMBERS

Reeve had loved these sorts of stories enough to use them to figure out a key portion of Iya's resurrection plan. Faron half expected him to sit up and do it again if she read them to him.

But seven days passed, and he slept and slept and slept.

"He will wake," Iya said from behind her. Though she'd heard him enter, she jumped anyway, because she was still unused to hearing Jesper Soto's voice blended with Lightbringer's. "You don't have to watch it happen."

"I don't want him to wake up alone," Faron said, swallowing. "After what I did to him, that's the least I can do."

"I—" Iya began, then seemed to think better of it. "Your next lesson is ready. Do you want to delay it?"

Faron held Reeve's hand between her own, checking for a pulse before brushing a kiss across his knuckles. His skin was warm beneath her lips, a warmth that lingered even after she drew back. She continued to sit there with her back to Iya, breathing until she felt more in control of herself. But it infuriated her, how he continued to act as if he cared about her while he worked to destroy everything she loved. He'd razed her home. He'd isolated her from her sister. He had held up a mirror to all the worst parts of herself, and he had told her that was all there was to her.

Reeve lay unconscious before her because of Iya. Because she'd believed that he cared about her, that he could help her defeat Lightbringer and save her sister.

Faron grew stronger with every lesson, but she still wasn't strong enough to escape. She wanted to be ready when Reeve woke up. She wanted to be able to get them out.

She let her breath out slowly, forcing cheer into her voice. "No, it's all right. Let's do it."

She changed into her riding leathers and coat before meeting him on the beach. Lightbringer was present, for once, which caught her off guard. Jesper's eyes were darker brown compared to Gael's hazel, but that was definitely Iya's warped cruelty staring at her through them. Gael, if he was still anything close to conscious in there, would not be her teacher today.

Still, Lightbringer's physical presence was unusual. She wondered if his control over Jesper's body was tenuous, requiring proximity to maintain, or if she was just being optimistic about Lightbringer's unfamiliar magic. If Jesper was fighting from within, more fiercely than Iya had anticipated, was there any way she could help him?

Then she realized Lightbringer wasn't the only presence on the beach. Lightbringer's tail shifted to reveal Gavriel and Mireya Warwick, dressed for a fight. Faron paused midstride, half-thrilled and half-wary. Thanks to Iya's own commands, Marius Lynwood had recovered from what she'd done to him, but, with Reeve in a coma and Elara the last victim of her power, Faron felt emotionally volatile. Her complicated feelings toward the Warwicks had only grown more complicated after she had learned what they'd done to their own son. She wasn't sure she could trust herself to hold back.

And no one here would stop her.

Lightbringer turned those massive green eyes on her, which jolted Faron back into action. It didn't matter whether she felt ready. She couldn't show weakness in front of a creature that had always dismissed her as a weakling. But at least now she knew what Lightbringer was doing here.

This was her final exam.

Everyone she had fought before had been her peer, students

THIS ENDS IN EMBERS

from the Hearthstone Academy who were unfamiliar with her magic and flush with the arrogance of youth. Gavriel Warwick was a seasoned soldier whose magical experimentation had cracked the bindings of Lightbringer's prison. Mireya Warwick was a weathered warden who ran the most secure and dangerous prison in Langley. Both were twice her age. Both were familiar with her summoning. Both had killed children and likely had no qualms about doing it again.

Gavriel Warwick still featured in her nightmares, skeleton pale and dripping with malice as he set her world on fire. He had surrendered before she'd ever gotten to fight him directly, and that had probably been for the best. The anger that flared in her chest, even after all these years, made it clear that the battle would have been a bloodbath.

She stopped yards away from the Warwicks. "I notice that you haven't visited your son."

"If he were awake, I'm sure you'd let everyone know," said Gavriel. "Must we make small talk? We're here only as a favor to our saint. My wife and I are leading our current operations in Joya del Mar."

Iya approached her from beneath the shadow of Lightbringer's wings, his hands behind his back. It still unnerved her, seeing what was his third face in the time she'd known him, but she stomped down the urge to flinch. Lightbringer continued to stare down at her. Watching. Assessing. *Show no weakness.*

"Based on previous lessons, you should be strong enough to face them," Iya said. "If not, we still have a few of the younger Riders that you have yet to spar with."

"Spar," Faron repeated dubiously.

"Well"—Iya smirked—"they can't hurt you, but you can certainly kill them if you like. Their magic is just amplifying ours, that's all."

Faron didn't think she and Iya needed as much power as they had, but she didn't bother to argue the point. Gavriel and Mireya were settling into defensive stances, so she copied them, searching for an opening. Gavriel was broad, his muscled body speaking of a brutal kind of strength. Mireya was all sharp angles and sharp stares, but that meant she was quick. Force and speed working in tandem against her, wielded by two adults who knew how to use them lethally. Her odds weren't great.

But when had her odds ever been great?

Faron was a survivor. She always had been.

Iya waited until he was standing on the grass, leaving them the wide swath of golden sand as their battlefield. Then he said, "Begin."

Mireya Warwick was in front of Faron in a second. Mireya's dragon relic—her wedding ring—lit up, covering her knuckles with golden spikes made of light. Her first flew toward Faron's face, and Faron barely managed to dodge it. The spikes trailed across her shoulder instead, dragging blood from the gouges left behind. Pain shot down Faron's arm, but she had no time to assess the damage. Gavriel Warwick was in her path, his own relic—a dragon-eye necklace similar to Reeve's—radiating a light that climbed through his chest and arms. He grabbed Faron, spun her around, and flung her toward the bay with so much strength, she soared into deep water.

Frigid seawater knocked her out of her body for a moment, making it hard to tell up from down. Her bleeding shoulder screamed, or maybe she was the one screaming.

THIS ENDS IN EMBERS

The hero of San Irie, so easily defeated. Was this what would have happened if she'd faced the Warwicks at twelve years old? Would San Irie still have won the war, or would the commander have displayed her corpse outside Pearl Bay Palace as a warning to her people? *Your saint is nothing. Stand down, or we will reduce your island to nothing, too.*

She reached the surface, sucking air into her lungs. Water and bile came with her next few exhales, and she struggled to focus. Gavriel and Mireya Warwick stood on the shore, watching her dispassionately. As if they were *bored*. Gavriel Warwick knelt down, placing a hand into the water, and his dragon relic glowed even brighter. That glow again traveled down his arm, into his hand, and then it traveled into the ocean...and one by one Faron saw fish begin to float above the waves, unmoving and scorched.

He was boiling the water. It didn't matter that she was in the depths. He would kill every sea creature between them just to get to her.

Anger overwhelmed her as she floated in the cold, salty water. Gael had warned that his temper had become volatile after bonding with Lightbringer, and Faron felt the truth of that in that moment. In all the moments that had led up to it. She felt as if her rage were always waiting to consume her, but now it ignited into an inferno as she thought of how much of her life had been defined by the kind of plan Gavriel Warwick was executing now. When rulers like the Warwicks saw something they wanted, they would destroy anything to get it. For them, it was not simply about winning. It was about the other side losing. San Irie had lost homes, farms, landmarks. They'd lost time, family, sanity.

Even now, San Irie continued to lose, because of a plan put in place by the Warwicks—a plan that had been delayed only because their son had been the sole member of the family with a conscience. An ancient god, once locked away, had returned to terrorize them all, because, even with their endless territories, the Langlish wanted *more* power. They could claim they had done it for their son, for their people, but their son was alone in an infirmary bed, and their own people would be dying in droves if they didn't bend to Iya's will.

Power was what everything came down to in the end. Power in the hands of people with poisonous hearts.

Would it really be so bad, Faron? To burn it all down?

No. No it wouldn't.

Flames rose before the Warwicks. Mireya Warwick gripped her husband's shoulder and pulled him to safety as the wall of fire cut across the shoreline, chasing them away from the water's edge. Faron swam until her feet touched the ocean floor, until she was running through too-hot water and back onto too-hot sand. She parted the curtain of fire until she saw the Warwicks, their magic already swirling from their dragon relics to face hers. But they were too slow, at least for what she really had planned.

Her soul surged beyond her body and gripped theirs. Sweat dripped down the sides of her face, beaded on her forehead. Blood dripped from her nose as the Warwicks fought her, a stronger fight than any she had faced before, but she pushed and kept pushing. They, too, began to bleed, their dragon relics so bright that she had to turn away. She could feel the pulse of their magic as it twined with hers, trying to sever her hold over them. But she was stronger. Iya was stronger. Lightbringer was stronger.

Mireya Warwick coughed up blood, as if Faron had punctured a lung. She wished she had. It was the least the director deserved.

THIS ENDS IN EMBERS

"Are you going to kill us?" Gavriel asked, and she could see his mind working for a way out of this. Red bled across his eyeballs, the vessels bursting as he tried to hold on to his mind. His voice shook, even as his skin was slowly leeched of what little color it had. "Is that what you truly want? To turn your back on sainthood completely? To become the very thing you've always despised?"

Faron almost laughed. Instead, she took a single step forward. "I never asked to be a saint. I only ever *wanted* one thing: to keep my loved ones safe. And they'll never be safe, not as long as you're still breathing."

Another step. A trail of fire shot from her foot in a snakelike pattern toward the Warwicks. Smoke began to coat the air, making them cough, making their eyes water, making them curse.

Faron smiled wide.

Justice had never felt so good.

"Do you even know how you've ruined my life? The nightmares you star in? The hope you've crushed?" she asked. Black spots began to dance before her eyes, and she knew it was because of the bond Iya had formed between herself and him, and that hurting the Warwicks would weaken her magic, would take away some of the strength she needed to ultimately defeat Lightbringer. But she didn't care. She didn't care, not when she had them at her mercy, finally, *finally.* "Does it make you happy? That you destroyed what San Irie could have been? We can rebuild, we can be better, but we'll always be different from what we would have been. Why should you have that much power over us even now? Why should you have any power at all?"

They had attacked her sister with slurs and violence.

They had destroyed her island.

They had resurrected Iya.

She could stop them, here and now. For San Irie. For Reeve.

Faron imagined Reeve awakening from his coma to find her sitting at his side, his hand in hers as she told him she had killed his parents. That they would never hurt him—or anyone else—again. Her heart stuttered as she realized she wasn't sure if Reeve would even be proud of her. The first and only time he'd seen her perform this new magic, he hadn't expressed an opinion either way.

I've always believed that what we know isn't as important as how we choose to act on it, he'd said then, newly recovered from the kind of beating that should have killed him. Would have killed him, if she hadn't intervened.

But this wasn't like that. Her power so outstripped that of the Warwicks that it was like fighting with toddlers. If she pushed just a little more, she could lock them inside their own bodies. She could make them present their necks so she could slit their throats. She could make them kill each other, then watch, paralyzed, as the other bled out.

Her hatred felt like a poison that made it hard to swallow. It would be so easy, so easy, so easy. . . .

Faron realized that she was shaking, and it wasn't from the effort of holding on to their souls. She was covered in a damp layer of sweat, fat droplets clustering atop her collarbone. Blood mixed with the moisture on her face, overwhelming her with the scent of copper and acid. Her heart was racing as every blink carried her to the past. She was standing before the Warwicks, but she was on a battlefield surrounded by burning buildings and mangled bodies, but she was on the beach outside Hearthstone Academy, but she was crying in a tent on the mountainside because she'd killed her first person and could still feel the warm slick of their blood on her hands.

What we know isn't as important as how we choose to act on it.

Faron may have thought these people did not deserve to live, but she didn't want to be the one to end their lives.

She was so, so tired of war. Of blood. Of death.

And she was angry—she would always be angry—but she wasn't a killer. Not when she had a choice.

She settled back into her own body, letting the Warwicks drop to the ground. Unlike Lynwood after their confrontation, they were both still conscious, if panting and bloody. Gavriel immediately lifted a weak hand to check on his wife, who gripped it and squeezed.

Faron's vision blurred, but she turned away before they could see the tears fall. She felt hollowed out. Without her anger, without her hatred, she was nothing but a husk of guilt and shame. Shame for the part of her that still wanted to finish the job. Guilt for having taken it this far in the first place. She would never forgive the Warwicks for what they had done, and maybe she would never forgive herself for letting them live when they would never have afforded her the same courtesy. But as she limped away from the beach, ignoring Iya's calls, she felt lighter than she had in weeks.

She may be a monster, but at least it was on her own terms.

CHAPTER THIRTY-ONE

ELARA

IN THE TIME IT TOOK SIGNEY TO AWAKEN FROM HER FIRST ATTEMPT AT breaking a dragon bond, Elara worried. It was what she did best, but, as hours turned into days that turned into a week, the fact that a single bond had drained Signey to this point made Elara wonder if it was even worth it. Iya could attack at any time; they couldn't afford for Signey to be out of commission.

She and Torrey took turns waiting by Signey's bedside while outlining the Night Saints' next mission. Her plan had worked: The tracking spell from the dragon relic made from Azeal's scales—a boot knife with the scales embedded in the handle—had pointed to Rosetree Manor on a map. Elara had worried that it was a trap, and Iya had to know that whatever he hid there wasn't completely hidden, but Mr. Lewis had been willing to take that risk.

Watson, the town in which the house was located, was on the edge of Iya's occupied territory, and previous attempts to fly into the Emerald Highlands had been chaotic at best. But at least they wouldn't go home empty-handed. Elara had suggested that they could harvest more of the building to distribute to their allies,

THIS ENDS IN EMBERS

protecting them from dragon magic, and that alone was reason enough to move forward.

Now, she set down the book she had been reading at Signey's bedside and tried not to despair. Even with Cherry's discovery regarding Signey's blood, even with the Night Saints, even with at least a short-term plan of action, it still felt as if they were twisting around in the dark. Before the Battle for Port Sol, they had managed to piece together the enemy's plan—and though they'd gotten a lot wrong, they had gotten enough right to fight to a stalemate. This time, they were no closer to understanding Iya's plan than they'd been before, while he annexed land and destroyed armies with Faron at his side.

She ran a hand over her face, feeling frustrated. So, she did what she always did when she felt this way: She prayed to the gods.

Of the three who could have answered her, Elara had not expected Obie. The god appeared in a cloud of white light that resolved itself into his trademark suit, the gold embroidery sparkling long after that light had faded. His hood was down, a rare sight that revealed his bearded jaw and white, pupilless eyes, and he was smaller than usual, likely because the infirmary did not allow for twelve-foot gods to stand comfortably within it.

Sorry, she whispered toward his feet, her head bowed. *You must be tired of me constantly asking for guidance.*

Obie said nothing, but Elara hadn't expected him to. He was the quietest of the gods, after all.

I'm doing as you ask, but I still don't know if I'm doing the right thing. Everything is so— She gestured vaguely, unable to find a word that could encompass the mess she had waded into. The people she thought were good only cared about power. The people she knew were bad only cared about power. Her attempt to save her sister had failed. Her attempt to break the bonds had hospitalized her girlfriend. She stood in a dark room, and every lit path led only to more pain. It was exhausting. *I want to be the Empyrean I promised you I could be. But sometimes I don't know what that means anymore.*

The silence continued. Elara chanced a look upward to find Obie facing the bed. Signey's chest rose and fell beneath her white sheet, her curls blanketing her head like a soft cloud. Elara smiled helplessly.

The first Empyrean sought to protect the world, a wish twisted into a desire to unite the world beneath his rule, Obie said in his deep voice. It had been such a long time since Elara had heard it that the words seemed to echo through her mind. *The second Empyrean sought to protect her loved ones at any cost, a dream turned into a nightmare by Iya's influence. You have seen the best and worst of humanity—the best and worst of the gods—and you seek only to protect with no qualifiers.* Obie reached up to scratch the side of his chin, a gesture so painfully human that it somehow made him seem even more divine. *There is no right. There is no wrong. There is only the endless effort to leave this world a better place than it was the day before. An effort I have watched you make since birth.*

Elara realized she was crying and turned back to the bed in a vain hope that the god wouldn't see it. *You were watching over me?*

Obie shrugged as if to say, *We watch over everyone.* Elara's shoulders relaxed, relief flooding her. If the gods hadn't been paying attention to her only since she'd become the Empyrean, that meant they had seen *all* her actions, good and bad, and still lent her their power. It meant that their disapproval, their reticence, their

THIS ENDS IN EMBERS

annoyance, wasn't because of her but because of those who came before her. It meant that she was not the failure she had feared she was, because there was nothing to fail at. She only had to try.

And the gods knew that all she did was try.

Thank you, she whispered, wiping away the tears.

Obie disappeared, but not before Elara saw his lips quirk upward in the ghost of a smile.

"Was I that sick that you're praying at my bedside?" a hoarse voice asked. Signey pushed herself into a sitting position, her lashes fluttering as if the very effort had exhausted her. Elara lurched forward to grab the glass of tepid water on the nearby table and hold it up for Signey to drink from. Signey finished the glass of water before she spoke again. "How long?"

"A week. How are you feeling? I should call someone—"

"I'm okay." Signey dropped back onto her pillows, yawning. "Did it work?"

"It worked, but—"

"Then I'm okay. When's the next mission?"

Elara raised her eyebrows. "It's adorable that you think you're coming on the next mission."

Ignoring Signey's protests, Elara went to call a healer and send a servant to fetch Signey's father. When she returned to the room, Signey had dozed off again, but there was color in her cheeks and her eyes half opened as Elara approached the bed.

"Just be careful?" Signey whispered, apparently accepting that she was too exhausted to argue any further. Still, she surged upward to give Elara a kiss, deep and lingering, her fingers curled around Elara's neck. "I hate not being there to watch your back."

"My back will be fine," Elara assured them both. She kissed the

285

corner of Signey's mouth and pulled away. "Concentrate on feeling better. You still need to break Stormborn's bond before Iya does."

Azeal carried Elara and Torrey into the Emerald Highlands, and this time they were both strapped into the saddle to keep from falling. Without being asked—not that either of them *could* ask—Azeal flew gently, gliding on the wind currents with minimal flaps of his wings as they followed the pull of the knife relic in Elara's pocket. Elara didn't feel as if she and Torrey were in danger of falling, not as long as they didn't meet with any other dragons on the way.

Ahead of them, Stormborn scouted for threats. Giles and Arran were still bonded to their dragon, just in case something went awry. It was a gamble, that Lightbringer wouldn't be present to induce the Fury in Stormborn or snap the bond entirely, taking out all three of them. But the deeper they went into the Emerald Highlands, the more Elara began to relax. If they could get in and out without being noticed, maybe she could finally sleep well tonight.

No sooner had she thought that than a furious roar cut through the morning sky.

Stormborn soared toward the sound, and Azeal stayed above the clouds where they could remain unnoticed. With Jesper's and Torrey's bonds broken, Lightbringer's forces shouldn't have been able to track Azeal—or so Elara hoped. If one of Iya's dragons breached their cloud cover, they would see him easily, a massive red smudge against the condensation, but Stormborn was every bit the soldier that his Riders were. He knew his way around military stratagem.

THIS ENDS IN EMBERS

Rosetree Manor appeared below. Azeal made a rumbling sound.

"Hang on," Torrey warned. Elara barely had time to tighten her hold around Torrey's waist before Azeal was diving. Her stomach leaped into her throat, and the wind became knives on her face. Somewhere behind them, she heard scaled bodies colliding and fires erupting, but all she could see was the ocean of grass rising up to meet them....

Azeal hit the ground at a run, stopping just short of the duck pond. The two of them climbed off, freeing Azeal to stand guard in the backyard while they made their way toward the manor.

The last time Elara had been at Rosetree Manor, she'd been a prisoner. There had been little time to admire the house, and now there was nothing left to admire. She and Signey had set Rosetree ablaze on their way out, but the Night Saints had leveled the building. Stone and wood littered the grass. Blackened soil and cracked tiles filled the center. Weeds already grew between those cracks, making it look as if the manor were being swallowed. Torrey began collecting parts while Elara walked where there had once been halls, feeling the ghost of her incarceration. Back then, she'd been so sure that Commander Warwick was painting her as the instigator of a war the queen had sent her to stop. Now she scanned the ruins for something, anything, that could get that job done once and for all.

"Elara!" Torrey waved her over to a jagged wall. Huge chunks of it were on the ground, creating a half-moon in front of the barely standing structure. "A little help?"

Elara stared at her blankly before she realized that Torrey needed help climbing over the rocks. She called on the gods, breathing around Irie entering her body, and then lifted Torrey off her feet and over the barrier. Instead of saying goodbye to the goddess, she silently begged Irie to stay with her a little longer. Azeal had yet to alert them of any incoming threats, but, if he did, Elara wanted to be able to fight.

Seconds later, there was a triumphant cry. Instead of lifting Torrey again, Elara drew on Irie's power to move the hunks of stone until she could see Torrey bent over four ovals that went up to her waist. They were partially buried in the soil, and they radiated a warmth that made Elara's body temperature rise even higher.

"Dragon eggs," Torrey breathed. "It's the stolen dragon eggs."

The only dragon egg Elara had ever seen had been the one that had once been in the center of Deadegg, scaled and blackened and as tall as a house. These were smaller, pearl white streaked with a rusty red, and lined with scales that looked soft, almost like the down one would find on a baby bird. She could feel Irie's power twisting inside her, disgusted to be so close to these creatures, and Elara did her best to radiate soothing toward the goddess. This was an even bigger find than she had imagined when she'd planned this mission.

"The egg grows as the dragon grows," Torrey explained. "The size before they hatch is a good indication of what kind of dragon will be born, before they get their first color." She frowned at the closest egg, scratching at one of the red-brown streaks. It flaked away beneath her nails. "Is this...?"

"Let's see." Elara withdrew the knife from her pocket. Before she could even point it at the egg, it lit up and flew from her hand. The handle stuck to one of the rust-colored smears. Then, it began to twist around, pointing its blade to the top, the bottom, the soil

THIS ENDS IN EMBERS

around them, the eggs left and right. There was so much blood in this corner that the relic didn't know where to focus.

Torrey stepped back, her nose wrinkling. "This is disgusting. Why is he using Jesper's blood to fertilize the eggs?"

"It's got to be some sort of blood magic, not fertilizer. They'll grow on their own. He must want them to grow a specific way." Elara stared at the stains, her eyes narrowed, until, suddenly, she realized the truth. "Wait. He's using Jesper's blood to *train* them. He's a Soto. He wants to make sure these dragons are born knowing him, recognizing him. He wants them to come into this world under his control."

Torrey's face blanched. "That's why I couldn't feel him. Iya's in Jesper's body now. Using Jesper's blood—their blood—to train the dragon eggs."

"We don't *know* that—"

"I couldn't feel him. Azeal couldn't feel him. We couldn't even *find* him during the battle—and that was long before the bond was broken. Where else could he be if not—if—" Torrey put her back to one of the ruined walls, a broken sob escaping her throat. "It makes sense. You know it does. He took Jesper."

Elara didn't want to say such a horrible thing aloud without proof, but she couldn't deny that it made a sick sort of sense. In Jesper's body, Iya would be free of Reeve—which might make Faron more sympathetic to him. In Jesper's body, Iya could spy on them or, worse, use Jesper as a shield to keep Signey from using blood magic against him. And it wouldn't matter that they had found his stash of stolen dragon eggs. The eggs had already been smeared with Jesper's blood. Destroyed, they couldn't be used against him; hatched, they were already in his pocket.

They were too late.

Elara pried the knife from the egg until it calmed beneath her hand. She wanted to stab it into the ground, as if that would relieve some of her frustration. Of course they were too late. Even if they hadn't waited for Signey's recovery, there was no telling how long the eggs had been here, leeching the magic from Jesper's blood. Distantly, she could hear the roars of the dragon fight coming closer, too close. She pushed away her hopelessness. Now was not the time. They needed another plan.

"We can't let him keep these eggs," Torrey said hesitantly. "But we also can't let them hatch, right? If—if dragons aren't meant to be in this world..."

"We're not breaking them," Elara said as she turned to face her. They weren't sure of much, but Elara could be sure of this. The tension leaked out of Torrey's body, but Elara didn't take it personally that she had assumed Elara's first plan would be to destroy the eggs. Shattering them, murdering the dragon hatchlings, would be the smart thing to do. It was what Iya likely thought she would do if she found them. But these dragons would hatch into innocents, under his control or not. It was not her job to decide whether they should live or die before then. "I'll just send them back to the divine realm."

Torrey moved out of her way as Irie flooded Elara with the magic to open a doorway between the mortal and the divine realms. She'd done this only once before, when she had threatened to send Iya and Lightbringer through until she could figure out how to save Reeve. It had broken her heart then, but she knew Reeve and she'd known that he would have made that sacrifice to protect the world from the god inside his body. Faron had stopped

THIS ENDS IN EMBERS

her from making that choice—though she'd done it by running off with Iya and Lightbringer before Elara could in turn stop her. But tearing a rift between worlds was easier than Elara could have imagined, and she already looked forward to locking Iya away within one.

For Reeve. For Faron. For herself.

The eggs sank into the glowing hole in the ground until they'd disappeared. Elara closed the path and then, gasping, ejected Irie from her body. She was breathing so hard that Torrey came to her side immediately, helping her stay on her feet. She'd almost forgotten that *easy* didn't mean it wasn't *exhausting*.

"Let's start packing up before our good luck runs out," said Torrey.

Elara was too tired for anything more than a nod. But though her body was weak, she felt like smiling until her cheeks hurt. *Take that, you bastard*, she thought as they picked their way through the rubble, *because you're next.*

CHAPTER THIRTY-TWO

FARON

R EEVE AWOKE THREE DAYS LATER.

Faron was dozing off when he surged up like a drowning man breaking the surface of the sea. His eyes were wild with panic, his heart frenzied beneath her hand as she touched his chest in an effort to keep him from toppling off the side of the bed. His feet kicked at the sheets, but he stilled at her touch, breathing like a cornered animal.

"I'm here, I'm here," Faron murmured, meeting his gaze steadily. "You're okay now." His eyes were so wide that his irises looked like a drop of ink on blank paper. "You're free."

They breathed together until the tension bled slowly, so slowly, from Reeve's body, his shoulders lowering from his ears, his pulse no longer a clarion call. When it seemed as if he was seeing *her* and not whatever nightmares had lived behind his eyes as he slept, she brought her hands back to her lap.

"Faron," he said. His mouth twisted. His breathing picked up. His entire body was shaking, so violently that she thought for a moment he'd sunk back into his nightmare. But then he continued speaking. "Faron, he killed them. Wayne and Aisha, he—they—"

THIS ENDS IN EMBERS

"It's okay." Faron reached out for him again, a weight in her chest that grew only heavier when tears streamed down his cheeks. "It'll be okay. We're okay."

"It's *not* okay." He held her tighter, his fingers unsteady where they dug into the small of her back. "Those were my friends. *He killed my friends.*"

"I'm sorry. I'm so sorry—"

"They're dead—"

"I'm here. I'm sorry." Faron climbed out of her chair and onto the bed, and wrapped her arms snugly around his body. The sound that Reeve made, as if his heart had been punched out of his body, made her want to cry with him. "I'm here."

It was surreal, to be with him like this. They had only kissed once before Iya had taken over Reeve's body, and for almost every day before then they had been enemies. The number of times he had held her could be counted on one hand, and yet Faron felt at home. She let him mourn his friends, murmuring insensibly because there was nothing she could say that would make this situation better. All she could do was hope that he was taking as much comfort from her as she was from him.

Faron hadn't realized how much working alone had affected her until she was finally promised the return of one of the few people she trusted. He was right. It wasn't okay. But it could be, in at least one definition of the word, if they were together.

She ran a soothing hand over his shoulders, again and again, until his sobs subsided and she could no longer feel the damp stain of his tears. He stayed there, arms tight around her waist, for so long that she wondered if he'd fallen back asleep, or if maybe he was thinking, possibly even about how weird it was for Faron to

293

be wiping his tears instead of doing her best to cause them. Would it be appropriate to kiss his cheek? Did he even still want her that way?

Faron shook her head. That should be the last thing on her mind.

The action jolted Reeve, who pulled back just enough to study her in that peculiar way he did, as if he were attempting to read her the way he would a book. Faron couldn't help smiling.

"I can't believe I actually missed that," she teased. "You're still an ass."

Reeve's mouth twitched as if he wanted to smile but had forgotten how to. "I don't know why I thought you'd be nice to me after that kiss."

"This is the nicest I've ever been to you."

He pressed his forehead against hers and huffed out a breath. "Point well made."

They breathed together, in their own little world. Faron wished that nothing could shatter this peace, but she had no idea how long they had left before Iya returned. For all she knew, he would never let them be alone together again.

"Iya has taken over Jesper Soto's body the same way he took over yours," Faron explained. "He's been experimenting with blood magic, apparently, and transferring from your body to Jesper's gave him his full power back." She bit her lip, the words *He did it for me* getting caught in her throat. Instead, she told him about Jesper's kidnapping, about capturing the Emerald Highlands, about the feral dragons, and about Elara's daring rescue attempt. She swallowed back any explanation of how she'd gotten Elara to leave; she'd given him more than enough to digest for now. "How do you feel?"

THIS ENDS IN EMBERS

"I don't—" Reeve dissolved into a coughing fit. Faron hurried to get him a glass of water and a roll of bread that she slathered with butter. He drained the glass in seconds, but he ate slowly, breaking off pieces with his fingers and chewing as if he had forgotten how. Panic sat in her chest, but she needed to be calm for his sake. "Weak, I think. Confused. But...better than I have in months. Maybe years."

Faron melted in relief. "Yeah?"

"Yeah." He took another slow bite. "Sometimes, it was like...it was so loud in my head. I thought I was just anxious. Turns out it was an asshole god."

Faron laughed, and, if it sounded as if she were on the edge of tears, he was nice enough not to say anything. "You could *also* be anxious."

"I probably am, yeah," Reeve said with a laugh of his own. Even after his laughter tapered out, a smile remained on his face, gentle and bright and impossible to look at directly. But when she tried to turn her head, Reeve captured her chin in a tender touch. She stared down at a blue like the surface of the ocean at midday, sparkling, sparkling. "I want to kiss you."

"Now?" She smiled. "You're not well. Your breath probably stinks."

"If you don't like me when I'm stinky, you don't deserve me when I'm minty."

"*For Irie's sake.*" Faron shoved him, wrinkling her nose at his answering laugh. "Go brush your damn teeth, and then we'll talk about kissing."

While he was gone, Faron rubbed her fists against her eyelids so hard that red burst against the black. Her face was hot. Her lips were dry. For the first time in months, she wondered if she looked okay: Her braids were limp, itching to come out, and she hadn't put on makeup that morning. Her day dress was rumpled from the chair, and her lower back ached. She wasn't ugly—though, admittedly, no one but Reeve had ever expressed that sort of interest in her, so maybe she was—but there were pimples breaking out along her hairline and jaw, and her mouth tasted of old jam.

Before she could flee to her room to brush her own teeth, Reeve returned.

As always, he looked amazing. Color was already returning to his pallid cheeks, his curls grown long and bouncing with every step he took toward her. They curved around his ears, brushed the back of his neck, and combined with his unshaved chin to lend him a roguish appearance that intrigued her. His smile held a promise. It made her feel warm all over.

Faron hovered next to the bed, unreasonably nervous. "Are you sure that you're all right? I mean, you were in a coma. If—if you need to take it easy..."

"Are you concerned or afraid?" Reeve asked, stopping a short distance away to study her again. Her nervousness shrank, shifted, until it felt more like anticipation. "You know we don't have to do anything if you don't want—"

Faron kissed him. His hands cupped her cheeks, and her arms wrapped around his back, her fingers gripping his shirt to keep her grounded. At first, it felt weird, their smushed mouths and their hot breaths and the way she wasn't quite sure whether she should close her eyes. Faron assumed she wasn't doing it right, that her second kiss was worse than her first, and that Reeve was disappointed.

THIS ENDS IN EMBERS

Then he tilted her head and dove back in for a third, and fire raced through her blood as if someone had lit a match.

Faron gasped, and Reeve's mouth opened, his tongue slipping between her lips and drawing from her a sound she hadn't known she could make until that moment. She pressed into him, hypnotized by the slick glide of their tongues, the soft brush of his hair against her forehead. Their kisses turned greedy. Desperate. Hungry. And all the while, Reeve held her with such soft hands, as if he knew she were unbreakable but he didn't want to take the risk.

He said her name in a way he'd never said it before, a low growl of syllables, and then his mouth was on her neck. Faron's knees gave out.

"Whoa!" Reeve caught her with an arm around her waist, his lips red and damp, his eyes glazed over. Faron seriously considered flinging herself out the window, just to spare herself the embarrassment, but his grip tightened around her as if he knew what she was thinking. His grin was annoyingly smug. "I guess I should have warned you that I'm a really good kisser."

"I'm going to bite your tongue off," Faron said peevishly.

Reeve sat on the edge of the bed, taking her with him, helping her rearrange herself so that she was comfortably straddling him. His thumb tapped patterns against her hip bone, and she was so sensitive to his touch that every tap felt like a bolt of electricity. At least his breathing was as ragged as hers, so she wasn't the only one affected by this...thing between them.

This love.

Faron pressed her forehead against his. "I really like you."

"I love you."

She froze.

"You don't have to say it back. I know it takes you a while, if ever, to feel those kinds of things, and I don't expect you to." Reeve's nervous but determined expression cracked her heart in two. "But, yeah. I do. I love you. And I'm afraid if I don't say it now, I'll never get the chance."

"You—" Faron managed before her voice gave out.

Reeve swallowed. "Yeah. Is that okay?"

"I—yeah, of course. Hey. *Of course.*" Now it was Faron's turn to hold his face between her hands, to look at him as if he were something precious. "You're allowed to do—and feel—whatever you want, okay? I was just . . . surprised."

Surprised and ashamed. He wouldn't say that if he knew everything that she'd done. No one would.

"Why? Because you're a nightmare?" Reeve asked, a smile growing at her indignant protest. He placed a kiss on the center of her palm, and that shut her up abruptly. "My whole life has been trying to please people. When I was sick, I didn't want to give my parents more reasons to worry about me. When I moved to San Irie, I didn't want to give people more reasons to hate me. But you—you were impossible to please. You hated me, and not for any good reason. I could tease you. I could snap at you. I could *breathe* around you. When I realized how I felt about you, it seemed obvious in hindsight. How much I looked forward to our arguments. How I'd think about you for hours. How sometimes I just wanted to—"

"Kill me?" Faron suggested with a raised eyebrow.

"Mm, something like that."

Reeve kissed the inside of her wrist before meeting her eyes again. Faron could still feel the warmth of his lips there, like a

THIS ENDS IN EMBERS

brand. She could feel the warmth of his words, too, wrapped around her very soul. It was more than she deserved. *He* was more than she deserved.

She lowered her gaze and climbed out of his lap, fidgeting with the cuff of her dress. Her abandoned chair awaited her, but she pulled it closer to the bed so he didn't take this as a rejection. Her mind played his confession on a loop, and the more it thrilled her, the more she wanted the ground to swallow her whole. Reeve had been awake for less than an hour, and in that time, he had already cried for his friends and made her feel loved in case they never got to be together. He was so *good*—and she was a monster.

"I...I have something to tell you," she whispered. "Well, a lot of things, and I'm not proud of any of them. But if—if you really love me, you need to know. Because after you hear this, you might not."

Reeve tilted his head. "Okay...."

Faron couldn't look at him, so she confessed her sins to the bedsheet. The village she had damned by finding their hidden children. The injuries she had caused Marius Lynwood and the Warwicks. Forcing her way into the souls of Jesper and Signey Soto...and even Elara. She told him about her failure to learn anything substantial, her failure to bond with Gael so he could emerge without Lightbringer's influence, her failure to leave Iya's side when she had the chance. She told him about her anger, that ever-present anger, that made her feel both out of control and more focused than she'd ever been in her life.

"I used to think this would all end one way," Faron finished. "Either I'd die in battle, or I'd be captured by Langley and imprisoned at the Mausoleum—if not worse. When the war ended, I felt like a dull blade, the kind you toss in the junk drawer between the

299

single earring and the old rag you keep meaning to throw away, you know? I didn't want another war or anything like that, but I lacked purpose. I thought...this was my purpose. To be the only person who could reach him, stop him. But all I do is hurt people. Destroy things. Make everything worse. He and I are co-Riders, which means our souls are the same. And he's a monster. I'm—I'm a monster."

"You're not a monster, Faron."

She closed her eyes. "How can you even say that?"

"Because I know you." Reeve said it as if it were simple. As if it were obvious. "I've always known you. Growing up, I was... torn. Between Langley and San Irie. Between missing my family and doing what was right. Between wanting to be your friend and knowing I should stay away. Picking on you was the only time I was ever truly in the moment. You were the only burst of color in the gray. I never knew myself, but I always knew you."

"Because you hated me," Faron said, a little too bitterly for it to be funny.

"I never hated you. I just didn't like you sometimes."

The reference to one of their most vicious arguments surprised her into laughing. She dragged her gaze up to his and almost gasped at the affection on his face. Even with all her sins laid bare, he didn't look afraid. He didn't even look disappointed. He was watching her as if he might never again get the chance and wanted to memorize her from the top of her head to the bottom of her feet. His hand was upturned on the bed between them, a quiet invitation. Faron's heart felt as if it might explode, but she placed her palm on his. When his fingers closed around hers, she had to swallow back the urge to cry.

THIS ENDS IN EMBERS

"I know that things are a mess right now, and I know this is hardly a fair comparison, but there was a time when I would look at you and imagine us just like this—a time I would sternly tell myself to wake up from that impossible dream," Reeve said, his eyes full of nothing but love. "When you kissed me that day on the airfield, I knew in that moment who I was, what I wanted, and where I belonged. Everything in perfect alignment. Everything beginning and ending with you. No matter where this war takes us or who this war turns us into, if we're together in whatever way you'll have me, we can do the impossible. I learned that from you."

"I love you."

Reeve smiled. "That was obvious, but I was trying not to be an ass about it."

"Well, you failed," Faron said, but she was smiling, too.

Somehow, she felt...calm, and she was afraid to lose that feeling. Reeve, so skilled at tugging her out of her own head, had always had this effect on her, but it was different when he used that skill in this context. Before, it had been annoying, how hard it was to remember that she needed to hate him, when he was the only person who seemed to be looking out for her sometimes. Now it was yet another reason for the ember in her chest when she looked at him, a quiet, steady warmth that kept her going on her most hopeless days.

"I still love you, though," she continued. "I'm sorry that I'll be bad at it."

His smile widened, too wide to be attractive, a dorkish spread of teeth that made him look like a little kid. "You, um...You can be bad at it. I don't mind."

"No, I want to be *good* at it," Faron insisted. "You deserve that, Reeve."

"I don't think this is about deserving. But I'm too tired to argue with you right now." His eyes fluttered shut, but he didn't let go of her hand. His thumb brushed her knuckles in a soothing rhythm. "He wants you to believe that you're a bad person, because if you're still good, after everything, then it means he just made all the wrong choices. But the difference between the two of you is that, at some point, Gael Soto stopped trying. And you're too stubborn to ever, ever stop trying."

"Don't think I didn't notice you complimented and insulted me at the same time."

"I'm serious," Reeve said, though he ruined it by yawning.

Faron wondered if she would ever stop smiling. "I know you are. Shut up." She waited until his breathing had evened out and his grip on her hand had loosened before she whispered, *"Thank you."*

CHAPTER THIRTY-THREE

ELARA

VALOR LOOKED EVEN MORE MAGNIFICENT NOW THAN WHEN THE drake had been newly commissioned.

While Elara and Aveline had been dealing with international politics, the queen had given the order for Valor to be airlifted from Deadegg and taken to Highfort to be restored. With war looming, and the threat of Iya's inevitable reaction to his missing dragon eggs, Aveline wanted San Irie to have every tool at their disposal—and it was much faster to fix a drake than it was to build a new one from scratch. The queen had been home longer than Elara had, but this was the first time either had seen the repairs.

All drakes were built to emulate the shape of the Langlish dragons that they fought, but the form that took was typically generic: four legs, a long tail, a triangular head, and a mouth that opened to throw blasts of magic at the enemy. But, as golden as the sun that glinted off the scalestone, Valor had been given the curved horns that some dragons had, an added level of defense for the upcoming battle. Elara thought it looked otherwise unchanged, if perhaps a little smaller, though she wasn't sure if that was accurate or if her memory had built up the drake to be something it never was.

The last time she had been this close to it, she had been hoping to be chosen as a drake pilot. Now, she was watching as yet another hopeful cadet failed to make a connection with Valor.

Beside her, Aveline chewed her bottom lip until it reddened. "I thought we would have found at least one pilot by now."

In the last week, the queen had readied everything on her end. With or without Valor flight ready, they would be taking the fight to Iya rather than waiting for his next move. Returning the dragon eggs to the divine plane might not have weakened him, but he would no longer have access to those dragons as part of his army. They wouldn't get a better chance to end this.

But it was clear from Aveline's fit of nervous energy that she'd *expected* Valor to be flight ready. Elara didn't know if their odds were that bad without the drake or if Aveline just needed the illusion of control, but either way she couldn't relax with so much stress radiating off her monarch.

"It took us months to find three pilots last time," said Elara. "Expecting to do that in a few days may have been too ambitious."

"We do not have much choice, Maiden."

"Are things really that dire?"

"I hope not. But why leave anything up to chance?"

Elara eyed Aveline, taking note of the queen's exhaustion. Aveline was always tired, but it seemed different somehow. There was a frantic edge to it that pushed it closer to a passive panic. "Is everything all right?"

There was a slight pause. "Do you ever wonder what it would be like if none of this were our problem?"

Elara's eyebrows furrowed in silent bewilderment.

"If I weren't the queen and you weren't the Empyrean. If neither

THIS ENDS IN EMBERS

of us was old enough to enlist, even if we wanted to, and all these wars and politics were someone else's burden to carry. What would that be like?" Aveline's eyes were on the drake, but she didn't seem to see it. "Back when I still answered to the name Ava, the revolution was something I heard about in whispers, in the papers. It shaped my life, but it wasn't my life. Some days, I miss that. There was the uncertainty of if we'd live to see tomorrow, but there was the freedom of endless possibility, too."

Elara could hardly remember a time before the fight. It had shaped her in too many ways, changed the trajectory of her life so that peacetime seemed like an illusion and battle was the only time she felt real. But she didn't say that. Instead, she asked, "What would you do with that freedom now?"

Aveline was quiet for a long time. Her cheeks slowly darkened. She cleared her throat, defaulting to her stilted formality. "I was only reflecting. Such freedoms are not afforded to the queen of San Irie."

A group of soldiers jogged past them. Aveline's cheeks flushed even deeper.

"Or," asked Elara with raised eyebrows, "do you just not want to be overheard?"

"Maiden—"

"Come on. I think that was the last cadet. Let's see the restoration up close, shall we?"

Before Aveline could protest, Elara grabbed her wrist and dragged her toward the drake. No one stopped them as they climbed up the exit ramp and into Valor's hollow flank. She released Aveline once the floor evened out. There was a cockpit in the head and another one near the tail, but Elara's eyes were drawn to the dark cockpit in the center of the room. This was where her dreams had died. This was where her friends had died. Swallowing, she took a step toward it but stopped herself before she could go any farther.

Her heart felt as if it were sinking, but she ignored it. This was *not* about her.

"So," she said, turning to the queen, "what *would* you do with that freedom now?"

Aveline was paying a little too much attention to the curved metal walls. Elara waited her out, letting the silence between them grow taut with expectation. The sound of marching soldiers, the clank of still-working drake mechanics, and the low bark of orders from officers swelled to fill that silence, but the air inside the drake grew thick. Finally, Aveline lifted her diadem from her curls, toying with the golden suns that decorated it.

"I suppose I thought by this age I would be...more certain of who I am and what I'm doing. My action and inaction affect so many lives, it's impossible to ever have that certainty." She stared down at the diadem, which twinkled in the light that poured in from the drake's windows. "I thought I'd have a place of my own. A partner. Maybe teach dance to children in Guirland. Stupid, small dreams."

"That's not stupid," Elara said. "I wanted to be a teacher at one point, too."

Aveline's grip tightened on the diadem. "Pilar Montserrat and I were once involved."

Another silence followed. Somewhere outside, the shriek of birdsong proved that life hadn't stopped, even if Elara's thoughts

THIS ENDS IN EMBERS

had jerked to a halt. Aveline's throat bobbed as she swallowed hard. The silence pressed forward like an unwanted visitor.

"Oh" was all Elara could think to say as several things fell immediately into place.

Aveline's brief glance was nervous, gone before Elara could fully process it. "It was just... she's very"—her lips pursed—"persuasive."

"And—and attractive."

"And that, yes."

"So, you"—Elara blinked—"you like women?"

"I like *people*. It doesn't matter to me how they present themselves."

"Ah."

More silence followed.

Aveline sighed loudly. "Please don't be awkward about this."

"I'm not! I'm not. I just didn't know." Elara cleared her throat. Maybe it was for the best that she hadn't known. She had thought her impossible crush impossible not because Aveline was queen but because she had been so certain that Aveline had liked men and only men. Her assumption had been based on the soldiers on whom Aveline's eyes had lingered, but it had still been just that: an assumption. If she'd known she'd had a chance, no matter how miniscule... "Is... are you and Doña Montserrat still...?"

"Of course not." Aveline said it so quickly that it had to be a lie. "I admit my self-control is often weaker than my resolve, but it's... We can't. I can't. But there was a time when—when I pieced her into that picture of my alternate future."

Elara moved closer, slowly, but Aveline didn't blink, even when Elara was right beside her. Her muscles were tense beneath Elara's fingers when Elara touched her arm. "What do you mean, you can't? Being queen doesn't mean you aren't allowed a partner."

"She's Joyan. Being the queen of San Irie means that I'm not allowed a partner from a country that *enslaved us.*"

Elara winced, thinking of Signey. "Well, I mean...that happened before we were born, so you can't really—"

"And a Montserrat, besides? How could I explain to my people giving the Joyan royal family such a foothold on the island? They would depose me immediately."

Elara's mouth opened and closed, because there were no words for this situation. The queen was right. Aveline was the ruler of the country. Anyone she chose to stand beside her would be scrutinized even more heavily than she was, and the island-wide protests that had arisen just from the Summit and conference proved she didn't have the luxury of choice. If she took a Novan woman as her spouse, there would be an immediate revolt, a civil war, leaving them as easy prey for one of the empires to swoop back in.

Tournesola Orianne had used Signey as a weapon to discredit the Maiden Empyrean's opinion. Their relationship had been used by Desmond Pryor as a reason Elara was unfit to represent San Irie at all. It would be worse for the queen, worse if she married another royal. Elara was only Empyrean until the gods took back her power. Aveline would be queen until she died.

"I'm so sorry," Elara finally said for lack of something better. Aveline had that look of profound exhaustion again, and it was that more than anything that pushed Elara to continue. "Have you ever considered that maybe Mr. Pryor has a point? An end to the Empyrean, an end to the monarchy?"

"Pardon me?"

THIS ENDS IN EMBERS

"Well, I mean—there are plenty of countries that are doing just fine without a monarchy. I know the Renards were gods-chosen to rule, but just because something has always been doesn't mean it should always be, right? I'm the last Empyrean anyway, remember? When this is all over, you could put power in the hands of a council of representatives or—"

"You want me," Aveline said coldly, "to give in to the dissenting minority, destroy my mothers' legacy, and become the first Renard to abdicate the throne without an heir?"

"I want you to be *happy*." Elara wasn't surprised when Aveline shrugged her hand off her shoulder, but it stung anyway. "You're an *amazing* queen, Aveline. You've done all that's been asked of you and more. But this doesn't have to be your life."

"One life—my life—is not more important than the rest of the world."

"That doesn't mean your life's not important at all."

Aveline's mouth trembled. She sighed, and it was a shaky sound. "I . . . will take this under advisement. Thank you, Maiden."

She walked down the exit ramp, a thoughtful look on her face. Elara should have followed her, but instead she looked back at the cockpit. She had wanted to be a drake pilot so badly, in the hope that it would give her some distinction beyond being the Childe Empyrean's sister. That hadn't been the first time she'd failed, but it had felt the most significant. Maybe Valor had sensed that her intentions were selfish, and that was why she had been rejected. She would never know. It wasn't as if drakes could talk.

Elara drifted into the cockpit, which looked identical to the last time she'd seen it. The cushioned chair with the double-strap seat belt and the neck pillow. The flat panel with its dark screen

309

and lack of levers. The whisper of magic that she felt like a physical touch, residue left behind from the drake mechanics who had repaired it. As if in a dream, she sank into the chair, her breathing slow and even.

So much had changed.

Had Wayne or Aisha sat here? Had their hands glowed with astral magic as they directed the drake into the air? Had one of them died right here where she was sitting? Her eyes burned at the thought. A tear ran down her cheek.

Elara placed her hands on the panel, sending a prayer up to Mala. *If Wayne and Aisha are with you, keeper of the astrals, please take care of them.* And then, as if they could hear her, she added, *I miss you both.*

She didn't realize she had closed her eyes until her lids went red with outside light. The panel was now illuminated, a shimmering screen showing the outside of the drake and the wide-eyed soldiers who had gathered around it. Her stomach swooped as Valor levitated only to drop to the ground with a worrying *clank*. She tumbled atop the panel, scraping her cheek against the edge of it, wishing that she had strapped herself in.

But why would she have? Valor had no pilots. Valor should not have been moving.

Footsteps clattered up the plank. Elara fumbled her way out of the cockpit just in time to see Queen Aveline and several officers staring at her as if she were a wayward astral with no ancestor to claim them.

"Did you just fly this drake?" Aveline asked.

"I . . ." Elara yawned, struck by a sudden desire to sleep. It warred with the building excitement in her chest, their shock mirroring her own. "I think I did. Did I?"

THIS ENDS IN EMBERS

"You lifted it several inches off the ground. Without any help. How did you do that?"

"I don't know," she said, unable to stop herself from grinning.

"Several inches? Are you sure?"

"Is that even possible?"

This question was directed at one of the officers, who stepped forward with a swing of her braided ponytail. "I...can't say we've ever had an Empyrean attempt to fly an unmanned drake, so I wouldn't have thought so until now. But if she can channel the power of the gods, who's to say she can't generate the power of three summoners working in tandem?"

"I wasn't channeling, though," said Elara. Despite all the impossible things she'd seen to this point—an Iryan dragon Rider, an ancient god rising from an inter-realm, her own girlfriend having the power to break dragon bonds—it seemed ridiculous that *she* could still be an impossible thing. She could be lucky, or she could be accidental. But impossible? Her excitement faded. "No, I just touched the panel—"

"And Valor chose you as its pilot, Maiden," said the officer. "I suppose we can still try to find more—"

"We don't have the luxury of time," Aveline pointed out. "If no one else is chosen by the end of the week..." She stepped closer, her dark eyes swirling with an intensity that pinned Elara in place. "Hey, listen to me. Can you do this? Can you pilot this drake?"

Could she? She would give anything to. She would have given *anything* to. She just never thought that she would do it alone. Like this.

"I..."

This was her dream coming true. This was a nightmare. How

could she balance channeling the gods with keeping a drake in the air? Why hadn't she been chosen before? What if her sister needed her on the ground? And after the war was over, would she be tied to Valor for the rest of her life?

She looked at Aveline, kind, exhausted Aveline, who had given up any chance of happiness to lead her country. She looked at the officers, most of whom she didn't recognize, and she forced herself not to mentally deflect their awe. She was the Maiden Empyrean, and she was meant to be a symbol of hope. A shield for the people who most needed protection. Now was not the time to be insecure.

Now was the time to be selfish.

This was her dream, and it was coming true. She would meet it with open arms.

"I can do it," Elara said. "Anything you need, I can do it."

CHAPTER THIRTY-FOUR

FARON

Hearthstone Academy was alive with the news that the dragon eggs were gone.

Faron skipped planning meetings to hang out with Reeve in the infirmary, but she heard about it even there as the healers gossiped in low tones about the saint's plan of attack while they gave Reeve's legs physical therapy. Just over a week in a coma wasn't enough for his muscles to atrophy, thank goodness, but he had lost enough strength in them that they had advised him against attempting to walk long distances until they were finished. Naturally, Reeve spent most of his time reading whatever books Faron brought him from the library.

It would have been like old times, if not for the gossiping Langlish women and the hand-holding.

Faron was still getting used to the hand-holding, but she had discovered that she really, really liked it. Before, her only experience with this had been when Elara or her parents had held her hand, mostly to keep her from running off and getting lost in the market. It was different with Reeve, much like everything was. It was as if he could tell how much she always longed to be touching him and he was more than happy to make it happen. Or maybe he wanted to touch her just as badly.

Her stomach fluttered with something like nerves, but the good kind. Like the anticipation the night before her birthday or the swoop low in her belly when she climbed the dragon egg that had once been in the center of her town. She wasn't a fool. She'd heard this feeling described in songs and poems, in books and legends. But it was still strange to apply these new feelings to herself. No wonder people walked around in such discontent, if they had to deal with this annoying *longing* all the time.

Thankfully, the healers soon cleared Reeve to leave the infirmary and withdrew. Faron waited until she heard their footsteps fade before she said, "He planned to hatch those eggs to add Riders to his army, but that was far from his whole plan. He has my summoning magic and his Rider magic. He has his blood magic. He's spent the last few weeks burning down the Joyan countryside, eliminating their access to their nature spirits."

"That leaves the Étolians, and their royal family won't fight. Especially since their only skill is in healing." Reeve tugged at the collar of his shirt and sniffed, making a face. "I need a shower."

"I'm not helping you with that," said Faron. Mischief curled her lips. "Unless you want me to."

Reeve's entire face went red. "I wasn't—oh, shut up."

Her laughter followed him out into the hallway, where there was a communal bathroom on the other side of the floor. In his absence, she placed her socked feet up on the bed and tilted back her chair so she could stare at the ceiling. Iya could wield three different kinds of magic, and he had made it difficult for the Joyans to wield theirs against him. Reeve had made a good point: The Étolian soldiers

THIS ENDS IN EMBERS

had no magic of their own, which likely meant that Iya considered them less of a threat. The only thing that he respected was power.

She remembered the first time she'd seen him, the real him and not just an increasingly corporeal projection. Using Obie's magic, she had cracked the dragon egg in the center of Deadegg, which had erupted with smoke and lava. Lightbringer had emerged from that egg, with Iya riding on his back. The Gael Soto who she had been working with had been gone, replaced by this human extension of Lightbringer's will.

Faron kept her eyes open so that she didn't see what had happened next when she blinked: Valor's crash and her neighbors dying in an inferno. But she could still hear the sound of the drake hitting the ground, and her own scream echoed in her ears....

"I feel better," Reeve said, returning to the room. "All things considered, do you think it's wrong for me to be wearing this?"

Faron turned to look at him and nearly fell backward. Reeve had showered and changed into riding leathers: clinging black pants, tall boots, and a fitted vest over a shirt with wine-red sleeves that emphasized the muscle in his lithe form. His red-brown hair was still damp from the shower, and a single droplet of water caressed his cheek and slid off his chin into the collar of his shirt. He was standing in the doorway with his arms spread, inviting her to make a judgment on his outfit, but all Faron could do was stare at him. The sound of the chair's front legs hitting the floor was louder than her heartbeat. Her entire body felt hot.

Maddening. These feelings were *maddening*. She would have been perfectly happy never experiencing them.

"What?" Reeve asked, but the curl of his mouth made it clear he knew *exactly* why she was staring.

"Nothing," Faron snapped.

Laughter danced in his eyes. "Should I change?"

"We need to deal with Iya before he deals with us," Faron pointed out, staring at the wall instead, "so you're dressed perfectly for that."

"Do you have a plan, or are we just going to run in and tackle him?"

"I have no idea why I missed you so much."

Reeve slipped between her chair and the bed, so close that Faron's knees brushed against his leathers. She peered up at him and his stupid wet hair and his stupid flushed skin and his stupid half smile, and she was so happy to see him being *him* that it was hard to breathe. "He must know I'm awake by now," Reeve murmured. "Maybe you can distract him by demanding my return to San Irie, and I can try and take him by surprise?"

"And then what?" Faron asked. "Lightbringer knocks down a wall to murder us both with a fireball? Or one of the Generals comes in and locks us up? Or he kills you?" Her throat closed at the very thought. "I won't let him kill you. *I'll* go talk to him, distract him. *You* should try to get out of here."

"Faron, we're on an island overrun by Iya's forces."

"You can steal a boat from the boathouse. There's no one in there anymore."

Reeve's eyes flashed. "I'm not leaving you."

"You have to." This time, it was her turn to whisper. She reached up, placed a hand over his heart. Once, his dragon relic had hung there, a blue eye with a catlike iris in a silver pendant on a chain. Now the space was bare except for the steady *thump-thump* of his heart beneath the leather vest. "He cares for me. That's kept

THIS ENDS IN EMBERS

me alive until now. He has no reason to keep you alive and every reason to use you to keep me in line. Don't give him that chance."

"Huh," Reeve said, his voice as low as hers. "You really do like me."

"I told you I did. Why would I lie?" Faron paused. "Okay, why would I lie about *that*?"

"I believed you! I did. It's just . . . I don't know." Reeve rubbed the back of his neck. "I wasn't awake for a lot of the time I was occupied by Iya, but I remember this . . . I remember feeling things from him that are . . . I don't know. I thought maybe the two of you—"

"*No.*" She wasn't ignorant. She had seen the way Gael had looked at her, the way he had protected her, the way he'd spoken to her. He felt *something* for her, that much was clear. But that was his mistake to make. Faron only felt sorry for him. "There's nothing between Gael and me. I don't look at people like that. Only you."

Reeve held her face between his hands and leaned down. Faron expected him to kiss her, but he pressed his forehead against hers. "When this is over . . ."

He said it like a promise. Faron had no idea what he was promising, but the possibilities made her shiver. He closed his eyes for a moment, taking a deep and bracing breath, before reopening them.

"Come back to me. I've held my tongue through a lot of unfair things, and I've had my fair share of losses. But I refuse to lose you. Not before we have a chance to see what this could be." His gaze burned into hers, a fire not of rage but of passion and raw determination. "I want you to be mine, and I want to be yours. I want us to be us. I'll leave now because you're asking me to, because I trust you to do whatever you think is best, but I would swim the

Crown Sea, walk through dragonfire, drag myself across the earth inch by painful inch, to get back to you, Faron. So come back to me. Okay?"

"Okay," she said, her heart in his hands. "I promise."

Faron found Iya in the library.

She'd only gone into this room before to grab books to read to Reeve, so it was her first time taking it all in. It was two floors, with a spiral staircase in the center to connect them. The rich wood paneling lent the library a cozy vibe, and cream-colored armchairs filled the space. There were long tables with chairs she assumed were for studying students, and gilded portraits of white people of all genders hanging on some of the walls. The high ceiling was painted with a map of the world, and the occasional arched window allowed natural sunlight into the space, though there were electric lamps to make up the difference when that sunlight was gone.

Iya stood in front of one of those windows, his hands behind his back. Faron's pulse jumped, but the view wasn't of the boathouse, as she'd feared. He was looking out at Serpentia Bay, which stretched between Caledon and the continent. Nova was an uneven line of mist and greenery in the distance, and the water before it was choppy and gray. The clouds threatened rain.

"The final battle will begin soon," Iya said without turning around. "You can sense it on the wind, can't you?"

"It's not too late to stop it." Faron stood beside him, keeping him in her peripheral vision. His new body was easier to read than Reeve's had been: Jesper Soto had a certain openness and

THIS ENDS IN EMBERS

expressiveness that even Iya couldn't hide. He was oddly at ease. Or maybe it wasn't odd. Gael Soto had been a soldier, after all. Iya was likely comfortable on the battlefield. "You must know by now that your goals are unrealistic. The world is so much larger than it was when you were forced into the Empty. You can't possibly win."

"Oh, Faron." He chuckled. "I don't need to win. I just want them to lose."

"I don't understand."

Iya lifted a hand, gesturing out the window. "These people have spread throughout this realm like vermin, and they don't know what it is to suffer. They tell themselves whatever they need to in order to sleep at night, knowing that they are *good* and *heroic*. They don't care about what was done to me or how my story has been twisted. I'm a myth. A legend. A villain. But when this war is at its end, whether I win or lose that final battle, they will remember me." His voice lowered, even as his hand hovered in the air almost uncertainly. "The victor writes the story, but they cannot write this one without me. Not again."

"You're *free*." Faron knew she was doing the verbal equivalent of punching a brick wall and expecting the wall to be hurt, but it didn't matter. This was no longer just about distraction. It was about the pain woven into Iya's voice, their shared fear of being forgotten, their shared anger at the tatters of their reputations, their shared thirst for vengeance. All those thorny, complicated feelings that kept them irreparably bonded together. All those thorny, complicated emotions that Faron understood better than anyone else. "You could do anything. You could be anything. It's not too late to—"

"Are you still telling yourself that?" Iya turned to face her.

"That it's not too late? That they'll welcome you with open arms after what you've done? That you can make up for the lies and the devastation?"

"Maybe they won't forgive me. Maybe I've caused too much harm. But that doesn't mean I'll stop trying to make it right." Her mind drifted to Reeve, who thought the world of her even though she'd hated him for most of their time together. She thought of her sister, who was so good that the gods had chosen her as their next Empyrean. And she thought of Aveline, who was a royal pain but never, ever gave up on her people, even when they were furious with her. "*That's* who I am. Someone who never stops trying. I may have forgotten that for a while, but that's why we're not the same. You gave up. You're giving up. And I won't. I can't."

Iya's lips twisted into a scowl. "I see my former incarnation has gotten into your head."

"He didn't tell me anything I shouldn't have already known." Faron risked a step forward. She reached for Iya's face, slowly, waiting for him to push her away. When he didn't, she settled a hand on his cheek, staring up at him with all the gentleness she could muster. "If there's hope for me, then there's still hope for you. Iya— Gael—please don't do this."

Iya tilted his face against her hand. She felt the rough scratch of his stubble, felt the warmth of his breath on her skin. His eyes closed, and for a moment she was back in the throne room at Pearl Bay Palace, making this same plea of a man who had just slaughtered so many of her people. Hoping against hope that she could stop him from killing any more just by appealing to his better nature.

And just as in that throne room, he pulled away.

THIS ENDS IN EMBERS

"I've given you far more chances than you deserve." Iya's hand gripped hers and blazed a sickly green. Shackles of the same color appeared around Faron's wrist, so tight that they began to bruise. "Now, I can no longer risk you interfering."

The library doors opened and Gavriel Warwick entered, Reeve unconscious and slung over his shoulder. "I found this one sniffing around the boathouse, my saint."

"'This one'?" Faron snarled. "That's your *son*." She turned back to Iya, even as chain links appeared from each shackle, winding around her arms and snapping them together. "Please, don't do this. Let him go. At least let *him* go—"

Iya shoved her to the floor. Faron landed hard on her side, pain striking up her spine. Iya's boot pressed against her cheek, keeping her down, keeping her where she was sure he thought she belonged.

"Leave him here," he said, pressing even harder. His boot reeked of mud and sand. Black spots danced in Faron's vision. "I'll deal with the girl."

PART IV

SAVIOR

CHAPTER THIRTY-FIVE

ELARA

ELARA LOOKED AT EACH OF THE NIGHT SAINTS AND FORCED HERself to confront the fact that this would be the last time she would ever see some of them alive. The final battle clawed toward them, blocking out the sun and sucking the air out of every room, and soon they would fly on Hearthstone Academy to stop Iya once and for all. Joya del Mar would march from the west, across the continent. Étolia would march from the north, down the Emerald Highlands. Langlish dragons would fly for Hearthstone with their Riders, keeping Iya's forces busy in the air. The first attack had been on a smaller scale. This time, they would hit Iya with everything they had and hope it would be enough.

With Aveline's blessing, Torrey had come to retrieve Elara on Azeal so she could be there when Signey broke the final dragon bonds. It felt momentous. And terrifying.

One by one, Elara said their names within her mind. Damon Smithers. Rupert Lewis. Giles Crawford. Arran Hyland. Their sage dragons, Nizsa and Stormborn. These were all the dragons and Riders who hadn't left with Iya, weren't in the hospital, or hadn't died long before. Three dragons and six Riders on their side, two

Riders incapacitated, and the remaining eight dragons and eleven Riders—because Elara doubted that Faron would fight her even now—on Iya's side.

The odds were so bad, they were almost comical.

But they also had the drakes: Liberty, Justice, Mercy, Nobility, and Valor. Elara had flown Valor across the Crown Sea just to make sure that she could, the other four following close behind her to make sure they could catch her if her magic failed and she was sent plunging into the ocean. All the drakes now waited in Beacon, where the queen and the pilots would meet up with the Langlish armies. Elara had left before she could take stock of how many soldiers each empire would send, but she hoped it would be enough.

No. It *would* be enough. She *needed* to believe that added power would match Lightbringer's ancient magic and endless malevolence. She needed to believe it to get through this day.

"The last time I did this, I passed out for a week, so bear with me," said Signey. "But I think that was a matter of scale. This should be easier with sages. Right?"

They had all arrived in the north of Langley, in the city of Tarragon on the banks of the Tenebris River. Mountains cut through the northern part of the sparsely populated metropolis, and the midafternoon sun made them glow like jewels. High cloud cover gave the impression that a monstrous fog was slowly eating away at the peaks. Giant brown rocks, slick with moss, littered the edge of the Tenebris, a wide ribbon of blue that raced south toward Serpentia Bay.

It was beautiful. A respite in the middle of an unfurling nightmare. More importantly, it was vast enough for three dragons—two sages and a carmine—to meet comfortably.

THIS ENDS IN EMBERS

Signey's back was to her, but Elara could picture the concentration on her face. The way she would whisper *okay, okay, okay* to herself before she got started, which was the only pep talk she would accept before she had to perform. Elara tried not to look as worried as she felt, but she couldn't get the image of Signey's unconscious body in the infirmary out of her head. A few feet away, Torrey looked similarly apprehensive. If it weren't for the war—weren't for the fact that Iya could easily turn bonded dragons and Riders against them in today's fight—none of them would let Signey do this so soon.

Of course, no one ever *let* Signey do anything. She would have found a way to be here even if they'd left her behind. Elara's stubborn, noble warrior.

Elara hoped this worked. She also hoped it didn't.

Her next breath came out shaky.

Wind whipped across the plain. At first, Elara thought it was an effect of the magic, but then she noticed Stormborn shifting uneasily, his tail swinging slowly through the air and creating a breeze. Even Azeal seemed agitated, though she couldn't properly read his expression. Stormborn settled after a touch from Giles, and the world was still again.

Then Arran made a sound like a dog being stepped on. "I can't hear him."

"I'm sorry," Signey said bleakly, moving on to Professor Smithers and Mr. Lewis. There was a pause as they whispered something to her that Elara couldn't hear over Stormborn's restless sigh. But whatever it was made Signey say, "I know."

The breaking of the final bond seemed to happen between one breath and another. Signey swayed on her feet, and Elara hurried

327

forward to catch her, but Signey steadied herself just as Elara reached her side. Her face was drawn, and her throat bobbed as she swallowed hard. She watched as Nizsa lowered her triangular head, pressing her snout against Mr. Lewis's side, and he and his husband ran their fingers over her scales in a loving goodbye. Signey watched them as if she'd been stabbed and she wanted this to be the last thing she saw before she bled out.

Elara touched her shoulder. "Are you okay?"

"I don't know," Signey replied without looking at her. "But I did it."

"You're still conscious, so that's a step up." It was meant to be a joke, but it fell flat between them. Her girlfriend didn't even seem to notice that she'd spoken, and the smile that Elara had dredged up died on her lips. "What does it feel like?"

Signey swallowed again. "Like severing a limb."

Her tone said, *It hurt*. Her tone said, *It will haunt me*. Her tone said, *I need you*, but she didn't say anything else to clarify exactly what she needed. Elara stepped closer, and Signey leaned against her. She didn't turn for a hug. She didn't reach for Elara's hand. She just stared at the results of her work, the Riders mourning the loss of something they had once thought impossible to lose. Elara had felt the same kind of grief when she'd realized that her bond to Zephyra had cut her off from her ability to summon astrals; she remembered the hollowness, the crisis of identity, the fear of navigating a world without such an integral part of herself.

With that in mind, she raised her voice. "I may have joined you late, but, in that time, we have dealt our enemy a significant blow. I hope you can trust me when I say ... I'm afraid. I'm afraid of what this battle will bring. I'm afraid we'll lose. I'm afraid that Iya will

THIS ENDS IN EMBERS

take even more from us before we manage to put him down. But none of that scares me as much as the idea that this is the last time you'll have your dragons."

They had known, of course, because Elara couldn't have kept such a thing from them. A choice made without all the facts was no choice at all. But the loss of these final bonds had made a concept feel all too real, and there was hollow sadness in every gaze.

"I'd do anything to keep them here, but we can't keep them here and have them remain *them*. As Azeal said, for years, they have loved and protected you in life and in death. For years, you have loved and honored them as best you could. No matter what happens next, that will never change. If they must return to the divine realm, let them return victorious. Let them return loved. Let them return with the memory of a partnership that grew beyond the need for a celestial bond: a partnership forged by choice and welded with love.

"And let us say goodbye to them knowing that the greatest threat to our world was destroyed by our combined power," Elara finished. "I wish I could take this sacrifice away from you, but I can at least give you the gift of a proper goodbye. And I'll be right there in the air alongside you—right there to watch us triumph. Are you with me?"

Cheers rang out, mainly from the two boys. However, there was a glint of pride in Professor Smithers's eyes. He gave Elara a single nod of acknowledgment before helping his husband climb into the saddle and then strapping himself in. On the other side of the field, Arran and Giles climbed onto the back of Stormborn and took off toward one of the distant mountain ranges, likely for the privacy to mourn their bond in peace. Then Nizsa carried Professor Smithers and Mr. Lewis south, toward Beacon, leaving Elara alone with her former den.

Well, she thought with a pang of loss, most of her former den.

"That was a nice speech," said Signey with a small curl of her lips. It was the closest she would come to smiling right now. "You would have made a fine officer, if you'd actually enlisted."

Elara wrinkled her nose. "I don't want death to be my whole life. I just wanted to do something good, and I am." She paused. "Right?"

"You're doing your best," Torrey said, joining them on the riverbank. "That's all any of us can do."

The Tenebris rippled and foamed, and the air was thick with the promise of rain. That rain would feed the soil and plants, but there were parts of the lands that would never again bear life. Lightbringer and his army had leveled farmland here and in Joya del Mar. San Irie still hadn't recovered from the damage Langlish dragons had done to their fields, but Elara knew now that wasn't the fault of the dragons. A dragon was only as good or bad as their Rider, and she had met the best and the worst of them.

"I'm scared," Signey admitted, glancing at Elara from the corner of her eye. She sounded as if she were confessing to a crime, and Elara's stomach twisted with guilt. "If Iya is in Jesper now ... If I have to face my brother today ..."

"I won't let you do that," said Elara. "Either of you. I'd rather fight Jesper myself than force one of you to do it."

"Jesper's been my best friend for ... I don't know. It feels like a lifetime," Torrey whispered, her head bowed. "He made me laugh when I was crying over my first breakup. He hid in closets and air vents with me when I wanted to spy on my parents. He read books with me and to me. It just feels like I failed him."

"And Zephyra," Signey added with a sigh. "We didn't save them in time."

"Jesper and Zephyra loved you. Even if they've lost themselves, they love you still. I believe that." Elara hugged first Torrey and then Signey. "Hopefully, we'll get a chance to say goodbye. But don't take on the burden of blame when there's one clear villain in all this."

Signey looked as if she wanted to argue, but something in Elara's expression stopped her. She and Torrey exchanged inscrutable looks, but it was better than the bleak hopelessness that seemed to cover them like a shroud.

"All right," said Signey slowly. "We have a plan. Torrey will ride Azeal. You're going to pilot Valor. I'm going to rip their dragon bonds away when they least expect it. We'll have all the armies marching on Iya's stolen land while I get Faron Vincent and Reeve Warwick out of the blast zone." The last one was news to Elara, and it was clear from the brief flash of a smile that Signey knew it. She would have kissed her, but she didn't think Signey would appreciate sharing such a moment with Torrey. Elara returned the smile, and Signey's smile widened before her voice lowered into a dark promise. "Then I'll face down my ancestor—whether he's in Jesper's body or not—and make him regret that he ever crawled out of that pit."

"*I'll* face down your ancestor, whether he's in Jesper's body or not, and make him regret that he ever crawled out of that pit."

"Without dying," Torrey added. "If either of you die, I'll figure out how to summon your spirits so I can kill you."

With artificial solemnity, all three of them promised to survive the upcoming battle. Torrey even affected a falsetto to promise on Azeal's behalf. If their ensuing laughter had an edge of desperate hysteria, there was no one else around to point that out. It felt good, to be children, laughing at a joke that wasn't funny. If she didn't think about the dragon behind them and that she was in Langley, it almost felt like old times in Deadegg with Wayne, Aisha, Cherry, and Reeve.

Elara could almost feel those friends with her now, as if she *were* capable of summoning their astrals. Perhaps Mala was watching, and, as keeper of the astrals, she was allowing Elara's friends a momentary glimpse at her. *I miss you*, she sent to them, hoping somehow, some way, they would hear her. *And I won't rest until he pays for what he did to you.*

The periwinkle sky stretched out above Elara, disappearing beyond the mountains, reaching out to where her sister and Reeve were. To where Elara soon would be.

This time, they would end this.

CHAPTER THIRTY-SIX

FARON

FARON AWOKE CHAINED UP IN A DUSTY ROOM.

The air was dank and fetid. The walls and floor were stone, and the only decoration was a single empty bookshelf with cobwebs trailing between the open spaces. Iya had removed the green chains and placed her in scalestone prison irons that were attached to the wall above her head. Her shoulders were already throbbing in discomfort, which meant she had been here for a while.

The battle could have already started.

Reeve could be dead or repossessed or hurt.

Iya could be dead, taking Jesper and the secret of her location to the grave.

And Faron was chained to a wall—with scalestone that Iya must have had since the Battle for Port Sol, waiting for the day she displeased him—trapped in some dusty room where no one but him could find her and forced to deal with the fact that hours from now or hours ago her sister would be at war without her for the first time in their lives.

Faron screamed until her voice went hoarse. She yanked at the chains until her wrists began to bleed. She twisted and cried and searched the floor for anything that might help her, but the room was still empty, and she was still alone.

She drew up her knees to her chest, pressing her forehead against them. It was hard to think of anything but feeling sorry for herself. She was familiar with this fear and helplessness. They had been her constant companions during the San Irie Revolution, long before she had become the Childe Empyrean. Elara would crawl into her bed, or vice versa, and they would huddle together as the world outside exploded in fire and ash. Some nights would be quiet, too quiet, the crickets and birds driven off by the constant threat of dragons. Some nights they couldn't hear each other over the sound of roaring dragons and clashing drakes. There had been times when the Argents, typically a misty blue, had glowed orange from the bushfires caused by the dragons. Lives and livelihoods destroyed in an instant.

Every day, new names of the dead in the paper.

Every day, people leaving to join the fight and never returning.

Every day, wildfires raging across the mountain, ever closer to swallowing Deadegg whole.

Faron had prayed, and the gods had listened. But she hadn't prayed for an end to the war. She hadn't prayed for her people to be safe. She had prayed for the power to protect her family, whose charred bodies she saw in her imagination every time she closed her eyes. She had feared being alone in this world, that the Langlish would take more from her than her peace of mind and her ability to sleep at night.

Everyone had deemed her a saint, but Faron had always been selfish. And that had gotten her here: alone. Imprisoned. Powerless.

THIS ENDS IN EMBERS

"I know you're awake," said a familiar voice from the hall. Marius Lynwood sounded so smug that his arrogance bled into the room like a miasma. "I hope you're enjoying the decor. It was so much fun to put this together for you."

Faron glared at the door without saying a word.

"I volunteered to stand guard," he continued, unruffled. "As wonderful as it would be for you to help us win, after what you did? I deserve this. I deserve to have you at my mercy."

"You have no mercy," Faron snapped. "You have no honor, no empathy, and not a single damn brain cell in your head."

"And yet I'm not the one chained to a wall."

"Let me tell you what's going to happen: Iya is going to lose. People like Iya always lose. You'll either die for him, or you'll spend the rest of your life in prison for betraying your own people. All the power you're enjoying now will be used against you and then stripped away from you. And you'll have to live with the fact that in thinking you're better than anyone else, you just proved that you're nothing."

Lynwood didn't respond. Faron imagined him breaking down the door, his fragile ego spurring him to come in to shut her up and, in so doing, give her the chance to take him down. But instead, he laughed.

"Clearly you haven't been paying attention," he said. "Iya is so much more powerful than you could ever imagine."

"Who do you think made him powerful?" Faron shifted on the floor, wondering if she could kick someone in the genitals from down here. "There's a reason he hasn't killed me. I'm the one who freed him. I'm the one whose magic he feeds off. I'm the one who knows all his secrets. Without me, he would lose even sooner. You'd be better off helping me than staying loyal to him, if power is all you're after."

"I'd rather die," Lynwood spat, "than owe anything to you."

"Fine, die. Until then, shut up."

Lynwood made a sound as if he wanted to have the last word but couldn't think of anything worth saying. Faron was done with this conversation anyway. There was no reaching someone like him, the type of boy who had spent his whole life being told he was special. The rise of a god who promised him a position of authority, a position he'd always expected to have without earning, was too alluring. Lynwood would have given his life to preserve the illusion that he was perfection embodied, because the realization that he was mediocre at best would have broken him.

This was who held her fate in their hands. People who cared more about how they were perceived than they did about their own lives—let alone anyone else's.

She was breathing too fast. Her lungs felt as though they had shrunken, and she couldn't get enough air. Every gasp scraped her throat on the way in and out. How could she be here again? How could she have been brought so low? How could Marius Lynwood be out there while she was in here, waiting for death?

She should have listened to Elara. She should have gone with her. Maybe they could have rescued Reeve together. Instead, Faron had charged ahead, believing she knew best. Believing she knew better than *the gods*.

Irie. Mala. Obie. Faron bowed her head, knowing they could no longer hear her but praying desperately anyway. *Do what I never could. Protect my people. Protect my sister. Protect Reeve. I built this prison choice by choice, but they don't deserve to suffer because of me. Please protect them.*

No one answered.

No one ever answered her prayers anymore.

Eventually, Faron slept. Her slumber was fitful, and her body felt as if it had been flattened by a dragon, but there was nothing else to do but cry or sleep. Blood had dried around Faron's wrists, and it now flecked off in rust-brown patches every time she moved. Her stomach begged for food. Her throat cried for water. Her eyes had given up on crying. All it did was dehydrate her.

Her mind continued to show her an intrusive reel of her mistakes. An entire lifetime defined by wars: the ones she feared, the ones she fought, the one she'd facilitated. After the war, she and Elara had been sent to a physician after one nightmare too many. Their parents had been scared, of the changes in them and of the idea of sending them away to a hospital for treatment. The physician had prescribed a change of air, which had resulted in a family trip to the beach.

Faron remembered gazing out at the gorgeous white-topped turquoise, listening to the *shh-shh* of the waves crashing against the golden shore, and wading in until the water swallowed her ankles. She had closed her eyes, had inhaled the brine and seaweed smell, and had felt her heart beating in her chest like a promise. *Alive, alive, alive.*

She hadn't known then, not yet, that alive, alive, alive came with its own challenges. Dying in battle was easy. It lent nobility to a soul preserved in death, a life snuffed out only to be rebuilt as a legend. Living through the war left her with far too much time and opportunity to tarnish her legacy. To disappoint her family, the queen, the gods. It left her frustrated and confused over what she was supposed to do, and who she was supposed to be, when there were no wars to be fought and no enemies to be defeated.

Obie had once told her that a chosen one didn't stop being chosen just because the war was over, but Faron knew now that this wasn't true. Her sister was the chosen one now. The asterisk had led to a footnote: If she could be chosen, she could be *unchosen*, as well. Either way, it was out of her control.

Other things out of her control: these immovable chains holding her to the wall and making her shoulder muscles burn; this impenetrable silence unbroken by the bastard guarding her from outside; a boy god she had thought she could save and who had repaid her mercy with a locked door and a threat. Was Reeve trapped, too, or was he looking for her? Was Elara even alive?

Would Faron still be alive after this?

"Are you going to feed me?" she called toward the door, her voice hoarse from disuse. "Or have you been given permission to starve me, too?"

"Food should be the last of your worries," Lynwood answered. The sound came from lower now, as if he was sitting down. "Don't you hear that?" Faron could hear nothing from this room other than his voice, but she didn't bother to point that out. Instead, she strained her ears past the vacuum of sound, her stomach dropping even before he said, "They're here. The battle has begun."

CHAPTER THIRTY-SEVEN

ELARA

THE BATTLE BEGAN WITH WHISPERS THAT BUILT INTO A SCREAM. Elara recognized the change in the wind, that innocuous moment that erupted into bloodshed, so quickly that it was impossible to trace the factors that had led them there. There was only survival—and she had to survive this.

She breathed steadily in front of the control panel as she guided the drake across the boundary into the Emerald Highlands. Her hands were steady. The anxiety that had followed her every day had ebbed. Battles like this had made her who she was, and she was comfortable with a direction, a weapon, and a bad guy. Swimming in the uncertainty of the past two months had made her feel like a fraud and a failure, but Elara had been a survivor long before she'd gone to war.

Iya wouldn't know what hit him.

Valor flew smoothly under her control, Irie's summoned magic so widely distributed across the drake that Elara didn't feel overheated. Considering the three-hour flight down the continent—and the four-hour journey across the Crown Sea before that—Elara had expected more complications. But the panel allowed her to see everything happening outside the drake on several little screens, the neck pillow was surprisingly comfortable, and she flew at the head of all the drakes, with Nobility pulling up the rear. She felt like a proper drake pilot.

And then a fireball appeared on one of the screens, forcing her to swerve out of formation or be blasted off course.

Irontooth, with his massive teeth and glowering eyes, met them flame-first with no quarter. His stomach and throat were alight, sending blast after blast toward them as his bloodred body blocked the path ahead. Justice drew up alongside Valor, shooting conjured fireballs back toward the Warwicks' dragon. Elara poured more of her divine magic into the drake, and Valor's mouth opened to create a shimmering shield in front of Justice to block Irontooth's next attacks.

There was no time to keep track of anyone else. Irontooth was fixated on the two of them, rolling through the air like a much-smaller dragon to attack them from every side. Justice used its superior speed to stay just ahead of disaster, but Elara could barely conjure shields fast enough, and every blast of fire that hit them felt like a punch to her gut.

Flying across the Crown Sea had been one thing, but it was much harder to keep her drake steady *and* combat sudden threats at the same time. Elara began to sweat, her heartbeat picking up as she overworked herself. This was something they should have practiced—a single person piloting a drake during a battle—but when would they have had the *time*?

Elara realized that she was panting, her fingers curled against the control panel like claws. She forced herself to relax.

Justice had Irontooth on the defensive, allowing the drakes and

THIS ENDS IN EMBERS

dragons behind them to get past. She had to focus. She blocked another fireball, giving Justice the room to send a bolt of conjured lightning that zigzagged through the air and carved a starburst pattern of black across Irontooth's side.

She hoped Gavriel Warwick was on Irontooth's back. She hoped he was sharing the pain, if not the injury. She hoped that somehow he could tell that she was the one piloting Valor—the girl he had dismissed as nothing but a stepping stone to her sister—and that he would feel the same fear he and his wife had inflicted on her back in Langley.

Justice blew past Elara's shield and collided with Irontooth, extending scalestone claws to drag down the dragon's body, and Elara remembered that she was not the only person with a grudge against the former commander of Langley. She dropped the shield to conserve what was left of her energy and flew on. She didn't want to have to land before she even reached the Hestan Archipelago.

By the time she arrived, the islands had erupted into chaos. All seven were connected by sloping bridges, and Elara had only been to Margon, the second in the chain. The rest she had seen from dragonback during her incendio, but it had been nighttime and all had been quiet.

That was not the case now. Buildings were on fire, smoke touching the sky from as far down as Avilion, the final island in the chain. It was several shades too dark to be mistaken for clouds, and she could see the flash of embers on the wind shed by burning structures. What she could see was overrun with soldiers grappling with one another on the flattened terrain. Some were Iya's forces, relatives of his Riders, conscripts from the Highlands and the Archipelago, or Langlish who had abandoned their country to follow their saint. But most of them appeared to be the opposing forces from Joya del Mar and Langley, with another handful from Étolia. They collided like toy figures, swinging swords and raising shields.

Hearthstone Academy was protected by the enormous serpentine pearl-white body of Lightbringer, whose tail curled around the fortress as if he planned to pick it up and throw it. He had done the same thing with Pearl Bay Palace, as if he needed to look over the carnage. As if he needed to be recognized as the reason it was happening to begin with.

Elara drew Valor up short when the white dragon turned to look at her with those ice-cold green eyes. She could see no sign of Iya—whether he was inside Reeve or Jesper—but she couldn't attack either way.

Hurting Lightbringer would hurt Faron. Until Signey found Faron, Reeve, and Jesper, she couldn't risk it.

Instead, Elara sent a protective wave of fire down between the soldiers. As far as she knew, most clothing in Langley was fireproof, and their forces had already been outfitted with uniforms in the same material before entering this fight, so her flames would be little more than a distraction. But she winced anyway, half because she could be killing innocents without seeing the damage from her magic, and half because Valor's fire sputtered unevenly like a striking match.

Are you all right, Maiden? The queen's voice floated up from the panel, an astral call from Nobility. *If you are struggling, I need you to be vocal about it.*

It had been such a long time since Nobility had been used for combat that they had decided to ease the decommissioned drake

THIS ENDS IN EMBERS

back into it by having the pilots survey the land without attacking. Nobility was somewhere high above, reporting the movements of Iya's army to the other drakes to maximize their strikes. Knowing Aveline, she was itching to get out of the drake and dive into battle to protect her people, but she was the only ruler on the battlefield right now. Elara was glad Aveline had been talked into sitting out a direct fight—for the time being.

And the last thing she wanted was to worry her.

"I'm all right," said Elara. "But Lightbringer has his eye on me."

Are you lying?

Elara winced, wishing for the thousandth time that she were a better liar. "No, he really has his eye on me."

Around her, dragons and drakes collided. Stormborn crushed Ignatz's windpipe between sword-sharp teeth, unaware of Goldeye approaching from behind. He had no Riders on his back, but that meant nothing in battle; sometimes dragons and Riders had to act independently to cover more ground. Azeal and Mercy attacked Blaze from two sides, while the medallion dragon twisted to avoid their flames. Justice and Liberty led the bleeding Irontooth in a false retreat toward where Nizsa lay in wait to ambush him, the emerald column of her throat alight with trapped fire.

Lightbringer continued to watch Elara hover before him in Valor, seeming almost bored by the chaos. If she could keep his attention on her—away from Nobility, away from Signey—then maybe he wouldn't get involved at all. Maybe they could win without engaging him.

Elara closed her eyes and allowed herself to *feel* the raw power of her magic, enhanced by the scalestone around her. She felt the wind that buoyed her metal wings and the smoke that obscured her view of the burning ground. She heard snarls and howls of hostile dragons and the whir and hiss of the determined drakes. She felt Irie's soul swell within her body, more power than the god had ever filled her with before, until she was no longer the one in control. It was shared control, in which they thought as one, moved as one, breathed as one, heard as one.

"*Hello, Irie,*" a voice like shattered glass said as clearly as if someone were in the cockpit with them. One divine creature in the ears of another. "*I wondered when you would show yourself.*"

"*Look what you've done to this world in your ravenous pursuit of power,*" Elara and Irie said together. "*This realm was never yours to rule.*"

Ahead, Lightbringer bared his teeth in a wordless snarl. "*You don't wish to protect humanity. You simply miss your dragon slaves.*"

Elara felt a deep well of sadness from the god. "*We were partners, not enslavers.*"

"*You called us beasts! I am no beast. I am a* god."

"*Lightbringer—*"

A cloud of fire erupted from the dragon and hurtled toward them. Elara swung Valor out of the way, but the flared ends of the flame caught Valor's wing. Instead of dodging, they tumbled in dizzying circles through the air until Elara could straighten out again. Fire washed over her, blocking her sight, knocking her toward the ground.

The same way that Wayne and Aisha had died.

Irie's power welled up again, like blood from a wound, but Elara had been channeling too much for too long. Instead of empowering her, the excess magic made her entire body feel hot. Too hot. She shivered as if she had a fever, black swallowing the edges of her

THIS ENDS IN EMBERS

vision. If she released the god from her body, Valor would plummet. But if she channeled Irie for any longer, she would die in here.

Valor curved around another wave of fire and jetted toward the continent. Lightbringer's tail swung at her, but Elara sank beneath it, racing out of range before the dragon could bring his enormous tail around again. Her vision narrowed to a single ball of light in the middle of the blackness as she aimed for an open patch of grass in the Emerald Highlands. All she had to do was land and she could let Irie go.

Land and let go.

Land and let go.

Land...and...let...go...

Alarms bleated around her. The screens warned that she was losing altitude, losing magic. She felt as if she were on fire, burning, burning, burning....

Valor jolted beneath her, once, twice. Then everything went black.

CHAPTER THIRTY-EIGHT

FARON

DEBRIS SHOOK LOOSE FROM THE WALL AS THE BATTLE RAGED ON. Lynwood had said nothing in what felt like hours, and every sound that reverberated through the prison made Faron want to vomit. She tested the give of her chains one more time, but all it did was aggravate the scabs around her wrists. Faron fought back tears, forcing herself into a state of resignation.

She would happily die here if it meant that Iya was gone. She would rather Elara be alive than for herself to be found. Death came for everyone eventually. Hers was just happening five years after the war that made her famous.

Something slammed into the door.

"*Fuck you,*" she heard Lynwood shout.

There was a sound like cracking wood and the kind of scream that Faron had only heard in radio shows—what hosts thought people sounded like when they fought a battle. Some kind of scuffle was happening out there, and Faron wasn't sure if this was good for her or bad for her.

She searched the room for a weapon she knew she wouldn't find, because it wasn't her first search. She wanted to hope that

THIS ENDS IN EMBERS

Lightbringer was losing and someone had come to rescue her, but it could just as easily be the Warwicks betraying him to murder her themselves, or a Joyan or Étolian come to kill her for working with Iya at all.

She'd had plenty of time to stew in despair, but now Faron gripped her anger close like a precious jewel. She wouldn't make this easy for them. She didn't want to die. She would fight with everything she had to get back to her family.

There was another crash, followed by a thud, and the hallway went silent.

"Faron? Reeve?" said Signey Soto. "Are you in there?"

Faron cried out, but her throat was scraped raw. She made another sound, hoarse and weak and desperate. If Signey moved on, never knowing where she was—

The wall imploded.

Rocks and dust crackled across the floor. The ceiling rained down more debris, a large stone dropping where her legs had just been. Signey Soto appeared in the dusty hole, searching the dimly lit room until she saw Faron chained to the wall and surrounded by gravel and grime. Her stomach chose that moment to rumble. She would have blushed if she hadn't been so relieved.

"Did you kill Lynwood?" Faron asked, trying to see around Signey for a body. "Please tell me you killed Lynwood."

"Forget Lynwood. Fucking *saints*, Faron!" Signey breathed. The dragon relic she wielded, claw rings extending and sharpening her nails, was still glowing. "I'll get you out of—"

"It's scalestone," Faron managed.

"Ah." Signey lowered her hand and bit her lower lip. With the wall gone, Faron could hear more sounds of battle: growls and screams, explosions and crashes. The air that wafted in smelled like dust and smoke.

And blood. Lynwood's blood.

"Okay. Okay, okay, let me just..." Signey stepped farther into the room, staring at Faron as if she were a complicated math problem.

"What are you—" Faron gasped. It was as if she had been underwater and was taking her first breath, as if she had been drowning without realizing she'd been drowning. Her shoulders dipped, freed of an invisible weight, and it was only the rattle of the chains that reminded her that she was not actually free.

"I healed you, but I can also break dragon bonds," Signey declared, sounding an odd mixture of proud and anxious. "I've been practicing—though admittedly I thought freeing you from Lightbringer would be a right bit harder."

"Our bond has never been as strong as his bond with Gael. I've fought him every step of the way. He and Gael...that's a different story. And now that he's in Jesper—"

Signey made a sound as if she'd been shot. "So it's true? He's inside my brother?"

"Oh," said Faron, wishing she had broken that news more gently. "I—yeah. He—yeah."

Signey's next breath came out shakily. She turned her back on Faron, even though it was far too late to hide the sheen of her eyes. Faron winced, scrambling for some way to make this blow a little easier...But how? When she had lost Reeve to Iya's influence, it had felt as if she were bleeding out, and her feelings for him had still been new and fragile. Jesper was Signey's brother. There was nothing anyone could say to make this easier.

Another explosion rocked the building.

All right. Maybe this didn't matter anywhere near as much as freeing herself right now. She stretched her fingers, took a deep breath, and summoned an astral.

It was like coming home, even though she hadn't done this since she was small. Yes, it took longer than it should have, about as long as a child first learning magic, but eventually she saw the cluster of her late aunts around her. She felt their love, the bonds of family and blood that tied their souls to hers, and she wanted to cry at how much she'd missed this. Missed them.

They all peered at her as if she were a stranger, and she supposed she was. After all, she hadn't summoned anything other than a god in six years. Aunt Vittoria settled beneath her skin, the scalestone no longer a barrier so long as the magic she was using was Iryan. She unwound the chains from the wall as if they were made of clay, smoothing them down into the cuffs on her wrists. When she was done, they had turned into a series of scalestone bracelets, ready to amplify her magic.

"Do you know where Reeve Warwick is?" Signey asked as Faron got to her feet. Any sign of her breakdown was behind a mask of determination. Instead of a grieving sister, Faron saw only a soldier. "I didn't find him anywhere in the building, but I assume that Nichol Thompson is guarding him, since—"

"No, he's with Gael," said Faron, crossing to join her. "Well, with Iya." She stretched out her fingers again, this time curling them into fists. "And, trust me, the first thing I want to do is pay them a visit."

Beyond the inner keep was mayhem. Signey explained that Torrey and Azeal had dropped her off just outside Hearthstone and she had made her way in on foot, avoiding skirmishes and breaking dragon bonds. Iya may have controlled the school, but Signey had walked these halls and navigated these grounds for years. She knew more than one way in, and most of Iya's Riders appeared to be on their dragons, unable to stop her. Meanwhile, Azeal, Nizsa, and Stormborn were already fighting without Riders on their backs; the former Riders were on the ground, aiding the soldiers, or in the drakes, contributing their knowledge of dragon weaknesses to the drakes' battle strategies.

Enemy dragons, newly freed, were confused, distracted, *unleashed*.

"Iya wakened their bonds," Faron explained as they hurried down the path toward the boathouse, using the trees for cover. "He used my magic to bind them all to him so he could draw on them for more power, which weakened their connections overall."

Signey looked nervous. "I don't know if I'll be able to break the bond between him and Je—and Gael, then. The first time I broke one, it was Azeal's, and it was so powerful, it knocked me out."

"We'll figure something out."

The dragons, Faron noted, did seem to be fighting with more ferocity than usual. Above Port Sol, they had knocked one another this way and that and spat fire from a safe distance. Above Hearthstone, they tore at one another with teeth and claw. The ground was littered with narrow rivers of blood and wet chunks of scaled flesh. Signey looked as if she were going to be sick, but Faron just noted that none of those chunks appeared to be the paper white of Lightbringer's skin. He was wrapped around the building from

THIS ENDS IN EMBERS

which they had just escaped, but no one had gotten close enough to make him sweat.

Not yet.

"Iya will be in the Emerald Highlands," said Faron, tearing her eyes from the scene. "Normally, it's a three-hour boat ride to get there, but thankfully I have my magic back."

There was a single boat in the boathouse, and it was being guarded by Nichol Thompson. He threw up his arms when Faron and Signey lit up their hands with trapped magic. "Just take it. I don't care."

Signey lowered her dragon relic first, rolling her eyes. "You are such a coward without your cousin to protect you, Nichol."

"Do you want the boat or not?"

"You don't need to give it to us for us to take it. The only choice you have is if you want to be unconscious when we leave or not."

Faron, who had no sympathy for Thompson, sent a blast of light his way. He crumpled to the ground. They took the boat.

The combined force of her summoning magic and Signey's relic magic got them back to the continent in half an hour. They hit the shore so hard that the boat made a worrying creak, but it held together long enough for them to escape it. Faron had thought the Highlands might be quiet, with most of the battle happening at Hearthstone, but she was swiftly proven wrong.

Everywhere, people were fighting, falling, dying. Swords clashed. Magic flashed. Fire sizzled. The sidewalk cracked open, allowing soil to spill free in the shape of a giant hand that dragged four screaming soldiers beneath the earth. A maze of thick mist surrounded another group of enemy soldiers, with only the glint of activated dragon relics visible in the fog. Faron realized, with a roll of her eyes, that she saw very few soldiers wearing Étolian colors mixed among the fray.

"They sent a skeleton army at best," Signey said, a disgusted curl to her mouth. "The tournesola felt that Iya was our problem to create and defeat and did the bare minimum while fortifying defenses at home."

The Étolian soldiers Faron did spot didn't falter, their swords carving a path through the enemies that swarmed them. But it made her profoundly sad how their ruler had failed to help them.

She and Signey made their way farther inland, toward the Snowmelt. Faron had expected more resistance close to the river, but the green field was broken only by the track made by the supply carts and the footprints of marching soldiers. In the distance, she could see the water sloshing along and several figures standing in front of it.

Her heart stopped when she realized that one of those figures was Elara.

"No," Signey breathed from behind her. "Jesper!"

They both broke into a run.

Elara was unconscious and trapped between Gavriel and Mireya Warwick, who each held one of her arms. Standing before them was Reeve, blocked from reaching her by Iya in Jesper Soto's body. Faron called out, causing all of them to turn. A malicious smirk crossed Gavriel Warwick's face.

They were still halfway across the field when the Warwicks threw Elara into the raging river.

And when Reeve immediately jumped in after her.

CHAPTER THIRTY-NINE

ELARA

ELARA WAS SLAPPED AWAKE BY THE SURFACE OF THE RIVER SECONDS before she slid under. Water filled her mouth, her ears, her nostrils. Water shoved her upward or downward or forward or backward. Water would soon become her grave if she didn't figure out which way the surface was.

Her head emptied of anything but the thought that she had to survive. Her weakened muscles burned as she tried to move her arms, her legs. Panic exploded in her chest. Her throat contracted as if it held a trapped scream. It wasn't as though Elara couldn't swim, but she didn't know where to swim *to*. The last thing she remembered was blacking out inside Valor's protective shell as they raced toward the Emerald Highlands, and now she was drowning. Had Valor sunk to the bottom of the Crown Sea? Was the battle still raging? How long had it been?

She slammed into a rock and almost didn't feel it. Every nerve in her body was already alight with the painful realization that she was going to die. Worse, she was going to die for nothing. Buried in a watery grave because she had overshot her own capabilities.

And then the rock moved.

Elara was yanked to the side, and her head crested the water. She inhaled watery air and then promptly began to cough as her lungs rejected the liquid. The river—because it was a river she was in—rolled vigorously onward, but she was inching closer and closer to the bank, something firm against her back and gripping her stomach.

As soon as she hit dry land, she threw up. Then again. And again. And again. It still felt as if she couldn't get enough air, and her chest burned. Adrenaline still made her pulse race as her body tried to adjust to the fact that she wasn't going to die after all. It was far from the first time in her life that Elara had thought she was going to die, but it never got any easier to deal with her own mortality. She had yet to leave her teen years behind and she had already seen two wars.

When she had scraped her stomach and throat raw, she collapsed onto the grass. It felt like a thousand little needles against her shivering skin. She was so tired. War or not, she wanted to rest here. She wanted to *rest*.

"Elara!" She knew that voice. She knew it as well as she knew her own. Her thoughts were like tree sap, clinging together and moving sludge-like through her skull, but *she knew that voice*. "Elara, are you okay? Open your eyes!"

She didn't realize she had closed them. They felt like weights, but she managed to lift her eyelids just enough for a rice-white face to swim into view. Red-brown hair clung to a pale forehead. Droplets of water slid down whitecap cheeks. Sea-glass eyes. Midnight clothes. Reeve. *Reeve.*

Elara reached weakly for him, and he scooped her up into his arms. She said his name again and again, like a prayer, and he

THIS ENDS IN EMBERS

whispered hers back, pressing his cold face against her cold shoulder and holding her as if he would never get the chance again.

"I love you," he said.

"I love *you*," she said.

"Your drake crashed somewhere near here," Reeve whispered against her shoulder. "My parents dragged you to Iya and then threw you in the river to distract Faron and Signey when they showed up. Although seeing Jesper was distraction enough."

"Signey found Faron," Elara said, her adrenaline rush shifting to powerful relief. "They're together?"

"Together and angry."

"And Iya—? He's—?"

"He took Jesper's body when he left mine." Reeve pulled back just enough to look farther up the river, expression grim. "The water carried us a fair distance away, but we should be able to get back quickly. Can you walk?"

"Can I—?" Elara's numb hands gripped his shoulders. She checked every inch of him for bruising, for scars, for even the slightest cosmetic difference. It was impossible to believe he was in such good health after being trapped in his own body, and yet he looked like her Reeve. Wet, but caring. "I can't believe you've been trapped by the enemy for two months, and all you want to know is if *I'm* okay?"

"Well," said Reeve, "you did almost drown."

"You found out your parents traded your body to a trapped god for power. A god that killed our friends. A god that wore you like a coat for—"

"*You almost drowned.*" It was so unlike Reeve to talk over her that Elara's mouth snapped shut. He seemed angry, an even rarer thing. "You're my best friend. All of it—*all of it*—would have been worth it to know that you were safe. And you nearly drowned. There will be time for me to deal with what Iya did, but I would never, ever forgive myself for what my parents tried to do to you."

Elara pressed her forehead against his. Reeve was breathing hard, but there was fear beneath the anger. She saw that now. Even before he'd found out what his parents had done, he'd been estranged from them. They had wanted him dead for treason— treason that turned out to have ruined their plans for him. Elara was the closest thing Reeve had to a family, and Reeve was one of the most important members of hers. He'd been just as afraid of losing her as she had of losing him, and he'd almost had to watch it with his own eyes.

"I know," she murmured. "I'm sorry. I can walk."

He helped her up, and, despite some trembling, her feet held her weight. She jogged in place for a few minutes, and when she didn't collapse, she nodded at Reeve. Together, they raced along the riverbank, hoping they weren't too late. She had promised Signey she would not be forced to face down her own brother, and Elara would keep that promise. If Iya had been able to leave Reeve's body, there was a way to expel him from Jesper's. She wanted the Sotos back together. She wanted Signey to survive this war without losing another member of her family. She wanted to stop Iya once and for all.

With Reeve by her side, it all felt possible.

There was still far too much distance between them and Iya when they heard the scream. Up the river, so distant that they looked like tiny figures, Signey and Faron were fighting Iya. Their hands flashed with the magic of astrals and dragon relics. They worked so well together that Elara was both thrilled and envious,

THIS ENDS IN EMBERS

terrified and sick. Signey moved like a tidal wave, giving Iya no quarter even though he looked like her brother. The few times she faltered, Faron was there to attack in her stead.

Without knowing it, Faron was upholding Elara's promise for her. And Elara trusted her to do it.

"I don't see my parents," Reeve panted.

"There," said Elara, pointing at the winding, rocky path that led into the mountains. Two figures hurried along it, disappearing around the bend of the high cliffs. "Signey knows how to break bonds. If she broke the one between them and Irontooth, they'd need to get somewhere high to catch their dragon's attention."

"I don't know if that's it." Reeve's eyes were cold as he stared up the mountain. "It's more likely that they're trying to escape. They're leaving everyone here to die."

"I wish I were surprised. . . ."

Reeve reached into his damp shirt, but he came up empty. He blinked down at his chest before making a sound of realization. "Right. I forgot that Iya got rid of it."

Her eyebrows drew together. She hadn't noticed the lack of that bump when they'd been hugging, but now it was obvious. Reeve had never taken off his dragon relic. She was used to feeling its weight. For it to be gone now was terrifying.

"Won't you need it?" she asked. "What if your parents are—"

"I don't need a dragon relic to deal with my parents." Reeve smiled, and even though he looked like a drowned animal, there was something heroic about that smile. A confidence she hadn't seen from him in a while. A confidence she could feel rising within her as well, now that she had been reunited with her best friend. "After all. I'm with the Maiden Empyrean."

CHAPTER FORTY

FARON

MAYBE VINCENTS AND SOTOS WERE ALWAYS MEANT TO BE LIKE this: moving around one another like water, strong where the other was weak, weak where the other was strong. A sword and a shield, trading off roles depending on the nature of the fight. Faron had never fought with Signey Soto before, and yet in this moment it felt as if she had been doing it her whole life. It was easy to put herself in Signey's shoes—reluctantly fighting the member of her family who she loved the most—and predict when Signey needed her to be aggressive. It was easy to moderate the strength of her magic so that she didn't burn out quickly, allowing Signey to take the lead. It was easy; so easy, it felt familiar.

Then again, Faron had touched the light of Signey's soul twice already. Maybe as a result, she knew her in a way no one else could.

Signey wielded the magic of her dragon relic like an extension of herself, no less dangerous for no longer having her dragon. Faron, with the magic of her aunt's astral at her fingertips, rained down swords of conjured light on Iya. When he retaliated with powerful waves of fire, Signey stepped in front of Faron to conjure a shield. When he cut through the shield with a sudden spike of

THIS ENDS IN EMBERS

flame, Faron called up a funnel of water from the river to wash him off his feet.

All the while, Signey spoke to her brother. "Jesper," she said as she twisted away from an attack, "you can fight him. You're the strongest person I know. You can help us stop him."

Iya never reacted with anything but flames and fury, but Faron knew him, too. Even with their bond severed, he had two kinds of magic at his disposal and he was using only one. Maybe Signey was getting through to Jesper.

All they needed was an opening, a long enough pause for Signey to sever Iya's connection to Lightbringer, and they could take him down. Tie him up until the war was over and they could figure out how to remove him from Jesper's body.

But Iya fought like an injured animal making a final stand, all ferocity and relentlessness. With the full power of Lightbringer behind him, they would run out of energy before he did.

Faron looked at Signey. Signey looked at Faron.

Faron raised an eyebrow. Signey nodded.

Stepping in front of Faron again, Signey drew upon her largest surge of magic yet, so large that her dragon relic covered her arms with bolts of light. Signey conjured a wall so blinding that Faron had to cover her eyes, and then Signey formed those bolts into massive battle-axes. With a flick of her hand, they began to fall, blade-first, toward Iya.

He jumped out of range, holding up an arm to block both the light and the dirt that flew from beneath the axes' blades.

So he never saw Faron coming until she tackled him to the ground.

They rolled around, warring for dominance, but she had the

element of surprise and the strength of an astral on her side. Iya glared up at her when he landed on his back, his arms trapped beneath her legs. She pressed her thumb against his windpipe in a dark echo of that night in Port Sol, when he'd left fingertip-shaped bruises on her throat. That night, he had leaned close and told her that she was nothing without him. Now she was the one leaning close, her knees digging into his rib cage, and she hissed, "You are *nothing* without Lightbringer."

"*Don't hurt him,*" Signey screamed from behind her. "He's still my brother."

Faron took a deep breath to corral her anger. Her fingers loosened, though she kept her knees pressed against his sides. "Jesper, if you don't help us, Iya will kill your sister. Gael, if you don't fight him now, he'll kill *me*. Is that what you want? Is that what both of you want?"

Iya writhed beneath her, but Faron fed more magic into her limbs to keep him down.

"Jesper, please." Signey appeared over her shoulder, blocking the sun. "I know you're in there. Please tell me you're still in there."

The writhing increased, until Faron could feel her strength waning. Signey was still appealing to her brother, telling stories from their childhood in a voice thick with tears, but Iya was minutes, perhaps seconds, away from freeing himself. They had no more time.

"Break the bond!" she shouted. "You have to do it now!"

Signey came up beside her. Her dragon relics were dark, used up. Her face was damp. But her arm was outstretched, and her eyes were closed.

THIS ENDS IN EMBERS

Iya *roared.*

He bucked off Faron as if she weighed nothing, and she hit the ground elbow-first. Stifling a cry of pain, she scrambled back to her feet. Jesper's body contorted on the ground. A light carved its way through his skin from feet to head, illuminating his shadowy internal organs, crawling up his throat like a glowing hand, and exploding from his eyes and mouth. His roar dissolved into a scream so pained that Faron's stomach turned.

And then it was over.

There was a thud before the light disappeared, leaving Iya strewn across the ground like a doll. Signey dropped beside him, rolling him onto his back, saying her brother's name in a broken voice. Faron inched closer, her magic still at her fingertips, and poked him in the side with the pointed tip of her shoe. He gasped like a drowning man and surged upward, blinking rapidly.

Hazel eyes found hers, wide and terrified. "What just happened?"

"...Gael...?" Faron asked warily. She had retreated to a safe distance away, but it was like looking at a child who had lost their parents in the crowd. Alone in the world for the first time, and feeling all the more vulnerable for it. "Is that you?"

"I can't..." Gael looked up at the sky. "I can't hear him. Oh, gods. I can't hear him. I can't *feel* him."

"Where's Jesper?" Signey asked faintly. Her face was a pale moon, so colorless that her freckles were stark against her skin. "My brother, is he in there?"

Gael touched his chest. "Yes. He was helping you. We fought together to help you break the bond. Now he's exhausted, but he's alive."

"Oh...Oh, saints..."

"You did it," Faron said triumphantly, turning to Signey. "You—*shit*."

Signey had collapsed in the mud, her limbs arranged haphazardly. Faron scrambled over to her, feeling for a pulse. Signey's skin was ice cold. Her eyes were open and unseeing.

"No," she whispered, grabbing Signey's wrist to check again. "No, no, no, no."

There was a hollow silence in Faron's head, a dangerous numbness spreading throughout her body. She checked the side of Signey's neck, and then she checked Signey's wrist, again and again, as if a pulse would magically appear where none had been. Signey Soto, who had made her sister so happy even in the midst of an attack on their island. Signey Soto, who had rescued her from her prison despite Faron's attempt to command her soul. Signey Soto, who Faron was only just getting to know but cared enough about to mourn anyway.

Signey had warned her that she didn't think she could break this final bond, and Faron hadn't listened. Now, she would have to tell her sister that her girlfriend was dead.

"Is she..." Gael trailed off at whatever expression he saw on Faron's face. "Let me see if I can do anything for her. Her body might just be overwhelmed by the magic, and it's put her in stasis until—"

"*Don't touch her*," Faron snarled, but it felt mechanical. Her mind was several steps ahead, imagining how that conversation with Elara would go. How many things would she take away from her sister? "You and your little friend have done enough."

"He's *not* my friend," Gael said darkly. "He's a power-hungry monster who needs to be stopped." He knelt beside her, prying

THIS ENDS IN EMBERS

Faron's fingers from Signey's cold skin. She was too tired to fight him. Tears ran down her cheeks, and her breath came out in soft sobs. "The last time I fought against Lightbringer, he got inside my head, and then he stayed. This time, we can end him. After that... whatever punishment you feel I deserve, I'll accept. But first let me help her. Let me try—with blood magic. Not just because we'll need all the help we can get, but because I did this to my family in the first place. This is a chance to make it right."

Faron finally looked at him, still crying. She felt a spark of emotion in her numb chest, something almost like pride. She hadn't been wrong about Gael Soto. He *had* been twisted by Lightbringer's influence. He *had* wanted to be free, to be a hero again. He *did* plan to redeem himself the only way he knew how.

They *were* the same, and she'd been right to put her trust in him.

It was too late, but it was never too late to take responsibility. And if there was a chance, no matter how small, that they could save Signey's life, then who was Faron to say no? If she had to have that conversation with Elara, Faron wanted to be able to say that she'd done everything she could. She could give her sister that much.

"Okay," she whispered, reaching down to close Signey's eyes just in case this didn't work. "Try your best."

CHAPTER FORTY-ONE

ELARA

THEY CAUGHT UP WITH THE WARWICKS HIGH ENOUGH INTO THE mountain range for the air quality to have changed. Elara hadn't been winded from the run along the river, but even she found it hard to breathe all the way up there. Her wet clothes stuck to her body, and the cold made goose bumps rise across her skin. She had channeled Obie to create stairs of shadow as a shortcut up the cliffside, but the heat of his power didn't prevent her body from having natural reactions to stimuli.

Not that it mattered. She wasn't going to let the freezing weather stop her from what they had to do; besides, if Reeve wasn't complaining about the threat of hypothermia, then neither would she. Whether the Warwicks planned to summon Irontooth to fight or to flee, Elara refused to let them get away.

Not this time.

Mireya saw them coming, and her wedding ring flashed with magic, seconds before a cascade of rocks tumbled down the mountain between them. Elara spread a wave of shadows over their heads, and the rocks bounced off harmlessly as if they were no

THIS ENDS IN EMBERS

more than pebbles. Reeve didn't even blink, didn't stop, didn't turn. He trusted her to protect them. To protect him.

Mireya conjured a small tornado between her palms and let it loose. It sucked up several stones and twigs and flung them in Elara's direction. Elara easily deflected them all and then threw the force of her magic forward, into the cliffs. More boulders tumbled downward, but this time they fell into the path ahead of the Warwicks, cutting them off from going any farther.

This and only this was enough to finally get Gavriel Warwick to turn. His face was a mask of pure contempt.

"Again," he said, "you choose these people, this girl, over your own family. Your own country."

Reeve stopped feet away from his mother and father. Elara couldn't see his expression, but the setting sun lengthened his shadow into something she could use if she needed to. She had her own grievances with these people, but she'd had plenty of opportunity to defy them. Reeve deserved to say his piece to his parents before they went to jail.

"Just stop it, Father," he snapped. "You don't care about me. You don't care about family. You don't even care about our country. All you care about is power and glory. You want victory, no matter how many bodies you have to leave behind. It's not about Elara and me. It's not about Langley and San Irie. It's about you and your *selfishness*."

"Selfishness?" Gavriel stepped forward to block his wife from view. Elara kept an eye on her anyway, but she didn't seem to be trying to run. "You would call me selfish after everything I've done for you? How I've kept you alive? If anything, you're to blame for all of this, you ungrateful little shit."

"Grateful for *what*? You should have let me die if this was the result." Reeve gestured over the plateau, where fire and smoke still coursed through the air. "I appreciate that you raised me, but it was your fucking job as a parent. You don't get to use your basic care as a knife to my throat to get me to do what you want. I don't owe you anything. Besides, the second you made contact with the Gray Saint, this was no longer about me. This was about dominance."

Gavriel's lips curled downward. His hatred made him look ugly, like a monster beneath his skin was finally letting itself out. "And what's so wrong about wanting dominance? Langley flourished under my control. You lived a life of safety and privilege because of us. Do you think such a thing just happened? I gave you a life I never had. I was a boy from a backwater village who worked his way up the military ranks, who worked for everything he had, who worked for everything *you* had. Is it so wrong to be tired of working? To take what was promised to me, no matter the consequence?"

Elara swallowed, hating how similar Gavriel Warwick's story sounded to her own. This man had once dismissed her as nothing more than bait for the real prize, the Empyrean, but all along they had come from the same place. And he had made all the wrong choices. Elara moved to Reeve's side, sliding her hand into his. His eyes were bright with unshed tears, but there wasn't a flicker of sympathy on his face. He gave her hand a squeeze, and she squeezed back.

"The second you started seeing power over others as something you were entitled to is the same second you lost sight of that backwater boy," he said coldly. "Instead of creating a world where boys like that didn't have to suffer, you became the very thing that caused all your suffering. And if you still can't see that, then this only ends one way."

THIS ENDS IN EMBERS

Gavriel stared them down. She could hear distant roars and see the occasional flash of light in her peripheral vision, but Elara was careful not to let that distract her. She curled her free hand, ready to channel Obie's power. Reeve's grip tightened around her other hand.

"You're right, son," Gavriel Warwick finally said. "This was always only going to end one way."

Then he jumped to the side just as a pillar of fire, larger and hotter than any Elara had ever seen a relic produce, zoomed toward them.

Elara gripped Reeve's shadow and converted it into a wall of obsidian blades, but he had already thrown himself in front of her. His hand slid from hers. His arm gripped her waist just as the fire and blades struck from different directions. Everything was light and heat, smoke and blood. Elara flew out of Reeve's arms, the collision of magic pushing her halfway back down the path. Someone screamed, and Elara didn't know who, and her heart stopped as her body skidded to a halt—

When the air cleared, Elara scrambled back onto her feet and ran. Her skin was stinging from cuts the rocks had carved into her, and there were pebbles falling down her back and hair. All she could think about was Reeve. Where was Reeve, that noble fool who had protected her when he had no magic to protect her with?

The rocks remained where she had dropped them, blocking the way up the mountain. Gavriel Warwick lay bleeding on the ground, pierced through by no fewer than ten of her shadow knives. Mireya Warwick was curled over him, her own back split open from several more of Elara's blades. Red dripped from her face onto his, as if she were crying. And Reeve...

Reeve was lying against the cliff face, one shirtsleeve missing. For a moment, Elara didn't understand what she was seeing, only that something was different about him that had nothing to do with his now-dry clothes. Then she realized that it wasn't his shirtsleeve that was missing. His entire right arm was gone, the stump at his shoulder cauterized.

Elara was at his side in an instant. He was so pale that he looked like a corpse, but his chest rose and fell with pained breaths. "Oh, gods. Reeve. Reeve, are you all right? Did I do this? Can—can I heal this?"

He rolled his head toward her, his eyes hazy. "I did this. I—I was acting on instinct, as if I could stop dragonfire with my arm...."

Elara searched the ground around him, but she saw no sign of his limb. It wasn't just gone. It had been annihilated.

"Nothing left...to heal," Reeve managed when she turned back to him. "Hurts..."

Tears dripped down Elara's face as she poured her magic into his charred shoulder, healing what she could. She was no medical summoner; she couldn't grow a whole new arm for him, especially not if his old one had been destroyed by dragonfire. But if she took away his pain, maybe after all this, they could fit him with a scalestone prosthetic in San Irie.

If they got back to San Irie.

Reeve's breathing slowly evened out. Color returned to his cheeks. He looked down at the right side of his body, and his eyes clenched shut. His own mother had done this to him. His own father had outright tried to kill him. Now they were both dying. She couldn't imagine how he must be feeling.

Mireya Warwick's body shuddered. She didn't move, couldn't move, even when Elara stood over her.

THIS ENDS IN EMBERS

"I told him...it wasn't worth it," Mireya croaked. "I told him that...we were dealing with something...f-far beyond our ability to control it."

"You still went along with it," Elara pointed out. "It's too late to be sorry now."

"Sorry?" Mireya turned her head. Blood was everywhere, her once-beautiful face now a crimson collage. There was sorrow in those dark brown eyes, but there was also wrath. "The only... thing I'm sorry for...is that we didn't let that wretch I gave birth to die."

Elara shook with rage. She stepped forward—to summon the magic to knock her out or to punch her in the face, she wasn't sure—but Reeve stopped her. He held her upper arm, staring down at his parents as if they were strangers.

For him, they had probably been strangers for a long time.

A single tear rolled down his cheek, but he just stood and watched as Mireya took one last rasping breath. Death took her away as Elara and Reeve waited. She didn't know what Reeve was waiting for, but part of her expected the woman to return for one last dig. Evil like that didn't die so easily.

Then again, evil like that was human.

Elara shook her head. Two of the figures from her nightmares had been reduced to this: hateful corpses who did not know when to quit. They looked so small. Maybe they had always been this small.

"Lightbringer," Reeve said, lifting his eyes to the horizon.

Elara pressed her forehead against his shoulder, a brief moment of indulgence before the fight to come. "Lightbringer."

CHAPTER FORTY-TWO

FARON

COLOR HAD RETURNED TO SIGNEY SOTO'S CHEEKS BY THE TIME Faron heard her sister's voice.

Faron had watched Gael's every move just in case. He'd taken a knife from Signey's holster and used that to cut his palm open. He'd swiped two fingers through the blood and closed his eyes until it began to glow a deep green, like moss. That same green had begun to illuminate Signey's body, spreading through the veins beneath her skin. Her eyes had fluttered, her body emitting a pained groan from somewhere so deep that even Faron had felt the phantom pain. Her pallid skin had darkened back to fawn brown, her breathing evening out to something healthier. Through it all, Gael hovered, unmoving, above her, and that was how the two of them had remained, right up until Faron heard Elara call her name.

She turned to see that Elara was helping Reeve across a series of shadow platforms that she had conjured over the Snowmelt. Faron was so happy to see the two of them alive that she almost missed a few key details. The first was that Elara was helping Reeve because

THIS ENDS IN EMBERS

Reeve *no longer had his right arm*. The second was that Elara had cried out Signey's name next, because she had noticed the body on the ground with Gael's magic pumping through it.

Faron stepped between them, holding her hands up in a surrendering gesture. "She's okay. It's okay. Well, it's not okay. But it's Gael, not Iya. Signey broke his bond with Lightbringer, so Iya is dead and Gael is himself again. It just...took everything she had."

"Is Jesper...?" Elara asked as she and Reeve stepped off the last platform.

"Alive," Faron confirmed. "Sleeping, apparently. It's Signey we should be worried about."

"Signey is...fine," said Signey, her voice cracking in and out like a bad radio signal. Tears ran down her cheeks, but she ignored them. "Worry about...someone else...."

Once Elara was sure Reeve could walk on his own, she ran forward. Faron expected her to go to Signey's side, but Elara threw her arms around Faron instead.

"You are such a fool," Elara said through tears. Faron started crying, too, feeling so relieved that her body melted into her sister's embrace. "Next time—and I pray to the gods there won't be a next time—we do this together. Got it?"

"I got it," Faron murmured. "I'm sorry about commanding you. I should never, ever have done that to you."

"You shouldn't have done it to anyone," said Elara, still holding Faron as though she were something precious. "But I understand why you did. And I love you."

"I love *you*. I'm so sorry."

Faron tightened her arms around her sister's waist and closed her eyes. She felt as if she were home for the first time in a long time, even though her heart was being torn in many directions at once. She had no idea how the battle was going—if Lightbringer had won or lost. She had no idea if Gael would actually manage to free Jesper once the war was over. She had no idea what had happened to Reeve's arm, though she felt the vengeful urge to attack whoever did it.

But she knew she was where she belonged: with her sister.

Together, they would end this.

Elara let her go, pausing to wipe Faron's tears and press a kiss to her forehead before moving past her to join the Sotos. Faron went to Reeve, unsure whether it was rude to look or not. He was still as obnoxiously handsome as ever, but he was standing oddly, likely because he was unused to the lack of weight. Faron pulled him into a hug next, resting her cheek against his chest so she could listen to his heartbeat. He was alive. They were alive. And, if they managed to stay that way, they had a chance to build something realer than her years of resentful hatred had been.

"Thank you for knowing me," Faron whispered.

Reeve pulled her even closer. "Thank you for trusting me."

"We can't wait any longer," Elara said, drawing their attention back to her. She held Signey's hand between her own, studying her girlfriend's face. "Obie says they need us at Hearthstone Academy to end this. Gael, will you fight for us? Signey, *can* you fight for us?"

"Of course," Signey said, struggling into a sitting position. Elara's arm came around her back to help, and her eyes closed for a moment. The tears Signey had been fighting fell in quiet streams before she reopened her eyes. Determination burned like flames within her sepia gaze. "I want to end this."

The green glow faded from Gael's hands, taking the bloodstains with it. He kept his head bowed, as if to hide the fact that he was still wearing Jesper Soto's face. "I don't have my Empyrean powers, or my Rider powers, but I can still manipulate blood for magic. I'm still a trained soldier." His tone was fierce, his eyebrows drawn together. "He destroyed my life. I want to destroy his. And I want him to know I was there when he finally lost."

"We need to get to Valor," Elara continued. "Faron, you'll stay with me. Reeve—"

"I'll work with Signey," Reeve said. "As soon as I can get my hands on a dragon relic, I'm sure we'll make quite the team."

Signey was watching Gael, and there was something in her expression that gave Faron pause. But there was no time to figure out if that should worry her or not.

"We need to find Torrey," Signey said, dragging her attention to Reeve. "She'll have extra relics, and she and Azeal can get us where we need to be."

"It's time to fix what we've done. All of us," Elara said, getting to her feet. She reached for Faron, who grabbed her hand without hesitation. "Good luck, everyone." She nodded at Reeve, at Signey, even at Gael, a sharp movement that said *We can do this* and *Stay safe* and *I love you* all at once. "We'll have to fly fast to get back to Hearthstone in time."

As they boarded Valor, Faron had so many questions, she felt about to explode. But when she asked about the whereabouts of Gavriel and Mireya Warwick, all Reeve or Elara would say was that they "were exactly where they deserved to be."

Empyrean? said Queen Aveline's voice when Elara had finished the minor repairs needed to get the drake airborne. Elara might have passed out, but Irie had managed to secure a safe enough landing that Valor wasn't in pieces. *Are you there? Report. Report.*

"Um," said Faron, "hi."

The long silence that followed her greeting made her wish that she'd kept her mouth shut, but Elara had encouraged her to answer, and Reeve, Signey, and Gael were up in the cabins. She abruptly wished she were up there with them. Elara nudged her in the side. Faron cleared her throat.

"Hi, Your Majesty," she continued. "I just wanted to say that I'm sorry for, well, everything that happened. Every life we lost is on my head. Every building destroyed. Every drop of blood spilled. I thought I knew what I was doing, but I didn't. And I returned your faith in me with betrayal. I don't expect you to forgive me, but I hope we get a chance for me to do better. On the other side of this war."

There was another silence, but Elara was smiling, so Faron supposed she hadn't done too badly.

You know, Faron, said Aveline, and that *was* Aveline and not the formal queen who looked down on Faron every time they met, *there were days when I hated you so much that I couldn't breathe, blaming you for everything wrong with my life.* Faron winced, but Aveline exhaled a breath that was almost, almost, like a laugh. *But I know you. We spent far too much time together during that war for me not to. I never once thought you'd actually joined him. Not once, Faron.*

Faron's eyes burned with the need to cry again. "Thank you. We're on our way to you now."

THIS ENDS IN EMBERS

There is an end to this madness. I will see you both on the long journey after it.

The astral call ended, and Faron felt so shaky that she went to sit in the front cockpit until she felt less like bursting into tears. There would be time to cry during the long journey ahead. For now, they had a war to win.

CHAPTER FORTY-THREE

ELARA

LIGHTBRINGER'S SEVERED BOND WITH GAEL MIGHT HAVE WEAKENED him, but it had made him as feral as he had been the moment he crawled into this realm. This was no strategic god clinging to the roof of the Hearthstone. This was an animal defending his territory. And that made him dangerously unpredictable.

Or maybe he was just made more dangerous by Elara's incompetence.

As soon as they had reached the Hestan Archipelago, Signey, Reeve, and Gael had been dropped off on the beach to use their combined efforts to find Torrey and Azeal from the ground. Elara and Faron returned to the air with a deceptively simple plan of their own. Elara could pilot Valor alone by channeling the power of the gods, but she couldn't do that *and* attack *and* watch Lightbringer's position. Faron had agreed to be her eyes, telling her where the dragon would move or attack next, so Elara could focus on flying and fighting. Faron knew Lightbringer the best, and she was sure she could predict him.

Valor flew around Lightbringer, all flames and ferocity, but Elara was still struggling. She had been summoning for so long,

THIS ENDS IN EMBERS

and she'd already been in one battle before this. Meanwhile, Light-bringer had stayed out of the fighting until now, and he moved his claws and teeth and tail with far more energy than Elara had in her. Valor's attacks seemed like minor annoyances, and Elara didn't know if that was because he was strong or if she was just that weakened.

Faron sat on the arm of Elara's chair, watching the screen intently. Several of Elara's attacks had gone wide as she had been forced to jolt out of the way of one of Lightbringer's limbs, but then the drake had dipped as Elara's energy flagged and her last blast had nearly hit *themselves*. Elara's cheeks burned. Faron had made fighting from a drake look so easy during the war, and now she was watching Elara fail.

I need to get out there, Aveline called from the panel as yet another one of Valor's blasts was dodged by the surprisingly nimble dragon. *I hurt him last time. I can hurt him again.*

"You can't go alone," said Faron. Elara was too focused to speak, but she hoped that the queen could feel the heat of her disapproval from wherever Nobility was. The astral call went silent without further response, and Elara and Faron exchanged glances. "She went alone."

A ball of golden light appeared on Elara's screen. Queen Aveline Renard Castell was surrounded by her royal astrals, and together, they soared in Lightbringer's direction. Her searing attacks carved bloody lines over the dragon's flank, distracting him from Valor. Elara's heart leaped into her throat as she watched Aveline fly past bladed wings and pillars of fire. She was nimble enough now, but Lightbringer was gigantic. Eventually, he would trap her. Eventually, he would kill her.

377

"The drake is dipping again," said Faron, dragging Elara back to her own problems. "Don't you know how to fly this thing?"

"I—I'm just learning how to fly it *and* attack with it."

"*What?*"

"We didn't have a lot of time," Elara said defensively. "And I'm doing okay!"

"If this is your definition of okay, I have no idea why your grades were so much better than mine," Faron deadpanned.

"It's because I actually study," Elara shot back, begging her body to hold on just a little bit longer. "And that's irrelevant to—"

The drake dropped again, leveling out near Lightbringer's stomach.

"For Irie's sake." Faron got up, running her fingers over the silver metal bangles on her wrist. "You fly. I'll fight. As soon as you get a clear shot at the soft spot under his chin, take it. Dragons are weakest there."

Elara felt stupid. Faron could summon astrals again, her magic made stronger by the scalestone bracelets she'd converted her shackles into. And one did not have to be a drake pilot to use scalestone to amplify and direct summoning magic. One only had to be Iryan. Yet it had never occurred to her to have her sister attack for her, to work with her like this.

Maybe they'd both become too accustomed to working alone.

Faron disappeared. A few minutes later, a light in the shape of a chair lit up on the panel, a sign that Faron was sitting in the pilot seat of the front cockpit. Valor's mouth opened, and fire burst forth, burying Lightbringer's stomach in red and gold flames. The dragon roared furiously and turned so that his spiked back was facing them.

THIS ENDS IN EMBERS

Elara threw all her power into directing the drake around and up, up, up.

Valor's conjured flame had blackened the white skin of Lightbringer's stomach, giving him what looked like a flaky bruise. He tried to lower his head, but there Aveline was again, golden blades stabbing into his skull and drawing blood. His wings spread so he could take to the air, but the queen was there, too, like a sun, like a star, like a comet.

She shone so brightly that she didn't see his spiked tail until it struck her in the side.

"AVELINE!" Elara screamed, shooting Valor forward as though she could somehow catch the queen. But Aveline did not fall. The spikes had pierced her through the center, sending a spray of blood over Lightbringer's battered body. The light that had surrounded the queen went out. She slumped forward on the spike, her diadem loosening.

Elara watched in horror as it tumbled to the ground. As Aveline's body followed shortly after.

She couldn't drag her eyes away. She couldn't even move.

The woman who had been her first love, who had become like family to her, who had believed in her even when Elara had had trouble believing in herself.

The queen who had once been a dancer, who had loved a woman she didn't think she could have, who had taken care of her people as if they were her world.

The girl who had grown up on a farm with parents who hadn't really been her parents and yet had stepped up to face her destiny with more grace than Elara could have ever imagined.

And now, she was dead.

"NO!" Faron screamed.

Through her tears, Elara saw the sky light up. Faron had thrown a blast of lightning that struck Lightbringer in the neck, climbing upward toward his chin. Elara felt as if she would never smile again, but Faron was a wrathful god, ready to see her queen's killer in his own grave. Elara drew strength from that rage, allowed herself to feel it. San Irie had lost so much. She had lost so much.

Lightbringer would lose everything. They would make sure of it.

CHAPTER FORTY-FOUR

FARON

BLOOD GUSHED FROM THE BLACK WELT FARON'S ATTACK HAD opened, slicking Lightbringer's body in crimson and green. Even with his chin hidden again, Faron continued to throw out lightning. Her world had narrowed to this beast and her power. He had made her stronger, even without access to the gods, even without the bonds, and now he would fear her the way he had sown fear throughout her world.

She wouldn't stop until Lightbringer fell from his perch, executed the way he had executed Aveline.

Tears dampened her face, and hate swelled in her chest. He'd wanted a massacre. They would bring him one.

Lightbringer was so distracted that he didn't notice the tiny black spot climbing up the column of his neck. Gael Soto was slick with substances Faron didn't want to give name to, but Lightbringer was being attacked from so many sides that he must not have felt the sword Gael was using as a piton between his scales. A scarlet gleam seemed to follow Gael's every movement, as though he were using all this blood to help propel himself upward.

Gael had been confident that he would be able to get close

enough to Lightbringer to climb his back, but Faron hadn't quite believed him until now. Until he'd gotten so close that now, more than ever, they needed to keep Lightbringer from becoming aware of him.

Faron swiped at her face before her blurred vision could become a liability. Every time she closed her eyes, she saw Aveline. Alive and raising one patronizing eyebrow as she corrected Faron's behavior. Dead and leaking blood around Lightbringer's massive spike. Alive and laughing beneath the stars during a rare moment of peace during the war. Dead and plunging through the air like an anvil.

The night before the official end of the first war had been Aveline's birthday. They had brought her a headscarf sourced from a stall in Seaview months before, and Aveline had held it in shaking fingers before asking if they were scared of what lay ahead. Faron had looked up at the young queen's face—so old, she'd seemed then, when she had been only seventeen, the same age that Faron was now—and she had said the same thing she still believed now: *When the queens died, when they took Port Sol, everyone in Deadegg thought that was it. We'd lost. We'd be Langlish again, and enslaved again, because we fought back. But then, Irie answered my prayers. She led me to you. And together, we'll win.*

Together.

They were supposed to win together.

And now Aveline was dead. Part of Faron had died with her.

"Faron, he's noticed Gael!" Elara's voice echoed through from the panel in front of her. *"Why aren't you attacking?"*

Shit. Shit, shit, shit. Faron shook herself free of the past and focused on the present. Lightbringer's neck twisted as he tried to

THIS ENDS IN EMBERS

spear Gael Soto with one of his sharp teeth while Gael tried desperately to hold his position. Faron blasted holes in Lightbringer's hide, strike after strike in Aveline's name, until the dragon's legs gave out and he collapsed on the rooftop. Nobility had even joined the fray to avenge their fallen queen, raining fireballs down from above to keep the dragon from trying to fly into a more advantageous position.

Gael got closer and closer to Lightbringer's head.

But the dragon refused to give up.

Lightbringer shook his head from side to side, trying to dislodge the smudge of black that was Gael, but Gael clung to the dragon's snout with the kind of tenacity Faron recognized in the boy who had told her he had only ever wanted to protect his people. Sometimes he slipped, but he never once fell. Every time she saw him, he had risen higher and higher, until Gael sank his sword into Lightbringer's right eye, dragging his weapon down until the organ collapsed.

Lightbringer's roar shook the world.

Faron grinned, teeth bared like a feral animal.

Crimson gushed over Lightbringer's face, joining the stains on his neck and body. He twisted his head even harder, but Gael had already yanked his sword from the socket. Faron aimed her next attacks at that eye, knocking Lightbringer back against the flat roof of Hearthstone.

Gael rolled to his left, bloody sword still in hand, and then came to a stop. His motionless body stretched out beside Lightbringer's like an offering.

"He's been hurt," Faron realized. "He's been hurt! If Lightbringer sees—"

"No, no, no," said Elara. "He's in Signey's brother. He can't—we can't lose Jesper. Not like this. I have to—I have to help—"

"Elara, *don't*—"

Faron had no idea how to end that sentence. They had a plan, but, with Gael out of commission, the plan was in tatters. How could she ask Elara to leave Jesper Soto in peril after all Elara had done to save her? How could she watch as Signey Soto lost her sibling after Faron had brought this on them all just to protect her own? They might have been safer in the air, but she wouldn't be able to live with herself if Jesper died like this, asleep in his own body as it fought without his consent.

She unstrapped herself from the pilot's seat and stretched her fingers, the scalestone bracelets rattling on her wrists. Ready for a fight. Ready for vengeance.

Ready as Valor shot toward the roof of Hearthstone, toward the writhing half-blind dragon who could spell their doom.

CHAPTER FORTY-FIVE

ELARA

ELARA RATTLED DOWN VALOR'S EXIT RAMP, HER MAGIC SWIRLING around her like protective armor. Lightbringer had yet to notice Gael—Jesper—protected, as he was, beneath a defensive hailstorm of fire from Nobility. Faron's footsteps sounded behind her, and then her sister surged past her, hurtling toward Gael's body without hesitation. Elara itched to follow, but the soldier in her refused. She needed to assess the situation. She needed to win this.

Her ears rang with Lightbringer's thunderous cries. His white body was stained with blood, not all his own. His tail swung back and forth across the rooftop, too far to strike Valor—for now. Faron ducked under his membranous wing, pausing only to shoot a line of lightning through it, and skidded to a halt at Gael's side. Lightbringer's throat lit up seconds before a stream of flames erupted from his open mouth, forcing Nobility to bank hard to avoid it.

The dragon rolled onto his feet, shaking the rooftop. Gael and Faron were on his blind side, but his head swung this way and that to catch as much as possible. Smoke flooded between his jagged teeth, transforming to threatening sparks. Everywhere they fell, a small fire flared, turning the roof into a hot maze.

It was chaos. They had to blind his other eye. But how?

"Elara, over here!"

Azeal had landed on the other side of the roof, tackling Lightbringer in a blur of claws and teeth. Even though the carmine dragon was the largest of the breeds, Lightbringer was in a class all his own. They took a chunk out of the stone, a tangle of red and white bodies, but it left a clear path from Valor to Faron. And her sister was no longer alone. Signey, Torrey, and Reeve had joined her, gathering around Gael with solemn faces.

"What's going on?" Elara asked warily. "He's not... Is he...?"

"No, of course not. No," Signey said. She wiped a hand over her face before glancing at Torrey. "We hoped it wouldn't come to this, but... we have another plan. A last resort. If—I mean, you don't have to—"

"I know I don't have to," said Torrey. "I want to."

"*What's going on?*" Elara repeated.

Reeve pressed his lips together and looked away. Faron refused to meet Elara's eyes. Torrey and Signey did that thing again, where they had a silent conversation that implied several conversations Elara hadn't been privy to. Elara's wariness turned to fear, curling in her stomach and slicing through her organs. And it had nothing to do with the dragons brutalizing each other mere feet away.

Faron tilted her head toward them, and Reeve followed her. He'd gotten a new dragon relic, she realized, an imitation dragon tooth that hung around his neck as his old one had. It took her a moment to identify it as one of Torrey's; she'd worn it that day in Beacon when they'd gotten brunch. Now it glowed with magic as Faron and Reeve helped Azeal keep Lightbringer at bay, protecting the pocket of space the rest of them stood in from attack.

THIS ENDS IN EMBERS

Torrey brushed her short blond hair behind her ear so she could loosen her ear cuff, another one of her favorite relics. She traced it with her fingers, a humorless smile on her face. "Jesper gave this to me, you know. There are a thousand ways to make a dragon relic, but he always made sure the ones I had were 'in my style.' Ferocious yet fashionable, he called it. He was always the best part of me."

Elara's fear began to scream beneath her skin. A gasp shook loose. "You want to take Jesper's place. You want to let Gael Soto inside your body instead."

"Jesper never got a choice. I did. And I'm choosing to do this." Those blue eyes were sad but determined. "Remember when I told you not to die?"

"We *all* promised—"

"And I intend to keep my promise. If Gael Soto is as good a soldier as advertised."

Elara was aware her mouth was hanging open, but she didn't know what else to say. It wasn't as though she hadn't noticed Signey and Torrey exchanging looks, or Signey's focus on finding Torrey after reuniting with Jesper's body, but she hadn't imagined this. How long had they been planning this? The day she'd broken the dragon bonds? Or as far back as when Torrey first suspected Gael might be in Jesper's body?

"You're agreeing to this?" she finally managed, looking down at Signey. Signey was cradling her brother's injured body in her arms, her curls blowing around her head like a flag. Elara couldn't see her expression from where she was, could only see the way that Signey's fingers were gently combing through Jesper's hair. "Why didn't you tell me?"

"I knew what you'd say," Signey murmured. "Because I said the exact same thing." When she lifted her head, her cheeks were slick with tears again. "Do you think I want this? Do you think I want to lose anyone else? Torrey insisted. For Jesper, she—" Signey's voice cracked. She bowed her head again. "This is her choice to make. I respect her right to make it."

Torrey's hand touched Elara's wrist, her pale fingers lined with dragon-shaped rings. "Jesper is my best friend. I know he would do the same for me, if he were here. But he's not here, and that's the problem. It's not fair to put him in danger like this. Even if I *know* he'd agree, the problem is that he didn't get to. My body and Gael's power . . . this is how we end this. Let me end this."

Elara expected Torrey to cry as well, but her eyes were dry. Her mind was made up. And it didn't matter what Elara said, she would do this with or without her permission. Elara swallowed.

Across the rooftop, Azeal slammed Lightbringer's head against the stone. Faron's and Reeve's magic twined together to chain the dragon's tail to the roof, keeping him from using it as a weapon. Lightbringer thrashed against his bonds, throwing fire left and right, fire blocked from hitting them by a shield that Faron had conjured. They were running low on time.

Beneath her, Gael groaned.

No, Jesper. Because he had taken over Jesper.

Elara realized that she was now crying and turned away. "Okay."

"Okay," Signey breathed, her voice thick with grateful tears.

"Okay," said Torrey, withdrawing a vial of blood from her pocket. "In Valor, I think. We have to hurry."

CHAPTER FORTY-SIX

FARON

FARON WAS FADING.

She had been channeling too much for too long, and even with Valor's scalestone and the scalestone on her wrists, she was beginning to feel the effects. Sweat coated her body, making her clothes cling to her form, and the heat in her blood was only made hotter by the tiny fires that speckled the broad roof of Hearthstone. Lightbringer refused to stop fighting, and so Faron refused to stop fighting back. But she had no idea how long she could keep this up before she overheated and collapsed.

At least Reeve showed no signs of tiring, but his dragon relic could run out of magic at any time. If they both lost their magic...

"Look out!"

Reeve's body slammed into hers. They rolled across the roof, stone scratching Faron's skin as they came to a stop dangerously close to the edge. Faron was breathing hard as her aunt's astral fled her body, giving her a momentary reprieve. The space where they'd been standing was blackened with dragonfire, so powerful that it must have blown a hole in their shield. Reeve's face was pressed against her neck, his body heaving with his own harsh breaths. One of his arms bracketed her from the roof edge. The other . . .

Faron touched his shoulder where his arm had once been. "Does it hurt?"

"Not anymore," Reeve said. "Are *you* hurt?"

"Always thinking of me," Faron teased as he carefully eased off her. Her braids flapped against her shoulders, and she looked up to see that Valor was taking to the skies without her. And standing below it, blond hair rippling in the wind, scalestone sword raised, was Torrey Kelley.

Or rather, Gael Soto in Torrey Kelley's body.

"They did it," Faron said as Torrey raced across the roof toward Lightbringer. "We have to help clear her way. Come on."

She helped up Reeve, wiping the sweat from her brow with a sleeve before she summoned another astral. Part of her wondered how they had gotten Elara—Elara, who had spent enough time with Torrey and Jesper that she surely had objected to trading one's body for another—to agree to the plan they had explained to her on their way up to the roof. The other part of her knew it didn't matter, not really, because her only goal now was to make sure that Torrey's sacrifice was not in vain. They had already lost Aveline, and Lightbringer still breathed. Whether they lost Torrey Kelley or not, Lightbringer would die here.

Faron would make sure of it.

Lightbringer's tail swung like an axe, but Faron threw a hand toward it, her magic cutting through the air. His tail was stopped by a platform of golden magic that exploded into shards. With a curl of her fingers, those shards rammed into Lightbringer's side, piercing new holes and making old holes wider. His answering

THIS ENDS IN EMBERS

roar was weak, more pain than fury, so Faron clenched her fists. The shards dug deeper and deeper, trying to pierce muscle and sinew, trying to cut down to the bone.

Nobility threw spikes of lightning, bolt after bolt, cracking what was left of the stone beneath Lightbringer. The dragon's body began to sink into the building, trapping him. Reeve tugged a string of magic from his relic and curved it in ropes around Lightbringer's neck, pulling them tight, choking the breath from the dragon's lungs.

And Gael Soto raced through it all like an avenging god.

With a mighty cry that Faron could hear even through the din, Torrey sank her sword into Lightbringer's remaining eye.

The blind dragon jolted as if he'd been electrocuted. His foreleg came up, talons extended. Gael jumped seconds too late. Light-bringer's claws tore through his body—through Torrey's body—seconds before connecting with his own face.

Her body hit the ground, then slid through the cracks in the roof, sinking out of view.

Lightbringer's own talons had carved a bloody line through his face and gotten stuck. Faron watched him attempt to pull them free, screeching all the while, and slowly she withdrew her magic until her astral dissipated. There was nothing further that she could do. It was all up to Elara now.

Valor landed gingerly on the roof, and Faron was unsure if it was because her sister's magic had weakened or because she was mourning her friend. Either way, magic erupted from the drake and then poured into the remaining surface of the roof, opening a portal to the divine realm. A black vacuum swirling beneath Lightbringer sucked him out of this world.

He was too weakened to pull himself free. Too blinded to find an escape.

Faron could hear Lightbringer's panicked cries as he was returned to his own world to face the judgment of the gods. Knowing the gods as she did, Faron did not envy him at all.

Lightbringer's teeth were the last things she saw before he disappeared completely. Finally gone, with nothing more than a snarl to remember him by.

The world became a blur of color: reds and golds, greens and blues. Dragons flew willingly into the hole, some carrying the limp or bleeding bodies of other dragons. It couldn't have taken more than ten minutes for them all to disappear, but for Faron it felt like a lifetime. She was seventeen and she was twelve, watching these creatures that she had feared and hated and pitied leave a world that had only allowed them to thrive as weapons to be used against other countries.

A final dragon hovered above the hole, her green wings flapping and her eyes kind.

Zephyra.

Faron bowed her head in respect for all the dragon had done for her sister, even when Faron had treated her like an enemy. Zephyra blew a geyser of fire into the sky with a triumphant roar, then flew down to join her brothers and sisters in returning home.

The roof returned to its black-and-gray state, the channel between realms closing without a sound. Faron collapsed to her knees, her shoulders shaking. It was over.

A broken sob escaped her.

It was over.

THIS ENDS IN EMBERS

But Aveline was dead.

It was finally, finally over.

Her chest and throat burned. Tears blurred her vision and stung her eyes. And no matter how many times she told herself that it was over, she had lost far too much for this to feel like a victory.

EPILOGUE

ELARA

WITH THE DRAGONS GONE, THE WORLD CONTINUED TO CHANGE. They buried their dead: Mireya and Gavriel in unmarked graves, Torrey cremated and her ashes kept by her parents, a commissioned portrait of Gael in the Soto family tomb beside Signey and Jesper's mother and older sister. Torrey and Gael received medals of valor for their sacrifice, at Jesper's insistence. In his opinion, no one had sacrificed more.

Then there was Aveline.

Aveline was honored in a state funeral attended by so many people that the streets of Seaview were packed. She was buried at her ancestral home, alongside her mothers, in a ceremony that carried on late into the night. In San Irie, a funeral was not just about the person's death, but about their life. Food had been served, music had been played, and stories about Aveline's legendary exploits had been told.

Afterward, Elara and Faron had stood in the back of Renard Hall, on the cliff overlooking the dark ocean. Elara had built an altar with a picture of Aveline on top, a candid photo taken during the war in one of the few times they'd all tried to feel like children

THIS ENDS IN EMBERS

again. Elara and Faron had pressed their cheeks against the teenage queen's, making faces while she rolled her eyes. After returning to San Irie, Faron had been the one to find the photo among Aveline's things, in her bedroom at Pearl Bay Palace.

Elara could still remember how hard they'd both cried, that picture in their hands. She had cried for Reeve, who had watched his parents die knowing that they hated him. She had cried for Faron, who had never learned how to trust other people and had made decision after decision that almost turned her into someone she had never wanted to be. She had cried for Signey, who had survived the war but still sacrificed so much. She had cried for Barret, who had lost out on years with his family, and Jesper, who had been kidnapped, and even for Gael, who had wanted to be a hero centuries ago and had achieved that only when there was too much blood on his hands to wipe clean.

Above all, she had cried for herself, and how she had resigned herself to there being no such thing as a happy life after war. There was only the struggle of living.

As one, Elara and Faron made a sign of prayer and turned their eyes to the stars. "Thank you, Irie," said Elara, "for bringing us together."

"So ends the Renard Castell line," Faron said. "May they be forever blessed."

"May they be forever blessed."

In Aveline's absence, a council of representatives from each parish was appointed to rule San Irie. Desmond Pryor was one of them, but Elara was confident in everyone else's ability to keep him in check. She was more concerned about Faron, who had declared that she was done with school, that she wanted to leave San Irie entirely and figure out who she was without an entire island to tell her who she should be.

Maybe her parents had been expecting it, though, because they didn't fight her. They'd only hugged her tightly and asked that she at least wait until her eighteenth birthday, so the family could have some time together before it was too late. After two wars, this peacetime looked as if it would be the one that would finally stick. They would have time to be a family again.

Elara had gone to the Port Sol Temple to speak to the gods. Though she was meant to give back their magic, she couldn't bear the idea. In the month since Lightbringer had been defeated, Étolia had begun to invade a weakened Langley. Barret Soto had been ousted in favor of the Hylands, who were already willing and ready to bring the country back to war. All the countries Langley had conquered were declaring their independence, and Elara knew that the power-hungry Hylands wouldn't take that lying down.

"Zephyra once told me that I want to fight for something I truly believe in. That I'm capable of great things," Elara had told the three gods spread out before her. Saying Zephyra's name still brought with it a pang of loss, but it was getting easier. War was loss. She'd known that for years. "It took me a while to figure out what that great thing was, but I think it's this. Protecting people. Fighting when I'm needed. Doing my best to do what's right. So if you'll continue to lend me your power and trust me to do the right thing, I'll continue to protect our people as best I can."

"Our decision has been made, Empyrean," said Irie. And then: "I am incredibly proud of all you've done. Yet I will not allow our magic to continue to influence this world, not now. But if things are ever this dire again...if you pray to us, we will come to your aid."

Since that was a better answer than Elara had expected, she bowed her head. "Thank you. Thank all of you. For everything."

Mala had hugged her for that. Irie had smiled. Even Obie had nodded once, as if he were unsurprised but pleased to be proved right.

And as they took back their magic, leaving behind a dizzying weakness that made her sway on her feet, Elara felt that pang of loss again. But at least this time, it was temporary. After all, she would see them again.

She just hoped it was later rather than sooner.

Luckily, the weeks hadn't yet brought with them any cosmic threats to San Irie. In light of the Hylands' rise to power, and with nothing else keeping them in Langley, the Sotos had decided to move to San Irie. After losing so much of their family in war, they wanted to learn to love San Irie as much as Celyn and Eugenia had. And with Desmond Pryor moving to Port Sol, they ended up buying the old Pryor house.

It was nice, having everyone in Deadegg: Faron and Elara back with their parents; Cherry on leave to greet them; Jesper, Barret, and Signey settling into the house on the block. Aisha's family, the Harlows, hadn't come to see Elara, but she hadn't expected them to. That pain might never go away, and she'd accepted that. They were at least willing to see Cherry, who reported that they were "as well as could be."

Now, sitting in the same empty field where Elara had once

practiced combat summoning, Jesper and Signey asked a perplexed Reeve if he was interested in coming to live with them.

"Oh," Reeve said, clenching and unclenching his metal fingers. Cherry had made sure he was fitted with a scalestone prosthetic arm sooner rather than later, and his physical therapy involved what looked like a lot of jerky movements and stretching. "I don't—I wouldn't want to impose. I can stay with the Hanlons."

He didn't sound as if he wanted to stay with the Hanlons. As far as Elara knew, they weren't *family* as much as they were *colleagues who lived in the same house.* They hadn't asked after him once during the war, likely assuming, along with everyone else, that he had turned traitor. At least Elara hadn't seen them at the rallies, so, whatever they believed, it hadn't stopped them from allowing him back.

"We're not being polite," said Jesper, sitting beneath the palm tree with a half-eaten guinep in his hand. "You . . . More than anyone, you understand what we're going through. We want to keep you close. And if we can offer you a home that actually feels like one, we'd love to have you."

"Unless you're happy where you are," Signey added, biting into her own guinep and then spitting the seed into the grass. Her free hand held Elara's, their fingers tangled together, both familiar and extraordinary after all they'd been through. "But it's just . . . it'd be nice. To have someone to talk to. About Gael and Langley and everything."

Reeve blinked again. He looked at Elara, who shrugged. He looked at Cherry, who told him to continue his exercises. Then he looked at the ground, and a small smile crossed his face. "Well, if you're sure. I'd really like that."

Elara hid a smile of her own as Signey leaned her head against her shoulder, her skin warm from the bright Iryan sun. "Hey, where's Faron? I thought she'd be joining us."

Reeve snorted. "She's bet your father thirty rayes that he can't beat her at dominoes."

And Elara couldn't help laughing. Some things would never change.

Two days later, Elara opened the door to Faron's bedroom to find her and Reeve tangled up on the bed.

She stared openly. She couldn't help it. She had seen Reeve kiss plenty of people before; he and Wayne had been so insufferable that she, Cherry, and Aisha had forced them to study somewhere else so they wouldn't have to watch them flirt. But Faron was not interested in kissing, or in boys or girls or sex. And yet here her sister was, her arms and legs wrapped around Reeve's body, while he held her face and kissed her as if the world would end if he stopped.

One of them made a sound that made Elara want to smash her head against the wall. She cleared her throat. "This... is going to be an adjustment."

They sprang apart. Reeve's scalestone prosthetic snapped out toward the end of the bed, but he still ended up taking half the sheet with him as he tumbled off the side. Faron tugged her shirt down over her sleep shorts, then covered her face with her hands.

"How long have you been standing there, you fucking creep?" she asked, voice muffled.

"Too long," Elara admitted. "Was this a goodbye kiss or...?"

"It was a mind-your-own-business kiss," Faron said at the same time Reeve said, "It was a goodbye kiss."

"You could go with her, you know." Elara helped up Reeve, unable to hide her amused smile. "There won't be much going on around here but crying and healing."

"You and I have been apart for long enough," Reeve told her, tossing the sheets back onto the bed. "The Sotos will need us. And Faron"—he glanced at his girlfriend, and the soft expression Elara saw there made her smile widen—"she'll come back to me. She promised."

Once he was gone, Elara and Faron lay side by side in Faron's bed, gazing up at the ceiling and silently basking in each other's presence. Elara wanted to squeeze in as much time with her sister as she could before they both had other promises to keep.

Eventually, they would be separated again, but at least next time it would be by choice. That was the nature of life, of relationships. Loved ones would always be separated by time or distance, but that didn't make them any less loved.

"Thank you," Faron said, her first words in hours. She did that sometimes now, falling into thoughtful silence and then breaking it with a statement that implied an entire conversation had preceded it. "You always believed in me. I needed that. I still do."

"I'm your older sister. Of course I'll always believe in you," Elara promised. "Besides, you've always believed in me, too. I'll never stop needing that."

"Is it wrong," Faron asked, "that I wish I'd saved him?"

Elara didn't need Faron to clarify which *him* she meant. "He died a hero. Even if no one else knows that, we do. In that way, you did save him."

"It's not the same."

"I know."

THIS ENDS IN EMBERS

Faron's voice was small when she spoke again minutes later. "Are we going to be okay?"

Elara thought about it before she answered. Had they ever been okay? Two wars, several losses, separation and doubt and fear and fights. They had both found love, but they had both done things that would haunt them. When Elara closed her eyes, she still saw Aveline and Torrey being torn apart. She saw Zephyra the day she said goodbye, and her heart cracked open with painful longing. Sometimes in the middle of the night, she woke Faron from nightmares about the people she had killed. About the chains that had trapped her and the dragon who had lived in her head whispering approval at all her worst impulses.

None of that was okay, and maybe it never would be.

But they were alive. Elara could take a drake to Langley and visit Professor Smithers, Mr. Lewis, and any of the Night Saints. They had astral calls and fire calls, letters and visits. They had life, in all its painful and proud moments, and that was a gift many people could no longer claim.

Elara reached across the bed and gripped her sister's hand in hers.

"We're going to try," she finally answered. "Every day, we're going to wake up and we're going to try."

Faron smiled, and, for once, it didn't look haunted. "Okay."

ACKNOWLEDGMENTS

This is my first completed series, and I haven't learned how to properly write acknowledgments yet, so just bear with me as I thank all the same people in slightly different ways.

First, I want to thank my best friend, Lauren. Every book I'm lucky enough to get to publish exists because she was the first one to believe in me, to read my work, to tell people that there was no doubt in her mind I would be on shelves one day. *Best friend* has always seemed like too small a phrase for how much of my life and heart you occupy; I'm so, so glad to have you on my side for twenty years and counting.

Second, all my love to my agent, Emily Forney. My books—my career—are as strong as they are because of Emily's hard work and dedication. Her brilliant mind, her collaboration, her belief in me—it all has pushed me to new and better heights. Every year, I become a better writer and human because I'm fortunate enough to get to work with one of the best agents in the business.

I cannot imagine having brought this series into the world with anyone else but my amazing Little, Brown Books for Young Readers team, who took my story and created a world I am so proud to have lived in for two books. Thank you to Alexandra Hightower and Crystal Castro for being the most supportive, encouraging, and evilly creative editors in the world; Lindsay Walter-Greaney and Lara Stelmaszyk for copyedits that asked the questions I was too

ACKNOWLEDGMENTS

afraid to face but that ultimately made the story stronger; Brandy Colbert for being the most thorough proofreader in the world; Carlos Quevedo and Jenny Kimura for this amazing new cover direction; and Patricia Alvarado (Production), Bill Grace and Andie Divelbiss (Marketing), Savannah Kennelly (Digital Marketing), Cassie Malmo and Hannah Klein (Publicity), and Victoria Stapleton and Christie Michel (School & Library). If I could, I would list every single person at Little, Brown Books for Young Readers, because you've all, in one way or another, made my publishing experience a dream come true.

Thank you to my cat, Sora, my walking antidepressant. What's the point in writing books if I don't get to kiss a cat on her little forehead?

Thank you to my sister, Dashá; my parents, Colin and Daisy; and my family in Jamaica, America, Canada, and beyond.

Thank you to my friends Brittany Pittman, Chelsea Abdullah, Tashie Bhuiyan, Chloe Gong, Christina Li, Laura R. Samotin, Taylor Grothe, Emma Lord, Jen Carnelian, Zachary Longstreet, Terry J. Benton-Walker, Rochelle Hassan, Kelly Andrew, Hannah V. Sawyerr, Betty Hawk, and Page Powars. In one way or another, you all kept me smiling while I was writing this.

Thank you to my unofficial marketing team: Ebony LaDelle, Jane Lee, and Tyler Breitfeller. Ebony, you are an inspiration to me. The elegance and grace with which you navigate the world makes me even more grateful that you allow me in your orbit, because the woman behind the legend is even better. Tyler, even though you won't let me pay you for all the graphics you make me, I love you with my whole heart. You are the smartest, funniest, most irreplaceable Leo in all the world, and I will never approve

ACKNOWLEDGMENTS

anything without your discerning eyes on it. Jane, you are my Aries soul sister and one of my favorite people in the world. Your energy and drive push me to be better than I was yesterday. I hope every day gives you a new reason to smile.

Thank you to the group chats: Joelle Thérèse, Ysabelle Suarez, Mel Karibian, and Maddie Martinez. Alaa Al-Barkawi, Arzu Bayraktar, Ryan Ram, Amani Salahudeen, Ale Massenbürg, Audris Candra, Nadirah Ashim, and Marwa Sarraj (and our honorary members, Mr. Meow and Baby Ale).

Thank you to Sophie Kim, Nadia Noor, Grace Varley, Pascale Lacelle, Lexi, May Cheng, and Riley Huntington. In one way or another, you pushed me to get this book done, and I'll never forget your support.

Thank you, once again, to Law Roach and Zendaya for the Joan of Arc outfit from the 2018 Met Gala that inspired this duology.

Thank you to myself. You did it, you pretty little fool.

And thank you, Readers, for following me this far. I hope that even once this duology is over, you'll follow me even further. I have so many more stories I want to share with you.

Lauren Banner

KAMILAH COLE

Kamilah Cole is the bestselling author of *So Let Them Burn* and *This Ends in Embers*. A graduate of New York University, Kamilah is usually playing *Kingdom Hearts* for the hundredth time, quoting early *SpongeBob SquarePants* episodes, or crying her way through Zuko's redemption arc in *Avatar: The Last Airbender*.